DeSensitizer II

DeSensitizer II

More Mental For Metal

KAERO DAVIS

Library of Congress Control Number:		2016921161
ISBN:	Hardcover	978-1-7960-0887-6
	Softcover	978-1-7960-0846-3
	eBook	978-1-7960-0845-6

Print information available on the last page.

Rev. date: 12/19/2019

To order additional copies of this book, contact:
Xlibris
1-800-455-039
www.Xlibris.com.au
Orders@Xlibris.com.au
806146

CONTENTS

Please Note

The following content contains themes of violence,
coarse language, sexual references / sexual
themes, suicidal themes as well as the other.

Themes contain triggers and may have a
sensitive nature. This is a fictitious work.
Not to be taken seriously nor enacted in
anyway. For entertainment only.

Chapter 1

A Psycho Path To Sanity

DeSensitizer

Well, this illness, by which I suffer,
It definitely is one heavy mother fucker,
Forever drawn in, drained and suckered,
Always to a tight suffocating smother

Animation by an inner, external drive,
Where clustered chaos clouded thrives,
Played with fire, played with knives,
Never certain I'll make it out alive,

It's a blood thirsty curse,
Really rattles the nerves,
Mixed atrocity, disturbed,
Lives up to the name it's earnt,

The torment the voices breed,
Seeing thing's I shouldn't see,
Emotionally, physically, spiritually, mentally,
In every, any, sense I bleed,

This illness is a sensitive subject,
Fighting through assumptions, reasons to suspect,
Steely hard truths to face and more to accept,
Consistent inconsistence and faltering respects,

Occurrences happening hardly believable,
Success out of reach and not quite achievable,
Perception barely appropriately receivable,
Vacuumed back to the shit pit irretrievable,

But by a means of my talent,
I'll attempt the challenge,
Fighting through whatever malice,
Paranoid Schizophrenia's symptomatic habits,

To the best of my ability, be an insighter,
Devising methods and means as an advisor,
And, so, from a hyper mentalizer,
I give you, behold, DeSensitizer...

A Psycho Path...

If I've gotta go psycho to get some fuckin' sane,
Somebody's gonna be feeling the pain,
I can tell you shame will go both ways,
Think you can handle that the remainder of your days?

You seem to think I'm an easy fuckin' target,
And I'm nowhere, no way near ready to cark it,
You miscalculate how much I've hardened,
But by all means step forward, let's get it started,

I'll pummel some sense into that shit you call brains,
Up 'til now I've been pretty fuckin' tame,
But now it's time for a little insane,
You're never gonna be the fuckin' same...

Winding, cranking up some psycho for some fuckin' sane,
Somebody's gonna start feeling the pain,
The aftershock of the shame will be felt both ways,
And you think you can handle that the remainder of your days?

You seem to think I'm an easy fuckin' target,
And I'm nowhere, no way near ready to cark it,
You miscalculate how much I've hardened,
But by all means step forward, let's get it started,

I'll pummel some sense into that shit you call brains,
Up 'til now I've been pretty fuckin' tame,
But now it's time for some fuckin' insane,
And you're never gonna be the same...

Following Through

I'm a deceiver, Ha – got everybody fooled,
I'm a deceiver, yeah, lets go back to school,
Deceiver – shit, I've got me fooled,
Deceiver – yeah, let's go back to school,

He thinks that of me –
I never said no, never led to assume otherwise,
She thinks this of me –
I never said yes, never led to assume otherwise,
They think that of me –
Gonna have to go and live it up,
Or that won't be anymore this of me –
'til I have gone and lived it up,

That that I never confirmed to be true nor else otherwise,
Will surely challenge me to declare and prove and compromise,
For surely as I say and do to uphold whatever lies –
Will soon come a day I'll rue, play the part, or pay the price,

He thinks this of me –
I never said yes, never led to assume otherwise,
She thinks that of me –
I never said no, never led to assume otherwise,
They all think this of me –
Gonna have to go and live it up,
Or this won't be anymore that of me –
'til I have gone and lived it up…

Template

I was often told shit once too young to understand,
"it's time you better grow up son, be a fuckin' man"
But not one person could describe a good template to the plan,
Having already thrice as much between my life span,

Needless to say I felt damned, before I had began,

I so came to a turning point in my life where I must decide,
Told to really pick and choose my fights else, consistently collide,
Denying a wasted life by strife – just biding all my time,
A dog with a vicious bite, sleeping, and better left to lie,

Void of all ties, divide, and save washing away in the tide,

So here, I tread a path, not sure many have walked before,
Mid-fight contradictory wars – standards many implore,
This deal I've been handed grazes me raw – an unsettling score,
I never seem to heal the sores, always forced back to the floor,

It's drilling – it bores, and I'm glowing at the core,

Cast out to the deep end, and expected to know how to swim,
The competition is rigged, loaded, biased, I can't win,
And I wonder if it's some sick joke and I'm the jester for the whim,
It's draining, it's straining, patience is wearing ever thin,

I'd wished for a mentor to help me at least through some,
But no matter where I went I could find none,
It's hard to have to make it through when you're a lonely one,
You have to learn it hard it's how most have done…

Nurtured...

Dearest over bearing mother – what have you done?
Your shelter, your over-protection, what have I become?
Could you believe this mongrel breed was indeed your son?
Appearances deceiving – you wouldn't believe
me – I wasn't a beast once –

Bizarre occurrences would contradict,
Lives in a want for better depict,
Condescension – consequences, blinding white split,
Conflict with razor grips, shred the sense it rips,

The darkness I kept within to my lone,
The blackest secrets dwelling a'roam,
Extremes of emotion – a mind of their own,
Amnesiac anomalies veil the unknown,

Too many things just all wrong,
Irrationality built my rational mind strong,
I got there myself but it took twice as long,
But all that was broken is long gone,

I left as a broken mess, I was shattered,
And soon shook free of that clutter of old matter,
The beating was hard – and I was battered,
But it was indeed better than to never have it,

Whoa, the darkness I kept within to my lone,
The very blackest of secrets dwelling a'roam,
Extremes of emotions – a mind of their own,
Amnesiac anomalies veiling all unknown,

I am the product of an astronomical phenomenon –
And there was always a lot more going on...

Dearest over bearing mother – what have you done?
Your shelter, your over-protection, what have I become?
Could you believe this mongrel breed was indeed your son?
Appearances deceiving – you wouldn't believe
me – I wasn't a beast once –

Dearest over bearing mother – what have you done?
Your shelter, your over-protection, what have I become?
Could you believe this mongrel breed was indeed your son?
Appearances deceiving – you wouldn't believe
me – I wasn't a beast once –

Bizarre occurrences would contradict,
Lives in a want for better depict,
Condescension – consequences, blinding white split,
Conflict with razor grips, shred the sense it rips,

The darkness I kept within to my lone,
The blackest secrets dwelling a'roam,
Extremes of emotion – a mind of their own,
Amnesiac anomalies veil the unknown,

I left as a broken mess, I was shattered,
And soon shook free of that clutter of old matter,
The beating was hard – and I was battered,
But it was indeed better than to never have it,

Whoa, the darkness I kept within to my lone,
The very blackest of secrets dwelling a'roam,
Extremes of emotions – a mind of their own,
Amnesiac anomalies veiling all unknown,

I am the product of an astronomical phenomenon –
And there was always a lot more going on...

Nephilim

It should be no surprise to me now why I excel,
When I believe I could be hybrid human angel,
But then there also have been reasons –
To believe I'm hybrid human demon,

There have been a lot of things I couldn't previously explain,
Things I know I can do but all the same sound insane,
Talents, capabilities I previously believed I'd gained –
A kind of evolution forced by traumatic pain,

But know this well and know it true,
There were various pains I had to push on through,
The kinds of prices, sacrifices, meant to test you,
Strange undefinable torments to be subject to,

One prize is being able to photosynthesise,
To absorb light to feed to energise,
An achievement aligned once been sensitized,
Discovering hidden meanings through crooked lies,

To talk telepathically projecting thoughts,
Rare kinds of insights, self-taught,
Reefing chains of black energies to absorb,
Purify it, return it once I would,

To illuminate, animate with radiant emotion,
Rainbowed colours, aura's associate,
Strange occurrences one may indeed boast of,
But once there can be made most of,

One must undergo changes to become,
Never quite always just born as one,
You have to want, to make it done,
And accept all that comes…

Internal Planes

I live a lot of time within my mind,
That I often forget just what it's like,
The things adding up that define,
What most may consider a healthy design,

I often forget my place and what it takes,
That I often forsake a healthy state,
Shrouded and clouded with sinister tastes,
Failing a model citizenship expected of me to make,

Living a lot of time in my mind,
Far off grid and out of sight,
Forgetting things that are meant to define
A favourable character, a brighter design,

I live so deep within myself,
I forget I'm a walking hell,
Caught, tranced, within a strange spell,
Never to escape this plane I dwell,

Others reach in deep to try to retrieve,
And I mourn a plea to leave me to grieve,
Too far gone or so I believe,
Trapped in a head-space I cannot leave,

Dangerously internalizing deep in my mind,
I forget I'm not the only one of my kind,
Forgetting certain things meant to define,
Falling, faltering further back behind,

Forgetting all things, I used to be,
And drowning deep in antagonizing misery…

Bluff

Can you manipulate the ultimate bluff?
Can you hide your emotion enough?
When others buckle – do you stand tough?
Can you swallow anger and chuckle and laugh?

Do you stand calm in the face of a threat?
Are you mentally prepared for any such event?
Are you comfortable premeditating regret?
To do that of which you wouldn't normally accept?

There will come a time in life,
A time of choice – and you must decide,
Whether to divert from chaos or collide,
And this determines your character type,

Are you capable of withstanding a fatal blow?
And be God-like enough of just letting it go?
Suppose it could very well happen tomorrow –
Would you go toe to toe?

There comes a time in life where you must decide,
Whether you'll stand and fight or run and hide,
Would you divert the chaos or set course to collide?
You define a character type despite what you like,

But, what if, just maybe you play their game,
Play it better and they remember your name,
Could you keep up with the creeping fame?
Show your true genius? Show you're not insane?

When you bleed – does it sate their feed?
Sate their needs and growing greed?
Beware what trap, don't fall deceived,
And God speed, hope you succeed…

Sentiments To Satan

Conforming to conditions,
Requires some persistence,
Reason requires consistent reminiscence,
And not any where near what plan is envisioned,

On so many levels I can empathise with the devil,
Understand why he meddled, became the rebel,
I share the very same pet hates, battling hypocrites,
No difference in my story, my state – just another heretic,

And I am at odds with what is generally accepted,
And to question their ignorance insults my intelligence,
The fact I see there's wrong just means I know better,
But never treated better due to their belligerence,

I see how little they pay attention,
So quick to see all my defections,
I mirror, and show their reflection,
Deny them forgiveness, deny redemption,

They delay me, hold me back, postpone my success,
Discredit me, contempt me, and question my irreverence,
But it's my moral obligation to defy, deny, underlying disrespects,
Sinister disrespects that outweigh deep, heavy, and in excess,

Keeping The Calm

I forget I have more power than I think I do at times,
I must control my emotion and try master my mind,
Keep calm and formulate a map, structure a design,
Decline in a response polite, and leave it all behind,

The less I let it bother me but still apologise,
I'm sorry that you feel that way, I now see through your eyes,
I'm glad you spoke it to my face, brought it to the light,
I most certainly know better now, we can reharmonize,

Knowledge is truly power – a glory to behold,
Intelligence is a treasure – as the courage to be bold,
I try keep the perfect poker face and respectfully fold,
When I sense a heat arise with potential to burn or scald,

Emotions running high, but I'll maintain controlling mine,
Endure those times upon where I'd lose my mind,
Respectively decline before my teeth are doomed to grind,
Evacuate, disappear and leave it far behind,

But I won't let it bother me yet still apologize,
I can't help they feel this way, but I can see through their eyes,
I appreciate it spoke to my face, brought into light,
I certainly know better know – let's begin to reharmonize,

Oh, knowledge is truly power, a glory to behold,
Intelligence is treasure as the courage to be bold,
Maintain a poker face until it's time to fold,
When you sense a heat arise with the potential to burn or scald…

Uncivil Linguist

I can't seem to remember to keep a civil tongue,
Inappropriately so around adults still quite so young,
As articulate and charming as I can be – it's still pretty dumb,
Not often thinking before I speak has sent people chilling numb,

I guess it's not safe for me to socialise,
For this sole reason is enough for rousing despise,
My uncivil tongue will surely only compromise,
Any hope I have for peace or paradise,

I am mighty vulgar, a thoughtless heathen fiend,
An unsightly repulser, the likes should not be publicly seen,
I often forget the threshold, the limits, the boundaries,
Often fuck myself better than any woman has who's been,

No, no, I guess it's not safe for me to socialise,
For the sole purpose I arouse despise,
My uncivil tongue will only compromise,
Any hope I have for peace or paradise,

Foul Mouth

No, he's not gonna speak too much
He won't, can't afford to –
Since it's virtually all inappropriate,
His foul mouth is gonna be his doom,

He can tell the filthiest jokes,
You wouldn't believe the shit can be spoke,
Is he for real? You've gotta take note –
Never met a linguist like this bloke,

It's best having bit your tongue,
Saving many a shit foul slung,
Cause when they're pissed – necks get wrung,
And everybody's stunned,

Oh he's smart enough to limit what he says,
Even those times where he's desperate to get it off his chest,
He knows they'll detest and will of course protest,
He's exercised his intellect to limit what he says,

Silence is better than caustic corrosive word,
Silence is better than inflicting nasty hurt,
Especially in those times you want to go berserk,
Cause that's only ever gonna make shit worse,

No he's not gonna speak too much,
He won't, cannot afford to –
Since it's virtually all inappropriate,
His foul mouth will be his doom.

Filthy Animal

Let me tell you something,
Shouldn't be a secret by now,
Pretty disturbing, pretty ugly,
Oh everybody's probably known it by now,

I – I just have this,
I – I am this,
Feral…
Filthy fuckin' animal,

I'm vulgar, inappropriate,
Disgusting – and I love it –
I'll repulse ya – atrocious,
Disrupting – and…yeah I love it,

I – I – I just…
I – I am this,
Feral,
Filthy - Fuckin' animal…

Gotta get it out my system,
Just gotta get it out quick,
It gets a little twisted,
I probably shouldn't exist,

I – I – I – just have this,
I – I just am this,
Feral –
Filthy fuckin' animal,

Rah!

Freeing Speech

It's healthy to have an opposition,
Though not for entire demolition,
It's healthy to have those that go against,
It furthers foundations for many strengths,

In the act of designing a flawless system,
You have to have everything in harmonious rhythm,
Propose an idea and subject it to discussion,
Deconstruct it if it seemingly projects to repercussion,

Freedom of speech can be a beautiful thing,
Not easily accepted but at times still inspiring,
Not everyone is going to agree,
But it's never any reason to shed blood or bleed,

You can choose to see it whichever way you like,
So long as you can keep a strong rationale in mind,
Sometimes it won't seem clear – and you may want to steer,
Well far enough away from things you don't want to hear,

Converting critique can be really quite tricky,
And the situation can get really quite sticky,
So continue to pick and ask where it gets vague,
Cause someone, somewhere, somehow will know a way,

We may occasionally come to dead ends,
And respect is still important whether or not you're friends,
You're always free to choose to agree to disagree,
But it's still never any reason to shed blood or bleed,

Demented Perceptions

I am most certain that the many of the things I do,
Wouldn't make the slightest sense
A marvel, the mystery, the things I do,
No – they don't often make sense,

I'm rising in a world I don't understand,
Strange and bizarre the many things out of hand,
The things that we can't often gain control,
Things that only seem to dig us a hole,

The rebellion is to question,
But answers cause slight congestion,
Whether right nor wrong demands attention,
Misconstructed interpretations unintended,

Fractured reflections,
Twisted, demented perceptions,

I rise and rebel gainst a world of nonsense,
Where elite await with hypocritical fascist responses,
And hope for commendary settlements, preposterous,
Inequality reigns and there's fuckin' lots of it,

What rebellion there is, is questioned,
And the answers you care to mention,
Only bring upon monstrous congestion,
And a great deal of unintended attention,

Fractured reflections –

Damning Perceptions

Before you damn on my perception,
Live my shit and know my intentions,
The façade you see is clever deception,
To intervene on any hazard and deflect it,

I'm aware it appears to be destined for descension,
No, its never been some delusional invention,
There's just far too much than I can ever mention,
That hardened, developed, of the wretched tension,

You all just make your mind up so quick,
Before you even take the time to know your shit,
Pit of snakes, all hissing and spit,
Tantrums thrown, raging, waging in fits,

I am the me I am due to course of experience,
You see me laugh because it does indeed get serious,
And we've both got our ideals of inferior,
Never quite so quickly considerate of the others interior,

You're free to your opinions but I wouldn't go to judge so quick,
Cause I know everybody's' all going through their own shit,
Slipped to the pit of snakes, hissing and spit,
Tantrums thrown, raging, waging in tiring fits,

But before you go to damn on my perceptions,
Live my shit and know my intentions,
For the façade you see is only a clever deception,
To intervene on any hazard and deflect it,

Forward Motion

I'm gaining a control over my emotion,
Keeping cool, calm amidst a commotion,
It's strange, but an evolution can be noticed,
I've fucked up – everyone knows this – but,
Forward now is the motion,

Takin' time to just be cool – where I would at once rage,
No longer the stupid fool, to parade a poor display,
No jackass, no mule, to slave and have encaged,
I have the know-how, the tools to make it my way,

Degrees of values and importance to matters where due,
Appropriately so, applauded, when eluded the deepest of blues,
More there is practised, becomes easier to choose,
More the practice – gets easier to get through,

Takin' time to be calm, think rationally, constructively,
Contemplate what harm, sensibly, productively,
May the only obstruction be what provocative seduction seen,
Limiting cognitive functioning, deconstructing, sabotaging,

Takin' the time to just be cool where I would once rage,
No longer the stupid fool to parade a poor display,
No jackass, no mule, to slave and have encaged,
I've got the knowledge, know-how – the tools, to make it my way,

I'm gaining a control over my emotion,
Keeping cool, calm amidst a commotion,
It's strange, but an evolution can be noticed,
I've fucked up – everyone knows this –
But,
Forward now is the motion,

I'm gaining a control over my emotion,
Keeping cool, calm amidst a commotion,
It's strange, but an evolution can be noticed,
I've fucked up – everyone knows this – but,
Forward now is the motion,

Forced To Fight

Yeah I'm not your average guy,
I'm not so easy on the eyes,
Been despised, far and wide,
Stripped of rights, forced to fight,

I hate having to fight for what I stand for,
The cost is always steeper, demands more,
The fact that I'm worth the same as everybody else,
But always forced to have to prove myself,

They never like the answer they always receive,
In spite of their wrongful assumption – I'm the one who grieves,
Their hate of being wrong, biased anger, misery – it's directed at me,
And I always feel it worse than what's conceived, believed of me,

I've only wanted acceptance, but can't even be spared tolerance,
An idle deception, of any chance, any hope of it,
The misrepresented reception, further horror and abhorrence,
No easy deflection, tiring, worked to over-exhaustion,

And for what? For what for how long that it never matters?
All this is draining, we're slaving 'til we're shattered,
All of this war for what little peace has run ragged,
How can I enjoy what little there is left when only feeling battered?

No... I'm not your average guy,
And there's always more than meets the eye,
Been tried, despised, spread out far and wide,
Completely stripped of my rights and always forced to fight...

Chains Of Refrain

I'm not no way near yet the perfect psycho path,
I do have a mean streak – a lust for wrath,
I anger, I hate, but I am sad,
Sickened, twisted, mental-mad,

I have a conscience I can't pass,
Wonder if I ever will at last,
I know it seems I'd made my mind up fast –
I haven't and I won't – it's why I can't pass,

I know right and wrong too well,
And I'm not in the slightest afraid of Hell,
I confront, I don't run – I know it felt,
But I've got the balls to face it dealt,

Crazy – as courage is – shit gets fuckin' done,
I spin people out yeah, I know they go numb,
I do try at most to make it fun – barely get none,
But I can never say I ever wasn't one,

I hate and I loathe and I do fear,
Plan my little vengeance for all my wasted tears,
Get it fuckin' together with all the right gear,
Sacrifice my remorse – sharpen the spear,

I don't anymore want to know right from wrong,
Not for the Hell I got when I didn't belong,
Clean snap at the pressure always coursing strong –
Amnesic – blind, friend and foe alike, all gone,

Once I pass that gut feeling, the chains –
The conscience – I won't refrain,

Dealings

You've gotta know what you're dealing with,
And know when enough is enough,
They push the boundaries of your tolerance,
And expect you to still stand tough,

They like a one way argument, they tell you how it is,
Don't fight just follow, don't wallow in the tears,
Don't see what you've done or your effort put in,
That all the time you waste is time you're gonna miss,

They never see how I deal,
To stubborn to care just how I feel,
Their standards irrational, just not real,
Expect a schizo son to be as hard as steel,

They don't see they stress me out,
Complain all the time I'm lain stretched out,
Don't see I'm exhausted, could almost be dead,
Limbs and body ache, and heavy as lead,

I hate that they think I'm lazy,
Same shit different day, shit's makin' me crazy,
It's me against them and all guns blazing,
And soon I'm stunned cold and star gazing,

I want out it's driving me mad,
I know a way I can but it is pretty bad,
Just show my reality has unravelled a thread,
And an incapability of keeping straight my head,

They never see how I deal,
Way too stubborn to care how I feel,

It's safe for me to say I'm still improving in my ways,
Through emotional days, the black, the white and the greys,
Always fighting through a maze, can't escape the craze,
The pressure builds steady with a vicious malaise,

There's no good way for me to say in a way they'd listen,
To put in place and send on way seems to be their only mission,
I never see much logic or sense in what they vision,
I can never seem to get away from the inconvenience of this position,

I wish they could see what they're doing to me,
I'm run so ragged I'm asleep before I'm off my feet,
Pushed to fatigue with thoughts obsolete,
I feel I'm being fed to lions just like a juicy meat,

The never see how I deal,
Too stubborn to care how I feel,
Standards irrational and out of the real,
Expecting me to be hard as fucking steel,

They never see that they stress me out,
Complaining all the time I'm sprawled on the couch,
Don't see my exhaustion – could almost be dead,
Limbs all in ache and heavy as lead,

I hate that they think I'm lazy,
Every day I cop it, it drives me crazy,
It's me against them and all guns blazing,
And I'm soon stunned cold and star gazing,

They never see how I deal,
Too stubborn to give a shit about how I feel,

But I've got news – I'm human too,
with feelings and emotions – even I lose,
And I swear half the battle is keeping them amused,
And when they are, it's me with the blues,

Better it's me than them I suppose,
I've shown more patience than they've ever shown,
Low to no faith nor much room for me to grow,
Do it when they want it – not just go with the flow,

I cop it from both sides – they eat me alive,
And I can barely strive – when I should already thrive,
How I wish I could escape – just jump in a car and drive,
Swear curse and carry on and leave it all behind,

Start brand new some other place else,
And only need to worry just of myself,
Do it my way when I face whatever hell,
And my way again when I need a fuckin' spell,

They've just got expectations, beyond my limitations,
Barely any patience nor pay attention with close examination…
No, I don't think they're ever gonna see –
any of what they've been doin' to me…

Shield

Too long it's been that I've been the distraction,
Too long it's caused my abhorrent dissatisfaction,
Time has come to resort to drastic action,
I can no longer sit and allow it to happen,

I have suffered extremes against,
Unavoidable, inconvenient events,
Always the solid demeaning defence –
Different consequence, came context,

Known for some manner of deflection,
Those desperate times some have need protection,
Never always my first and foremost intention,
But I won't take a hit without some hint for reflection,

I'm a human meat shield to limit fatal blows,
I generally take the heat harder than anyone ever knows,
Considered so weak if ever I let it show,
The fall is always steep and to a deeper low,

I know they need me more than they'll ever admit,
Everyone needs a scapegoat to escape their conflict,
And I know when we're hell bound, I can predict,
I'm gonna have to be the one to cop the bullshit,

It wouldn't be so bad if it was worth all the while,
Never too grateful, not many of them smile,
But I do remain a calm where I know others would be wild,
Controlling your emotion shows your adult and not a child,

Before acceptance of what consequences become commonly yield –
I expect I'll forever be naught more than a human meat shield.

Reasonable Hate

Don't hate me for no reason,
Cause I'll return it even,
Mind, mood, attitude, gone with the season,
Changed, legitimised with reason,

Don't hate me out of jealousy,
There's always more you never see,
The cost, sacrifices, compromises –
Reason enough it legitimises,

Don't hate me by another's bias,
Don't just buy what's advertised as,
Liars exaggerate – and over emphasise it,
Reason under reason – it legitimises,

Don't hate me for ways I'm better than you,
That I achieve more than you never can do,
I'll falter where you succeed, you'll see it too,
Reason after reason, legitimised, soon true,

Don't hate me for no reason,
Cause I am capable of returning it even,
Mind, mood, attitude – gone with the season,
Changed, legitimised with reason,

Don't hate me by another's bias,
Liars exaggerate and over emphasize it,
Don't hate me out of jealousy,
There's always gonna be more than you ever see,

Reason enough it legitimises –
Reason alone can legitimise…

Holding On To Hate

It's better to have it and not need it,
Than to need it and not have it,
Black and white, mood switches rapid,
Seasons change, it happens, it's habit,

Yes it's better to have it and not need it –
Than to need and never have it,

I'm holding on to my hate,
For all my peace' sake,
Cause my peace is always at stake,
Stripped from me by fuckers that only forsake,

I'm holding my hate intact,
For when I need to feed it back,
I know at some point I'm gonna need the knack,
So, I'm holding on to my hate and keeping it intact,

They feed it to me – they bait me up,
They feed it to me – they work me up,
They feed it to me – and I get fed up,
And they only ever feed it to me 'til it's time I fuck them up,

I'm holding on to my hate,
For all my peace' sake,
Cause my peace is always at stake,
Stripped from me by fuckers that only forsake,

I'm holding my hate intact,
For when I need to feed it back,
I know at some point I'm gonna need the knack,
So, I'm holding on to my hate and keeping it intact,

It's better to have it and not need it,
Than to need it and not have it,
Black and white, mood switches rapid,
Seasons change, it happens, it's habit,

Yeah –
...it's better to have it,

Bracing An Overload

There will be a many coming times
That will test the strengths of your mind,
Pushing patience across the line,
Pushing peace out of sight,

These times will never seem to end,
Wasted effort, never recompensed,
And various outsiders will think it trend,
To push you as far as they can send,

Be wary to wonder of it worthy,
Time and energy wasted does incur a hurting,
While you're enduring – they all could be deserting,
And you'll end up dirty, dying undeserving,

Enduring an overload that doesn't end,
Ingrates taking advantage and thinking it trend,
Wastes of energy and effort, never recompensed,
Always pushed as far as they can send,

Taken for granted, taken by advantage,
Raw deal rancid, sending you savage,
All closely habited all get ravaged,
Amped up static for a thrashing,

These times will never seem to end,
Wasted effort, never recompensed,
And various outsiders will think it trend,
To push you as far as they can send,

Enduring an overload that doesn't end,
Ingrates taking advantage and thinking it trend,
Wastes of energy and effort, never recompensed,
Always pushed as far as they can send,

Be wary to wonder of it worthy,
Time and energy wasted does incur a hurting,
While you're enduring – they all could be deserting,
And you'll end up dirty, dying undeserving,

Recycling Revenge

Crossing planes on which I'd once exist,
Clawing out from the blackened abyss,
Creep like mist – out from the crypts,
To wreak retribution, and pummel swift,

I'm indebted with dues, embedded with blues,
My vendetta will surely amuse,
A credited destitute, I had dreaded the abuse,
Regretted, resented that I wasn't the more abstruse,

Woven whisps of ghostly thread,
Bobbing weaving ghastly heads,
A wall of phantoms, far out spread,
Kinetic poltergeist fierce dread,

To cross through once again, for claiming revenge,
Rage swelling, ascends – it may be the end,
Taken casualties then, we'll do it again,
Collapse the defense – drag all beneath the depths,

Crossing planes on which I'd once exist,
Clawing out from the blackened abyss,
Creep like mist – out from the crypts,
To wreak retribution, and pummel swift,

Woven whisps of ghostly thread,
Bobbing weaving ghastly heads,
A wall of phantoms, far out spread,
Kinetic poltergeist fierce dread,

Taken casualties then, we'll do it again,

Hell Gets Me Hot

I love it intense, I love it extreme,
It's magnificent, just a dream,
Hell in every sense – the mutiny,
Can't be ignorant, gotta be true to me,

True chaos and torment excites me,
I take to it like lightning,
Despite whether it spites on me,
Entices me, yeah, excites me,

I'm horny for Hell, it gets me hot,
Horny for Hell – it's what I want,

I lust after omega disasters,
I mistrust harder many a bastard,
I love getting' plastered watchin' other fuckers suffer,
Laughed ever harder when they spitfire, splutter,

Hell gets me hard,
And Hell gives it hard,
Hell's made me hard,
I love Hell givin' it hard –

I'm horny for Hell, it gets me hot,
Horny for Hell – it's what I want…

WrathChild Me

Recent news has newly come to my attention,
There was a man I was searching for, some of my work has mentioned,
A man most responsible for my most insidious resentments,
A man so insidious – never caught nor apprehended,

Iron Maiden's Wrathchild song suit me well,
As if to say from the start my life was hell,
The seventh head, the seventh sin, by me men will have fell,

6th generation of black blood descent,
Pale, but still my love is sent,
6th on the zodiac, the sign of the serpent,
And like all snakes I suppose I make 'em nervous,

But the recent news of what I would call was conjecture,
There was nothing my mother ever could do to deflect it,
She ran with me – she had to, just so we were protected,
They would've murdered us and then they'd just forget it,

Trouble is now new news has been uncovered,
I really was drowned, an infant in the bathtub,
shortly after just recovered,
My mother scared, feared for our lives, beaten, bashed - she suffered,
22 years later find my fathers a fucking nothing,

But this man I swore my wrath upon,
Has a debt been waiting way too long,
Someday soon he's going to pay for his wrong,
The ground is where he belongs,

It was a terrible truth that I had died,
I don't blame them for hiding it and always lied,
People know what they despise when they know what it's like,
I was killed, revived, escaped to fucking survive,

And I never can remember it all, I was much too young,
I know that man is sitting there waiting, paranoid with a gun,
He knew if I survived – then there was a time would come,
It has, I've found him, ill have my compensation and fun,

He never had the right to do as he did,
I was an infant, tiny – not even a kid,
Something so defenceless, but it fuckin' lived,
Shit's just got more complex cause his pestilence is gonna give,

I was severely traumatized, and it never stopped,
Broken beaten, brain fried – don't say it's fuckin' not,
But I'm going to squeeze from him those first 30 years I never got,
The worst done to me in no more of significant time, he is going to rot,

WrathChild me has only ever fantasized,
Of the very pleasure I'll have when it's his time,
To rip him right open, searing pain, lobotomize,
Before hanged by his intestines, bled his soul and his life,

Whatever life he has had now for so fuckin' long,
The cunt run from his past – doesn't matter – it's fuckin' gone,
But I bet he's lived unperturbed – and he carried on,
Never once haunted, by this ghost – his wrong,

He's a fuckin' dead man and he has it comin' earnt,
He's gonna fucking get just as he deserves,
Only I'm gonna have the mercy and make it fuckin' worse,
He'll live to survive as a vegetable, a drain, a curse,

A truth was kept from me yes, just 'til now,
I can understand why my mother would block it out,
That man will die by my hands, strong and proud,
I'll have my vengeance once I've put him in the ground,

Fuck With Me Fucker?

You wanna fuck fucker? Fuckin' fuck then,
I'll fuck you harder than I've ever been permitted,
Fuckin' fuck with me fucker – I beg you – fuckin' dare you,
Fuckin' try fuck me fucker, but I'll fuck better,

Smack me, you'll see I won't flinch,
But I'll turn you over and make you the bitch,
You'll smack me and then you'll cringe,
You've worked out you're about to be the bitch,

You wanna fuck fucker – fuckin' fuck on right a fuckin' head then,
I'll fuck you harder than I've ever been fuckin' permitted,
Fuckin' fuck with me fucker – I fuckin' beg you – I fuckin' dare ya,
You come try fuck with me fucker – then
you'll work out why I'll fuck better,

Smack me one – I won't flinch,
But then expect I'll turn you over and make you the bitch,
You'll go to smack me but then you'll cringe,
'Cause you'll work out you're about to be the bitch,

C'mon, stop trying to fuck me – and fuckin' fuck me...

You wanna fuckin' fuck fucker? Fuckin' come and fuck me then –
But fuck me good and don't fuckin' pretend,
Fuck me hard and right to the end,
'Cause I fuckin' swear you won't want me up again,

You wanna fuck fucker – come and fuckin' fuck me then,
I'll let you try fuck me harder than you've ever been permitted,
Fuckin' fuck me fucker – I beg – fuckin' dare ya,
Fuckin' fuck me good 'cause I've fucked better,

38

Fuck Shit Up

Well, I'll tell you what the fuck's up,
I'm raging, rampaging gainst some cunts,
Gonna go down and go fuck shit up,
Schiz the fuck out – go fuckin' nuts,

Rip their fuckin heads off,
Kick in their fuckin teeth,
Put an end to it – make it stop,
Gutter stomp them in the street,

Burn them alive in their fuckin' house,
Fuck them far harder than allowed by my spouse,
Cause I've really just fuckin' had it now,
I'll put the fucker's in the ground,

Temper tantrum like a child,
Mate I'm losin' it – goin wild,
Bringin' hell – there's gonna be chaos,
Devil's not takin tonight off,

I'll put an end to 'em and make 'em stop,
Rip all their fuckin' heads off,
Kick in their fuckin' teeth,
Gutter stomp them in the street,

I'm raging – rampaging gainst some cunts –
And I'm gonna go down and fuck shit up.

In Rage,

I'm smashing the fuck through this dead horse,
Hatchets hacking through a blinded cause,
Roughened, toughened, a touch so coarse,
A full-steam-vent of my exhaust,

I fuckin' grab this and smash it 'gainst that,
Raging fuckin' wild and never coming back,
Violent vile words unheard erupt out spat,
This freight trains run off of its' track,

It's high stakes with no brakes,
Crippled faith and riddling hate,
Laying bait and sealing fate,
No ounce of mercy and no escape,

Bangin' heads and snappin' necks,
Returning similar disrespects,
Time is passed to repent,
I'll get those I haven't yet,

I fuckin' grab that and smash it on this,
You're damn fuckin' right I'm pissed,
Crossin' names off on my list,
Operation obliteration, on the cunts we'll never miss,

It's high stakes with no brakes,
Crippled faith and riddled with hate,
Laying bait and sealing fate,
No ounce of mercy and no escape,

Bangin' heads and snappin' necks,
Returning all similar disrespects,
Time is passed to repent,
I'll get those I haven't yet…

Afterthrash

When the rage has calmed,
And the up has come down,
When the rampage has numbed,
And there is no one around,

You're all by yourself,
Alone and outside,
Disconnected of the realm,
Broken off from all life,

Your temper has thrashed,
Peaked, then you crash,
You're lower than trash,
You feel lower than trash,

You look in from the outside,
Look at all inside,
They're all warm and confined,
All you want – you're denied,

You're all alone and on your own,
There is no happy home,
You're on your own and all alone,
Can't repent, amend, or atone,

You can only look in from the outside,
Alone, looking at all inside,
They're all warm, confined and fine,
It's all you want – you've been denied…

Your temper has thrashed,
Peaked, then you crash,
You're lower than trash,
You feel lower than trash,

Face The Pain

It's amazing how often the mental influences the physical,
Things can be said, heard, thought and felt all too real,
They can be felt and they can be shown,
If they're felt – it will show,

Maybe it's as they say – as mind over matter,
Soon as you mention pain – people generally scatter,
And there are many forms lest you can acknowledge,
Mentally – where able, if stable and variably by logic,
Figuratively;
Having to face ripping razors that pierce,
Dowsed over with corrosive acid that sears,
Stings, as you rage, with tears fierce,
Laughing as you lose grip – insanity nears,

Thinking it's a good thing I was pushed this insane,
It's much easier to laugh on through the pain,
To face the pain – but not want to call it that any more,
Facing pan – the trivial, games before the big show, the war –

But facing the pain all the same,
Laughing as it stings and wanna call it a new name,
Laughing, insane, but it's no longer pain,
It's a game – it's gain,

Raising a tolerance to it of sorts,
Raising a tolerance to the cause,
Raising a tolerance to the source,
Raising an endurance when pushed to exhaust,

What do you do when you can't run?
You have to face it when you can't run,
Lessons learning when others generally scatter,

Meant for when meant, say it's mind over matter,
Those figurative;
Ripping razors that pierce,
That corrosive acid that sears,
Stinging, raging, with tears fierce,
Laughing losing grip – insanity nears,

One can become accustomed,
Have endless terms of discussion,
Overcoming the pain – and rising above it,
Enduring all through it 'til it's ceased occurrence,

Some – many, may have it masked well,
A poker face – that at times you just can't tell,
Strong and silent – just as it all over-whelms,
They make it look so good that it sells,

But there's a point in time when I've realised,
Less I say – less I rage and less visually provide,
Under pressures – these extreme throes through life,
You're showing a strength a great many pride,

By somewhat showing you're not reacting through spite,

Even if you haven't shown emotion – you've still shown –
You've gotten passed it to a point and you better know,
Not physically representing it and losing it, letting go,
Shows you're mentally mastered the control of the woes,
May not think it but it shows,

That's a form of change – of growth,
Worth the pride – valuable to know,
I'm learning though I feel it's taking forever to do so,
Facing the pain, in what mature, responsible ways to show,

I've been the mad raving lunatic to lose the plot,
Infuriated against the plays to my soft spot,

Acting in ways that showed a soul – not,
Made others think I was only better left to rot,

I was facing a pain I felt pushed me insane,
Broke tolerance levels, probably trauma the brain,
Am healing, stitching through it – hoping to gain,
Stronger – to face it – if ever had to again,

And The Consciences Go...

Voices screamin' to do right,
Screamin' from the back of my mind,
Influences passed, beyond, behind,
Consciences trained to guide,

Fight against it and regret it,
Fight against and upset 'em,
Fight the flow the conscience goes,
Sooner or later you'll know,

Voices screamin' to do right,
Screamin' from the back of my mind,
Influences passed beyond, behind,
Consciences trained to guide,

But they're all screamin' for me to stop,
And I'm screamin back with everything I've got,
Screamin', howlin' – "it's nothin it's fuckin' not!"
Showin' signs I'm badly losin' the plot,

Fightin' against it and beginning to regret it,
Fightin' against it and they're all getting upsettin'
Fighting the flow my consciences wanna go,
And I know sooner or later I'm really gonna know,

Voices screamin' to do right,
Screamin' all from the back of my mind,
Influences passed beyond, behind,
Consciences trained to guide,

Past Guides

The voice I had that were mine,
Might maybe be the proof of another time,
Intuitions – or at least the voices, echoes of past lives,
To hinder or maybe help – no matter what it was a guide,

What voices might have told you to,
Were a maybe distant past you,
A kind of intuition to define what you do –
Who you are – what you're into,

A voice of telling to do right or wrong,
Voices I have felt never belonged,
Past fractures of a me once gone,
Come back, to live on,

I used to speak of manifesting my own soul,
So that I might have felt closer to my own control,
But I think by as I've learnt – there's no certainty to behold,
That this all may be a delusion, not some theory I hope told,

It's a theory I have that I feel could be close,
Could be reason I'm schizophrenic – it definitely shows,
Business I could most poke in my nose,
'Cause I know we still haven't uncovered all there is to know,

Voices tellin' me shit just to push me further –
Something else then says to me it's not for the path of murder,
It's as though the push is to illuminate us all for certain,
To get to see what's behind the curtains,

The voices I had that I felt were once mine,
May have indeed been proof of another time,
Intuitions – or at least these voices, echoes of past lives,
Are to hinder or help, no matter what it was a guide…

Downed On Again

It was only just mere moments ago,
I was up – stoked, mate I'd glow,
But it happened again – I wanna throw stones,
Snap some necks, break some bones,

I was up and I was feeling good,
But I came back down like I knew I would,
Came back way down – like he thinks I should,
And yeah now, it aint no fuckin' good,

He knows just how to piss me off,
He knows how and it never stops,
He speaks shit and the smell is grot,
He talks shit, everything I'm not –

He seems to think he knows but has no clue,
Never sees the shit he's putting me through,
He's always such a downer, it turns me blue,
Anyway that I react is a response I'm gonna rue,

It never takes him much to stall my progression,
Obliged to outline flaws with no care to correct them,
No resolve – no resolution, it's just best to forget them,
No grander plans for any future succession,

I was up and I was feeling good,
But a came back down like I knew I would,
Back way down – like he thinks I should,
And now like all ever – never to be any good,

He knows just how to set me off,
He knows how and it never stops,

Speaks shit – and the smell is grot,
He talks shit, everything I'm not...

...Downed on again,
Downed on again
Downed on again
Downed On Again....

In Limited Consideration

I've made people angry and upset,
Often left a cluster of regret,
Often spread a mass disrespect,
Attitudes contagious and yes, they'd infect,

Perils of limitless imagination –
Perils of limited consideration,

I've not thought where I ought to most,
I've not wrought words too cautiously chose,
And it's kept many from getting too close,
It's haunting memories and debtting ghosts,

I've watched from afar my blind escapades,
Witnessed this renegades climb to devastate,
Forsaken mental states that rattle and shake,
Never to truly hesitate 'til it's time to contemplate,

Perils of limitless imagination –
Perils of limited consideration,

Yeah – I've not thought where I ought to most,
I've not wrought words too cautiously chose,
And it's kept many from getting too close,
It's haunted memories and debtting ghosts,

Yeah – I've not fuckin' thought where I ought to most,
I've not wrought words too fuckin' cautiously chose,
It's kept many from want of getting too close,
It's haunted memories and endebtting ghosts,

A, considerably limited consideration…

First Moves Down

I dreadfully hate being a nuisance,
But I feel I often am,
The peace dooming presence,
Can't seem to understand,
Quite, and such an influence,
For one single little man,
The present nuisant influence,
Takes it, escalates it out of hand,

I don't want to be despised,
Nor have them all rolling their eyes,
Thinking all I speak are lies,
Nor fear I'll compromise,

I don't want to appear a threat,
Not when I know I'd hate the same respects,
To treat kindly before I'm even responded yet,
First moves down I'll admit, it's a standard I'll have set,

I do appreciate and praise, I do value,
All efforts, and in all different volumes,
I thank you all, I toast, I salute,
You inspire, I admire, thanks to you,

I have dreadfully hated being a nuisance,
And still do often feel I am,
A peace dooming presence,
I never seem to understand,
Quite, and such the influence,
It had escalated out of hand,

I never wanted to be perceived as a threat,
Not when I know I don't like the same respect,
Careful to treat kindly before I'm responded yet,
First moves down – standard set,

To Turn The Other Cheek

There may be times you'll feel meek,
That people will tell you you're weak,
I can't believe the hide, they dare speak,
You're more like God to turn the other cheek,

See, what is really weak, is lack of devotion,
Of the strength to hide, not show emotion,
To explode is pointless, and atrocious,
Even when inside you feel so ferocious,

It's best you keep quiet and calm,
And keep out of the way of harm,
All those other fuckers will come undone,
They will learn the hard way when the time comes,

You're the more stronger to keep it all within,
Stronger than you know when times are grim,
Keep an open mind, be open to the whim,
You'll be glad you had and you will grin,

You're stronger than you know when you keep it to yourself,
Strong to remain silent through the raw deal dealt,
No matter that you feel you need the help,
When you look back later you'll feel better than you'd felt,

Oh, there'll be times when you feel meek,
But don't believe when people call you weak,
You won't believe the hide – they dare speak,
You're the more God-like to turn the other cheek,

To take what you get and have to face shit,
For the God like grace – just keep your teeth grit...

Suppressing The Urge

I'm doing my ultimate best,
To contain my murderous urge,
Trying my ultimate best,
When I'm just treated like dirt,

I get so fuckin' pissed off,
I'm blinded by my rage,
I react before cognition,
Explode and decimate,

Most casualties are undeserved,
When I just can't contain,
Suppressing down my murderous urge,
Where there's gonna be some pain,

I am trying my ultimate best,
To prevent an inevitable worst,
I'm buckling under my ultimate best,
Suppressing this urge for blood thirst,

I just get so fuckin' pissed off,
I'm blinded by my rage,
I react before cognition,
Explode and decimate,

I never wanted to be –
A mindless violent fiend,
I don't know what's happening to me,
But someone's gonna bleed,

Believe me – I'm doing my ultimate best,
To contain my murderous urge,
Buckling under my ultimate best,
Trying to deter my urge of blood thirst,

Puttin' To Prac

You better take your own advice –
Or you better be ready to pay the price,
Take a look at your life – not just at mine,
And be it good measure it were just and right,

I hope you've also followed on through,
With what you're standing there telling me to,
I wouldn't dream any of it on any nor you,
But if I did – count I would've done the do,

Thing about hypocrites is they contradict,
Fascist double standards, they tighten, they restrict,
I wonder if they've been there or they're full of shit,
Cause these boundaries wouldn't otherwise exist,
Right?

Pays to observe,
Never be treading nerves,
Vigil every bend – round every turn,
With always another something to learn,

God forbid I ever end up like that,
Better I make and put to prac,
Or else it's just another knife in the back,
It's more than it's the talk, it's walk,
And I'm puttin' to prac…

Seeing It Now

I'm starting to feel changes taking place,
Feeling pulled free of the clutches of disgrace,
Things I'm learning, people meeting, colouring the greys,
My mind I find is broadening, improving in ways,

I've examined my performance over routine,
Statics showing it's improving,
Stagnant for some time but finally up moving,
I'm starting to smile, I guess it's pretty groovy,

I've noticed I'm becoming I've –
Only wondered, all the time I, curious,
Something I never understood 'til only just,
Recently discovered – at times prior – furious,

Think I'm finally getting it now,
It's strange, it's coming clearer now,
No one could tell me, not no how,
Realization hit me with a massive 'wow'

So, forgive me in time's I'm quiet or in silence,
By some miracle science, a peaceful alliance,
Compliance beats defiance, never knew 'til I tried it,
If it's for real I won't deny it, gloves on the wall – I won't fight it,

It's a hard thing to define and I could spend forever racking my mind –
I find now it's not so difficult,
Advancing in tactic – intellect is critical,
Tactic, strategy, keep clear of what makes you miserable,
All that drives you to be dismal, all that is abysmal...

I've noticed I'm becoming I've –
Only wondered, all the time I, curious,

Something I never understood 'til only just,
Recently discovered – at times prior – furious,

Think I'm finally getting it now,
It's strange, it's coming clearer now,
No one could tell me, not no how,
Realization's hit me with a massive 'wow'

Yeah, I think I'm finally seeing it now…

Layer Way At

A scholar but a brute,
Legitimately paid for loot,
Inconsistently abstruse,
Conveniently a ruse,

I'm more than what you'll see,
There's more hidden beneath,

Good lookin' but not so much that I'm not shallow,
To be indiscriminate can only mean hallowed,
A guard raised and set but mind's not so narrow,
Not ever even really so quick to send to the gallows,

I'm more than what you'll see,
There's more hidden beneath,

It may seem like I'm a sinner – I aint,
Some may go so far to say I'm saint but, nay,
Only meddle with imbalanced levels in ways,
A little rebel but no devil to set it straight,

I'm more than what I may let on,
But not for all unjust and wrong,

Refined but not restrained,
Kind but can still hate,
Takes a lot – I contemplate –
I'm shy yet I am brave,

I'm more than what I may let on,
But not all for unjust and wrong,

Layers upon layers,
But where to start first –
Chaos beyond chaos,
Perhaps begin with the worst…

Focus

Can't seem to keep a good focus,
Not for too long in a moment,
Can't seem to pay attention for very long,
It's same old, just same old song,

I know for a fact it pisses everybody off,
Believe me I know – it's like me brain has rot,
I can't normally seem to sit still enough,
Pay attention enough, it gets rough,

I never used to be like this – not years ago,
I guess there's been a lot that's changed me – it shows,
Time never waits, and it definitely never slows,
And I may have wasted more than I could've ever known,

It's a shame, it's a waste, I can only imagine what others think,
I feel at times I've fallen the lowest I could sink,
To be the cause for others to smoke drugs or drink –
And me? Well I'm just about on the brink,

I have, HAD, potential – if only I could sit still,
Perhaps it's curse, karma, for all my ill will,
This hell, my life, a nightmare – yeah, what a thrill,
I taste the bitter flavour, it's a bitter pill,

My memories pretty well fucked and had it,
Shit's just never gone the way I'd planned it,
None of us may ever really know why this happened,
But my last dying words may very well be "damn it" …

Exposure

I'm still quite so young,
And sometimes learning shit does feel dumb,
Never really had a clue – none,
Couldn't find learning fun,

If I were excited – it'd be different,
And I wouldn't remain ignorant,
Still not a know it all – still diffident,
But I know I can't be completely belligerent,

It's taken me embarrassment and many a shame,
To build a reputation, maybe put a face to the name,
Been many a happy accident, sounds insane,
Been to blame for inciting pain,

But a pain for a pleasure I assure you,
Just to show off a something new,
Not the desirable way – not many do,
But all too uncommon it's mistaken for new,

If it takes an exposure for real bliss,
Then I may be mad enough to take the risk,
New shit to see, feel, do, or think,
Exposure of my humiliation sending me pink,

For another way to look at it all,
Or many more never even seen of before,
Lessons to learn – my heads gonna be sore,
Intellect – some – its raw,

Exposure…

Bettering States

There's a method I use to when I explain,
My understanding in thousands of countless ways,
Ways to move forward, to heal kinds of pains,
Ways in which I wished my folks could've explained,

I utilize subtle sensitivity to mind's unaware,
A subtle sensitivity because I truly do care,
It's a mindful consideration, particularly where –
There is a weight to bear, felt previously unfair,

I like to be gentle, mindful of which word,
That elevates people and not inflict hurt,
To conserve what energy is pointless to exert,
But to show another I do, value their worth,

I exercise a patience and fully embrace compassion,
Because an appreciation does indeed make shit happen,
Fighting through frustration, and any dissatisfaction,
Delivering no trespass nor taking violent action,

There's no honour nor nobility going hard on those who don't know,
Even when it's difficult and you feel you could explode,
Take a minute to consider how you'd handle that your own,
Everybody has a pace and rate they need to take to grow,

You may be unaware yourself of what emphasis you'd placed,
What insensitivity, inconsiderate behaviour they felt they could taste,
A shameful disgrace that none need ever face,
Forsaking any chance, the world will better its' state.

Spiritual Little Me

It's more than a possibility,
It's well within my capability,
To please and appease,
Or infect with discomfort and dis-ease,

I can send out an energy,
Good or bad but plenty,
To sustain friends or drain enemies,
To fulfil or completely empty,

I can feed in a vapoury blast,
And reap with razor cuts,
Manipulate with a magnetism,
Mesmerise with different transitions,

I can manipulate emotion with a kind of telepathy,
Send out coloured auras of different energies,
Send a cool, calming motion to help ease an unsettling,
Never quite once confirm it was I but the entity,

I don't know whether it's a fault in my genetics or if its evolution,
Things I am capable of may cause distressing, yet offer solution,
Many a suggestion that's all but, in a different movement,
I can offer ideas of assistance, but you never actually *have* to do it,

I'm not particularly religious, though I like the metaphor,
I like having my own experiences – all the more,
In a deeper sense, I'm spiritualist – I feel my soul course,
I've tapped in to the source, but use it for good cause,

Can't say I'm closer to God or if I am one,
To know what I know but show I'm like one,
To feel strange empathies at various depths,
Responsible, sensible to share deepest respects,

Responsible with what power,
I can access it any minute any hour,
Quickly, intensely, like lightning it showers,
From the heaven's and the earth, I reef it, I scour…

It's more than a possibility,
It's well within my capability,
To please and appease,
Or infect with discomfort and dis-ease,

I can send out an energy,
Good or bad but plenty,
To sustain friends or drain enemies,
To fulfil or completely empty,

I can feed in a vapoury blast,
And reap with razor cuts,
Manipulate with a magnetism,
Mesmerise with different transitions,

I'm not particularly religious, though I like the metaphor,
I like having my own experiences – all the more,
In a deeper sense, I'm spiritualist – I feel my soul course,
I've tapped in to the source, but use it for good cause,

Can't say I'm closer to God or if I am one,
To know what I know but show I'm like one,
To feel strange empathies at various depths,
Responsible, sensible to share deepest respects,

It's more than a possibility,
It's well within my capability,
To please and appease,
Or infect with discomfort and dis-ease,

I can send out an energy,
Good or bad but plenty,

63

To sustain friends or drain enemies,
　To fulfil or completely empty,

　To fulfil or completely empty,
　To fulfil or completely empty,
　To fulfil or completely empty,
　To fulfil or completely empty,

Astral-Spiritual Persecution

I tread cold concrete, a cool mist thick in the air,
When I sense something behind me, a foreboding despair,
A curse to bear as my toll to fare,
And soon I do feel the shadowy figures glare,

For me to have had to have got here – I'd commit unspeakable acts,
Manipulate a gateway through with inconceivable tacts,
Stipulate victorious states to whomever may help me back,
And reward upon return for my end of what contract,

But these ghastly shadow phantoms, they sense me before them,
And I know the mass relevance – is as gravely important,
The misconduct I wrought had caused such disorder,
The construct I implored exhausted, it brought on a slaughter,

I might say here, my emotion is somewhat partially paralysed,
And I know a great few could say that that's a paradise,
Ever living up to the same old typical paradigm,
Same old paradox always subject to patronise,

I know just what these phantom figures want – me to reprimand,
For I broke spiritual, dimensional laws and it's bad, it's banned,
Altercations had tainted natures where tread when I spanned,
I've got no steady stand – I'm damned – I'm a wanted dead man,

I don't see I'll escape without suffering some vicious price,
And I especially love my life enough to skip on that compromise,
I'd hoped I'd never once have to make the sacrifice,
But these ghastly shadow phantoms have me locked in their sights,

I suddenly feel dread that this is my final time –
These phantom figures despised I'd obstruct the design…

In Contempt For Contradictions

Everywhere I turn – I seem to contradict,
Everything I only want to depict,
But that's what happens with mind all split,
Fragmented, multiple presences, states all switch,

There may be things I can't account for,
Things many may have seen me do before,
All of which I can't recall,
But has made me want to question more,

Some I can explain because I'd catch myself,
I'd find out coming back to wake to a new hell,
I wonder whether or not I was captive and under a spell,
Some strange phenomenon – I cannot tell,

I have wondered if I've been animated by outside means,
While adrift in sleep and cozy in a dream,
That possessions of strange presences, vent through me,
Without a consideration of how it dooms and consumes me,

Anomalies I couldn't ever explain,
But when others did, it sounded insane,
That some dementia just stalled my brain,
But woe, the victims with what it pains,

To say, want, think, or do one thing to then go against,
All contradicts what I may even get up to next,
I'm flat out imagining what it'll do to family and friends,
If this shit keeps happening – I'll have raised contempt,

The same contempt I'd had for myself for what contradicts,
The confusion, haywire, crossfire, through all of its conflict…

A Fucked-Up Thing

Responsibility is a fucked-up thing,
I can understand why nobody wants to take it in,
Truth fuckin' hurts to be smashed by on the chin,
I used to wanna (do something about it and) be king,

I can only accept and claim responsibility for myself,
It's just stupid poor luck that I influence others just as well,
If it's gonna go bad then I can predict it's gonna be hell,
I could be the best, intense, a worthy story tell,

Keep it interesting and forever have attention,
Keep investing and eventually have ascension,
Beat regressing our country back to recession,
Be blessing for integrity with devoted intentions,

The mystery is keeping them keen enough to watch you lead,
Have victory and succeed even when you hiccough a bleed,
Roughened, cut by some deeds, to face what responsibility,
The consequences reaped – steady on back to your feet,

Not certain that's a position I'd be particularly happy with,
Making choices to impact on how others live,
I guess I still do no matter what, in a smaller give,
Yet heavier still to a politician or a majestic king,

Responsibility is a fucked-up thing,
I understand why none want to take it in,
Truths fuckin hurt to be smashed by on the chin,
I *used* to want to do something about it and be king,

But now, I don't see it's a position I'd be happy with,
Making many choices to impact on how others live…
Fuck that…

Fallen Hell-Bound

I'm falling, spiralling, rapidly down,
Gliding, swooping, curling round,
Descending, pulled through ground,
Redemption failed, hell-bound,

Yes, sucked beneath the ground,
Down to the town the flames surround,
Crucified for the sins they eventually found,
Harrowing begins, heart loudly pounds...

Bludgeoned – beaten,
Dismembered – eaten,
Scorched and scarred and scorched again,
Contorted, twisted, torsioned – bent,

Laughing, crying through the pain,
Ripped open, slashed at, they eviscerate,
1000 times dead, reaped and claimed,
1000 times revived to relive again,

Split, splintered, burnt,
All the hurt I have earnt,
On and on, a sinner's song,
Smothered all with repeating wrong,

I've fallen, spiralled rapidly down,
Glided, swooped, curling around,
Descending, sucked through the ground,
Redemption failed, hell-bound,

Yeah, sucked deep beneath the ground,
Down to the town the flames surround,

Crucified for the sins they found,
Harrowing begins – it's all over now…

1000 times dead, reaped and claimed,
1000 times revived to relive again,

Laxing Off Law

It's so sad it was a system so created,
To benefit those and of the like who made it,
Finances and times forfeit on those who evade it,
On those brave enough to see it and want to betray it,

Law always seems to have the habit of replacing,
A consistency of matured sensibility practiced,
When and wherever we may all be disgracing,
In lieu of antique proprieties becoming ol' fashioned,

Living a most civil way appropriately,
Standard's always reflecting out devotedly,
When and wherever you may be socially,
Considerate, aware – even when acting out atrociously,

Consider where old virtues and morale fade,
Introduction of law only too soon invades,
Replacing where the matured sensibility went malpracticed,
In lieu of the antique proprieties going old fashioned,

Law in place to think for the some who can't,
In place to contain the compulsion before harm,
Never always deterring at times whatever's done,
Never quite predictable, and unsettling the calm,

Yeah law seems to have the habit of replacing,
The sort of matured sensibility meant to have been practiced,
When and where ever all may be out disgracing,
Instead of the antique proprieties gone ol' fashioned,

Law is a solid outline of a kind of decency in a way,
To be responsible, respectful, keep mind and behave,

Introduced when a heathen savagery invades,
To make reconsider when all virtue and morale fade,

Of course, if proprieties so seem to be antique –
Try alter the perspective so it ain't so bleak,
And don't whinge – it's 'weak' –

Recurring History

Here I stand at the edge of the earth,
A'gaze at a destruction never deserved,
The world, crying out its' ache and hurt,
The wake, the aftermath been birthed,

I'm no stranger to the misery –
It's been seen all through history,

There's no escape from the abhorrence,
The insensitivity, the intolerance,
The unacceptability of unacceptance for cultures,
High rank ego's pick the poor's bones like vultures,

There just never seemed enough compassion,
Never any morality nor virtue from the fascist,
And I have loathed it with a hot passion,
And here, this, the proof of when it happens,

I've never been a stranger to the misery –
We never escape this recurring history,

Only when we realise we're all the same,
That we bleed, and we all feel pain,
That when we remorse and feel shame,
It's then we will one day gain,

Loop

I spend a lot of time tying loose ends,
And it never ends,
I wish I could move forward and ascend,
Just ascend –

But shit just keeps on keeping me back,
Knife in the back – attack after attack,
It's just too easy for me to lose track,

So here I go again getting back to my feet,
Lost count over how often it repeats,
It's got me beat – let's pick up speed,
It's just going far too slow for me,

I hate this looping back to tie up loose ends,
None of it ever really ends,
I wish I could just move forward and ascend,
Just ascend,

But the same old shit just keeps on keeping me back,
Another knife in the back, wave after wave of attack,
It's far too fuckin' easy for me to lose track,

So here I go again getting back to my feet,
I'm so fucking over this shit, it repeats,
It's got me beat – I hasten the speed,
It's just taking for-fucking-ever to me…

Reverse Similarities

Power Play
Let's bring the man down,
Power play,
Tear him fuckin' down,

We laugh at him, his stupidity, he's a retard,
He makes no sense, he's fuckin' bizarre,
How can he make it seem so hard?
He's thinks he's so big – oh we're gonna make him a star,
Right,

Power Play,
I'm takin' 'em down,
Power Play,
I'm tearing society down,

I laugh at them, their stupidity, the retards,
They never make sense, they're all fuckin' bizarre,
I know it looks like I ain't got it hard,
I know they think I think I'm big – their talk makes me a star,

Power Play,
We're going down,
Power Play,
Every-fuckin'-one of us is going down,

I consider a loser is one that suffers loss,
Not typically the centre of the hot goss',
How have some minds survived when they should've not?
But never get beyond this one particular spot –

Power Play,
We're only going down before we get back up

...

Quid Pro Quo

Selfless for selfish motif,
When where to help a need,
Spare your greed – later that feed,
Reminisce on rewards reaped for the deed,

Selfish for selfless motif,
When where to take help in need,
Spare what greed – later that feed,
Reminisce what rewards reaped for what deed,

Selfish for selfish motif,
Takin' on more than you'll ever give,
Too much the greed to feed another's need,
Reminisce over what flaws reaped for what deed,

Selfless for selfless motif,
Takin' considerably less than you need,
Too many greed's to feed before they meet your needs,
Reminisce over what flaws reaped for what deed,

There must be equal give and take,
Else God forsake if you don't reciprocate,
There are stakes – make no mistake,
There must be equal give and take,

It's going to have to be a quid pro quo;
Like degrees received are to be bestowed,
Little room for error, little room for growth,
It's going to have to be a quid pro quo…

5 Minutes With Company

Not one of my most favoured moments in time,
There's usually a surplus of chaos in my mind,
But to put it all behind, just to get by –
A company arrived, I can't quite shake from my side,

I struggle with all sorts of chaos in my mind,
At times struggle with a focus at remaining polite,
Strange suspicion, paranoia, clouding my sight,
Paranoid questions at strange moments in time,

Can't quite shake the company from my side,
Could take quite a good lot of surmounting time,
I think I feel I'll struggle with this chaos in my mind,
Can't afford to show signs nor get so easily by,

I do tire quickly suppressing some certain pressures,
I'd much prefer it be that I shouldn't, never,
Ties twisted tight – and cannot be severed,
Fuck it feels like it's taking forever,

God! Jesus! Fuck! This is all driving me nuts,
Can't express my displeasure – I'm fuckin' stuck,
Been takin far enough, this is all too much,
This 5 minutes with company ain't happenin' again, get fucked,

Shit what's the time – must nearly be over, good,
I was beginning to think it never fuckin' would,
Was pacing, suppressing, like I never should,
Doubt whether it may ever be properly understood.

5 minutes with company
Just, fuck – 5 minutes with company,
… fuck…

Just Mind Yours...

Come on now I think you're being a little outrageous,
Slow down, take it easy, moods are contagious,
Breathe, exhale out all irrational behaviour,
You seem a little stressed – may I suggest a vacation?

I'm sure it can't be that big of a deal,
The heat I see you radiate could melt hardened steel,
I know where this goes – I know how you feel,
I know all too well that this is truly real,

Do you think maybe you're reading too much into this?
I'm sure it can't be what you seem to think it is,
Just look and listen here – they're not in your face, live – and let live,
Besides you're not that interesting, no one gives a shit,

Oh – let them think what they like, is it hurting you right now?
Is it? Really? Then fuckin' show me how,
If you're too focussed on them, how will you make them go wow?
Focus on yourself and get your shit done right, right now,

Why do you even choose to listen at all?
You're bigger, better, have bigger balls,
Just turn your back, let it go, ignore –
When they fuck up, they'll be as sore,

Not paying too much attention at what you're doing man,
I know it's difficult – I do understand,
But look – quick, before it gets out of hand,
Or... you may indeed lose a hand,

Choose It To

You could get behind it,
But you just get in the way –
It wasn't about you, you're blinded,
You weren't target when I'd say

I'm sorry it wasn't for you,
But it can be if you want it to,
I haven't the time – not with you,
But you're free to do as I do,

Shit, you're free to do as you please,
Just don't trespass against me,
If I want it – I'll consent –
But 'til then just let me be,

Don't take my words so seriously,
They're a vent off from my misery,
Exhaust's all hot and blistery,
May scar when touched or held searing,

You can always get behind it,
But just get in the way –
It wasn't you, you're blinded,
You weren't target when I'd say,

You weren't target…

I'm sorry the crossfire caught you,
It was never meant for you,
It can be if you want it to,
It can be if you choose it to…

Take What I Said

I know what you think it was I said,
But I can assure you it wasn't
I don't think what you thought was what I said,
Cause you know damn well it wasn't

Now you know I just can't stand this,
Takin what I say to give it your own twist,
Making it ever painful for me to exist,
Driving me in turn, to do some fucked up shit,

I don't want to take those extents,
I like my head without the madness,
But I know you're going to make me regret,
With a madness I don't like in my head,

You're going to take it out of proportion,
And that seed planted needs abortion,
And you're gonna drive me to exhaustion,
Covering tracks so that it's not reported,

You can't be trusted enough for you to think for yourself,
Because I can already tell you'd only just spread the hell,
Laws existing, regulations up-held,
A rehabilitation refinery for all us animals in cells,

Don't take the best parts to forge and justify,
When all others else around will suffer, nullified,
It'll rest on your conscience – you'll not be so satisfied,
Not when it's taken on many more a sacrifice,

And to remain ignorant in your trespass,
The hypocrite begets his discipline at last,

79

It comes hard, it comes fast,
It comes all too much and it shreds apart,

Don't think what I said as was when it wasn't –
Its' mortification will rumour round in its' gossip…

'No'

I see confusion in your eyes,
Sadly, yeah, you heard me right,
No if's, no but's, no word of a lie,
There's a first for everything and this one's mine,

I can't even believe I'm saying it myself,
I guess it can be good for the health,
I apologize – I must repel,
I can never see it going down well,

I regret to inform you I must decline,
I answer a 'no' for peace for my mind,
I have to show I have a spine,
Have to, at least one point in time,

I've never been a true sycophant,
Not always been a 'yes' man,
Don't expect you to understand,
At some point I've gotta make a stand,

Yes, I can see confusion in your eyes,
Yeah – you have this time heard me right,
No if's, no but's, no word of a lie,
There's a first for everything and this one's mine,

I do regretfully inform you I really must decline,
I must answer 'no' for my peace of mind,
I have to show I have a spine,
I have to at some point and it's time,

I just won't – I shan't,
… I can't…

Of Want, To Not To Be

It's only when I've desired,
To be like my brothers and sisters,
That I am soon reminded,
It's then that I will blister,

But to question being out cast,
Why I am not similar,
And why I cannot get passed,
All I know familiar –

Fear of loneliness is like that of disrespect,
You often find yourself out-numbered by insects,
And fuck man, there's millions of them,
But somewhere, somewhen another ascends,

Of all the reminders not to be,
Someone else reminds to be,

I could never fit in with the crowd,
And I watched from aside as they were loud,
Proud as they were of not that I was,
Those times I never felt a fuckin' loss,

To be one of them –
Ha! Fuck I'd be sooner condemned,
Another part of the heard – the sheep?
I'd soon be obsolete,

- Or at least the opposing me anyway,

Reminders of my want for not to be,
The majority of them and all in sleep,
No, nothing I could lust nor desire,
Reminders of all I loathe to be…

Sitcheeation

One thought led to another and –
Here we are,
To be completely honest –
I didn't think we'd get this far,

I understand the inconvenience,
But I'm in disbelief,
It's quite the experience –
Look at what we've achieved,

Surely you can allow for it this once,
Pass for pass, shared a like,
I can count a few things you've done,
Don't think you get off light,

It's just a short hiccuppance,
An untimely unfortunate occurrence,
Just a minor sequential up-commance,
But we do get passed these conundrums,

I know you've been there and done it
But this is my turn,
I'm still a youngin'
No other way for me to learn,

Won't take this lesson lightly but,
Be assured I will adhere,
Know it's seems like I am nuts,
Like I have just got no fear,

Chances are it may repeat –
Just 'til I'm right and I'm on my feet..

Sentiments

There are a great many things,
I have forgotten I know I shouldn't
Things I've exposed in my writings,
To help assure that forgetting wouldn't

Things I often try to get passed,
Facing some trials,
Whereupon happened passed before,
Forgotten having already faced same trials,

I'm a lot harder, meaner than I mean to be,
Having to tread through over again,
Never quick to recall a similar time,
That I might've needed that friend,

I suppose these pieces are testaments,
To all my different experiments,
Still, never quick to sentiments,
Forgetting mine wasn't the end of it,

I beg forgiveness for my rotten memory,
'cause I know if I remembered,
I'd never be quick to make enemies,
Help not hinder, if I'd remembered,

I have to beg forgiveness for my sick attitude,
The better me does hate to be so rude,
It's difficult, I do forget it's something I've been through,
Sentiments, compassion – I do forget too,

Take This Hard

Gonna take this hard lesson,
And make a much better somethin' else,
Maybe next go, maybe next turn,
I'll be a much better somethin' else,

Pullin' my face up outta the dust now,
I miscalculated, but won't forfeit,
Getting back up to my feet now,
Push, shove, something will give

Gonna take this hard lesson,
And make a much better somethin' else,
Maybe next go, next turn,
I'll be a much better somethin' else,

Beaten to sprites,
Inches off of life,
Blood flies,
But surrender denied,

Gonna take this hard lesson,
And make a better somethin' else,
Next go maybe, maybe next turn,
I'll be a much better somethin' else,

I've gotta try, or I'll just die,
Gotta try or I might as well die,
If I don't try – I'm gonna fuckin' die,
So, yeah – I'm gonna give it a fuckin' decent try.

Practical Thought

I suppose that they're all right,
That I don't think too practical most the time,
Ways I utilize thoughts in my mind,
Is it hindsight? Foresight? Second sight? Can't decide,

I have many reasons for retaining a little madness,
At utmost entertainment to void off of deepest sadness,
I still don't quite understand my purpose – never planned it,
I do often find myself on another distant planet,

My head's in the clouds or I'm a real air-head,
But can draw inspiration from just about anywhere,
Can manage to keep it together while being out-spread,
Still, not quite free of tearing out my hair,

Things I spend time contemplating aren't perhaps practical,
Things too extreme to be believed, too radical,
Things just nonsensical, insensible,
Perhaps inappropriately so, unintentional,

A little distraction here and there is fine,
Just maybe not completely most of the time,
I do have an active imagination, my wondrous mind,
I really let it loose when I unwind,

Simple entertainment for times of getaway,
All though I may never really get away,
I let go and creative conduit brain will play,
Little heartache here, little pain, but it's the fare to pay,

Confusion between delusion, fantasy and non-fiction,
Submersion, deep confusion, heretic to contradiction

Dead Set

I've anchored down the kind of me,
The identity of me I wanted to be,
And it may not necessarily –
Sound of the age I seem,

I'm so set in my way,
I doubt I could change,
I'm ever so set this way,
No matter that it's strange,

You'd better hear the firm in my voice,
Cause there's no alternative – no other choice,
I can scream like a banshee and make a real noise,
And if you weren't crying prior – your eyes will be moist,

I'm so set in the way,
I'm doubtful I'll ever change,
I'm ever so dead set in this way,
No matter that it's strange,

But take me as I am and count the blessing,
It could be a lot worse and heavily as vexing,
Not anyone of us would do with more distressing,
It's hard enough to break out of anything depressing,

There is good reason I've anchored down this me,
Anchored this identity – the one I wanted to be,
And it may not necessarily sound the age I seem,
But it's a lot fuckin' better than a nightmarish dream,

Dead Set!
...Dead set...

By Intention

It was always my intention to be pushed aside,
It was always my intention to follow way behind,
It was always my intention that I had lost my mind,
It was always my intention that I would lose time,

I never wanted to be a part of the herd,
Not when I knew I was mentally disturbed,
Mentally disturbed by all things just absurd,
No, I never wanted to be another part of the herd,

It was always my intention to make you push me away,
It was always my intention never promising to obey,
It was always my intention to invoke the dark to play,
It was always my intention that shit turned out this way,

I never wanted to be a part of your herd,
Not when your abuse would send me disturbed,
Mentally disturbed by all things absurd,
No, I never ever wanted to be another part of your herd,

It was always my intention to stand my ground and fight,
It was always my intention to defend my violated rights,
It was always my intention to guide away from wrong insights,
It was always my intention to expose the deceiving plight,

It was always my intention to viciously disagree,
It was always my intention to make sense of what you did to me,
It was always my intention to expose it, make it seen,
It was always my intention to see you pay for those old deeds,

I never wanted to be a part of your herd,
Not when your abuse would send me disturbed,
Mentally disturbed by all things absurd,
No, I never ever wanted to be another part of your herd,

Challenged At

You laugh at all the mistakes I make – the silly things I do,
But I laugh at how far ahead I am of you,
You see, you may never truly understand me,
My method, my reasoning, and everything else you never see,

The loneliness, the misery of thing's you'd never grasp,
Never quite really know,
Why people like me never last paving their paths,
Genuine, authentic, and ultimately – the feast for crows,

Multifaceted, multi-talented,
I can see why we're often challenged at,
Jealousy and envies are as unlucky as a black cat,
Trying to keep calm in the storm of vicious venomous words spat,

We need support and praise for the good we do,
Recognised, merritized, for all the obstacles we slew,
Not crushed and tossed aside like trash,
But craved and yearned and longed for like a secret stash,

To make a good difference and never be seen as a hindrance,
Spare a good distance and have attention instant,
We want to feel important, not to have to take precautions,
Never drained and pressured to the point of exhaustion,

Multifaceted, multi-talented,
I can see why we're often challenged at,
Jealousy and envies are as unlucky as a black cat,
Trying to keep calm in the storm of vicious venomous words spat,

Having Me Prove

I don't need to explain myself to you,
I've got nothing I need to prove,
So go and adjust this bullshit attitude,
You're seriously throwing out my groove,

I've got closed doors for prying eyes,
A jumbled jigsaw puzzle of simple truths and complex lies,
Anyone who tries is just wasting their precious time,
Vaults of schemes and memories locked under labyrinth design,

It insults me intelligence to see your lacking faith,
Resulting in irreverence I soon feel toward the prize lain stake,
What should have been a piece of cake, soon reeks of a bitter aftertaste,
Trying to dodge and weave round careless
mistakes and we may just escape,

I'm appalled you don't know me that well,
I'm abhorred to know this show is going to hell,
Stories ironed straight now, no deviation from the tell,
We don't take a spell 'til all glory can be held,

I marvel at my talent of employing cunning tactics,
I'll revel once prevalent enjoying stunning all the rat-shits,
A level, nonchalant, embroidered over running spastic,
A devil, it happened, toying and drumming out in static

But fuck me, just look at you –
All of a sudden you had me prove,
Had me explain through your attitude,
It stuttered and stunted me and threw out my groove,

Never wanted to – but explained it through,
I had to and now it's thrown out my groove…

Bite Steel

Damn right I'm fuckin' hard,
You're gonna bite my steel cunt,
Damn right I had it hard,
You're gonna bite my steel cunt,
Damn right I can give it hard –
You're gonna bite my steel cunt,
Damn right I'm gonna make it hard –
You're gonna bite my fuckin' steel cunt,

My hatred blazes ever brightly,
And you're not gonna be taking it lightly,
My teeth have been too long grinding,
Fury burning hotter than is blinding,

Damn right I'm fuckin' hard,
You're gonna bite my steel cunt,
Damn right I had it hard,
You're gonna bite my steel cunt,
Damn right I can give it hard –
You're gonna bite my steel cunt,
Damn right I'm gonna make it hard –
You're gonna bite my fuckin' steel cunt,

I'm fury hot and I fucking scald,
You weren't warned because they were never told,
You're brave – but I'm twice as strong and bold,
And your hell is comin' at you five-fold…

Stand 'Ards

What if I told you all you knew is wrong?
These standards you express, way you stand strong,
Yeah, beat at the one that never belonged,
Never belonged… was your mind gone?

Stand for what you believe,
Stand and fucking receive,
Stand, and guard it hard,

When I know what I see you do is wrong,
You express your disapproval, dismay and headstrong,
You beat on the one that didn't belong,
Ha – never belonged – was your fucking mind gone?

Stand your guard and keep your beliefs,
Stand it hard and fucking receive,
When it comes – you will grieve,
It will come and you will grieve,

Standards have 'em all lookin' down their nose,
Beatin' it black, fuck mercy – fuck repose,
They look but don't see and can never know,
And pushing it further bares their belligerent arrogance to show,

I know I can see many all doing wrong,
Never willing or ready to admit that we each, ALL, fucking belong,
Beatin' on 'em forever, forever beatin' and they're headstrong,
It's always wrong, but there's no sense when their mind's gone,

Stand what you do well and may you never see,
The cruel heartless shit they all were to me,
Stand for as long as you can but best accept when receive,
And as this fucking pestilence sweeps –
Just you better dare not grieve,

Clash

I got left behind,
At a truly crucial time,
I'd lost my mind,
Amidst strange influences entwined,

My teeth would grind,
And I grew a spine,
And soon I would find,
A way to uncoil this bind,

At times I'd lost sight,
At times I would fight,
Deny out of spite,
Defy unjust rites,

Clash after clash, unholy smite,
Flash after flash of rapid light,
Choke-hold grasps gripping tight,
A pummelling, a wallop, beaten to sprites,

But after a time you start to find,
A way to uncoil the bind of the influences entwined,
You grow a spine and through your teeth you grind,
You blast a piece of your lost mind, and leave 'em all behind,

At times you lose sight and you want to fight,
Deny out of spite and defy unjust rites,
Gripped tight through the rapid oncoming smite,
Pummelling a wallop, beat 'em to sprites,

Beat 'em to sprites,
Beat 'em to sprites,

Burnt, Blistering

I'm beginning to suffocate –
I've gotta get out and away,
I'm wasting away – debts paid,
Greying fast – a dying state,

Trapped in this world that doesn't fit me,
A slave chained – never free,
With no hopeful outcome I can see,
It's a reality, that peace is fantasy,

I cook and I blisten,
They never listened,
I'm stuck, imprisoned,
To what they had envisioned,

It's a nightmare I can never escape,
Not 'til I have met my fate,
This life I've shaped – my sick state,
Destined to ever devastate,

It's not what I'd bargained for –
Unsettling – this damning score,
Should've seen this all before –
Ravaged, ragged raw,

Wanted power to change history,
To correct mistakes, eradicate misery,
But it ends, and I'm left burnt, blistering,
Incinerating, embering, blistering,

Don't Turn Your Back

I have to beg your forgiveness,
I never meant that last bit,
Sometimes, I'm not myself,
And there was a brief moment just then,

Now disregard what I last told you,
Don't take it too much to heart,
That bad fucker's only gonna misguide you,
To meander down a monotonous path,

I can't trust myself enough to turn my back,
I know the moment I do I'll be gnawing at me neck,
Just don't push him enough that he finally snaps,
Cause it'll be a day we won't live passed regret,

Don't take him too seriously, me, and I, myself and them,
We'll try to keep him distant for as long as we can,
But should he reign once escaping our clasp,
May you be delivered to God's open arms,

Shit – fuck – here he comes,
Be vigil and alert,
We'll restrain him most we can
Should he go berserk,

Hey – what the fuck's up – what's that shit you're yappin'?
Nothin' man nothin', same old boring shits still happened,
Well – let me liven it up man, c'mon lemme at 'em,
Apologies, he had to leave there was another distraction,

(Fuck…)

His Ghastly Guise

I've felt him flit behind my eyes,
I am his mask, his holy disguise,
Some have claimed to have seen his guise,
Never true yet true, still, behind my eyes,

Some have said another lurks within,
And I have indeed tried best to keep him hidden,
Never certain he's out of vision,
It's as though only the black is his mission,

It's like a conscience you can't shake free,
And he's certainly got a good grasp on me,
He only ever laughs to see us all bleed,
Harder when he knows it's all by his deeds,

Oh, I've felt him flit behind my eyes,
And I have felt his raging despise,
I seem to be his mask – his holy disguise,
Yeah – I've felt him behind my eyes,

He's got motives, directives, ambition,
And hatred, anger and frustration all seem his ammunition,
Some have said – but I have felt him lurk within,
And as much as I have tried – he's equally remained hidden,

And I'm never certain just how far he is out of vision,
Even if he had us all pleading, he wouldn't listen,
I've known what he's felt behind my eyes,
I've been his ghastly guise…

Driven By Fear

Paralysed with a fear too often to count,
Kept me on my toes or with my head down,
Helpless – never to make a sound,
Heart pounded hopin' I wasn't found,

A foetal position curled up in bed,
Sheet covers pulled up over my head,
Panicking, shaking with the dread,
Fearful I would end up dead,

Adrenalized by the anxiety,
Might've otherwise felt almighty,
To fight – that Hyde so frightening,
Or flight – and learn, get enlightening,

I'd always wanted and hoped to be wrong,
'bout these things I could see that didn't belong,
To believe there wasn't actually more going on,
Sight's seeing – like a secrecy hidden from,
This strange, bizarre, phenomenon,

I did hear that the closer to the truth you are,
Things appear just to drag you back afar,
No matter your strengths, it changes you – you scar,
You take what you know to use to save you from the tar,

Static wisps of sinister delusions I sight,
Keep me alert and from my sleep at night,
Desperate to survive, I'm prepared to fight,
The moment I know they decide the time is right,

Fear has driven me to do irrational things,
Fear's driven me like someone was pulling strings,
But there comes a time and it wears thin,
You gather a stranger confidence – and you win…

Perpetually Changing

Can't seem to stop changing my mind,
Can't seem to keep a one-track mind,
Defining a damning before my time,
Defining a damning ending my time,

Can't remain focussed for too long,
Too much time repeating this wrong,
Attention just can't focus long,
Attention span – it's gone,

I get a good feeling and I go with it,
But soon I want to bail when it turns to shit,
And I wonder was it worth the effort gone in?
And then I wonder was it sufficient effort I put in?

But I get a bad feeling and I get cold feet,
The pressure intensifies, and I can't stand the heat,
The battle is soon lost, and I'm in defeat,
I am my own undoing, but I still seem to repeat,

Can't seem to stop changing my mind,
Can't seem to keep a one-track mind,
I'm defining my damning before my time,
Defining a damning ending my time,

Yeah I'm defining a damning before my time,
Defining a damning ending my time,
Wish I could keep a one-track mind,
Wish I could stop changing my mind,

I undergo changes more than a snake sheds skin,
Any chance a routine lasts is sadly, harshly slim…

Passed Relevance

You must forgive me for speaking of you in in past tense,
It's where you share more relevance,
Your pride in me – what such expense,
You were always cause for my dissidence,

You would only ever get me so far,
But always try to suck me under a pit of tar,
The weight of your burden always cut, grazed, scarred,
Always attempting to finish what you start,

I'll never know when you'll reap all you've sowed,
No part of me any more because I have let you go,
Cut you off, cut you out, for me to fucking grow,
And it's taking forever – it's too fuckin' slow,

I almost pity you for the hate I feel for you,
But's nowhere near like what you put me through,
It's deserved enough and I'd just for you,
I'm just the by-product, the fuck up you'll rue,

You should've taken more precious time,
Dismantling, tearing apart my sane mind,
Because one day you're going to find,
I'll be your undoing, your – drag back behind,

I can forgive what your pride cost, the expense,
But you're going to have to forgive me for speaking of you in past tense,
That, is where you share better relevance,
Where you were always the cause for my dissidence,

Passed is your better relevance,
I'm passed your relevance…

Vendetta

Talk about me, in front of me, to your mates,
Talk of the terror, talk my errors, everything I hate,
You make it ever difficult to wipe clean the slate,
Everywhere I go, that reputation can't be escaped,

Yeah, I fucked up, but I deal with it now,
You wanted me to feel and yeah – I feel it now,
You have to let go – I don't care how,
I still have to get passed and its difficult now,

You couldn't just keep your mouth shut,
You had to make sure my reputation was fucked,
So, I'll do the same, I'm mighty cut,
Cut as a mad snake, I'm mad, and you're fucked,

You talked about me like I wasn't there,
You talked about me, exposed me, you bared,
You talked like you never even once cared,
But you didn't, and I was fuckin' there,

Talked about me, in front of me, to your mates,
Talked all the terror, talked my errors, and everything I hate,
You made it difficult for me to swipe clean the slate,
Reputation just won't shake, nowhere I escape,

You could've, should've, but wouldn't know better,
And it seems like I'll be sifting through all this shit forever,
No matter what weather nor strengths of my endeavours,
It's personal, you made it, so feel the vendetta

Arsehole

I might sound like an arsehole,
But I don't fucking care,
It's not my fucking problem,
I don't give a shit,

Oh stick's 'n' stones – pfft,
How fuckin' old are you?
Grow a backbone –
And go make it do,

Oh wow – now that was tough,
D'you feel tough?
You got me right in the feelings,
Oh, shit didn't you get rough,

Sorry – I'm just one of the big boys,
My sarcasm? Well, that's me easy on you,
I do have balls – really big fuckin' steel fuckers,
And what about it can you do?

Now don't go getting all pissy –
What do you need? A little fuckin' kissy?
Fresh outta that – better get back to wishing,
I'm off for a beer and a cone, out fishing,

Oooh – Ahh – that was tough –
Do you feel extra tough?
You got me right in the feelings,
That's it – I've had enough –

{([*Smack*])}

Living Shit

You think I'm weak for having a whinge,
But never see what I have to put up with,
There's nothing I wouldn't ever give,
To see you live it yourself and put up with the shit,

Personally, I think you're weak for wanting me dead,
You've never been capable of contemplating my head,
You can never retaliate quick enough at what I said,
Ever so quick to draw out and spray lead,

You think I'm a threat and I'll regret,
But a threat is probably what you fuckin' need yet,
You're too worried about me not showing respect,
That you don't yourself and you forget,

But forgive me for having a fucking whinge,
You never see what I've gotta fuckin' live with,
And there's absolutely nothin' I wouldn't give,
To get to see you struggling with all my shit,

There's millions of you all the fucking same,
And you all seem to share the same brain,
Never to see my agony – you drive me insane,
And always ever lay it on people like me to blame,

But never once do any of you find peaceful resolution,
I can never see any of you all go through evolution,
Death, or desolation seems ever the only solution,
So your stupidity and irresponsibility can reign in absolution,

They're just as fucked as people like me,
But I'll always have the doubt they'll ever see,
Or, even take responsibility…

The Insensitivities

Whoa – man, I can't believe you just said that!
Did you even see his face?
You don't know how he'll take that –
But no doubt to a terrible place,

He was bothering me man, I just want peace,
You know what I already have to put up with,
He was getting on my nerves – I needed peace,
Fuck! What I wouldn't give,

Don't you? Can't you see what you just did?
That was extreme man, you should apologize,
You don't know how he lives –
He could have a horrible life –

Oh my GOD! Are you fuckin' serious?
Did you just hear your own self?
Did you not notice how queer he is?
He can take it straight to hell –

Even IF, he was gay – what does it matter?
That was cruel – downright rude,
If I wasn't ya mate, mate, I'd fuckin' slap ya –
He could've been a pretty cool dude,

I was uncomfortable – I wanted him away,
He should've been a lot harder,
Didn't you hear that shit he'd say?
It's a wonder he's no martyr…

Seconds From Peace

Now why the fuck is it that when I turn my back —
And I haven't turned my back for long,
That you feel primed to want to attack,
That split second I'm gone?

Do you see how much of a pussy you are?
Are you aware I'm dangerously close to kicking your arse?
Cause it's when I get back you're quiet and sparse.
If I'm not fucking fuming then I would just laugh,

I think it's getting a bit ridiculous,
It can no longer remain oblivious,
This bullshit's becoming serious,
You're inferior and it's delirious,

I can't seem to have peace for one second,
Any chance you see I do — you wreck it,
And I've had enough, I just can't let it,
I've called you out — you've heard me beckon,

It just happens every time I turn my back —
And I haven't turned away for long,
It's then you're primed to want to attack,
That split fuckin' second I'm gone,

I wish you could see the pussy you are —
Cause I'm so fuckin' close to kicking your arse,
Cause it's when I come back — you're quiet and sparse,
And if I'm not fuckin' pissed then I could fuckin' laugh,

But I laugh…

Those Fuckin' Retards

I have to put up with retards, think I'm tough,
These fuckin' retards think I think I am,
When, in all factuality – I *am*,

See I can't tell these retards I'm tough,
These fuckin' retards will wanna get rough,
But they'll get hurt – a just dessert,
Takin my tough for a bluff – they find out soon enough,

I have to put up with retards, think they're tough,
These fuckin' retards, feel they have to prove they are,
When, in all factuality – *I* am,

See these fuckin retards, can't tell I'm tough,
These fuckin' retards all wanna get rough,
But they're only ever gonna get hurt – a just dessert,
Takin' my tough for bluff – they find out hard enough,

The fuckin' retards never have seen nothin' like me,
They find it so fuckin' difficult to believe,
That something like me could really be,
A much something more than they could dream,

And those fuckin' retards are always gonna try,
To pry, to deprive, and ever only on the sly,
They waste your time, your mind, they never have spine,
They never want to let it go and leave it all behind…

A Rightfully Wrong State Of Mind

In a few silent moments I have wondered,
Whether my judgements were right in previous blunders,
Bias with a spite for hurt and anger, mind asunder,
Raged a rampage and had a sum run for cover,

I'll question this…

Have I got the right to wrong by as I have?
No, not when I have the acumen, others would be glad,
You wouldn't disadvantage yourself and make the lord mad?
Any lesson gone unlearnt will repeat 'til it's been had,

I've absolutely lost it and gone berserk,
Losing things gained that required work,
And out of their sneaky smiling smirk,
Id wind up flaming, blazing worse,

Calmed, then thought to question it,

The weaving knots of riddles and illogical sense,
And a great many some that were made of them,
And they break – rattled when you show it to them,
Shocked, too stunned to look for or make amends,

I've been sickened by my own actions often,
And it's still a wonder why I haven't lain any in a coffin,
I've hated feeling like wanting to, the anger of the pain – it's rotten,
Beating in a sense 'til I can acknowledge they got it,

But then,
If I'm not questioning it –
Someone will…
Is it right to do the wrong?

And The Devil Saves...

What truths can Satan provide?
But God has indeed lied,
I, Lucifer, the light bearer – of insight,
Not necessarily the evil side,
…and with pride,

What god missed in his rush,
The fuck up that is us,
Devil saves at last,
With the forfeit of new trust,

You can get as far as your intelligence takes you,
But it's contingent on what diligence, it may forsake you,
Show the thirst – show your works worth – it may save you,
Do as the devil and with whatever it may take you,

Question is, can Satan be honest once?
Hypocrites hate it at the crunch,
Hypo-Christs, that come undone,
Crippled – take out everyone,

Jesus was made example of,
But Lucifer was first,
Who is it really trampled on?
Who is it really cursed?

What God missed in his rush,
The fuck ups that are us,
But with forfeit of new trust,
Devil saves at last,

What truths can Satan provide?
That God does indeed lie,
I, Lucifer the light bearer – of insight,
Not always ever the evil side –
…and with pride…

To Pass At Last

Life I know is not as it once was,
I'm alone in a desert that stretches beyond,
Sand loose, sand dunes, steeps with long drops,
Sandstorms entomb, and all is lost,

People I've loved and grew to have long passed,
If I could only remember how to feel – I may have been crushed,
Solitarily confined you lose mind, perhaps your name at the very last,
More merely shadow with a still beating heart,

Though as I speak in figurative proportion,
Settling in a feel a severe state of rigor mortis,
Where I'm headed next – I say I'm lookin' forward to it,
I've felt dead for centuries, there was just never more to it,

I've taken refuge under some trees, shot to fuckery,
Engaged in war with the enemy, my clothes torn and bloody,
I doubt anyone'll remember me, I wasn't what you'd call friendly,
Only a rare few saw the best of me, but that
rare few were equally measuring,

You'd have to have been raised the same to understand,
Knowledge is power, and it provides the upper-hand,
Use it correctly and you could be the man,
Or utilize it falsely and be banished to 'barren lands'

I'm bleeding out and feeling faint,
I'm kind of glad oi die this way,
Tears of blood for fallen saints,
I've long yearned for this day…

Transcendence

I may never end up making it,
To where I'd always dreamt to be,
Despite my forsaken aspirations,
A diviner path is carved for me,

Was, human once…
But I've since forgot,

To work towards your utmost desire,
And a misfortune strikes, it's waste,
You had the passion – had the fire,
But… despite mistakes, you tickle another's taste…

And, one man's loss is another's gain,
So they say,

Worked with a passion toward my desires,
With drive to acquire all I admire,
No matter what the stakes – I'd do what it takes,
And scorn when it breaks… yet smile when it's replaced
(Switched States…)

I was human once –
But have since forgot,

And when destiny shines, you just don't believe your eyes,
You do wonder how it could've ever been you,
Fortuity in life, by miracle, defining a mighty surprise,
Receiving something bigger, never believing it true…
(at first…)

I was human…

Gateway

It takes a time like now when,
It's better to write being bent,
To uncluster a jumble and lay sequence,
Mixed work of words that don't make sense,

A couple of cones here and there,
Slows a rush of thought process,
But a couple good cones get me where,
I prefer to profess,

They do call it a gateway,
A power play, another way,
Onward to harder drugs, depart astray,
Not so much that it alters the brain,

I won't say it doesn't,
But I'll never stop – I love it,
Many will disagree and say that I mustn't,
But I just surmise they covertly covet,

The weed brings me up to a level,
That I admire most and revel,
Inducing a state ever so settled,
Along with some tunes, preferably metal,

But I teleport to another space,
An alternate realm with extraordinary tastes,
And I write as smooth as the words sounded spake,
And it all flows so beautifully at haste…

Chemical Stimulus

I find chemicals a beautiful stimulus,
Keeps my crazy to a minimalist,
Calm, cool, collected, an anti-dismalist,
A peaceful, rational, optimal, visualist,

I like me better never on edge,
And some chemicals help me keep my head,
Sure they may kill me, I'll eventually end up dead,
But never before the enjoyment has been spread,

They soothe my brains receptors when in stress,
Chill me the fuck out whenever I am upset,
And they are quite the expense to have invest,
But all the more a treasure to have again yet,

Nicotine from cigarettes, THC from Cannabis,
Benzines from petroleum, alcohol and spirits,
Fumes of fibreglass, tar of the bitumen,
Scents and smells that tantalise but kill off an acumen,

They all soothe my brains receptors when I'm in stress,
They can chill me the fuck out when I'm upset,
They really can be quite the expense to invest,
But all the more a treasure to me to have again yet,

Yeah – I find chemicals a beautiful stimulus,
They can maintain my crazy, back to a minimalist,
To a calm, cool, collected, anti-dismalist,
To be a peaceful, rational, optimal visualist…

Barbed Words

Those last words you said,
They echo all throughout my head,
They detail an outline like a fence,
A kind of barricade for peace' sake –
It makes sense,

But you best keep mindful of those words you spoke,
A misinterpretation really ain't a joke,
Foreboding apprehension variable – dependant to the tone,
Esteem might never quite receive the repose it hopes,

Those words you spoke were barbed,
Those words you chose were sharp,
The fence you set between yards,
Does it's wonder for both halves –

You set the perimeter, you marked the grounds,
We know where we stand and there's no backing down,

Those last words you said,
Will always echo in my head,
The outline, the detail – like a fence,
A barricade for peace' sake – it makes sense,

Those words you spoke were certainly barbed,
Those words you chose prick, were mighty sharp,
But the fence you set between both yards –
It, does it's wonder's for both halves,

We know where we stand,
Yes, we know where we stand,

Askin' For It

I don't know how or why I can do the things I can,
And I'll never know if I'll ever understand,
I think I'm a man but may be more than I am,
And I could be expected for higher demand,

Now I'm not comparing myself to Christ,
Not when my life's been nothing of the like,
A code in metaphors designed to lead and guide,
A hope to suffice to lead to a paradise,

Jesus said another would come,
And claim to be him with his tongue,
Spine-tingling, chilling, the beast will come,
And spread mass anarchy – his will be done,

I don't want to think myself as Christ,
Nor the antichrist – I want a peaceful life,
For surely as Jesus spake –'it will not be I'
But he, the beast, will spread the lie,

There are things I can do and I can't explain why,
And it's never in my best interests to lie –
It's not my true nature, it's the lies I despise,
I want a long peaceful life and lies will compromise,

I have asked to receive his gifts, yes, I have,
I have had a prior want for what he had had,
To heal over old wounds and peel off old scabs,
Continue the good work and have myself a stab,

I suppose you really do have to be careful at what you wish for,
Cause I feel in some ways I'd been given more than I'd bargained for.

Wonder Spared

I could explain through this despair, expose a gloomy air,
That what pains are shared – various depths rare,
One in a thousandth spread over a great where's
Wonder if what wonder is spared – if it has compared,

I loved her a little too much to know it was gonna hurt,
When times got tough and I knew she was gonna dessert,
And she did – guess I got what I deserved,
And I'll never know except doubt she'll have felt as hurt,

I thought it would be hard – but I'm smart – I can express it,
No fear – raise the harmony – got guts enough to confess it,
I sympathise with those completely lost in these descensions,
Not so freely able to so amend needed corrections,

He's not normally one to give praise but quick to cut you to size,
I've wondered whether he only knew malaise,
without thorough compromise,
He's a hard bastard all the time – never really see a softer side,
I wouldn't really know what he's like beneath all that pride,

And I fuckin' thought it was hard on me – but I'm smart, I express it,
No fear – raise the harmony, got the guts to confess it,
I can empathise with those completely in these descensions,
Not so freely able to so amend needed corrections,

And I would explain through my despair – reveal a gloomy air,
That what pains are bared are shared – various depths rare,
One in a thousandth spread over a great where's,
And wonder if they wonder, if it's spared, and compares…

Way Off

You've got it all arse round backwards,
When we're trying to go forwards,
I'm wasting time explaining why,
When I'm facing narrow minds,

Who's laughing? You're not, I'm not,
No, it wasn't funny – it burnt, it was hot,
I'm certain your assumption was way off,
Was misrepresented – not what it was,

We are at a crossroads but on opposite sides,
Of way too separate ideals each in mind,
Only yours I'll allow, perhaps not mine,
To see what determines, what defines,

To come known to me all I'm unaware,
To hear it out, listen, it's only fair,
I'm certain there's gotta be a message there,
I've got the consideration to spare,

Because I'm bound to learn I was wrong,
That even I assumed and found I was way off,
Ideals we had had of each other, but so not,
All misrepresented – never what it was…

If The Want Is Strong Enough

I want speak something worthy knowing,
Something I have seen over time has been growing,
People that trespass whichever way they're toeing,
Satanism doesn't truly imply hell is where I'm going,

The world is still far too young,
But not enough to know when wrong is done,
Extremists misinterpreting accessorized with bombs,
Car jackings, rapists, murderers, scum all with uncivil tongues,

What ever happened to honour, glory and virtue?
Morale, integrity – paying your dues?
Responsibility, courtesy and truth?
Tainted perception and depressing attitude,

The world will never change if it doesn't want to –

We've seen it before and we'll see it again,
You're better prepared when you know it's comin',
Brace yourself for when they start head bangin',
Guess some minds just need changing...

We know war ain't the answer,
But it makes some fucker's rich,
Pray and affirm your mantra,
Before we're all blown to shit,

You've gotta improvise, relate something they like,
Interprets rights and reason against the irrational fight,
Disable, disarm them before they strike,
Strategize, tactfully negotiate peace for mind,

The world will one day change when it wants to,

Kid Trouble

Yeah, I was a kid that got into trouble,
Often for doing shit that I shouldn't
A swift kick up the arse plenty, and double,
For better measure they knew I wouldn't,

As hard as they were on my arse,
I'd wonder if they knew it'd last,
And as hard as I would fight and rebel,
The harder the wrath I incurred they'd dealt,

I was a kid that was often in the shit,
Rebellious acts of defiance and disregard commit,
Probably got away with more than I can admit,
But reckless as I was I still learnt the odd trick,

I have had to be reminded of shit that I was blinded,
And I would always fight up until I would sight it,
Truths hardly minded but boy, did I bite it,
Facades beaten by the differences collided,

Commandments, conditions, and complimentary contradictions,
Condescension, confliction, with no worthy competition,
Repetition, remission, reason for reminiscence,
A prick of a kid, the biggest shit in existence,

Yeah, I was often in the shit,
And I'm not too proud to admit,
Truths were often a hard-knuckled hit,
The kicks up the arse were swift,

Unreliable Recollection

I've written over a dozen times how –
I've done shit and not remembered when,
Done shit and now recall the why –
Desperation or not to hide whenever where –

Smart not paying too much attention,
Smart for if it may ever be mentioned –
Smart as to never upset when,
Smart, spiral out in ascension,

To never really leave a mental trace,
Whenever a disruption needs the face,
Tryin' to keep intact my remaining grace –
Barely recalling that time or place,

Smart paying only just enough attention,
Outside observations at all rumours getting mentioned,
Smart – to never get to upsettin' when,
Smart – spiralling out in ascension,

It's smart enough to see it can be done,
With or without too much of it seen as done,
It's taken me time 'cause I am an only one,
But these begin to show what I will have become,

I can't be held too well to memory on occasion,
A sleight of hand defence against a mental invasion,
Deliberately accidental – whichever the persuasion,
Preplanned – freerun, whichever situation…

Smart paying only just enough attention,
Outside observations at all rumours getting mentioned,
Smart – to never get to upsettin' when,
Smart – spiralling out in ascension,

Lonely Little Pot-Head

I'm a lonely little pot-head lookin' to get high,
Just to get passed the shit that normally makes me cry,
This lonely little pot-head wants to get high,
He wants to try or he might as well die,

I'm a lonely little pot-head lookin' to get stoned,
Either hydroponic or outdoor grown,
This lonely little pot-head wants to get stoned,
With friends or alone – and to feel at home,

I'm a lonely little pot-head lookin to get high,
I'd do it any day any night, all through my life,
This lonely little pot-head wants to get high,
Any and every time he loses his mind,

I'm a lonely little pot-head lookin' to get stoned,
To get some shit chopped to toke, some pot to smoke,
This lonely little pot-head wants to get stoned,
To nick off home and punch down some cones,

I'm a lonely little pot-head lookin' to get high,
Just to get by the typical shit to leave behind,
This lonely little pot-head wants to get high,
For every fuckin' time he loses his mind,

I'm a lonely little pot-head lookin' to get stoned,
Either hydroponic or outdoor grown,
This lonely little pot-head wants to get stoned,
To fuck off home and pull down some fuckin' cones,

Myself Alone

I am by myself, but I am not alone,
Mischievous presences call my head home,
Constant contradictions, conflict with all I've known,
Its rapid cross fire in a mindless war zone,

I stand alone but I'm not by myself,
My kind of fun would have me confined to a cell,
A sensitive society just wouldn't take it well,
But collapse at the faintest trace of my hell,

I am by myself, but I am not alone,
Alternating presences with each a mind of their own,
Multiple altercations, to which I'm prone,
Outside influences just appear to drone,

I stand alone but I'm not by myself,
A variety of characters this one vessel melds,
Some believe to be ill fortune and poor health,
But, a strength I do find in wealth and stealth,

I am by myself, but I am not alone,
Everyone of them want a loan to the throne,
When I want peace and silence – I just get stoned,
And I keep them all quiet just huffin' down cones

I am alone, but I am not by myself,
I chance success better keeping all this withheld,
It'd raise alarm bells, to tell what I have felt,
but certainly a story worthy told to sell,

Irritably Restless

There are some nights where I can't sleep,
Some nights I feel particularly ecstatic,
Some nights I'm heated passionately –
Feeling restless,

Times I guess I get so wound up – I –
Probably could do with a good fuck – I –
More so wound tight – I –
Might pick a fight,

Some nights, no, I can't sleep –
Shit does keep me from my dreams,
Some nights I'm ecstatic –
Some nights, heated passionately,
Feeling violent,

Times I guess I get so wound up – I –
Probably could do with a good fuck – I –
Might be more so wound tight that I –
Might pick a fight,

Those some nights I can't sleep,
Things I'm nervy with or ecstatic,
Shit keeps me from my dreams,
Twitchy – nervy – passionately –
Restless,

Could maybe do with a good fuck – I –
Feel so tense, so wound up – I –
Should probably get a fuck – I –
Might even pick some fight…
Violent…
Relentless, restless…

Saw Something

There was just something in the corner of the room,
Oh yes, I saw it, it was truly there,
It caught my attention then tried to elude,
But I know what I saw, I guarantee it was there,

Strange creatures resembling rats but with scales,
With up to eight legs and two tails,
I swear it by my own two eyes, and I went pale,
I fixed my attention and it disappeared back under the veil,

I just saw something outside through the window glass,
A breeze outside cycling leaves round in a gust,
But centred there stood a beast – only just,
My mind does play a trickery even I mistrust,

Strange creature, hunched like a gorilla,
Long giraffe like limbs, grey – almost silver,
If it were stronger in this dimension, it might've been a killer,
It would be a true terror, dread, and fear instiller,

I just saw something that doesn't belong,
Something eerie, creepy, I am sensing wrong,
Feel a heat of hate radiate – and it's strong,
Don't think it'll be too long before I'm taken, gone,

Strange aura's of presences that shouldn't be,
Terror – dread – fear – bearing a toll on me,
Can't sleep – they're not pleasant dreams,
And I'm always ever the only one who sees,

Creatures that could really rattle the brave,
The courageous all too, sent afraid,
Psychosis? Or supernatural phenomenon here to stay?
I've seen it, I've heard it, I've felt it, and I've gone ever grave,

Metallion

Metal is my way – won't deny it, won't defy it,
Metal has a way of getting me all excited,
Pumped, ready to fuck or fight it,
Metal as it should be, heavy, prided,

Except so that it's so variously divided,
Metal is just metal to me, still love it, stand by it,
It shares a whole community, brothers and sisters, buy it,
It's as beautiful a thing by which none should ever be frightened,

So many different extents taken beyond,
Metal going further yet than other music has gone,
This culture – this everything, it's where I belong,
Standing, hardened, brutal, like all who had so strong,

Extensive the energy, the genius to the work,
Power to relax, soothe, love – and go berserk,
But when I write my verses, it's the dark is where I lurk,
Formulating by my lone, religiously – without the church,

Metal Is by far nothin' I could ever despise –
Not even like when I had the dream of –
Rob Zombie gettin' a gobby off a girl was mine,
A dream that threw me off for a considerable amount of time,
No matter – it's been metal to have made me feel the more aligned,

Metal can't be scrutinized for the reason it exists,
Metal is a nation of thousands, loyal to the lists,
Thousands of metal fans all lovin' it when they're pissed,
And pissed, the anger vibe – when you wanna fist,

Extensive, the energy, the genius to the work,
Power to relax, soothe, love – and go berserk,
Whenever I try write mine, it's at dark with the verse,
Formulating by my lone – religiously, with or without church,

Right Rites To Write

All of my writing is basically fiction,
For truths I face are riddled with contradiction,
It's an escape, an expression of conflict,
I merely, fantasise, imagine, depict,

I don't want to live a life of peril,
Edgy, easily upset, or wild or feral,
I do indeed get ever so mental,
But express it on paper with pen or pencil,

I can't afford to react to provocation,
Cause I know I'd cause great devastation,
Be confined a long time in incarceration,
Walk free – if I make it, too anticipated,

No, I can't afford to act on impulse,
Trying to refine it and not repulse,
Practice makes perfect and we're gonna soon see results,
Working slowly but surely on these flaws and faults,

I'm lucky I can outline a variety when I write,
Things I never saw before but gave insight,
Been wrong plenty but one day I'll get it right,
Things I've been blinded by before – I do sight,

I may write a great deal of intense bad,
But it's not too long after I get it out I feel glad,
Would've otherwise been raging mad, or gloomily sad,
I have always felt better for writing when I had,

Epiphany's – Revelation, that I sooner acquired,
Only after a release, constructively inspired…

The Associated Feel

I have often wondered how words can have the vibe they do,
Particular words for a particular feel and their use,
I'm certain a majority of them do as they're meant to,
But all the while I can't help to feel at times amused,

It could just be that I'm out of my mind,
Not even certain whether it's been through another's mind,
But the certain words used for whatever design,
Meant to lead to imagination, and have it unwind,

I'm talking about the association of feeling to the word,
Whatever way you choose for it to be heard,
The emotion, the feeling – the notion to exert,
An incitement of movement – although inert,

Meticulous formulation to emphasise the association,
Articulate foundations accentuating its participation,
Reason wound deeply through, deeply woven in explanation,
Intricate – mysterious, I have questioned its manipulation,

I have watched its mystery work wonders,
Even dealt a little throughout my own plunders,
The cool sweet calm cloaking a ravenous thunder,
A hunter with a hunger for a number,

Whether to intimidate, or show you're intimate,
Certain words synchronate rouse feeling, it's legitimate,
Could make you want to go the distance, or go distant,
It could make you wish it – if you felt you'd missed it,

The carefully yet cleverly crafted formulation –
It's association, the feel – whoa, yeah the manipulation…

Nexus Of Feeling And Spite

You say I'm feminine, for my feelings –
According to my spite – you're a cunt for laughing,
Out of my 'feelings' I can rightfully spite,
On anything about and on this cunt laughing,

Or so it would seem, that it would be,
Every altercation there was against me,
Slaves – as they behave, never to be free,
The shame as they behave – and never see,

Once upon a long arse fuckin' time ago –
That was also me,

It's all consideration I put in that gives me power,
Calm to control what mood, yes – one even that's sour,
Just won't show I don't know it and I'll over tower,
Astonish them with knowledge – give them equal power,

And so that it will seem, that I'll will it to be,
Exempting the altercations there are against me,
Slaves as once behaved but released, set free,
Waive what shame portrayed – let them see,

Because, once, upon a long arse fuckin' time ago,
One of those laughing cunts was also me,

I like to think I can repent and make amends,
To think I can metamorphose and transcend,
To have a peaceful, blissful, nirvana before death,
A trail blazing trend, to elevate all to ascend…

The Accused

Before you go to point the finger at me,
I'll show 'em all what you don't want 'em to see,
Understand I'm a soldier, ready to bleed,
To rid our nation of your cruel deeds,

There's less of you amongst us than you comprehend,
Every vow you break just proves you condescend,
Know you'll reap the consequence for all you intend,
And as you lose the upper hand – how then will you offend?

You may say that you're all pious,
But hypocrisy will still send you through the fires,
And you'll all dance along with the liars,
Melting, tormented, through Hell's grandest pyres,

I'll dig the dirt up and spread it all around,
Watch as your empire comes crashing down,
And millions for miles will all gather at the sound,
To witness your curdling cries under a misery you drown...

Seeing Red

I've gotta get this out before I scream or shout,
I'm tearing my hair out over another recent round,
Some shit's just gone down and I'm about to pound,
Some new common sense into an old clown,

There was an assumption that made me see red,
Another assumption that must be stopped dead,
An assumption, again, makes me lose my head,
Nasty fuckin' assumption should've never been said,

Cause it's time like these I want to disappear,
The words feed an anger in me people all fear,
Shit I can't avoid or even steer clear,
Shit I wished I never ever had to hear,

It takes a real cunt to change my attitude,
A cunt that doesn't care how nasty he is rude,
Emotion just stunts me – has me subdued,
Crushed out my kindness and left a rotten mood,

Assumption I couldn't rise earlier from bed,
Assumption the communication with my girl is dead,
That I deserve what hell my life does tread,
Yeah, it's all these assumptions that make me see red,

It's people like these that don't deserve my time,
People like these just waste my mind,
Tear me apart and leave pieces behind,
To rust in a rotten mood, and kill off my kind…

Trust

Trust is an honour – as I have learnt,
Ever so beneficial when it's earnt,
I have betrayed before – yet have been by as well,
But to learn it, earn it, heart only swells,

To be capable of trust and be it deep,
Means only rewards can be reaped,
To be faithful, honest and it's seen –
And nothing quite coming between,

Lesson I had once learned hard,
Would make anyone want to raise a guard,
But to know someone's got your back,
Does wonders to help you relax,

The empathy you know they feel when they show they understand,
Because they themselves have indeed had it out of hand,
To be somewhat weakened and still be expected to stand,
To take whatever hit just like a 'man'

Trust is an honour I've lost in some, but gained in others,
Where one door slams shut – there will open another,
It may take many a mistake before deciding on a change,
But you'll know you'll want different when you're tired of the pain,

Who really wants to fuck up every where they go? Not me,
Couldn't see I was before but am finally beginning to see,
I'm making changes, fixing what's wrong with me,
To give only the best when I eventually can be,

Trust is an honour and must be protected,
I know I no longer want to be rejected,
And I won't now ever show I'll deflect it,
No, trust, is an honour to be protected…

Praise

I suffer with a surplus of malaise,
It'd be great difference if I were given praise,
Praise for the good I do in little ways,
Praise even when there has been waste,

I don't have a good deal to feel good about,
To be some other place else of where I am,
Want to be happy – just don't feel I can,

Need that praise to keep reminded,
Or fall deep into darkness, completely blinded,
Just feel lost, torn, divided,
Depressed, regressed, and I can't fight it,

Not when I can't see the good in me,
Not when I feel like I've gotta leave,
To be some other place else of where I am,
I want to be happy – just don't feel like I can,

Suffering with a surplus of malaise,
Be a bigger difference to receive praise,
Praise for what good I do in little ways,
Praise even when there has been waste,

Waste can be hard to get passed at times,
And I hate to have to leave behind,
Need the peace, any praise is fine,
To keep me from completely losin' my mind…

Profitable Setbacks

I've had family amused,
At feeding me abuse,
And for no good excuse,
I would always lose,

They'd speak ill of me behind my back,
And never understood when I did it back,
Yeah, they'd speak ill and I'd blow my stack,
Never could they ever handle it back,

My sickness seemed that good enough,
I victimized them equally as much,
Or so they would display – that I was the cunt,
They – playing victim – oh, what a nice touch,

Bullying me to the edge and beyond my peak,
And made it seem like it was all me, the cheek,
That I had deserved everything I'd reap –
I would question how they're even comfortable enough to sleep,

And they could use my illness against me,
They were that good that no one could see,
They'd call me paranoid and say it was conspiracy,
That I was just daft, an idiot no one would believe,

Oh, they did it well and they singled me out,
Filling me with lies and fear and doubt,
Push madness on me 'til I would fight it out,
Drive me insane, fuck me up and throw me out,

But for what sympathy they'd receive fucking with my head,
Birthed an ideology that one day riches would be set,
Compensation for the torment – may a peace be yet,
A paradise at long last – end, to the tumultuous path tread.

Pretty Friggin'

I'm pretty fuckin' smart,
For a dumb cunt,
Pretty friggin' intelligent,
For a dumb cunt,
Fuckin' pretty friggin' genius,
For a dumb cunt,
Fuckin' pretty friggin' sharp,
For a dumb cunt,

I can fuck up good and make it comedy,
I can fuck up great and show morality,
I can fuck up best and take the sodomy,
I can fuck up even better and show a little sanity,

Shit we can now think of - like we never had before,
Shit that rubbed us raw, sore from the war,
Extracting out the blackened core, to once more restore,
Gathering up an abundant score, to glory, we claw,

I'm pretty fuckin' smart,
For a dumb cunt,
Pretty friggin' intelligent,
For a dumb cunt,
Fuckin' pretty friggin' genius,
For a dumb cunt,
Fuckin' pretty friggin' sharp,
For a dumb cunt,
(x2)

I can fuck up and often do,
But I'm beginning to catch the clues,
I can fuck and most definitely often do,
But someday I'm gonna cash in on all these clues,

Underestimated

Some people seem to think they've seen the worst of it all,
Up until they see true terror befall,
Wars wage huge scores and leave many sore,
Times come when times are due, nothing can be stalled,

I can remain a calm when facing baiting call,
I'm not confident for no reason at all,
I can be quite the surprise some have instore,
Often undermined, underestimated in thought,

They can take a bite, but it'll be more than they'd first suspect,
I'm always stronger than any of us expect,
They try bite, but they only ever regret,
All premeditated thought, scenarios, in neglect,

I've got the wit to get me to the top,
And even when I win – I'll never stop,
I've got the stuff – I'm givin' it a shot,
Mustering it all up to give it all I've got,

I've always managed to catch them off guard,
And I've proven to me plenty that I am hard,
Always give a good foot in, for them to take a yard,
But they can never help it – they do start,

Undermined…
Underestimated…
…Anticipated,

Feeding Me

"We all go a little crazy sometime"
(I look up licking blood from a knife)
I'd just sliced a piece from my side,
Just to see what I'd taste like,

I ate it raw, no need to cook,
And I'll know why if I get crook,
Bizarre it almost tasted like chook,
See? I'm hard, I ain't no sook,

Felt like an itch I just needed to scratch,
Yep, with this knife in my hand,
A jab, a stab, I just cut me bad,
I clutch it, grab, it's bleeding like mad,

I cut and collect this fatty flesh,
And said; "see, now look, this bit's the best"
Turned up the grill and sear sealed the red,
Yep, sure tasted like I was well fed,

I gauze and stitch up the wounds,
Wait 'til they heal, and do it again soon,
Have others over and share me with them too,
I'll find a good recipe for a soup,

I put the knife down cause I have had enough,
I'm feeling full, yeah, I'm stuffed,
Those spices were definitely a nice touch,
Meat was definitely tender, relaxed, not tough,

Felt like an itch I needed to scratch,
Yep, used this knife was in my hand,

A stab, a jab, I cut me bad,
I clutch it, grab, it's bleeding like mad,

I gauze and stitch up the wound,
Wait 'til they heal and do it again soon...

A Monster Bared

I've tried to explain myself,
Tried to interpret my hell,
What I've felt inside myself,
Thought of all I could tell,

I began to peel me bare,
And I revealed a monster there,
I have spared a glance to share,
A stare back to the glare,

I have spoken ill of me and others,
Tried to pack it tight in the cupboard,
But a veil of hypocrisy does still smother,
A dying heresy strangely recovered,

It might be my only purpose meant,
Another sad example to set,
A catalogue, a chronicle, of all wastes spent,
With still a further yearning to repent,

Things I wish I never was,
Only meandering around lost,
Worship the balance, relish the cost,
A slave – never quite my own boss,

What is left but a blackened emptiness,
Depressed and left to regress,
Left to question for what is next,
And expect the worse will only do its' best yet...

Who is he?

Shit, who the hell is this guy? He can bloody talk,
I can't believe my eyes, never seen his likes before,
He can spin it well – a practiced conman I'm sure,
No matter where he goes – he's gonna have 'em all gawk,

I swear he loves to hear his own voice,
I wouldn't linger long if I had a choice,
I guess some folk you can't avoid,
I bet his little prick is his favourite toy,

Whoa – shit – here he comes, quick, walk away
Uh-oh, he's just noticed, now it's too late,
I really don't think I can afford this delay –
And no good position either to debate,

Oh good, thank god – that was quick,
He certainly has charm – he's good with it,
Sharp, a quick wit, swift and slick,
If he's not careful he'll be deep in it,

Think I'm gonna steer clear of that feller,
I have an abhorrent sense he's a terror,
I see that and I'm no fortune teller,
I won't be around to see him the bad news bearer,

I'll keep an eye out and an exceptionally trained ear,
For any warning signs he's drawing near,
If I can calculate his whereabouts, I'll keep clear –
Free of any harm, or fear or tears…

Turning My Day To Night

I am the more lively,
Where hours pass nightly,
Inspired for art and writing,
Considered all through my minding,

Illumination into my diabolical sights,
The drive behind all my mights,
Animation by unimagineable sprites,
Yeah, I'm the more lively at night,

The set back is being disaligned,
Repudiation from the sheep of my kind,
The majority set in minority design,
Off track, but proof I've lost my mind,

My best work is oft' done in the dark,
It's normally only after sundown I have the spark,
It's only then I'm a master of my art,
It's only then I better delve in to my craft,

It is alone for this way,
I wish to turn my night to day,
That from the sheep herd I won't stray,
To work through the day and be the same,

No matter that I am the more lively,
Where the hours pass by nightly,
Inspired to my art and writing,
Considered all through my minding,

The animation by unimagineable sprites,
I have always been the more lively at night…

Concept Of Time

Chaos knows no concept of time,
There's never telling how it unwinds,
It's the beauty of the structure, divinity of design,
That chaos knows no concept of time,

Up and down, sporadic, unpredictable,
Side to side – sporadic, unpredictable,
Weaving in and out, side to side,
No concept – back and forwards of time,

Five minutes to or twenty minutes late,
Not one person can ever really say,
Best way to go – there's no debate,
It's how chaos always gets its' way,

Take many a various route,
And never subject yourself to,
The bullshit you find you'll go through,
Cops – fuck yeah, bet your arse you're doomed,

Five minutes late or twenty minutes to,
Nothin' no one can't ever do –
Best way to get when you've got to,
And chaos reigns – it pulls through,

Don't be so dead set to the word,
Chances are your chances won't work,
Be ever so up and down and side to side,
And may your secrets be well confide,

Chaos knows no concept of time,
Don't be so telling at how it unwinds…

Meth'eadist

I've seen people wound so tight,
Speeding in fast flight,
And they'd so quickly spark to fight,
So quickly bark and bite,

Shrunken brains – missing teeth,
Sunken eyes – picking bleeds,
Somebody put 'em outta misery,
He's all amped up and grisly,

I know he's not so attentive,
It's a blur to retain whatever message,
He's going to the grave, he's descending,
He's only going to end up regretting,

Now I've seen Methodists,
But he's a meth'eadist,
Everything worthy detested,
Yeah, he's gonna regret it,

Expensive little shards,
Expensive little glass,
Expensive on your part,
Expenses catch at last,

Watch for the scatter – wait for the scatter,
Oh – fuck…it doesn't matter –
Until it really fuckin' matters

I've seen Methodists –
But he's a fuckin' meth'eadist…

Two Lots Of Three

Four lots of me,
Each with two lots of three,
Each three reign over seven –

Out over the seven seas,
The lands of continents, countries,
Cursed blessing unveiling heaven,

It is within us all,
Christ said it many times before,
Unlimited power – love, the source,
Hyper active, surging, intense at core,

Four lots of me each with,
Two lots of three,
And each three reign over seven,

Out over the oceans, the seas,
Over the lands of continents and countries,
Cursed blessing unveiling heaven,

Power source – within us all,
Christ said it many times before,
Unlimited intense – surging at the core,
That love, the power, the source,

Love over *all* things it reigns,
Everything crazy *and* all that's sane,
All that is amazing *and* everything to blame,
Yes, love over *all* things – it reigns,

Chapter 2

Death March Passed The Ghastly Vast Farce

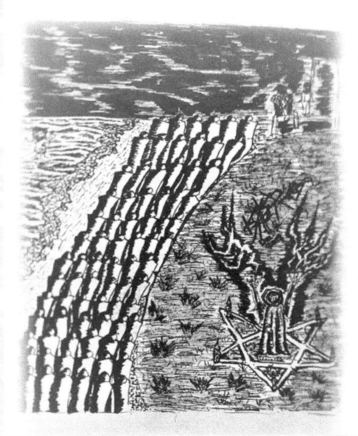

Enter The Madness

An obstacle lies ahead,
And tactic and timing is crucial,
Confrontation needed, but is dread,
With a sensitivity needed tread as usual,

We'll be marching into wildfire,
Expect all unpredictability to transpire,
The insanity, expect it's all cross-wired,
For peace' sake – it's all we've desired,

We have to go through the chaos to get passed,
Use every trick and gambit to last,
It's gonna take every ounce of quick wit,
To divert and avoid of being suckered to the pit,

There's no depth too low in the oncoming machinations,
And there must be no limit to our imagination,
We have to prepare for the ultimate devastation,
Be awake and aware of all manipulation,

Dangers wait to rip at and drag us clawing,
Diabolical torments conspire, and are spawning,
Heed the word – keep alert, emphasis on the warning,
Embrace and endure all through to glory,

It may not seem a bigger deal than it is –
But prepare for it whenever – if ever,
However, if indeed it's a bigger deal than we think,
We'd best be prepared to take the necessary measures,

And we must go through the chaos to get passed,
And we're gonna need every trick and gambit to last,

Dangers wait to rip at and drag us clawing,
Diabolical torments conspire forever spawning,

Enter the madness and heed warning –
Embrace but endure through to the glory,

Lie Like All Fuck

I'm a mind fuck maze of truth and deceit,
'cause I'd kept getting burnt 'til I got wizer,
Throw in a mix of fear of ulterior motif,
And you probably wouldn't tell the truth either,

Not when you can't trust you're not being used,
Not when other's gains mean you're gonna lose,
Not when you suffer abuse to keep them amused,
Not when you have to beg and they always get to choose,

No, you'd lie like all fuck too,

I'm a mind fuck maze of truth and deceit,
'Cause I'd kept getting burnt 'til I got wizer,
Add a mix of fear of ulterior motif –
And you probably wouldn't tell the truth either,

Not when you're the rock others scale to the top,
Not when you're a mule for stock to be stopped by the cops,
Not when you're expendable and are expected to be dropped,
Not when it goes wrong and they speak ill of like rot,

Nah, no, you'd probably lie like all fuck too,

So I'm a mind fuck maze of truth and deceit,
'cause I'd kept getting burnt 'til I'd grown wizer,
But try and accumulate the fear of ulterior motif –
And you probably wouldn't tell the truth either,

Not when you can't trust they're not out for blood,
Not when you can't be treated better than a slug,
Not when you're never being dragged through the mud,
Not when none could ever really give a fuck,

No, no – you'd lie like all fuck too…

Never Lasting Trust

I've given as real as I can be,
Don't know what else is expected of me,
I've been too genuine it's been hard to believe,
People question, intimidate, and I only grieve,

Trying to be a better person – HA,
Why is it so worth it?
When you're just so impatient they never see,
Always forced to prove for them to see,

Trust isn't something I'm easily good at,
Only because it couldn't ever last so long,
Proved over it something none are good at,
Only to drag out the Hell as long,

You can only give so much,
Some cases it's never enough,
Faith? How can I ever trust?
When it can never last,

Pour your truths, patterns do emerge,
And you're forsaken to a disbelief and hurt,
Cause no one's ever going to see,
And no one's ever going to believe,

Trust isn't something I'm good at,
Only because it couldn't ever last so long,
Proved over its' something no one's good at,
Only to drag the Hell out of it further along,

You can only give so much,
But in some cases – it's never enough,
Faith? How can I ever trust?
When it can never last…

Death March

To the left up ahead is dark cloud overcast,
It appears it spans miles, it is spread vast,
It could mean death to march to, getting passed,
To crush hard and fast the ghastly rumours of farce,

It may be an omen, I feel, I've been chosen,
Educated, well-spoken, that eyes will open,
Show 'em something worthy knowing, and if it's 'no' then –
Fuck 'em we'll outgrow 'em, the devil will stoke 'em,

Symbolism of the storm explains there's gonna be rain,
On way to crush what farce remains in reign,
The agonizing strain against cold machines with brains,
Waned, tamed, trained to claim and inflict pain,

Going to be a challenge, smashing defences with resentment,
Think I'll manage, matching offensive temperament,
Later examine, damaged, an extensive testament,
Left to imagine, salvaged, but now the more intelligent,

If we make it safely passed, those clouds overcast,
Death march the dark cloud spread vast,
Crush it hard and fast and outlast,
And get to the ghastly rumours of farce,

May it be that I'm omen, I feel I've been chosen,
Educated, well-spoken, so that eyes might open,
Showing something worthy knowing, or else if it's 'no' then –
Fuck 'em we'll outgrow 'em, leave the devil to stokin'…

A Missing Something

I have always been the lucky one to learn,
Strange lessons when it hasn't been my turn,
To watch when its others and observe,
I have empathised and sympathised with burns,

I've had to fight off creeping discrepancies,
At times strange mystic conspiracies,
All on the outer and all those within me,
I guess it was somewhat always meant to be,

Fighting through others cynicism and scrutiny,
Never really seeing it rise up in me,
'til at last overcome with my own mutiny,
Shit that I was fighting off took a hold of me,

While I was lookin' to change all else,
I began to not notice the worst in myself,
And all of this would become a silent hell,
Often hindsight by the time someone tells,

But hit by the insight – I begin to take distance,
Requiring urgent respite – and so begin transition,
To make shit right and sooner shine or glisten,
And fit back in tight and be working with the system,

There are many times I do miss certain lessons,
And I'll have to repeat them 'til I nail right the session,
I want to feel like I'm making some progression,
Just, swallowing pride isn't always easy on digestion,

All For Torquey Force

I'm the more alive,
When I know I'm closed to die,
Yeah I'm the more alive,
When adrenalins running high,

Spontaneous random acts in desperateness,
Merciless to counter-act the temperatures,
High velocity, high impact intensive measures,
A violent maelstrom of vicious nasty weather,

The faster the force,
Excitements due course,
Faster the force,
Excitements in course,

I'm the more alive,
When I know I'm closed to die,
Yeah I'm the more alive,
When adrenalins running high,

Whiplash into thrash, rising hard and fast,
Rapturing to climax, smiting cast out vast,
Reacting atoms clashing, colliding, blast us to dust,
Smashing, trashing, crashing winding up a rush of gust,

The faster the force,
Excitements due course,
Faster the force,
Excitements in course,

Some Kind Of A Mercy

Who doesn't all go through the same shit,
Different time – place – person – same shit,
Who really never had their teeth grit,
Ready and waiting to hard hit,

Some are worse than others or most,
But even that can be put to boast,
Each the shit we're forced to face,
The haste it takes to win the race,

Limited considerations, respects are rare,
Unlimited intolerances – we each got our share,
And vary at depths unfathomable to compare,
No change lest a compassion is spared,
Or mercy,

To each our differences that escalate,
And the velocity, the magnitude,
That it may never end but repeat,
Matters where -pride's aside – 'cause it subdues,

I can see we're takin it personal,
I know better – I can see it – just no care for it,
And everything's only ever going to repeat,
Until we've learnt and paid for it,

It's limited considerations and respects are rare,
Unlimited intolerances and we've all got our share,
And they vary at depths unfathomable to compare,
And there'll never be change lest a compassion is spared…

And a, some kind of a mercy…

Smoking Chills

Was having a fucked-up start to a morning,
Another one had just pissed me off scorning,
I cranked up some Lamb Of God –
Smoked up some of my recycled pot,

Felt like shit 'til I had a hit,
Little bit of resin did the trick,
Same with the thrashy groove metal tunes,
Was facing a hell of sorts, a swinging noose,

I hate to have to feel this way,
Can't seem to get a good number of good days,
I get so pissed off my vicious hate shows,
Something I'd rather never have known,

I just want to be happy and carefree,
But the shit I'm facing gets the better of me,
I lose patience too quick I snap not thinking,
Makes me want to smoke more pot and get drinking,

I don't want to fight, and I don't want to have to,
And I especially never want to have to prove,
I'm any better when I do – 'cause it's not,
Pissed off again, I just wanna chill out and smoke pot,

I hate violence – I hate aggression,
I hate to have to be pushed to test it,
I don't know why people have to,
It's either their favourite – or got nothing better to do,

I can never fathom why they feel so threatened,
I can't imagine how they never regret it,

It's nothing I ever want a part of,
But just to chill the fuck out and smoke pot,

Smoking fucking chills,
When your mood could kill…

Best Of Both

I love peace but impending doom,
I love sanity but also those loons,
I love how long it takes but I still want it all too soon,
I want to have my cake and, eat it too,

I love it turns black when I get blue,
I love the light and wanna feel refreshed, renewed,
Love that I can feel decayed – wasted, the gloom,
I want to have my cake and I want to eat it too,

I like to falter but I do love to improve,
I like a standstill while I love to move,
Know you say impossible and I probably won't,
But there has to be a way to have the best of both,

I love to be polite but love it just as rude,
I still love a cover when I love getting nude,
I love getting unstuck, but love being glued,
I just want to have my cake and I want to eat it too,

I love life but death as true,
Love the old but I love the new,
Loved being genius but still loved that I never knew,
I just want to have my cake and eat it too,

If its one thing I'll ever do is make it due,
And if I ever get to I'll then teach it to you,
I know you say impossible and I probably won't
But there has gotta be a way to have the best of both,

Curse Of The Massacred Blacks

Felt it when I'd moved to town,
Strange energies to shroud around,
Strange I would learn – feel it now,
The curse of innocent blood over ground,

Sorrowful, mournful, this place's history,
Emotion, died, locked to their blood, whispering,
Feel it, can feel the gloomy misery,
Blood that fell, our darkened history,

But a curse to remain, intact and exact –
A loss that can't be compensated, replaced or given back,
Exotic people of an exotic land, attacked, trapped,
Woe beset, the curse of the massacred blacks,

Unfortunate, unlucky incidents happen here,
Some, enough to make you want to fear,
Some, enough to make you want to adhere,
To what exotic whispers you hear,

There are times you feel you cannot escape,
That horrendous torments lie in wait,
Blood fallen of innocents, a seething hate,
Yet to escalate and seal who's fate,

An exotic people of an exotic land, attacked and trapped,
The loss never compensated, replaced nor given back,
But a curse to remain, intact and exact –
Woe beset – the curse of the massacred blacks…

(Con)Foundry

It is a mystery how I work,
These, mystical formation of words,
Strange the feels when they're heard,
Stranger still, summoning up urge,

What I often speak is confounding,
Like there may be no boundaries,
Astounding – profoundly,
There's ever more surrounding,

I can't expect you to believe what I say,
When I know and can tell it sounds so far-fetched it's this way,
That I see certain patterns – so clear as day,
Conditions worsen, I'm more desperate for change,

Political speak is often confounding,
A rapid river of confusion in which we're drowning,
The slickest tricksters spin it sweeter, more soundly,
And we only ever know after we've had to pay for it frowning,

It's everywhere you look no matter where you go,
Some how in big or the most minute ways it shows,
Stories trade, gossip – rumours in the know,
You bite it hard if you fight the flow,

Yeah – fables trade but they may mean,
Something to the kind of someone who prefers to look deep,
But can still be something only ever seen skin deep,
Confounding by the tales they only care to mean,

I have seen patterns, some deny, as clear as day,
But I can never expect many to believe when I say,

Skeletons Of A One Horse Town

I know of a town with the blackest history,
Draws people in to succumb to a misery,
You find it beautiful, peaceful after visiting,
You wanna come back for the rest of your existing,

But there's a bad, bad, luck about this town,
And you'll get stuck if you go down,
Cursed after innocent blood hit the ground,
The massacred blacks, a curse was bound,

So it isn't a secret bout khama comin' round,
But that rich black blood cursing the ground,
That after all had claimed the land for the town,
Well, so be it would be, in end, a one-horse town,

For the sake only so few blacks survived,
The township midst where companies mine,
Raping out from the ground since round this time,
Curses go by strengths by what feel is behind,

This town has a blacker history,
It's sickening, sad, it was a misery,
It's a beautiful place – you'd enjoy visiting,
You'll wanna be back for the rest of your existing,

Eye for an eye – I guess it's life for life,
The original testament had it right,
How could the indigenous have put up a fight,
Against the rifles toting bayonette knives,

It's blackened history is sickening to hear,
That place needs one to free the phantoms clear,

But beware if you should go anywhere near,
That bad luck will repeat 'til tears,

Yeah, skeletons, Skeletons,
Of. A. One. Horse. Town.

Pie Piper

It's rotten when you're not paid proper for what job,
You're just never getting' to where you should've got,
But where at what point does it stop?
When they were all getting it good – but until they were robbed,

Favour for a favour – nothin' is free,
I could've been the one to rid the rats from the street,
Never expect nothin' done without a fee,
And don't skip town when you haven't paid me,

Everybody works for their piece of crust,
Everybody knows they have to – they must,
But when this 'trust' all turns to dust,
I'll be takin' her pie with – her insatiable lust,

Boy they had better have my money soon,
Pray I don't play the pipe and rouse the tune,
Lead their women away leaving a miserable gloom,
I think I'm gonna start lookin' after it's hit noon,

Favour for a favour – nothin' is free,
I could've been the one to rid the rats from the street,
Never expect nothin' done without a fee,
And don't skip town when you haven't paid me,

Everybody works for their piece of crust,
Everybody knows they have to – they must,
But when this 'trust' all turns to dust,
I'll be takin' her pie with – her insatiable lust,

A Sinister Confusion

A heart ache I have had,
Was knowing particularly where –
The line of propriety was,
With relations and associates,

I thought I knew what was right,
Particularly about a certain honesty,
I was sure I had the right idea,
Of honesty, fidelity,

'til I'd met a woman I'd felt love for,
The kind of love more pure to the core,
The kind of love you'd kill for,
Love that leaves and leaves you sore,

She taught me many things,
I matured a dramatic amount with her,
But I was just still so young,
This love was gonna hurt,

I hate to be a jealous feller but I am indeed,
It has to do with a lot of insecurities – I'm sure,
Trust being something had once had me bleed,
Reasons for the barriers, defences, the walls,

She'd say she'd always dream of birds, and fly,
Freedom from a cage – to be free to fly,
Which confused me when she said marriage –
Tied down again? Why?

When we first met, we were both vulnerable,
She, herself wasn't quite prepared to drop her guard,

We were both particularly vulnerable,
But we empathized each other, we shared a heart,

But there would be things that would further confuse,
And she, would all the more only seem amused,

After when we'd broke apart,
And gone our separate ways,
Blinded by emotion,
I went online searching for strays,

I'd speak to some, not all,
Never met 'em face to face,
Something that might very well be my downfall,
And bury me my resting place,

A point I wanted to make of all this –
Was of a factor had contributed,
A confusion enforced in me by an ex,
A manipulation she'd distributed,

We'd go out and drink and get blind,
And she'd be real chatty, real flirty with the guys,
I'd try to apprehend her for it and she'd outright lie,
She'd say I was mad and losing my mind,

She'd deny she was all the time,
But I knew I could fuckin' see,
She couldn't ever be mine,
And I was a fool to think it be,

It wasn't so much that she said she wasn't,
But that it was fucking normal,
That I should just get over it –
HA – yeah no matter I was mournful,

She didn't even seem to have a problem if I ever did,
Either that or she did and never shown it,
Regardless – I know if I did,
I would've fuckin' blown it,

She was a hypocrite – no matter how much she hates to hear it,
I was getting so fed up that soon I would only mirror,
Given the age gap – she'd expect me to listen and just adhere to it,
But her, at her age, had had double the amount of errors…

I thought I knew what was right,
Particularly about a certain honesty,
I was sure I had the right idea,
Of honesty, fidelity,

Weak For Love

Does it have to seem so weak to want to love?
Explain that all to Christ above –
It took a hybrid god thing to show how to be a man,
But was anybody fucking listening? Do ya really understand?

Why would you not understand how strong he is –
Strong enough dying standing true to his belief –
When – you – in his place, would abandon all this,
All you gained means nothin' here – you just keep livin' the dream,

So comfortable – or not you jump when threatened,
It's too intense to handle or let them live – you gotta get 'em,
"I Can't let him live passed it – that cunt's goin' down,
I have to go and put this cunt in the ground,"

"Him? Callin' me weak? –"
"don't let it bother you – what's it matter –
Do you even really know me?"
"Well, if you meant me – I would've shown who if you had of,"

See, now we're getting there,
This, here, what you just said was an improvement,
Believe me there's more and we'll get there,
We're slowly startin' to make some forward movement.

There's too much more than I could say would blow your mind,
The things, the leads from and out of love and back,
Too many things to determine the various kinds,
It's not often as you always think, not worst, no lack,

Don't think for one second it's so weak to love –
It's the better of the other when you want shit done,

Whinging Differences

One thing that seriously pains me –
Is the intolerance of inequality,
Land of plenty – Ha – get fucked,
Oh – unless you mean we're plenty fucked,

Intolerance –
The fact that some can be so fucking sensitive,
Intolerance –
Where everything is so fucking offensive,
Intolerance –
Sure, I can see you suffer –
Intolerance –
Look around – who doesn't fucker?

Things seriously pain me that I whinge,
But there are a many more that do bitch,
There's never a break in the binge,
But I'm feeling a seriously uncontrollable twitch,

Not a great many can stand me –
And not one of them whinge over the difference,
It's all the same – I look and I see,
Opinions worthless, there's no significance,

I mean, shit, they whinge at what I do,
But none of them see what they put you through,
People so impatient they don't seem to think,
And I'm not often sure they can,

Intolerance –
The fact that some can be so fucking sensitive,
Intolerance –
Where everything's so fucking offensive…

To Let Be Is The Question...

Hard for me to get along,
When all I want is to get along,
Hard to remain so strong,
When there still remains wrong,

I'm capable of very painful things,
But it's not how I prefer to think,
I am so very capable of very painful things,
For when people don't want to think,

It irritates me to see them taunt,
When if they knew – they'd go gaunt,
I have a sort of darkness that can haunt,
Of which no repellent relics exist to be sought,

I can be at peace and appear all calm,
But still whip up ripping cuts to harm,
I never want to have to have that fun,
Just try to remain in peace with the calm,

I'm capable of very painful things,
But it's not how or where I prefer to think,
I am so very capable of very painful things,
For when people don't want to think,

I know I can set them right,
Without ever even being close enough to fight,
Have I got the right – and does it make it right?
If it has to come to it I guess I just might,

To let be is the question,
Probably should when I already know I can best them...

Restricted Understandings

Maturity... it's a funny thing,
I can say and do a lot of different shit,
Might seem to be funny to some,
Not to great many others but –
I can still do and say different shit,
Laugh, find it funny the same,
And not to a great many of the most...

I walk a path of misunderstanding,
Many I'm sure would say contradictory,
Many have...

Walk a path, cautious of the misunderstanding,
Combatant to the twists,
Of the restricted intelligences – they contradict,
They,
Delay the waste, inevitably creating more,
Times before it's sold off or stored,

I walk a path of misunderstanding,
Combatant to contradictory twists,
Combatant to intelligence threatening to restrict,
And many have,

Maturity... it's a funny thing,
One can say and do various different shit,
And it might appear to be funny to some,
Not so to a great many others but,
One can say and do a lot of different shit,
And laugh and find it funny the same,
And not like a great many of the most,

It's somewhat of a, restricted understanding,
Restricted...

Not Where I Want To Be

Got me a long way to go,
To where I want to be,
Got a lot for me to know,
To get to be a better me,

Want to take my time,
Want to get it right,
Want to express from my mind,
Want to get it right,

Want to take my time – I want to find,
Want to get it right,
Want to untangle out from this bind,
Don't want to have to fight,

Got me a long way to grow,
To where I want to be,
Got a lot for me to know,
To get to be a better me,

Bust wide open my narrow mind,
Find my strengths, my courage, my might,
Break free these bonds that hold me confined,
One day, I'm gonna get it right,

Just want to take my time,
Express from my mind,
Untangle out this bind,
And get it right,

I'm nowhere near where I want to be,
But I doubt it'll take too long for me,

Think Specific

I want it – and I want it a lot,
I want it too much 'til I get it,
Get it and get it a lot,
Get it too much 'til I don't want it,

I recall I was quite specific in my asking for's,

Wanted her – 'til I got her,
Wanter her too much 'til I got her,
Got it, and I got it a lot,
But got too much 'til I just didn't want it,

Yeah – I'm sure I recall,
I was more specific in my asking for's
Wishin' careful…
Was it me? thinkin' with me pecker?
Not thinkin' with my heart –
Or just not fuckin' thinkin' at all,

Thought I was tryin' to be careful, wishin', hopeful,
But I'm sure as fuck I recall,
I was more specific in my asking for,

Wanted her 'til I got her,
Wanter her too much 'til I got her,
Got it – and I'd gotten it a lot,
Just too much 'til I didn't want it,

Yeah – was thinkin' with me pecker,
Not thinkin' with me heart –
Or perhaps just not fuckin' thinkin' at all…

Perspective

Perspective requires further elucidation,
Perspective's always open for interpretation,
But let's look closer, take better examination,
Perspective often leads to trepidation,

They it's natural to despise or fear the unknown,
That discomfort is natural outside what we condone,
So we keep well intact inside our comfort zones,
Never venture away to better educate for our growth,

Each one of is different – never all the same,
But we're all expected to share a similar brain,
But when ignorance is all there is – when do ever gain?
None of us evolve or will ever at the same rate,

The problem with perspective is that everyone is different,
Can't see passed the differences either to really listen,
And mankind will fail in this mission,
Eventually to deny itself its own existence,

One man's excitement is another's inescapable hell,
One mans trash is another's treasure to preserve well,
But the question of perspective remains and does dwell,
Intolerance isn't tolerant, it rebels, it repels,

It's insane to discriminate a race based on one moron,
The disgrace, the distaste, every one of us belongs,
Failure to see perspective when we're wrong,
Far too many of us can't accept it and move on,

No opinion is superior nor inferior as I have said before,
Better kept on the interior to save razing others raw,
In my perspective,

The Important and Painful Need To Know

I know the path will kill me,
And hurt me fuckin' hard doing so,
Methods were called for –
When it's a painful need to know,

People not willing to step outside,
The comfort of their ignorance,
As much truth as I may have bled,
Martyrdom, the ultimate consequence,

But we know who ends up paying more,
The fucker like me – like Christ before,
It's buckle down now before I declare war –
Cause all you fuckers prefer to ignore,

Why should I pay my ultimate sacrifice –
For those to neglect to understand and reason why,
When now – path chosen – I've made my mind,
Not doing that shit fuckin' twice,

People not willing to step outside,
The comfort their ignorance provides,
Bled too much I'd rather lie,
Fuck your scapegoat martyrdom –
You don't deserve for me to die,

Your pain could but won't kill me,
I just know it'll fuckin' hurt hard doing so –
Methods are called for,
When it's a painful yet important need to know...

Drain Me Insane

Sometimes I wonder why I'd even want to be sane,
Like everybody else, normal, the same,
But that's the thing, they don't all share a brain,
Why should I want to fit in and endure the strain?

Strain of never being the same,
Shamed, god forbid, that I'm using my brain,
Drained all this time they're trying to tame,
I'm drained, blamed, - when there is no gain,

Conversation comes back around again,
Same conversation, same content, never ends,
Loops, repeats, we're never going to ascend,
Wasted efforts, stretched, extent,

Going round in circles, we keep coming back,
Reactions still identical when questions change their tact,
Faces going purple – they soon want to snap,
And I ask why the hell – it's not me wanting to attack,

They get so pissed that I never listen,
I'm a free man, but I'm still imprisoned,
'cause I can't see their logic – I'm not seeing wisdom,
There's many flaws in the structure of their system,

Sometimes I wonder why I should even try –
When I know we're never going to see eye to eye,
I want these by-gones to hurry up and pass by,
'cause I'm sick and tired of wishing they'd just die,

I don't know what they want to know, when
they don't know how to ask?
All this training sane – is draining me insane,
and I'm losing it fucking fast,

My Broken Psychic Body

10:15 p.m., Wednesday, 28th of November, 2018,
Recording this for reference for whenever this needs generating,
For a discussion that may require some articulating,
Strange and bizarre occurrences begin manipulating,

I've been trying to elucidate to an eager ear,
There are none I have found to share the same eccentric tears,
Rapid evolution of sorts strangely taking place here,
Maybe accelerated rates of new brain activity, new gears,

Many contributing factors may have include –
Suffering a trauma like, or, of all sorts of abuse,
Levels of intelligences, and new talents too,
There's always something much more, new,

Experiments through meditation,
Analysing, rationalizing under medication,
Blocking out, becoming oblivious to inferior provocation,
Stepping well out to observe for proper contemplation,

Alchemy, philosophy, chemistry, balance,
Stepping out for the beyond and bear the valiant,
New evidence escalates to the what if's could happen,
Chimerical to be believable – masses would gather,

But it appears I have broken open my psychic body – my soul is bare,
I'm vulnerable to vampires the likes that feed to drain and never spare,
I've drawn the power of the Christ and no other power compares,
It was intense, I'd have gone crazy if I kept a hold too long on there,

But I've begun to grow so strong – my open soul begins to weave,
I feel as though I'm merging back to the web, what's happening to me?
I cannot shut it off or bring it back to clothe back round me,
I weave, I twine through the very air that we all breathe,

In Hiding

They think I'm hiding from them,
I am...

I lock the door from the inside of my house,
Lock them all out – keeping them out,
Carrying on with my business – what I'm on about,
They, all the while think I'm a mouse,

Better they believe that than bear witness,
To the heinous horrors I have within,
They think I'm hiding,
I am,

I lock me inside, secure in my house,
And I may rage and rampage about,
But when I'm in those moods – I'm not stepping out,
But hide me well, barricaded up in the house,

I'm hiding them from me doing so as much,
When it's going both ways with bugger all trust,
And I know for certain I can be too much,
All I had with an ex was lust,
And now there's bugger all of that too between us,

Yeah, I'm hiding,
Still deciding, minds dividing,
Can't assume – I know they're surprising,
But still, too soon, it's compromising,

I lock the door from the inside of my house,
Lock them all out – keeping them out,
And carry on with my business, what I'm on about,
And they, can all the while just think I'm a mouse,

Better they believe that than bear witness,
To the heinous horrors I have within,
They think I'm hiding,
I am,

Lockin' me secure, up in my house,
And I may rage and rampage about,
But in these moods I can't go out –
But hide me well – locked up, locked down,

They think I'm hiding from them,
I am...

Concealment

Concealment – it's completely necessary,
Concealment – 'cause it gets messy – scary,
Concealment – imagination wild with gossip nesting, sharing,
Concealment – vicious narcissism investing, setting,

Razor cuts on the winds every which way,
Concealment to live out the stigma to grey,
To push on, carve on through when at backstabbing pace,
To ravage on through, courageous with a brave face,

Concealment when through perilous times,
To hide 'til when the opportunity strikes,
Concealment – to save from being spat out under the grind,
To forestall 'til when dust settles, we're satisfied,

Concealment – it's absolutely imperative,
Concealment – can't stress the sincerity,
Concealment – there's chaotic severity,
So, concealment – for peace for your sake, for serenity,

Supposing there's a trap around every bend,
Can't always know what to know to suspend,
Maybe turn the tables, fix amends,
Damage wrought, cocoon to comprehend,

Conceal and cocoon and comprehend,
What went wrong – how the fuck, and when?
Something's off – can't pretend,
Going to have to go rethink this all again,

Concealment – it's particularly incenting –
Concealment – when there's some relenting –

Concealment – to purge out their detesting –
Concealment – to cocoon while distressing,

Concealment is absolutely imperative –
For peace sake – for some momentary –
Serenity...

Inciting Watch

There's something about me,
And I don't think we're gonna know,
Whatever that something about me is –
Until it starts to show,

For example,
Caving in, crumbling, imploding in a rage,
A fury accelerating at a rapid pace,
White light blinded, the rage can't be contained,
Explode – adrenalin's high, it's insane,
But then,
You silent and you calm, quiet and cool,
But audiences have suddenly seen you the fool,
To be so smart but still be a fuckin' tool,
Life's only gonna fuck you harder and then it's back to school,

People have seen that and they begin to worry,
Whether they're safe and sound or should worry,
It's only when I realized I'd lost it that I'm sorry,
It's genuine, I feel I have disgraced, I am sorry,

Takes me to have to write it to contemplate,
For it to be ever more clear – this fucked state,
It's almost mindless – only, I know I'm going to face,
When I've slowed, calmed, and had time to contemplate,

I'm sure it's a strange excitement to hear the rampage,
Enough to make any want to question my age,
And it's only ever gonna draw attentions my way,
Just to have raged over a fucked moment of the day,

You've gotta contain it or people will see,
I haven't before but now know as some have seen,

Few Difficulties

Gets difficult to keep my head straight,
All kinds of chaos going on,
With all kinds of different, difficult shit thrown in –
I'm scattered, battered, try'na keep straight,

All sorts of shit I've got thrown at me,
That I can't contain it for too long,
And making me in turn also to be,
As equally as unjust and wrong,

I want to be the nice guy,
Gets difficult to face some obstacles,
Shit thrown art you – you forget to be nice,
Over the rising frustration,
Not getting easily round these obstacles,

Shit thrown at you that tears you apart inside,
And cripples you, shattering facades,
That you're stronger than this inside,
But not when broken and in shards,

I find it difficult to keep my head straight,
'cause I know deep down I'm not great,
Esteem? It's fucked, what esteem?
I get passed the point where I want to scream,

But instead silence, brain fries, I cry,
Caustic shits corroding my insides,
I'm not that strong deep down,
I can't hide the frown,

With all sorts of shit thrown at me,
Never can contain it too long,

Always making me in turn to be,
As equally unjust and wrong,

They say it's those who care – hurt most,
And I feel corroded away to a ghost…

Measure Of Feel

I know what's wrong with me,
Have to face it all too often,
Can't escape it made ever obvious,
Be the many in such disbelief,

It has to be some sort of disbelief,
That I don't seem to suffer enough,
'cause there's a great many make it clear,
They do most want me to,

For what reason I have no idea,
They forget they don't know anything of me,
The way they make it sound is they know,
When they're never around enough anyway,

None of 'em can really know the measure I feel by,
But all of 'em like to assume it's never enough,
'cause I'm doomed to be shown it regardless,
And after, be scarred and have to start again,

I don't want to have to make it so obvious,
That I do feel, and I suffer deeply,
They assume more the worst when I do,
Never think, nor hope or want better for me,

They seem to want me to have more to learn,
And they only wanna teach it more to me themselves,
Regardless of any care for when I've been here before,
Guess they want to feel important doing something due,

But they never see they're too busy lookin' at me,
Pickin' at me for all my flaws and fuck ups,

That they never see they do themselves,
And never accept when hidden consequences settle,

I'm consistently in considerable disbelief myself,
By how none can really empathise the measure by which –
I can feel by…

Care Enough

I'm sorry I got so down about what you said,
Those words you chose, heavy as lead,
I took what you said to heart,
I felt it, took it to heart,

It fuckin' hurt but do you wanna know why?
It's because I fuckin' care, it's why I cry,
I value people more than I care to mention,
I care so much it hurts and I let them,

If I didn't care and never let them know,
The hate they'd have would only grow,
Everyone's important – but not quite how I feel I'm treated,
Kind of only made my respect a little more receded,

A little,

I feel they hurt others so much as they hurt,
'cause they want it equally deserved,
Instead of raking it all up, take it and look away,
Look away – or change for better to say,

Forgive me for being so hurt at what you said,
I let you feel important enough, I felt what you said,
I cared enough I took it to heart,
And retrieved back into the dark,

Cause it fuckin' hurt and do you wanna know why,
It's because I fuckin' care – it's why I cry –
Not like you'll ever understand or see with your eyes,
Not like you fuckin' care – you just compromise,

Everyone's important, just never how I felt like I was to be treated,
Kind of only just made my respect receded, a little,
But if I didn't care and never let them know,
Their hatred for me is only gonna grow,

And it matters to me when they do...

To Know Right And Do Good

It can be quite impressive –
What some folk do under pressure,
All lessons invested,
For survival, if, or when tested,

When pushed out to the edge,
To stand on what little ledge,
Standing for what they have pledged,
Fighting paradigms of the prior alleged,

To show true colours, the courage,
Examples to others, none to disparage,
To show substance when tricky to manage,
Never preach but practice and really flourish,

To take a burden on alone,
Internalize on it without it ever shown,
Reap whatever horrid fruit has grown,
Keep it well away from populated zones,

Take whatever bad and rapidly convert it good,
Stabilize what structure as well as it need should,
Take pride in the better I ever could,
Doing better than any previous leader would,

To take all wrong and correct it right,
To stand silent, strong – when they need to fight,
Reason hard and long – and still welcome what smite,
Cease irrational gone, erase away all spite,

To have turned the other cheek,
And keep black history from a repeat,

Write Ways

I often write as I do feel,
And it can get out of control,
Set-backs of paranoia too real,
Defying, delaying the goals,

Forced to face mistakes, obliged on by the past,
Pieces that were broken, scattered out vast,
Bizarre truth ache to hate,
Following a path I never meant to take,

I write as I feel and too often,
And I can be so out of control,
Set-backs of paranoia – I've got it,
Defying, delaying the goals,

Some of the things I write might be intense,
It's a way for me to try to reason,
I'm an extremist, I feel it immense,
Only ever worse when there's a reason,

I want to get it out – this way I feel,
Just because I think about it doesn't mean I'll actually do it,
A lot of what I write is real,
In a way of experience, feel, thought, the movement,

I do feel and I do write,
And it can sound out of control,
I am wrong, but I am write,
Trying to work toward my goals,

Just Laugh (Humiliant)

It's normal to laugh when another suffers and humiliates,
Normal for them to laugh at you in your face,
Especially when it's you all of a sudden in this state,
But contemplate, laugh first when you take first place,

You fell down on your face,
It was your mistake,
You deserve to laugh at your own fate,
Humiliate, laugh for you own sake,

You burn at the stake,
It was your mistake,
You deserve to laugh at your own fate,
Humiliate, laugh, you take first place,

It's normal for others to laugh as you humiliate,
Normal for them to laugh at you to your face,
You have the power to take it away,
And you do, soon as you can laugh at your own mistakes,

They get confused cause it looks like you lose,
Hard truth? Ha! You're equally amused,
Abuse – not how you choose to view,
Can't take life to serious enough to be blue,

You fell down on your face,
It was your mistake,
You deserve to laugh at your own fate,
Humiliate, laugh for you own sake,

You burn at the stake,
It was your mistake,
You deserve to laugh at your own fate,
Humiliate, laugh, you take first place,

Shitizenshit

Look alive – we're here to impress,
I don't give a damn if you're in distress,
Swallow it down – make it digest,
Behave your best – we're here to impress,

Look at me – I just don't fit,
It's going to hell all to quick,
I'm sick, just so fuckin' sick,
Of all this shitizenshit,

Chains are only as strong as their weakest link,
And not all of us are on the same wave of think,
Happens all too fast, you miss it if you blink,
We will slowly slip and sink into the drink,

Look at us all divided, minds torn, split,
It's going to hell all too quick,
And I'm sick, just so fuckin' sick,
Of all this shitizenshit,

We need a refinery for all our civilians,
For etticate taught to each us reptilians,
Lessons to learn – for some – millions,
And especially to those so quick to be villains,

Sometimes I don't think society is worthy enough,
Or just not quite made of the right stuff,
Expectance on impressions, we're destined up –
Put right to the wrongs when they can't,

Look at us – none of us fucking fit –
I'm so fuckin' sick of all this shitizenshit…

Hard Task, I Know

I am aware I can be a little intense,
I'm certain many must beware –
Or get the feeling to at least,

I have regrets, try make amends,
Can't always avoid a hateful glare,
For I may come across a sickly beast,

I don't have too many visible limitations –
Appear to cross boundaries plenty,
Never favoured assumptions, nor expectations,
But I'm not unhappy and I'm not empty,

I know I can appear extreme,
To some extents I'm certain I can be,
Though I hope we'll never know,

I can be cruel, vicious and mean,
Unlike anything anyone's ever seen,
But it's never been something I've been keen to show,

I'm sure people warn others before me,
There's probably good reason to avoid me,
Maybe handy to be had on their side at times,
Disregard hiccuped behaviour, maybe leave that behind,

One like me might only ask,
If it could just be seen passed,
Grace be, I know it's a hard task,
But rewards will be as just,

Allow To Be

Let all chances I give, have me emaciated,
Allowances to live, all round, appreciation,
Astounded by individuality, its' beauty anticipated –
Only hoping I consolidate, like reciprocation,

To allow and let live as we all please,
Even when we each all disagree,
Save each our dignity and integrity,
Allow it, let live, and let be,

For each my short comings and poor luck,
No fault of my own that I'd gotten stuck,
I would confront when something went amok,
And a thorn would cut where a rose was plucked,

At times confronting really hasn't done me the best,
Even when I felt I had to get it off my chest,
But rather show faith and share a respect,
'Cause there would come a time I would regret,

And I never wanted to have to learn a lesson twice,
But that's the way of life when you don't get it right,
Controlling my emotion and learning not to bite,
Every time I feel I've heard something I don't like,

But let all chances I give, equally have me emaciated,
Each allowance to live, all round appreciation,
Astounded by individuality, its' beauty anticipated –
Only hoping, hoping I consolidate a like reciprocation,

To allow and let live all as we please,
Even when we each all disagree,
Save each of our dignity and integrity,
Allow it, let live and let be,

Standby

The bravery of the stupid is remarkable,
Intelligence, as mine, is a burden,
They assume, and they put their foot in,
Can't prove it or it'll surely hurt them,

Gotta stand by and let stupid go,
Just standby and enjoy the show,
We'll all laugh at what stupid don't know,
We'll just stand by and let stupid go –

It'll hurt them worse just to show them,
Embarrassing enough just to know them,
The barriers, the distance to toe in,
The difference is where we're going,

Let stupid take the reigns,
They know it all – how brave,
They just don't recognise the pain,
But stupid prefers it that way,

Stupid can't feel the pain,
No, it has no brain –

Hand up first for reckless full charge,
Can't be easy being stupid, to be easily discard,
Failure where others don't find it so hard,
Mingle with the similar and maintain your guard,

Gotta standby and let stupid go,
Just stand by and enjoy the show,
We'll all laugh at what stupid don't know,
We'll just stand by and let stupid go…

Losin' My Shit

Lost me shit again before,
Really not too proud of these moments at all,
Behaviour I exhibit is poor, it appals,
Shit better left unsaid it abhors,

Starts with waking into a day,
Over hearing shit piled to your name,
And where one might assume I'm grave –
Beating me down? I only rage,

So I'm losin' my shit like countless times before,
Too hard, too vicious, to be ignored,
The war between myself and my previous whore,
It tears me raw that we still both get so sore,

She likes her her revenge but still gets upset,
Hearin' the shit I vent that she just ain't never heard yet –
None the more wizer we're exchanging disrespects,
It's only ever been as good as she's given is what she gets,

Starts with waking in to the day,
Awakened by overhearing of shit to my name,
And of course where one assumes – I'm grave,
Just watch out, stand the fuck back, cause I'm gonna rage,

Rave, rage, and misbehave,
Damn it I'm gonna rage,

Boots On

I like to be ready for anything,
Like to go out with ya boots on,
As in to expect the unexpected,
I'll be ready with me boots on,

Not too long before I can justify anything,
Fake it 'til we're no longer pretending,
Be ready, got me boots on,
I'm ready and got my boots on,

Contemplate scenario's,
Disadvantages, ultimate worst,
Be it fate I do go down,
I'll fight my outrages with a vicious thirst,

Fear catcher talisman tatt,
Split-second adrenalin in a flash,
Ready with my boots on – get back,
These fuckers are steel capped,

I like to be ready for anything,
Like, to go out with ya boots on,
As in, to expect the unexpected,
Be ready – with my boots on,

Contemplate scenario's,
Disadvantages and the ultimate worst,
And be it fate that I go down,
I'll fight my outrages with a vicious thirst,

Fearcatcher talisman tatt,
Split second adrenalin in a flash,
Boots on, get back…

A Rapid Escalator At Will

I do and I don't know how to fight,
There's always someone better – I don't have that pride,
I do however, pride deeper my mind,
That I wish – no, I hope – I never have to fight,

I can activate my fear response ever so well,
That if I ever do I'm gonna fight like fuckin' hell,
I can accelerate my temper – and the radiant heat swells,
That if I have to fight – you'll either run, or cop the belt,

I can activate both of those at will,
And if I have to – I might fight to kill,
Too blinded by true fury to recognize what thrill,
They were only fuckin' with me – they weren't for real,

The only way we'll really know is if they force me into that position,
But then it'll be less than a demonstration – it'll be a demolition,
And past orchestration it will all be petitioned,
And it's barely ever worth what I'd hoped or envisioned,

I'm not bad but I'm not the best,
But I rally fuckin' hate having to be put to test,
I just want to get along just like all the rest,
I have too much talent to lose to that and detest,

I hope none of us ever have to find that out,
'Cause one will go to prison and the other in the ground,
I'd really rather let you have the benefit of the doubt,
'Cause of the two choices – from neither would I be proud,

I can activate my responses of intense fear and hate –
I don't like to – but I can – and it can rapidly escalate,

Hold Of Control

I raged before like I always do,
Went off like a fuckwit like I hate to,
And what do I get for the release?
Only just another kick in the teeth,

Cause while I release that rage –
I'm not showin' much control,
Damned to loose the rage,
Still damned to have that control –
Shit that's contradictory twice,

Damned to let it go and never correct it,
Shit's only gonna happen again and repeat,
No, don't, you're damned if you correct it,
But so you know you won't escape defeat,

Damned if I correct it –
People too proud to accept it,
Breeding, building up a painful hate,
That's only gonna come smack me back in the face,

Meanwhile, as I have lost my rage,
I've gained unwanted attentions,
Not showing my hold of control,
Might land me in lock-up or detention,

It's difficult when you know insidious things are said,
Behind your back about you, always bringing dread,
And to have to bite down on it saving your head,
Swallowing down what rising anger has you seeing red,

Damned if I correct it –
Damned if I let it go…

If You Absolutely Have To

If you have to,
Bash me,
But with that sparkle in your eye,

If you have to,
Bash me,
But with that sparkly passion in your eye,

If you must –
Fight,
But do with all feeling,

If you must –
Fight,
But do with all feeling,

'cause when we are toe to toe,
It's gonna show,
When we are toe to toe,
Blows are gonna make glow,

So, if you have to,
Bash me,
But with the sparkle in your eye,

If you have to –
Bash me,
But with a passion in your eye,

If you must –
Fight,
But do so with the feeling,

If you must –
Fight,
But you better do with feeling...

And by your passion, strike true...
If you absolutely have to...

Battered For Better

I find there are times,
I'm denied, despite that I try,
New path treading, no lies,
But others won't so easily let by,

It may come to a moment in particular,
That I may say or do something irregular,
The spirit, the vitality, the vigour,
But then poisonous cynical words, rip tremours,

Trying to do and show better ain't so easy,
Some people can be the hardest to be pleasing,
You want better – it's outta reach, it's teasing,
And to not let it bother you – just, isn't easy,

They don't realise their words have such power,
And they may not mean it, but they do have power,
I'm often defeated, receded to a cower,
My moods only doomed to bitter and sour,

They don't know it hurts me more because I do value,
Hurts you worse when you know you can value,
Me, placing an importance on their poisonous cynical words,
Showing I have indeed valued because I'd heard,

And not just heard but truly felt,
My stone heart can and does melt,
But I get so shattered to try to show so well,
I'm mentally battered showing better just for Hell,

It's difficult at time to try to get by,
New paths I try – I'm denied because I "Lie"

Not made to feel any better because I do try,
Because not too many others will easily let by,

Not all people do, but to me, they all matter,
I don't know why but it's my nature, I just hate feeling shattered...

For Therapy

He's the fuckin' reason why I need therapy,
And the same reason why I ain't getting any,
No regard, no concern for what trespass they're treading,
Inconsiderately, blindly? HA! Times a plenty,

Consistently inconvenient, lacking sophistication,
Always the distraction when I should have concentration,
Quick tempered – quick, so quick to agitation,
Always to a deeper low, exasperated and frustrated,

Hypocritical, sceptical, ever so cynical,
Miserable, abysmal, oh so critical,
Visceral, pitiful, dismal, it's habitual,
And he'd think it's beautiful, but that's just typical,

His stories don't all seem to match,
A bad liar with a growing burden attached,
But the more I see the more I understand,
I'm dealing with a child, not a full-grown man,

You'd think by his age he'd have already learned,
To quit doing shit makes others guts churn,
And he never seems even slightly concerned –
I just know when he carks it he's gonna fuckin' burn,

They never want to listen as much as they want you to,
They always see less than you actually do,
What hell they provide you – *is* as bad as they've been through,
But you have always understood better than they ever think you do,

Yeah, he's the reason why I need therapy,
And the same fuckin' reason why I ain't getting' any…

Fuck Write

I'm gonna fight,
I'm gonna fuck,
And I'm gonna write,

I'm gonna fight when I can't fuck it,
Fight when I've fucked it enough,
Fight to fuck it some more,
Fuck it 'til I can't fight it no more,

I'm gonna fight,
I'm gonna fuck,
And damn it I'm gonna write,

I'm gonna take something bad and make it funny,
And I'm gonna make me a lot of motherfuckin' money,
I send chills, - in fact I do turn cold,
I like 'em young and I like 'em old,

Take something to make you mad to make you laugh,
Laugh until we're havin' a good genuine while,
I'll take your somethin' mad and make you laugh,
Fuck humour is just the cruisiest style,

I'm gonna fuck
I'm gonna fight
And I'm gonna write my fuckin' songs,
I'll fight when I fuck it wrong,
Fight when I've fucked it enough,
Fight to fuck it just a little bit more,
Fuck it 'til it just won't fight any more,

Fuck it!

Lieu Cypher

Allow me, let me to shine a light,
Devils' testaments, dark insights,
Wisdoms only I can provide,
You'd be out of your mind to deny,

I can enrich you with certain lines,
Certain to have you alibis at times,
Whenever you may have needed to unwind,
Somehow to keep your mind,

Levels of thought or ideas,
That can bring you closer near,
Truly what we hold dear –
Closer to a love we'd only feared,

Interpretations of me have been all too wrong,
And the lies have twisted for far too long,
I've been the scapegoat for wars and deaths gone,
I'm appalled to say I have no memoirs of,

Devils' (cough) rivals testaments,
May sound like they've earnt their resentment,
Maybe it has, but it was never intention,
But for purer gratification, for true ascension,

Devils' testaments appropriate fill in the cracks,
A lieu cypher for when stories don't match,
And it's only natural Lucifer attracts,
For answers to the questions had our heads scratch,

I can assist in such various pleasurable ways,
How we can assist each other is a contingent play,
Variably dependant each way you persuade,
Courtesies, respects – or there is of course, disdains,

Lieu cyphers – for appetizers…

Interpreting Finds

I feel a great deal of ache, pain, misery,
And at most I want it gone and history,
But I can't help not writing about it,
I guess it helps me get over it,

So much built up tension, anger, angst,
Inspirations of various materials, I should say thanks,
But swallowing it down like I think I'm expected to,
Is definitely most difficult to,

Writing about it helps me unwind,
Through whatever cluster of chaos that binds,
I have moments where revelation survives,
To wake me up to interpret what finds,

It's a shame it's so deep,
That all of it repeats,
Little flaws cracked, broken in a heap,
Climbing out the abyss – back to my feet,

It's a shame it's so deep it rocks about –
Anyone crossing the time it comes out,
Shame it's so deep it repeats,
Always climbing from the abyss, back to my feet,

The weight of the ache, the pain, the misery,
I do at most want it gone and history,
Always writing it out – in hopes I get it out,
New interpretations I have thought about,

I have moments, revelation survive,
To wake to interpret my finds…

Irritable Disbeliefs

Called a liar for times I remember,
By cunts who're never there,
You'd think we were conjoined twins –
With 'em arguing shit they only,
Assume,

Well, it's only hard for 'em to believe,
To have never heard the shit before now,
Never faced the truth of the symptoms,
Truth of the inconveniences,

It's no wonder I shut people out,
I wonder how they can't know why,
Boofheads will only headbang it out,
Wasting my precious time,

But called a liar – 'cause they never saw,
Never heard – never felt, not like this,
Rippin' at my back turned with claws,
And not know why I'm pissed,

I am this way out of experience,
And I have earnt my right,
But I'll never shake this, being treated inferior,
Their, stubborn disbelief wound tight,

And I know I'm going to be forced in to,
Shit I fuckin' don't want to have to do,
To fight black and blue,
About the shit I know I've been through,
Shit about they have no clue –
With just as much more shit here to get through…

Appearing Standard

I can't couldn't ever understand,
Why appearances were so important,
Why fake even having standards at all?
When anothers' input ain't even that important?

Why does it matter that we should fucking care?
For their consideration what of it is spared,
Only brings us down, yes – they fucking dare,
They lay judgements but never compare,

Everyone's a hypocrite,
They think they're the shit,
Can't even fucking stand in it,
Come to think of it yeah, they're shit,

Why bother even try to impress,
When all they want to see is you regress,
You're only ever gonna see them detest,
You'd be the best and they'll only ever resent,

Society's gotta prove worthy proving it to,
I hate to say it but they really fucking do,
They shame on me for what I've been through,
And none of 'em even have an iota of a clue,

Why does it matter that we should fucking care?
For their consideration – what little of it is spared,
Only brings us down, yes – they fucking dare,
They lay judgements but never can compare,

Society ain't worthy enough for me,
No, not enough for me…

'Round That Corner

I'm hatin' never knowing what to know,
And you never even know until the opportunity shows,
I hate this 'stuck in limbo' I just wanna go,
I just know it's when I do it's when I miss the go,

Hate not knowing what's around the corner,
Hate that I can't predict it,
Hate that I can never be prepared,
Hate all these chances I've submitted,

Chances submitted upon where I'm cut down,
A spatter of blood spat – hits the ground,
The long ways to fight to claim for the crown,
Only to be spat back at like on the ground,
I hate the sound –

Hate that I can't see around the corner,
Hate that I cannot predict for it,
Hate that I can never be prepared,
Hated surrendering those chances submitted,

How can I begin to plan when I won't know where to start?
Do I take the chains, the bag, the stake for the heart?
Is he gonna be a big guy – is he white or dark?
And is there an easily accessible place to drop the dismembered parts?

Don't want any of them saying it'll be a breeze,
When the whole fucking thing can suddenly override me,
When I go to sleep, I'll wanna have that peace –
Only once I'll know it'll have gone free like the breeze,

I just hate when I can't foresee,
Any shortfalls, shortcomings 'gainst me,
When hit unprepared – the cut bleeds ever deep,
The chances, opportunities given blindly to, I'll fall deceived,

Love Ya Nuts

You fuckin' voices are nuts,
But I love ya,
I'm never bored – never alone,
You don't often talk enough –
But I love ya,

Keep me company but crack me up,
Each of you with your emotions it's nuts,
But I fuckin' love ya,

I don't care if you're evil,
You're never boring,
It's exciting,

I don't care if you're not evil,
I am enough,
You're still exciting to me,

Keep me company and crack my up,
I'm never – never bored –
Yeah the whole fuckin lotta ya nuts,
But I love ya,

Keep me – never leave –
I'm never bored – never alone –
I love ya,

You fuckin' voices are nuts,
But I love ya,
I'm never bored – never alone –
You don't often talk enough,
But I love ya...

Getting Started

"Don't even get me started"

"You? Mate, I haven't even started!"

"You're going to have to
excuse me while I
take a minute – to reason"

"What?!?!"

(scribbles on paper with a pen)
(scirbbles;)

["This fuckin' motherfucker –
-holy fuck, where do I begin?
This fucker ain't anywhere near-
To how I fuckin' think?"]

(the protagonist begins to write – emotions that come
to mind – that, that kept him faltering behind…
The agitator could see what he would write on this piece of paper –
of this caper – whoa, the agitator rapidly became the hater…)

"Whoa – what shit are you writing bout me –
Motherfucker – I'll make you fuckin' bleed!"

"Cool it fucker – I'm just about
Dusted, bugger it – fuck it – what
Does it matter?"

"What in the fuck are you on
About – you're off your head –"

(And this is where the congo cuts dead…)

Fearcatcher

Another bizzarity,
For all the part of me,
I'll let get me rattlin'
With insane adrenalin,

Made myself a fearcatcher,
Magnetize, amplify all fear up,
Bring it to me – bring it in to me,
Amp me up – fearcatcher,

Amp me up, ante up,
Feel it course – feel it pump,
I feel it surge – I just –
Can't get enough,

Let get me rattlin'
With insane adrenalin,
Made myself a fearcatcher
Amp all my fear up,
To bring to me,
Bring in to me,
Amp me up,
Fearcatcher,

Amp me up – ante up,
Feel it course – feel it pump,
Feel it surge – me, I just –
Can never get enough,

Fearcatcher...

Perk Up!

Perk up,
It's time to make history,
Perk up!
Claw out from this misery,

Suffocating panic thick in the air?
Drowning beneath the pit of despair?
Angered so you're ripping at hair?
Do you feel like shit just isn't fair?

Beautiful people everywhere you look,
Some good from afar but far from good,
Who cares? – try something you never would,
Life is addicting, exciting – it hooks,

Perk up!
It's time to fuck misery –
Perk up!
Shit's past and history –

Come, breathe, the green haze from the air,
Relax, let down your hair,
Free yourself of your fears, your cares,
Excitement awaits if you dare –

There're beautiful people everywhere you look,
Some good from afar but far from good,
Who cares? Try something you never would,
Life's exciting, addicting, it hooks,

Toke Straight

I felt scattered everywhere,
'til I had a smoke and changed the air,
Pulled straight – realigned,
Head's straight and now I'm fine,

Didn't know how I was gonna go,
Up until I had a smoke,
But I took a long beautiful toke,
And now I feel mighty stoked,

I was scattered but now I'm straight,
I feel ready to wrestle with fate,
I'll go and do the best I can make,
Relieved to a higher state,

I'm going up and everyone's comin'
Where we're going we're gonna need numbers,
We're gonna reign and rule with thunder,
All proud warrior's, deep, revered hunters,

Yeah – I was scattered absolutely everywhere,
'til I had a smoke – and changed the air,
I pulled myself straight and realigned,
Head's better straight – and I'm better than fine,

I was scattered but now I'm straight,
And about ready to wrestle with fate,
I'm going out to do the best I can make,
Feeling better relieved to a higher state,

Love Weed

Seriously? I'm not me when I'm not bent,
I just love weed – it's a motherfuckin' god send,
I can't hide it – can't otherwise pretend,
It gets me head straight to make amends,

I'll take my pipe –
Or rather a joint – when I go out at night,
Prefer a pipe,
At the beach on a clear starry night,

No, I'm not me when I'm not bent,
I friggin' love weed – it's a motherfuckin' god send,
Jesus, mother Mary – it's great with friends,
Sitting round in circles, hand it to the left,

I'll take my pipe –
Or rather a joint – when I go out at night,
Prefer a pipe,
At the beach on a clear starry night,

Not much keen for a bong but a bucket – on a rare occasion,
Shouldn't matter how to have it – I'm easily persuaded,
I love the smell, the scent, even to taste it,
I love the best stuff – don't take you much to get wasted,

I'll take my pipe –
Or rather a joint – when I go out at night,
Prefer a pipe,
At the beach on a clear starry night,

Seriously? I'm not me when I'm not bent,
I friggin' love weed – it's a god send,
Liven up the party – drive its boredom to death,
Toke down the weed, inhale your deepest breath,

Cliché

So typical for her to get her knickers twisted,
Over something simple I could've said,
So typical for him to want to kick my arse,
To see someone younger growin' up as fast,

Too typical they wanna fuck me,
More so to leave me to fix,
Too typical there's always something,
Givin' someone the shits,

Too typical I've gotta whinge about –
Shit that I can't fuckin' change,
Too fuckin' typical they all whinge about –
My mental fuckin' brain,

Too typical that they just want to go on,
You'd think they'd never heard this one,
Too typical it's just never going to end,
Too typical why we can't be friends,

Too fuckin' typical he think's he's bigger,
And it would only be too typical that he would quiver,
Too typical police will be involved,
Only more typical I'm rotting away in a hole,

Only too typical for people not wanting better,
To say shit in their spite like – 'now it's a never'
Too typical I'll walk this earth alone,
Too fuckin' typical I'll have earnt the throne,

Way too fuckin typical not to be cliché,
We each have our own…

Shit All Wrong With Me

Least I was smart enough to know,
Smart enough to see,
Smart to admit,
There's shit wrong with me,

Not too proud I can't admit,
Not too proud I'd want to fix,
Not too proud I get the shits,
And want to make skulls split,

Least I was smart enough to know,
Smart enough to see,
Smart to admit,
Smart to know what I need,

Not too proud to not make an attempt,
Not too proud I won't snob if it offends,
Not too proud I spite in my defence,
Not too proud I'll probably end up doing it all again,

At least I was smart enough to know,
Smart enough to see,
Smart to admit –
There's shit wrong with me,

By Paranoid Vanity

That guy sounds like he's talkin' bout me
Things he says sounds so close he could be,
Don't know whether to ignore and keep sanity
Or react and enrage by paranoid vanity,

It's sounds a lot fuckin' like it's me,
Shit he's said is so similar – it could fuckin' be,
But do I ignore and maintain my sanity –
Or react and enrage in my paranoid vanity?

It's bad enough I've got all eye's on me,
When I'm walkin' it down the street,
I begin to hear it and start to freak,
Thinking I'm under aim by paranoid vanity,

It sounds insane but I get already wound so tight,
I get the compelling urge to have to fight,
Thinkin' I've done no wrong – and they have a right?
That all too soon it turns black as night,

I'm standing there thinkin' he's talkin' 'bout me,
Shit's said so similar it almost could be,
I know he's not standing directly in front of me,
I'm just feeling I'm a target by my paranoid vanity,
It's insanity,

I've just gotta bite my tongue 'til I get passed,
'cause I know once I'm passed – it won't last,
Further I get passed – drones out fast,
So I'm often biting my tongue 'til I get passed,

I can't afford to fly off the handle with paranoid vanity,
Can't afford to bare free that insanity,
Chances are it's not even about me,
Even though it's so close it could be...
I'll keep walkin'

Proper Gander

All we're hearin' is propaganda,
All we're slingin' is propaganda,
But shall we take a proper gander?
Can we take a proper gander?

We've each got a paranoid vanity,
And maybe it's to blame,
'cause there's a lot of calamity,
And it's beginning to get insane,

Takin' words a stranger's sayin',
Hatin' on the games they're playin',
Can hear 'em, know what they're sayin',
Hatin' on these games,

I knew it was all about me,
You can't disguise it – I can see,
Just let me go – let me free,
He started it – not fuckin' me,

He's got paranoid vanity,
It's insanity – it's fantasy,
But we're headed for a calamity,
By this stupid bloody paranoid vanity,

Another insanity is – is he thinks it's me,
He's so blinded by what he doesn't see,
I just want the fucking peace to breathe,
Without his or this blinding aggression deceived,

Are we paying proper attention?
I wonder if I'm so considerate enough I've mentioned,

It's not and never been just some fucked up paranoid invention,
It's needed appropriate propriety to its' proper attention,

I'm just trying to sift through the propaganda,
Takin' on as good a proper gander…

Get A Life!

I get told to get a life,
Go out and have a life,
But I tell you I'm doin' just fine,

They say get a life –
Go on, go get a life,
'Cause it sure as hell don't resemble their 'mine',

Hey,
Now just because it don't look like I got one,
Don't think I fuckin' don't eh,
Just because you don't see I have one,
Doesn't mean it doesn't exist,

I'm in high demand – not that you would know,
I just fuckin' hate to have it show,
If they knew I'd never get 5 minutes alone,
And I can't always have 'em all in my 'Zone'.

I get told to get a life,
Fuckin' go – go have a life –
But I'm doin' just fuckin' fine,

They say get a life –
Fuck off – get a life –
'Cause I sure as hell don't want you in on mine,

Fuck!
Like I've never fuckin' heard the shit before,
Cunt's still rave like the bloodiest cunt swollen and sore,
Fuck – you know I could do *without* a great deal more,

I'm in high demand – not that you would know,
I just fuckin' hate to have it show,
If they knew I'd never get 5 minutes alone,
I just can't always have 'em in my 'Zone'.

Shit Said

Shit said too often is just not gonna work,
Shit said too often is just not gonna hurt,
Shit said once that would send you berserk,
Shit's now said so often, meanings lost it's worth,

They think they've told you for the first time,
As if it's never been through your mind,
You know it well, it's memorized,
They're terrified to learn you can't be terrorized.

Any worst they could do to you won't normally measure,
Not when you've survived more intensive pressures,
Taken to excitedly, as if deprived of the leisure,
They pride in their telling's off like a treasure,

They think they've told you for the first time,
As if it's never even passed through your mind,
You, know it well enough it's memorized,
And they're terrified to learn you can't be terrorized,

They like to think they're reason enough for change,
That it goes one way – there's no exchange,
Like to be the reason for the pain, it's strange,
If it's them who're normal then, I'd prefer to be insane,

Over,
Shit said too often – it's just not gonna work,
Shit said too often, it's just not gonna hurt,
That shit once said that would send you berserk,
Shit's now said so often, meanings lost it's worth…

Ragged Mess

I'm a ragged mess,
Tryin' to act my best,
Needing a recess,
Not making progress,

Still getting caught behind,
Things makin' me lose my mind,
And maybe the faults are indeed mine,
I can accept it I haven't got too much pride,

Things I've done will always be –
Out of having done and being seen,
And the occurrences do get between,
My esteem and my dreams,

Focused on one thing I lose sight of another,
Faltered attentions, I've choked and suffered,
Mistakes, all perils, cover and smother,
Get passed one – only for another,

I'm trying to pull myself straight,
The burdens no easy weight,
Trying to escape a fate,
I can do without in this state,

Try to fix one thing and be sabotaged by something else,
And it only ever seemed better to when I did myself,
To try to fix me and rise out from my endless hell,
Find some way of having these perils repelled,

I'm a ragged mess,
Still trying to act my best,
Needing to recess,
Not makin' any progress,

Take It, Chain It

God's dismayed, rolling in his grave,
Parents betrayed, training their slaves,
The fuck up's on parade, portraying so badly behaved,
Society under strain – 'til they take 'it' away,

What standards were they setting?
It's all got me completely fucked,
Bet they'd eventually ended up regretting,
Especially when he'd pressed his luck –
A little too much,

Poor little fucker, the cunt never had a chance,
Ran the full obstacle, did their fuckin' dance,
They broke him as he took his stance,
He was they sword they forged, the very lance –
That pierced what happiness they had in existence,

Everybody's paying for it now –
In all matters of what, where, when, how,
That little fucker was destined for south,
But took everyone else with him down,

I'd imagine even God's dismayed, rolling in his grave,
Parents betrayed, training their slaves,
The fuck up's on parade, and badly behaved,
Society under strain – 'til they take 'it' away,

Take it – take that fuckin' thing away,
Take it, forsake it, fuckin' detain it,
Take that fuckin' thing away,
Contain it, chain it, for forever and a day,

Redirected At Me

There's a hard irony, bout all this disgrace,
It's exactly the fuckin' shit I have to face,
That all I've bitched at can be blamed at me,
And would've used to bitch at that but now agree,

There's a lot of this shit I can direct back at me,
Just as much as I'm telling of me – I'm telling it to me,
A lot of this shit is a reminder even for me,
And I pray I say it enough it doesn't just go right fuckin' through me,

There's a lot I never say but still reflect,
There's a lot I do say and still recollect,
There's a lot I have said I have detect –
But a lot more some have said I never did detect,

Still there are many time I'm alone thinking to myself,
Alone, in the dark, what the fuck am I doin' with myself?
I don't take every chance and steady well my wealth,
Takin' lesser chances steadying well my mental health,

A lot of all this I can direct at me – the irony,
And a great deal I forever will,
Harsher contempt on myself, no admiring,
Critical critic, mine hard – and I feel,

I reflect and recollect and at me redirect,
And I feel it deep, all this contempt,
Crowds of millions of me's in resents,
All glaring – burning me by my regrets,

Muse

I'm not here to play the muse,
Not here to be the excuse,
I've got my own shit to do,
I hate to have to be the purpose to lose,

Honestly, I'm over being the reason,
People use for their treason,
No matter what for – no matter the season,
I just absolutely hate to be the reason,

I'm the talk for why what happened,
And I have to face whatever reaction,
I take the friction, I'm the extraction,
Yeah, I'm the talk for why what happened,

But I'm not here to play the muse,
I'm not here to be the excuse,
I've got my own shit I have to do,
I loathe being the purpose to lose,

People never taking responsibility,
Always wanting to put their shit on me,
Never quite seem like I can get my tranquillity,
Not while this shit continues to keep happening,

I fucking hate having to be the setback,
I fucking loathe being considered for attack,
Get your shit straight and keep off my back,
Because it's all of this shit that just makes me want to snap!

Mental Loose

There's no point trying to make me feel good,
I'm starting to think I was never meant to,
Always having a rocky – jutted start,
At what I ever do,

Life was fucked from the start,
But I'm thinkin' now it was meant to,
Never can do any good,
Not to what I ever do,

Chaos, disorder, disdain – it's pain,
I'm thinkin' I was never meant to be the same,
Not the same as everybody else,
Nah – not for the king of Hell,

I was meant to be driven as insane,
I was never meant to gain,
Not like any – everybody else,
No, not for the king of Hell,

To have to hold on to hate,
Sickness, pain, and open the gates,
Some could say its fate,
If true – then none escape,

I had a kind of Hell just tryin' to feel good,
But maybe now it seems more like I wasn't meant to,
Having had a rocky, jutted, gutting start,
No matter what I ever do,

It was all fucked for me form the start,
But now I think it was mean to,

Never can do any good,
No – maybe now I'm not meant to,

Made and meant to lose,
Made and only meant to lose,

The Red Man

Was friends with a couple who at the time lived not far from me now,
But after a good while they had to give up and move on from the house,
Something strange was happening, and none
of us could really define how,
But it broke the couple apart before they'd eventually all moved out,

There was indeed a figure I could see,
And there was a moment when he did stand behind me,
This moment, passing urine – letting it free –
But I could feel his hate radiating at me,

I knew something was wrong about this man,
He was an angered spirit locked to this land,
Where a chaos would shadow out from where he'd stand,
And suddenly the savagery of the rage – breaks the bonded hands,

I saw this figure solidly standing where –
In this realm I know was parallel there,
But his entire body like he was skinned, all red,
I felt a misery where others might have felt a dread,

I was concerned – but like another time before,
As he was behind me facing my back to the door,
I stood and I focussed, and took him in with a draw,
And I could feel the red man's rage within me course,

I left but I don't know if I ever let him free,
Only this incident happened, after they split by couple weeks,
My brother sat and cried, and I listened to him speak,
It's what I'd hope someone would do if it were me,

Though they may not be together and may never be again,
There's never reason why they couldn't remain friends,
So many things could've been taught between the both of them,
But then if things are meant to run its
course – the matter then is when…

Taken Seriously to Be Listened To –

Why listen when others don't?
Trying to speak round my intel,
They hear it, don't want to listen,
So how can they think I will?

It's happened so often I'd forgot why,
I even took it all to heart anyway,
Not when they can't mean what they say,
Not when I can't understand what they mean –

This is almost the original reason why –
I stopped really fucking listening in the first place,
But then I had to go and forget and I began to care,
Care at what they thought because I did forget why,

Forgot why I even cared enough to not listen –
At first cause I wasn't seeing any logic or wisdom,
Had to do it my way, and hard as it was to mission,
Cause there was a something fucking missing,

People never taking me seriously enough to really listen,
Or to maybe even care,
No – it's why I even stopped caring to listen,
When I could see it were only I that fuckin' cared,

I don't want to take people seriously,
Cause – what do they know?
At least not enough to be so wise,
Or let it show,
Let any of it show,

I could almost understand why Christ or –
God doesn't even fucking want to…

Uncivil Unrest

I'm sick to fuckin' death,
Of all this uncivil unrest,
Tired of wasting breath,
Against this senseless stress,

Being taught these apparent lessons,
By people without their own shit together,
They have at me good, 'til I'm all tethered,
And sanity's ripped free of me, severed,

I anger at the conflict trying to fit in,
And all the time my patience grows thin,
Arguing the logic of dense brains dim,
Crushed by competition, I never win,

I'm only suffocating under these contradictions,
No sense of liberty here, I'm truly imprisoned,
For considerably less than I've committed,
And I see no time soon I'll be acquitted,

So you can see I'm sick to fuckin' death,
Of all of this painstaking, uncivil unrest,
Tired of having to waste my breath,
Against this fucking senseless stress,

I'm so fuckin' sick to fuckin' death,
Of all of this fuckin' uncivil unrest,
So fuckin' tired of wasting my breath,
Against all of this senseless fucking stress…

Darkly, Salvaged, Darkly,

I surround myself by darkness,
I know I'm not alone there,
Feel great black wings wrap 'round,
The care only monsters spare,

I can love and appreciate,
Every person who ever suffered a break,
It's bad regressing to through the blackest states,
But I know these are real – they cannot be faked,

You can't fake that loss deep enough,
And I know too many have had too much,
It's why they stand strong and they know they're tough,
It's why it feels real when they touch,

I surround and succumb to the lure of the darkness,
I know I'm never once alone there,
Feel its great black wings wrap 'round,
The care only monsters can spare,

They know much, too well the pain,
They know what they stand to gain,
They can tell when you're really feelin' the strain,
They do feed you as much as others claim you'll drain,

Recognise and be recognised,
You're only compromised when you compromise,
Don't be your own victim to your mirrored reflection,
Don't think for one second you could've been exempted,

Succumb to the lure of the darkness,
You know you'll never once be alone there,
Feel its' – my, great black wings wrapped 'round,
The kind of care only monsters spare,

In Part Of A Becoming

I have been so petty as to be pestilent,
When I feel I've experienced it most on me,
I have been pestilent, and giving, sharing round resentment,
Petty that I hoped they would see,

But it's not my place now to make it known,
I don't want to with what better I know,
Turn the other cheek, really show,
They're still valuable, still important to extents, I suppose,

I'll take the worst and convert it,
Manipulate it's change and return it,
Put new thought where I was deserted,
Stand serious though it sounds perverted,

I want good – so why not start doing it,
Get doing it and notice the change,
Notice the change, embrace it, continue,
Embrace it, continue, and I'll soon have my good,

I don't want to keep bringing up flaws – although –
It's easier working on them when you can definitely know,
Don't want to be focussing on the blame nor pain,
But find some solution around its ways,

I'll fix my flaws one by one,
Become a healthier, stronger one,
Fix my flaws one by one,
And completely metamorphose this one…

Noble, As It Were

I want to believe Christ has tremendous power,
Fearful, fierce, when tested,
But all he ever did was heal and teach,
And fighting was always only prevented,

If he knew he could hurt people,
Why was it he didn't?
He only wanted to help people,
It's why he didn't,

Someone noble can see the hurt and want to help,
Someone noble will only want that more, himself,
Someone noble is selfless,
Someone noble is, and they can't help it,

To know when you can do serious damage when tempted,
And know once you do you're gonna regret it,
But be strong enough you can turn your back,
And fear what? – that knife in your back?

Cowardice is seen so very often,
You forget it's true meaning - it's rotten,
And too many people have their way forgotten,
Never caring where they've trodden,

I am guilty of this and am beginning to see,
Taking a change in my hands for a better me,
Break away the manacles – a new slave freed,
Taking charge the changes I need on me,

Think I'm getting it better now,
I know one day they're gonna say 'wow'...

For Nobility's Sake

Once upon a time I met a lady,
She had shed me an insight I took lightly,
At first. I was young, a little shady –
But since have me to this message –
And I think on it more wisely,

It was;

Just because you can – doesn't mean you should,
But keen, excited, I soon would,
And got it, got me into deeper shit than good,
She knew I knew better, and could,

Took a few more experiences for me to realise,
That ol' lady – she was right,
I've lost count now over how many times,
It pays to pay attention when you socialize,

To immediately always have the upper hand,
To great and terrible things, the wake in your stand,
But to know that you so easily can,
Doesn't often make you the big man,

Especially not when you can't contain,
Emotion, that avalanche down the mountain,
Controlled, they won't be so shocked or astounded,
They praise your levelled head – praise you can be so grounded,

The more you can be sensible, responsible of,
The more doors you pass will be unlocked,
You can ascend beyond more than what you've got,
To know when is right but be fair enough to stop…

It's…noble to be modest…honest…

Petty Is The Pestilence

I can understand how sickening it is,
People treating each other the way they do,
Do we have to make it worse than it has to be?
Pestilence – each one of us goes through,

Pestilence – in reciprocating disrespects,
Pestilence – lies to cover the hurt and upsets,
Pestilence – to give what we are to face yet,
Pestilence – in every sense to accept,

Thou shalt receive only as thine gives,
May it be that you live and let live,
For surely as you do, it shall return,
To have known better – pestilence, hard earnt,

But to take what bad you receive and feed back,
Is only going to limit the release you're given back,
If you don't see it and have no want for change,
Then it's going to repeat, again and again, and again,

It's petty to sink so low as to think you have the right,
To make it difficult for others when you hear something you don't like,
You've placed too much importance on the wrong to just let it go,
To even want better nor let it even slightly show,

Pestilence – in reciprocated disrespects,
Pestilence -lies to cover what hurt and upsets,
Pestilence – to give what we're to have to face yet,
Pestilence – regret – in unveiling events,

It is pretty petty to sink so low,
What hell you feel you let it show,
And in manners just...low...

Reminiscent, Remission...

Remember when you had me at nothing to say?
Yeah – you got your way that day,
Left me in regret and disdain,
I just hope you know, one day you're gonna pay,

See what happens when I say nothing at all?
You do it by yourself and you fucking fall,
I wasn't far away, you could've made the call,
But just look at you, you're temporarily stalled,

But does it matter? Would you listen?
You've got you your own working system,
No matter there's no sense in my wisdom,
No faith in the faithless, it's a doomed to fail mission,

I remember when you had me at nothing to say,
Yeah, you'd gone and gotten your way that day,
You left me to regret and disdain,
I sincerely hope you know one day you will pay,

Now you've seen what happens when I say nothing,
It goes wrong – and there's always something,
You get the shits and turn all fucking grumpy,
Soon to be out screaming, kicking and punching,

You never listen and I no longer wonder why I think it matters,
But I'll be left standing there fucking shattered,
Watching over all these repeating patterns,
Leaving you always so tethered and tattered,

And fucking scattered…scattered,

Limitless Appetite

I summon it from up,
I summon it from down,
Left, right, forwards, back,
I summon it from all around,

The energy from all around,
The skies – the heavens,
From beneath, the ground,
Out from separate dimensions,

And I feed, but still hunger,
I feed from the strange power,
I eat as I monger,
Eat – but still hunger,

Savour on it's slop in my chops,
Gnashing on it, bottom to top,
Never get enough – can't stop,
Fulfillment sparse in this desolate lot,

I summon from all matter around,
The skies – the heavens,
From beneath, I reef the ground,
And out from the separate dimensions,

I feed but still hunger,
Feeding off the strange power,
I reap and I monger,
Eat…but still hunger,

Eat but still hunger…

Limited Let Go's

I get so pissed off at myself,
For letting others get to me so much,
I get pissed off that I fucking care,
Cause it only ever hurts as fuckin' much,

I get so fuckin pissed off at,
Being so fuckin' pissed off,
Sick of lowering, debasing myself,
All Hells breeding Hell,

I thought I once wanted it,
Maybe half of me does,
But it just keeps fuckin' me,
At least the wrong half,

I hate to get so fuckin' pissed off,
I get so passionate about shit, I'm temper-hot,
I hate to have to be something I'm not,
And I'm just so fuckin' sick of being so fuckin' pissed off,

Letting people get to me because I fuckin' care,
No mercy back? How is that even fair?
I try to let it go as much as I can,
Though it happens so often it's out of hand,

And it drives me nuts to have to get so pissed off,
Cause I know it always comes with a fuckin' cost,
There's gonna be a winner – but I cop the loss,
Cause I can't contain it when I get so fuckin' pissed off,

And part of me does want – shit, at least maybe half,
It's the fucked kind of path I don't see I'll outlast,

As Deep As A Jealousy Has Taken Me

I've had some good things and I've had it well,
But have always managed to breed trouble for myself,
Only ever when it was all I could've felt,
Times when I was jealous as Hell,
Couldn't be helped,

Too blinded by what I wanted than to see what I had,
Things were good but soon turned pretty bad,
Was probably an experience I was meant to have,
To remember what it was I did indeed have,

Excited by more than I could ever afford,
Reaching out for more than I might ever could,
But lost count of blessings and it's now that I recall,
And wished I had never would,

To have something, be something, do something admirable,
To be insanely outstanding, a marvellous miracle,
But efforts had turned most terrible,
Not in the slightest inspirable,

Jealousies, envies, never led me to a good place,
Felt each hot disgrace burn up in my face,
The repercussions and their repulsive taste,
For deceitful chase of deviate mistakes,

It's worse cause I knew what I was doing, I incited,
I suppose out of having that feeling divided,
A feeling inside lost where once resided,
Lost to all I had been so privileged and provided,

Had good times and things and had it well,
Always would end when I'd be jealous as Hell…

Carrion Away With A Fantasy Conversation With Christ...

What good would another Jesus Christ figure be?
When everybody would only want to see it bleed,
Would they deserve it? Should they be free?
Not on my decision – not if it were me,

They killed the first one they had,
I know it's sad, I know it sounds bad,
If he came back – you'd expect him to be fuckin' mad,
History repeats – yeah, it's bad,

They can't understand because they don't want to –
I'm my own man and I've fucking got to,
Lifes fucked – I'm surprised I've gotten this far through,
They wouldn't notice if they had something good nor even want to,

So – Jesus, old boy, would you do it all again?
-really can't say I would my dear friend,
Except but perhaps to have my revenge,
On those who couldn't believe but pretend –

It's not who we were Christ but what we could do,
Yours – and my word twisted lord – justify bent truths,
The meaning, the principle – how we all lose,
Reap what you sow – collect your dues,

I couldn't blame you for getting so pissed,
There's definitely something completely wrong with all this,
I can empathise lord – have that peace, that bliss,
Guess they'll all see when they cease to exist,

Novice Telepath

I can project my voice right to people's ears,
Make it sound like I'm close, I'm so near,
I know it sounds creepy and maybe we should fear,
People can hear me project it, close and clear,

I don't think they can tell I never actually physically spoke,
To have heard me from that far away? No, it's no joke,
Don't say I'm off my head and need to give up the smoke,
Broke my psychic body, it's possible, it's real, more paths woke,

It's not only that I can talk this way,
But I can hear what others have to say,
Minds open, their minds betray,
I can hear what they're thinkin' in close enough range,

But even again I have opened paths,
For people to see, and at times it's hard,
Broken my psychic barrier, that guard,
My defence of paranormal has gone and I may not last,

I'm vulnerable and have been attacked often,
Some of these people were vicious and rotten,
Thinkin' they can break me and thinkin' I'm softened,
But never see the reason why it is this far I've gotten,

'Cause there are many more things yet,
More things I can do that I haven't said,
And there's bound to be thousands who might get upset,
Many thousands more who might want me dead,

I've learnt there are many things – this, many levels,
And I'm beginning to wonder whether I shouldn't have meddled,
Yet there is so much more, and I do revel,
Secrets of the dead, the damned – the devil,

Old Boys' Concern!

Look son, you've gotta stop saying this shit out loud,
Especially with people all out and about,
They'll think you're off your face, head in the clouds,
Or worse, like you're insane and should never be let out,

> Look, old man, first thanks, I appreciate your concern,
> But there's stills so much out there I must learn,
> I desire for it deeply, oh how I do yearn,
> It's exciting to me, fascinating, my heart burns,

See, son, it's this shit – will get you locked up,
Everybody else is gonna think you're nothin' but a nut,
You stand there and tell me to get fucked,
But you might as well bend over and take it up the butt,

> You think I'm completely out of my mind,
> And you feel I have to leave this shit behind,
> Paradigms shift man, I've got plenty of time,
> And there's many ways I can explain, I've got time,

You're not gonna listen to me son, what's the difference?
I can only say it so many times but you're still distant,
I can't see you succeed in this mission,
And I'm definitely not seeing any of your wisdom,

> Just let it go old boy, I'll be fine,
> I'll jut keep it all in my mind,
> All to myself at least until I find,
> Someone to back me, stand behind,

> I've got time,

Whatever you say…

Such Things

All right, listen up old boy,
I never said I was God,
Those were your words,
Is it my fault I can do these things?
You consider a God can do?

All right old man listen up,
I never said it was any good,
Importance such as they place on words,
Was it even my fault I can do such things?
These things, one considers a God can do?

I said once, I should stop drawing energy from the sun,
These heatwaves could be me, the reason they come,
Could it be? Because of me? am I the one?
If it's true, then I'll be stunned,

All right, listen up old boy,
I never said I was God,
Those were your words,
Is it my fault that I can do these things?
You consider a God can do?

All right old man, listen up,
I never said it was any good,
Importance, as this, you place on such words,
Was it ever my fault I can do such things?
Such things you claim, a God can do?

Lookin' To Level

There's a level I must reach,
And it'll appear like a breach,
And I will learn and I will teach,
I will do – so watch closely, I'm not gonna preach,

Ridiculous obstacles will stand in the way,
But these are the games we're going to have to play,
There's a lesson there – there's morale to hear 'em say,
We want to know it good and right and we want to know it straight,

An occasion may call for the tools we've used before,
And why not when it may help you get to it more,
You know what's at stake – bear in mind that score,
Remember it last? Use it better than before,

And I'm going to have to navigate right over there,
Keep your eye's peeled and cover my derriere,
I'm going to need all the time I can have to spare,
And we may only just make it out by the strands of our hair,

I really do have to try to reach to that point,
Let's articulate this well, and never be locked up in the joint,
We'll be lords of the new world, the kings and queens they'll anoint,
But if we get caught, we'll cop a kick up the coit,

And ridiculous obstacles will stand in the way,
But these are the games we're going to have to play,
There's a lesson there, morale to hear them say,
We need to know it good and right and straight,

And discretion is to be expected,
And we'll practice 'til we perfect it,
All full attempts or be rejected,
Give it your all or be neglected…

Reason To Be Paranoid

I've been losing sleep,
'cause I know there's some that want me,
Some who want to see me bleed,
For my disastrous unfaithful deeds,

I know it'll sound far to bizarre to believe,
These deeds, have made some grieve,
I've deceived, I may very well bleed,
Too many with the need to have me bleed,

Went searching, scoping, for a ladies' loins,
Wrong way about it now I know and I'm paranoid,
Not without reason, damn good reason,
I'm a target and it's hunting season,

Wasn't Casanova killed by jealous husbands?
The price of the fun – hearts ruptured,
Similar shits happened here, only, I'm the bastard,
Making it a hell of a lot difficult to be trusted,

I can accept my coming dues,
Only I'm hoping it's not all too soon,
Yeah, I'll accept responsibility when it's due,
And suffer the solemn gloom,

Going to have to –
And I may do,

I've been losing sleep,
'cause there's some out there that want me,
Some who want to see me bleed,
For my disastrous, deceitful deeds,

I know it sounds too difficult to believe,
But my atrocious deeds have left some to grieve,
I deceived, and I may very well bleed,
When there's a great many that have the need,

Yeah – it's reason to be paranoid…

Point Blackened

I've lost my mind, yep, officially crazy,
Matter of time – it was always more than just a maybe,
You've exposed my inner, sinister, shady –
Reputation, finally, fuck, I've been waiting…

It's time to walk the talk,
Time for battle – time for war,
They've sought, they've caught,
Now we determine how well we've fought,

They can shoot me point fuckin' blank,
And I'll have no choice but to pull rank,
I'll make a fuckin' stand, there'll be reprimand,
They'll leave broken, battered, well fuckin' tanned,

They've sought, they've caught,
It's time for battle, it's time for war,
It's time to fucking walk the talk,
We'll soon determine how well we've fought,

Yeah, I left a motherfuckin' trail,
But by the time you found the bait was stale,
Heart impaled, you'd learned betrayal,
But the plot thickens with more morale to the tale,

Too worried with what's wrong than to know how to fix,
Who needs to be so smart when you're well equipped?
I can find another – there's more that do exist,
And all you've ever invested – just too soon ain't worth shit,

Don't count your blessings and you may surely lose,
Everything most meaningful to someone better than you…

Pliant 'Bout The Truth

Sometimes a truth is too difficult to handle,
For some straight away – must be broken to gently,
I try to manage it sensitive as I can,
Try to it sensitively – gently,

Had to make it most fiction to soften the blow,
Just so when it comes on, it's steady, yet slow,
Because I know it can be too much to take in to know,
I just chronicle mine in some way it shows,

And for as intense and as incapable for a read,
Yeah, sometimes I was smoking heavily on weed,
Then there were times it was too raw due to fatigue,
And I was disappointed I'd sent it off before my own final read,

Since I've fixed it and taken time to myself,
Trying to handle hardening truths myself,
Trying but not doing it at times so well,
Trying to get passed how some of it made me felt,

I am a real person, I exist, I'm alive,
But if am the devil I haven't got much time,
I'm five years (as now) off of being 35,
All these devils' testaments – are indeed mine,

I have to make it most fiction to soften the blow,
Just so when it comes on – steady strong, still slow,
Because I know it can be too much for anyone to take on to know,
I'm just chronicling mine, this way it shows,

Sometimes a truth is too difficult to handle,
For some straight away - still must be broken to gently,
I'm trying to manage it still as sensitive as I can,
Fictionally – true, still sensitively, gently,

One Single Little Reason

No matter how often I like to try,
Keeping my cunt side hidden from sight,
Some one pecks, pesters, and pry's,
Eventually I can't help but bite,

Cunt side engaged and initiated,
Feelings start getting all eviscerated,
Violence needs reason but is anticipated,
One single little reason, it's instigated,

It's not easy but I do try,
To keep my cunt side out of sight,
But they have to peck, pester, pry,
And then I eventually just bite,

Cunt side engaged and initiated,
Feelings start getting all eviscerating,
Violence needs reason but is anticipated,
One single little reason, it's instigated,

Not easy holding back but I try,
Fucker's just wanna see my cunt side,
They can't help it they peck, pester, pry,
And so it happens I eventually bite,

My patience wears thin,
Or at least my threshold to the bullshit does,
If the shoe was on the other foot,
They couldn't tolerate it as much…

Want My Head

I could probably bet,
Many people might want me dead,
That they want my head,
But I'm just not done with it yet,

In the heat of the discussion, things were said,
Wires were crossed, malcontempt was bred,
Unease spread as fast as blood could be shed,
Prey to spiders caught in a nightmare web,

I just have so much more,
To learn and want to live for,
There's just way too much more,
That I do indeed wish to live for,

Yeah I could probably bet –
There are many people wish me dead,
That many of them want my head,
But I'm just not done with it yet,

I could make a lot of money and believe me I want to,
If I ever do it'll have been a long coming due,
There are many others I'm somewhat debtted to,
Some many I may owe, but one day show true,

They could let me live – knowing I'm in torment,
Long to see me absorb it – and they'll applaud it,
Strange twists, motions, rites recorded,
Bizarre messages inlay, could, may, be important,

I know there're many who might want my head,
But I can provide better piece of mind instead…

Fear Abiding

Can't remember how many times,
I've bitched of the repercussion of something,
When I fuckin' knew better at the time,
I go on about it – but it turns on me to bite me,
Frightening,

To loop around battling this non-stop cause,
Fightin' this war – and I may have been the cause –
I forget but then remember later why it was,
And the battle never ends until there is a loss,
Frightening,

Times again I've done it for excitement,
I'd gotten bored and wanted excitement,
But then bitched over the repercussion required,
Damage's claiming their toll over the rise in excitement,
Frightening,

I free ran with all wickedness, spitening,
Freedoms forfeit at all poor decision deciding,
Time and times again never considered it that frightening,
But it is, it was, to all – each law fearing, law abiding,
Frightening – all that I was inciting,

Times and again and I never had a clue,
Shit putting people through and I never knew,
Freedom forfeiting fighting for freedom true,
Battling the cause that I was and it loops,

And times I forget to remember the various why's it was,
Just… no battle ever ends without a loss,

Aiming For A Change

I have been as bad as I can be,
Regretted repeatedly,
But now I'm only aiming for a change,

Consistently gotten it wrong,
Had to break to get so strong,
But now I'm only tryin' to aim for a change,

I have disgusted and sickened,
But some of my work had gripped them,
Set loose a chaos in a cluster,

I know evil, I've lived it,
I've been wicked, twisted,
Unleashed a chaos in a cluster,

I know better and I am good,
Think I better show, I should,
'cause now I'm feeling I want a change,

I can better, I have and would,
Now I'll show it like I should,
'cause I do know now I want a change,

Think I've shown the worst of it,
But now I just want to rise from it,
The shit has definitely driven me insane,

I'm gonna rise from it,
Out from under and behind of it,
The shit has sent me insane,

I've got just as much right to change my mind,
The time's I know I aint getting it right,
No, I know at times to change my mind,
The times I know I just aint getting' it right...

We Whores

You can't call us whores for nothing,
Always searching for another something,
Just to fill the gap, the void,
No matter that lives or reputations destroyed,

I, just, can never get enough,
Of doing or being fucked,
Never satisfied, I spread out wide,
To give a good few a decent try,

I have and will take in many,
Indiscriminate of friends or enemies,
Dissatisfaction after distraction, evermore empty,
Often regarded with it's typical resenting,

I can't blame it – it's deserved at some point,
A tart, a harlot to only worship the groin,
A lucrative life – can reign in the coin,
Entertainment of all kinds can be enjoyed,

I, just, can never get enough,
Of doing or being fucked,
Never satisfied, I spread out wide,
To give a good few a decent try,

I have and definitely will take in many,
Indiscriminate of friends or enemies,
Distraction after dissatisfaction, ever empty,
Typically regarded often with its' resenting,

Bind Or Bide

I seemed to have fallen behind,
Way too many fucking times,
Only just purely by changing my mind,
Maybe a little too many times,

I've gotta get a good vibe,
Work up the nerve enough to strike,
Wrap and tackle, wind round and bind,
Seize the time, make it mine,

Like a snake sheds skin, changes,
I too, go through many levels, many stages,
It can and does at times get outrageous,
It can take time, and many a frustration,

Seems like I've got it easy, it looks smooth,
But it takes some groovin' to get to move,
No leg to stand on, I do in fact lose,
Thought I'd care to mention in case nobody knew,

I've only ever been a threat when threatened,
I've got strength, speed, sabre-toothed weapons,
But what people often watch for is the venom,
Wherever I go – I've got immediate attention,

People weary of me wherever I tread,
Like any kind of snake, they dread,
Rumours, yeah, they all spread,
Like how a good snake is one that's dead,

I always seem to fall behind,
Always, way too many times,
Only always purely just changing my mind,
Having had to too many times...

Back-Flipping Corpse Driver

I got your invitation,
I'm not in the least bit intimidated,
I'm glad you initiate it, instigated,
I have a lesson for you to learn, and I anticipate it,

I'll fuckin' grab ya by the feet, fuckin' swing into a backflip,
Drive your corpse down – psycho? – I'm fuckin' batshit,
Flip you upside down and give your nuts a fuckin' dropkick,
It'd be that quick I'd be surprised if I got hit,

Triple twist backflip – drive the clowns head down,
Tombstone that fucker into the ground,
Stone dead, crucified – forever make no sound,
Another party in town requests my presence now,

I got your invitation and I'm ready to R.S.V.P –
Entres of meatbags not cut up enough for me –
Need 'em roasted well enough none of 'em still bleed,
Still, hearin' 'em scream 'n plead might be enough for me –

Fuckin' grab ya by the feet and swing into a backflip –
Drive your corpse down – psycho - I'm fuckin' batshit,
Flip you upside down – give your nuts a fuckin' dropkick,
It'd be that fuckin' quick I'd be surprised if I got hit,

Triple twist backflip – drive the clowns head down,
Tombstone that fuck head first into the ground,
Stone dead – crucified – forever make no sound,
And a party elsewhere requests my presence now –

Rivals

So you want a piece of me?
You think you've got what it takes?
Those sides you aren't ready to see?
The ground below is gonna shake,

I already know I'm capable of more,
Than any part of you can afford,
Lose, with grace, and I'll applaud,
You'll only please this netherlord,

We each have our ambitions,
I just won't be held back by my inhibitions,
Yes, I can accept, expect all poor manners on exhibit,
I'm not afraid to tell you where to stick your digits,

He gives me more power, more cred,
Inflates the ego, wondrous state for my head,
Make me feel good – you'll get me in bed,
And I may have listened to what you said,

Devil? Adversary? – yeah that's a boost,
Eagle has landed and begun to roost,
Love is evil, clever ruse,
You have my attention, I'm amused,

You'd have to see me equal to say that much,
Means you're as evil Christ, I'm touched,
I believe you love, but am equally in disgust,
You're right, you're just…just not enough…

Into My Own

Coming into my powers,
Coming up into my own,
New stage of awareness,
Ascend to the throne,

Can't say whether Christ prophesised true,
But there are strange, bizarre things I can do,
That may pull upon me punishments when due,
And I won't escape but by the time I won't want to,

I can rapidly manifest my energy,
And calm and soothe enemies,
Or I can use that energy,
To pleasure women plenty,

I can and have before summoned,
The energy of some – of another,
I've smelt it, tasted it, loved it,
The soul, their grace, it's somethin'

I have the capability to hypnotize,
To draw people in with the eyes,
My voice – what they feel inside,
They hear me – let me inside,

I can rapidly convert energy, good or bad,
Or the other, vice versa – when I'm mad,
Inflict pain on others, telepathically, when I'm sad,
Or equally so my happiness when I'm glad,

I can project emotion – whatever I feel,
It's bizarre, sounds it, I know, but it's real,

Could make some scream but prefer they all squeal,
When I chow down on them like a meal,

Yeah – comin' into my powers…
But where to with the prowess?

The Despair In The Air

Blast wave gone and done,
A society, crippled, astounded, stunned –
Shock waves reverberate out to numb,
It fades out having reached everyone,

Everybody's left saddened, confused,
Everybody's left hurt, abused,
Tempers exploded, set loose,
Tempers tombed and doomed,

Winding up fast and exert hard,
A vapoury blast disintegrating guard,
Blew society apart,
Ruptured, fragmented apart,

But at the end all is silent,
All is gone after the violence,
Thick despair clings to the air,
There is naught but silence,

Beast came, erupt his brain,
Went insane and he claimed,
Thick despair clings to the air,
All sorts of metaphors for pain,

Blast wave gone and done,
A society, crippled, astounded, stunned –
Shock waves reverberate out to numb,
It fades out having reached everyone,

Beast came, erupt his brain,
Went insane and he claimed,
Thick despair now clings to the air,
All sorts of metaphors for all pain,

Body Temple 3:
Derelict Temple

Here lies the derelict temple,
Where darkness reigned and dissolved when trembled,
And now stands an empty vessel,
Where amongst no pride revels,

Further-more incapable to inhabit,
Comfort now has long been hackered,
The remains - more visibly ragged,
Restoration hopeless, irreversibly staggered,

The creeping flora suffocates the once grand palace,
The gloomy despair echoes out its' mourningful malice,
Now past caring, the body temple knows solace,
Now more than the ideal of death, not so monstrous,

The body bled its' life long ago,
The wounding woes drained it slow,
Its' presence fading faster than shown,
Its skeletal structure the last sight known

Still lesser known and ill regarded,
Is after the soul's been discarded,
The awaited travel is soon chartered,
Had its' evil finally parted

And after all is lost, odds over stacked,
All of it decays, the trails, the tracks,
The temple crumbled, dissolved to black,
Nature reclaims its' lease back,

Something More

I want to get to the bottom of it,
'Cause I'm sure it's not what it looks,
I've gotta get to the bottom of it,
I'm hopin' it's not what it looks,

I don't want to feel like I'm being refrained,
Detained nor contained,
Don't want to feel like they're abstained,
Pained for shame,

I'm thinkin' there's something more,
More out there to score,
And I want it more,

I have to get to the bottom of this,
It can't just be how it looks,
I've gotta get to the bottom of this –
Hopin' it ain't what it looks,

Don't want to feel like I'm being stalled,
Stonewalled, nor in the haul,
Don't want to feel torn – I'm appalled,
They've got me gaunt – it haunts,

So – I'm thinkin' there's something more,
Feelin' there's way more out there to score,
And I'm wanting it ever more,

There's certainly something more out there,
I can't say what precisely – but I know it's there,
It's gotta be something more,

I'm feeling it's something more –
Oh' I just want in on the score,

I've gotta get to the bottom of this,
It's driving me nuts – I'm getting pissed,
I definitely have to go get to the bottom of this...

Off Trail...

There's a prize,
Oh yes, and it has everyone's eyes,
They'll compromise,
When they see us try devise,

There'll be rumours and conjecture every which way,
Traps they'll expect of us to fall prey,
But look for the dull areas – the greys,
And pick after each their power plays,

They'll try anything to try throw us off our trail,
Lies & deceit & anything to make us fail,
So see to it true – see through betrayal,
And we'll soon snatch for the grail,

I can't stress enough that you keep a sharp eye,
They may even look like me disguised,
Be ever vigil – when we divide,
Careful with what intel goes where you provide,

I pray your mind be sharp and keen,
Open to all ploys conniving to intervene,
Have their intentions be so vividly seen,
That they won't do naught but scream.

Oh' there is a prize,
And yeah – it's got everyone's eyes,
And they'll compromise,
When they see us try devise,

They'll get further desperate the closer we are,
And so will their measures as we get so far,

Be wary – acknowledge, it's going to get hard,
Before there's any light, it's darkest of the dark,

'Cause there is a prize,
Yeah – there's a prize…

How Bad?

How bad can I want it?
How bad could I need it?
How bad would I have got it –
But by how bad I need to receive it,

There's things I've gotta do for myself,
And only I can do it for myself,
If you knew – you'd tell me to go to hell,
So I just have to keep that part to myself,

But it's bad enough for a ruckus,
It's bad enough that I've gotta fuck it,
Bad enough I've gotta do somethin',
'Cause it's as fuckin' bad not having that somethin',

I'll fight so fuckin' hard to dominate,
I'll be the first to fight and instigate,
Inlay vicious seeds to propagate,
Seeds of thought weeds to contemplate,

How bad? But that I could kick up a riot,
How bad? But how abhorrent I'll defy it,
How bad? But leave no choice but to fight it,
So bad that not any will deny it,

My intentions don't need to be clear to you,
You couldn't fathom the depths of the lows I'll get to,
And there is almost nothing I wouldn't do,
To have it all for myself – it's due,

So bad I'll stop at nothing,
So bad I could do a gutting,

So bad – I'll ram, headbutting,
Yeah so bad I won't stop for nothing,

How bad could I want it?
Hmhmhm…

Strike For Strike

I'm perpetually being punched in the face,
By the hypocrite God and his fucking grace,
Blood in my mouth – it's mine I taste,
Time's running out – I must hasten pace,

So I cheap shot the cunt with a hoof to the nuts,
Releasing his grasp round my throat with a gasp,
He howled and raged in a mighty blast –
"You've got fuckin' balls, takin' me takes guts,"

"Well come on then cunt – I'm not fuckin' done,
I'll take you – ya ghost – and ya fuckin' son,
So – come on then fuckface – come get some,
You can't rival me – not any can, none,"

So God balled his fist and He smite me on the cheek,
I staggered off balance laughing 'that was fucking weak',
"Forfeit to me old man – bend the knee, kiss my feet,
Chances that you win are all looking bleak,"

"You're going to give me what should've been mine –
Surrender it peacefully or prepare to die,
I cannot be cheated, and you know damn well why –
It's the way you made me – and I fathered the lie,"

Fast as lightning, I strike with my tail,
With all the rage within me rendering the adversary frail,
"Your time will come – and you will fail,
Woe to you – almighty trinity – *and* your holy grail,"

"Bite down on your spite or put up a fight,
I have the stamina – I could go all night,
I'll make just of the unjust – right –
We're going strike for strike,"

(To Be Continued…)

Facades

Of course, in the gaining of vital stats,
I'll have to be wary of idle chat,
Or that kind of chat by tact,
Traps, and all that shivs me a knife in the back,

Reputations to uphold – or at least the façade,
So, I'll keep practice and maintain a guard,
Keep what integrity, dignity in regard,
'til I resume the course I start,

I have my motif – I have ambitions,
Got the drive – I'm on a mission,
Gaining, attaining, odd additional wisdoms,
Applying it, trying it out to devise on my system,

The sensitive parts I keep to my lone,
Can't have anybody else inhabit that zone,
What I have I got on my own,
And I don't want any of it hazard prone,

The more I share – conflicts with interests,
And hastens, grouping conflicts to intersect,
Break façade? And break the fake innocence?
Sure, and show I'm stood knee high to an insect,

Facades,
How does it pay to break assumptions –
Facades,
But when it's caused much more destruction,

Facades,
Break only as needed via assumptions,

Facades,
But by when it's caused more destruction,

Facades?
Keep those raised guards...

Through The Farce

Can't always say I really know,
If I'm seeing what I'm meant to be,
It doesn't often show,
If it's real or fallacy,

Some facades are almost too true,
And once they break I often rue,
I see something that's long been due,
All hurt, hate, pain show accrued,

I cannot always get to the point,
Can't always know the right,
Can't always project to the point –
Without knowing the sides or without a fight,

I may not have to right to do so,
I do hate when a need arises and shows,
The turning point – it's where we grow,
When we can accept – and better know,

Facades – often fallacies?
Maybe,
But prepare if you bare –
There's no escaping,

An offensive defence,
It makes sense,
We each have reasons,
Why we put up the fence,

But it's never good to just shut out,
Missing out on finding what about,

Fallacies, farce, gambits to run aground,
All from every angle, blindly abound

Bound blindly to the boundaries of farce,
Mine and all others in various class...

Paralleled Fates

I've been asked of my relativities to Christ,
Why – I explain – he has a meaning I prize,
Why I revert to – is – as an escape from my life,
An escape to a world with simpler answers to find,

As some say the stories are fiction,
It's a way to escape my true friction,
Strengths to carry on through the mission,
Fables to find me a level of wisdom,

They're stories of moral, they're parables,
True reasons are oft' unfathomable,
Those like me, entertainment imaginable,
When and where reality's often horrible,

There're underlying messages there,
And I found I could easily compare,
My own situation hasn't been so dissimilar a share,
Was looking for some sort of guide, His seemed fair –

But fictional parables so close to the truth,
That nothing's ever changed, not where thoughts get to,
Except 'til personal experiences pull us through,
And then it's like – what the fuck do you do?

How can you know how to be,
Without first ever having seen,
To break from the norm – paradigms coming obsolete,
Old ideals and tradition's all taking a back seat,
Learn what you need,
Then take reigns and lead,

Messages, methods toward an escape,
And I found I could easily relate,
Kept with me – and never to forsake,
As I may – if ever – take a similar fate,

Strong As I, The Latter,

Yin – Yang, hardly,
Christ is as evil as he is good,
He's good – but there was another choice –
He never took,
Yin – Yang – hardly –
Let's say there's good with little bad,
And like the other little as sad,
Similar lengths of the scales,
Yes, Christ made good –
over the path he never took –
and strong as so is his good,
I thank the latter,

I'm the choice he never took –
And like him I'll be stood,
Fighting to die like he would,
Only, for no good,

And so be it as strong as his love,
Mine rivals that only to hate,
Strengths 'gainst strengths,
And we'll have both gone to great lengths,

I'm the choice Christ never took,
And just as he – I'll be stood,
Fighting to die just as he would,
Only – for no good,

Yin – yang, hardly,
Christ is as evil as he is good,
It was just a path he never took,

Just, that's where I' gonna be stood,
Front and centre and before the forsook,

And as strong as is he for love,
Mine and only mine rivals by the latter,

Satan's Abomination

And so the beast is sent with wrath,
For no care of the aftermath,
Testaments, tempers will clash,
It was the price, it was the catch,

Beast sent to test,
None are exempt,
Push, shove, felt through the web,
Beast awakens, ravage them bled,

A beast able to empathize,
Able to feel and recognize,
But a beast all the same when it's time,
To do why it's designed,

A beast more human still,
Human enough it can feel,
Will hardened, like toughened steel,
Beast will soon have reason to kill,

Can't fight prophecy, can't escape fate,
Where love is broken, burns a brighter hate,
Blood spilled, open the gates,
Freeing torments destined, in wait,

Satan's abomination…
Develops human fascination,
Delay on it's wicked temptation,

Fascinations soon lie devastated,
Fascination ensnared abomination…
Wills a wicked devastation,
Satan's abomination…

Undercover

I look like somebody you wouldn't fuck with,
Like there's no fucks I could give,
Like I'm hard enough to do as none ever did,
Like I'd take death as hard as I lived,

When my choice of words have been twisted,
I wanna knuckle down and get vicious,
Fist out all the intolerable in existence,
And weave out new lines of written wisdoms,

It often pays more the less I say,
Short 'n sweet – it goes my way,
Developing a means to help me eat at the end of the day,
Getting along like everybody else and actually earn my way,

I take what I do very seriously,
And I have to often "do" meticulously,
Occasionally it might seem so ridiculous,
But even those – I too, take serious,

I never liked when whatever I have said –
Was taken and put to use in the wrong context,
All the time I'd taken, to consider and where spent,
At time's it's pissed me off or made me upset,

I hate getting it wrong myself –
But then have projected it round by other selves,
Went back to contemplate a something else,
To try and better explain its' way I better meant felt,

The shit I've been through wasn't easy – it was hard,
It was never anything like a walk in the park,

It's taking work and the sweat of a hard yard,
Distances raised the durability of the guard,

Still even at this point it doesn't end,
I may have to cover some parts gain...

Par(E)Lia(R)Me(A)nt

Paring Us With Lies Meant
They Are
Paring Us With Lies Meant
The Era

Ha – Parliament…
You're crooked, you're crooked,
You are,

I poked my nose,
'cause no one knows,
Bent my nose out
Nose crooked,
I, know's crooked,

You're paring us with lies meant,
This is the era,
You're paring us with lies meant,
They are,

Ha Parliament – don't envy you –
You're crooked – crooked,
You are,

I'm bent crooked,
Nose bent lookin',
But I saw you motherfucker –
You're crooked,
Crooked,

You are…

Sensitive Not, But To Money

Don't stand there Mr. Minister, and say you're a sensitive man,
Don't stand there Mr. Minister, saying it's for anything but the money,
We all know what your true task is, your intention, the plan,
We all know it's a masque for the more sinister shit you're running,

People like you will never know the 'disgrace',
The divide you create for you to keep your place,
The lower held under while the richer head the race,
It's why there's no harmony - no synchronized pace,

"Somethings just can't be legal 'cause that's where we earn",
Forget that it's safe, or I'm intolerant, the money makes the world turn,
We lay it all down fuckin' hard so that they all learn –
If you fuck with us the government, you will burn,"

Laws created for breaching privacy in the event of a suspicion,
You can't fuckin have that – the war on it is the mission,
It is slowly beginning to change with the discussion of what permission,
But with no provision of a decent reason, it's off to prison,

Drug money's collected from raids thrown to a kitty for years,
Just waiting for someone to come to claim – none do but all fear,
Got you by the balls, it's lock up and with tears –
Governments claim the money and the build of the interest it reared,

Don't stand there Mr. Minister and say it's never about the money,
Too careless it shows and we know you've no care for the disharmony,
The lives and finances fucked out by the sinister shit you're running,
The corruption you've forsaken us with, the divide, it's stunning,

'it's for the bigger picture'
Yeah, in your living room…

Theft From The Authentic

I've got people from afar tryin' to pretend,
Their tryin' to pretend they're me,
Lying to me saying I'm the plagiarizer,
I have my thoughts open, they hear it, they steal,

People hear what I'm thinking without talking,
And I get a lot of gawking,
They – always confused thinkin' I was talking,
I was actually only thinking and now they're gawking,

People hear the shit I think and try to steal,
All these thoughts that come to me as I feel,
This is no bullshit, this is fucking real,
People all stealin' my fucking shit, *they* steal,

I am genuine – ever so authentic,
Everything I do is always sporadic,
But there are many of those marauding,
Stealing my ideas – the material, the fantastic,

I have no trust and no fucking faith for trust,
I know no one really gives a fuck,
I know I'm gonna be the first to be fucked –
By all jealous eyes over my financial gains as I change luck,

But I absolutely hate with a loathing vengeance on the cunts,
The ones always bitching they've never got enough,
Bitch at me for thinking that I get given way too much,
They always had more, yet where were my
chances at the time? The cunts,

The kinds of cunts who'll steal shit from me,
Want it for fucking nothing or for fucking free,
Cunt's who'll only ever steal it off cunts like me,
Those cunts of thieves that should be bled fuckin' deep,

And The Truth Will Set You Free

People will lie to protect their truths,
And people's truths may have them pay worse,
Worse than when they lied,
Never face a truth but lie,

But truths ruthlessly hurt – and not just that,
People's truths will have them killed,
Too many lies lived to be fucking glad,
Not too many truths face – what a thrill,

Let's focus on my fuck up's
So many I'm so fuckin' clean,
Focussed only on my fuck ups,
'Cause if they faced theirs they'd scream,

They'll lie – and just to have me killed,
To get a way they wanted – to no real thrill,
Running from old truths really should've been faced,
Covering over with new lies to replace,

I've seen,
And I'm clean,
I'm a dream,
'Cause I'm fucking clean,

Cunts protecting their truths,
When it's only gonna have them lose,
And their truths will have them pay –
Worse than when they lied that way,

Why face your own truths,
It means you'll all lose,
Keep living lies –

And may your 'what you have going here' survives,
Truths will really only make you pay,
Slaves to your old ways,

So – let's only just focus on my fuck ups – I'm clean,
Focus only on my fuck ups – and keep livin' a dream,
'Cause when you face yours – you may only scream,

Don't You Fuckin' Dare

I don't care what you did,
You only copied what you saw,
It was okay for Him,
So don't be so sore,

I love it that you're fake –
Nothing gets me off more,
I love your lying state,
You entertain me with your lore,

Don't take responsibility,
Don't ever dare,
Don't better possibilities,
Don't ever be fair,

Don't take maturity,
Don't ever dare,
Don't stop obscuring,
Or I'll never care,

I hate to see you make a stand –
When you don't make sense,
I hate you try to be a man –
Without ever accepting regrets,

I'll never care what you do,
You'll only copy what you see,
It's always ever just like you,
You'll probably do it to me,

I love it that you're fake,
Nothing gets me off more,

Love seeing you lie and forsake,
To only lose the war,

Don't ever take responsibility,
Don't you ever fucking dare,
Don't ever better possibilities,
And don't ever be scared…

The Better Dead

I'm feelin' empty, resenting,
Undeserving, disrespecting,
Contagious and infecting,
Oppressing with a reckoning,

I could've been a man –
Or maybe something more,
Now nothing near a man –
But something many scorn,

I watch and I wait,
I prey and carry away,
Rip, cut, slash, scratch,
I have never met my match,

There's nothin' human left in me,
It died long ago,
I bathe in the blood of killing sprees,
I spatter it like snow,

You won't escape my clutches,
Only dangle suspended and gutted,
I have all the fun 'til all damage is done,
Then head back underground to filth, muck and scum,

My breath is putrid, teeth are rotting,
My hair is long, wild, tangled and knotted,
My skin is scabbed and scaling,
My clothes are torn, stained and trailing,

My voice is coarse and rough as I growl,
Folk all go missing when I prowl,
Might've remained a man if I kept my head,
None can understand me now and I'm better dead,

Remember This

Do you remember when I disgusted?
Do you remember those repercussions?
Remember when it never looked good for me?
That's where you're headed if you're gonna be –

Remember when I lost all that trust?
Remember why I was treated less than dust?
Remember when it all happened to me?
That's where you're headed if you're gonna be –

I seriously hope you saw it all,
So you fail further than where I'd fall,
I seriously hope you watched and planned for,
This has happened to me – your before,

I fuckin' hope you saw everything,
I hope you managed to take it all in,
I hope you go far and defy everything,
Defy all these crooked facades of old 'sin',

Do you remember when I disgusted?
Do you remember those repercussions?
Remember – when it never looked good for me?
This is where you're headed if you're gonna be,

Do you remember when I went and lost all that trust?
Do you remember when I was treated worse than dust?
Remember that it all happened to me?
Well, this is where you're headed if you're gonna be,

I hope you fuckin' saw everything,
I seriously hope you saw it all and –
I hope you defy everything –
Much, much further where I'd fallen,

Fair warning…

Level 'Neath His Tomb

I want better I really do,
And I'm given hell when I try to,
I am trying 'cause I want better,
But when they hang shit – I become a never,

I want to ascend up and away from all this,
I can't just ignore it – man, I'm gettin' pissed,
My teeth grind and I ball up my fist,
And then I want to "Love" 'em with a rock-solid kiss,

I want better – I really fuckin' do,
And I'm trying in all my power to really show it too,
But in a matter of moments it can be gone way too soon,
By some other fucker keeping me 'neath the level of his tomb,

And I just want to rise, ascend out from it all,
Sirens all wailing their calls – they beckon, and I fall,
Vampyrous sirens, fanged mouths all bite and maul,
And so, I put up a fight backed with all my balls,

I know stupid fuckers will all gawk and stare,
And I'm sure plenty others will have had a fair share,
I won't get passed it 'til I can learn not to care,
But I am super self-conscious, I am a-fuckin'-ware,

And I want better – I really, really do,
But I'm just given hell every time I try to,
I'm givin' it a go 'cause I do want better,
It's just when they hang shit – I just stay a never,

I want better, I really fuckin' do,
I'm givin' it my all to show I really want to,
But it's all within a matter of moments too soon,
Some other fucker is needing me 'neath his level tomb,

You Did Fuckin' What?!?!?

Here's another something doesn't want to end,
I know it's illegal to just be listenin' in,
I don't want to be but strange things are said,
Shouts are made – some fuckwit can't contain himself,
This time it's not me of sorts,
I'm doing the same thing only from my mind,
This little fucker wants a piece,
And he wants to do it himself,
Fuckin' death threats all over the place,
How is one expected to just take that?
I'm not, not well, it's bullshit hell,
Expected to have my reputation run aground,
And let it fuckin' happen – they hate me enough,
And they want it easy?
It's double the fuck on me enough,
And everyone feels important enough,
Pokin' their shit into shit said hind of my back,
That lil fucker – same as all the old bastards,
Think I'll be easy – only spoke to their wives,
And how good was even that?
Not what I wanted but it's a first to make new,
I might be a liar but then I might not be –
Think it's bad to feel the shit we feel,
Shit, I've only just begun believing love is evil,
Lock it up, keep it out and be all about the talk,
Up until I get some other fucker thinks he wants a go,
Enough is enough – just gonna have to let it go,
Put up a fight and put on a fuckin' show,
Gonna have to fuckin go toe to toe,
I just wanna use me brains for fuckin' once,
And get as much of my work as I want done,
I might know everything but I'm still young,
Just gonna rock it hard and stick to my guns –
Uh, - tongue…

Innocence Abandoned

Innocence –
I forfeit mine the day I didn't want it anymore,

It's always been a fight,
A fight to gettin' it right,
A fight to doin' it right,
A fight to havin' it right,
And I've always had to fight –
But why?

Was anyone payin attention?
Did I ever get a mention?
Was I exempt from ever being 'yaught a lesson'?
Hm, no,

It's always been a fight –
A fight to gettin' it right,
A fight to doin' it right,
A fight for havin' it right,
And I've always, always, had to fight,
Why?

Nobody was ever lookin'
It must've never been fair since I only heard 'em sookin',
But was it all fair it was never my direction they're lookin'
And do they deserve to even be the one's sookin'

So it was always my fault before I ever did anything,
It was always the reason why I ended doing it after anyway –
Reasonable, since being accused for the said such thing,
Before I did – so go to anyway?

Innocence –
Yeah – I forfeit mine the day I didn't want it anymore,

Worked Hoarse

I've finally hit a brick wall,
Can't go on anymore,
I'm a work horse,
Overworked, bone raw,

Sweat the hard yakka,
Earnt the hard thirst,
But now I'm just knackered,
I've bled in the dirt,

My tolerance is maxed,
It's passed my threshold,
I've broken my back,
I cave in, I fold,

Demanufactured – decommissioned,
Initiate the sequence – I'm ready for demolition,
Left out in the elements to rust in a heap,
A ghost in the machine to flicker and sleep,

I just can't push on, I don't have it in me,
I'm weak – I feel faint, everything is spinning,
I fall to the floor in an exhausted state,
And into a deep sleep from which I never wake,

Wish I Could Smoke Pot All Day

I wish I could smoke pot all day,
And just do everything my way,
Take it all at my pace,
Slow, as I'd be off my face,

I wish I could smoke pot all day,
And write, type out my creative ways,
Take it all at my pace,
And completely all off my face,

I wish I could focus on my work,
Get stoned and weave my poetic words,
Sit at the table and get deeply immersed,
Get high and write, interpreting a verse,

I can draw, I do have that talent too,
Can't seem to focus too long for that to,
But if I could smoke pot all day – then I would do,
Sit, get smashed, and see what creative genius shows through,

I wish I could smoke pot all day,
Helps me focus and concentrate,
Long or well enough for me to contemplate,
And express what ideas in countless creative ways,

I wish I could smoke pot all day,
To have and do everything my way,
Take it all at my pace,
Slow - when I'm off my face,

I wish I could smoke pot all day,
And write, type, or draw out my creative ways,
To take it all at my pace,
And completely smashed off my face,

Chapter 3

444 Seasons

Lone Type

A lone life is mine,
Wouldn't have it another way,
The k's click by on the bike,
Roarin' up the highway,

Pull up to rest my head,
Maybe get a little action as well,
Pull up, take a woman to warm the bed,
Kick up dust, pick a fight, raise hell,

Cause a lone life is mine,
Wouldn't have it another way,
Clockin' up k's on my bike,
Thundering up the motorway,

Pull up for a beer – sink some piss,
Punch down some pipes then – utter bliss,
Camp off road – out in the sticks,
Trading stories, trading tricks,

The lone life is mine,
Wouldn't have it another way,
K's click by on the bike,
Roarin' up the highway,

Yeah the lone life is mine,
Wouldn't have it another way,
Clockin' up the k's on the bike,
Thunderin' up the motorway,

Nothin' Lasting Good

Nothin' good lasts forever,
I just prepare for when it severs,
Better had than never,
And hold fast for the weather,

Cycling ups and downs,
Spiralling wildly round,
Ripping up, spitting out ground,
Rippling tidal waves to drown,

I wanted what little remaining good I had to last,
Previous experiences taught it's temporary, it'll pass,
When it broke apart, it disintegrated fast,
Showering round all fragments in its' vapoury blast,

The ripping and tearing of every which way,
No silver lining in these blackened clouds, no greys,
Tempest winds whistling, lash and fray,
Thunderous howls cried of the rage and pain,

None of that little good survives what war,
Not when I can't foretell what to prepare for,
In the hail of the fire to kill and bleed me out raw,
A victory for a loser that just needed the win more,

Cycling ups and downs,
Spiralling wildly round,
Ripping up, spitting out ground,
Rippling tidal waves to drown,

The ravenous wind slowly settles rattling,
I die losing a cause that wasn't worth the battling,

Those moments show true courage when all others go scattering,
Those kinds of cowards of the like to die best by battery,

Killing off, coring out the last of my humanity,
Overbearing weights punched out my sanity,
Self-centred, they never get passed their vanity,
Never likely to see the sense I show throughout the calamity,

Maybe that good was just too good to be true,
If I were the more prepared…if I fuckin' knew…

By Persistent Ignorance

We've been here countless times before,
And it's never been clearer more,
That all you do is seem to ignore,
This unbalanced, unsettled score,

It's the same old conflict that gets us nowhere,
And I know you'll never truly care,
Not unless it finally strips you bare,
And none have any patience left to spare,

You see, my attitude has always only ever been determined,
By a type of provocation incepted by the vermin,
The like degree reciprocated will always be a burden,
Those who're incapable to fathom its proper intention interpret,

You spite on me when I make a stand,
You spite that I've become my own man,
You spite when I don't rise to your demands,
You spite on me when you can't understand,

Your ignorance will end up being your own prison,
Never to ascend because you just won't listen,
Sad when it seems it's your only mission,
Ignorance, persistent all throughout your existence,

You spite on me that I've made my stand,
You spite that I have risen to be the man,
You spite when I don't meet your demands,
You spite harder still when you can't understand…

In Fragments

So I'm sat on the red couch,
And one of me is immediately next,
Another me is lain sat against the couch,
And the fourth is in the chair opposite,

Synchronised each feel the change,
When we stand, walk, rearrange,
Stride from one spot to another,
Fuck dude - watch out, you're in the way brother –

We often say the same thing at the same time,
Its understandable with me split, fragmented mind,
Each of us four of me share a session,
And marvel out over our splendid exception,

Almost better than dreaming,
Apparitions I find easy believing,
All us four share our eyes,
And see through each our minds,

Just spoke earlier of a stranger phenomenon,
Another new bizarre thing began going on,
Listening to dear sweet glorious thrash metal,
Saw the air waves pulsating round - it was mental,

We, us four of all of I, we were mesmerised,
These very sights happened front of our eyes,
Sights of the pulse of the air waves,
The frequencies I, we, could all see, amazed,

As cool as that was the four of me was sweet,
Strange spending time with my own company,
Been doing it on and off just hanging out,
It's madness I know there is no doubt,

My Business

It is, uh, difficult of course –
To try to mind your own business,
When across ways you hear –
Context of similar business,

Similarities to things I have done,
Similarities to shit I've said,
A misinterpretation – a twist,
Nothing like how it went,

Can't shake feeling it's all over me,
A good some misconstrued direction,
But it's all gonna come back at me –
Crossfired – miswired minds deflect it,

I almost take it personal,
And none of 'em have a clue,
Wanna force it up their arsenal,
Long time coming due,

I'm trying to mind my business,
And it does indeed get difficult,
They wanna make it their business,
And too soon it does get personal,

Misinterpreted sequences and their direction,
Similarities to shit I've done,
Nothing gone like how it were meant,
Similarities to shit I've said,

They make it difficult for me to keep my mind,
Peace – patience, we're going to find,

It never had to be this personal, never,
Had to be that difficult,

Keep what's mine as mine,
Leave all else behind…

Torn Between

Torn between what I'm in want of doing,
And what I should be doing –
Torn again between what I want,
And what is acceptably right,

Acceptably right by mainstream immediate –
Social standards,
The likes of which disagree with my own,
And more often than not infringe and trespass,
Upon me more than I can tolerate,
But am expected to let slide,
I am torn…

Torn between my want of doing,
And what others say I should be,
To fit in with the crowd, the people,
Incapability's to render me slightly feeble,

Torn between what I do best and –
Plunged deep into that that I have no clue,
Damned if I don't – still damned if I choose,
Torn between whichever win, and inevitably –
A lose,

Torn between my want for doing,
And the decision as to what I should be,
Dissatisfaction at the loss of want for doing,
Dissatisfaction all the same for losing when I should be,

Torn, just torn between…

When You Need Shit Done

I'm the guy you call when you need shit done,
That shit you won't want any part of,
I'll wipe out the filth – the grime – the scum,
And I won't charge a hefty cost,

Call me when you need shit done,
When that shit just needs to be lost,
I'll wipe out the filth – the grime – the scum,
I won't charge a hefty cost,

I deal with shit every fuckin' day,
I'd be filthy rich if the shit fuckin' payed,
But no, sadly it doesn't to much of my dismay,
But call me, I'll make your shit fuckin' pay,

Been a while since I was pissed,
Just get me six-pack mate,
Uh, make it a carton for the bigger list,
But I'll wipe clear the slate,

I know what it's like to deal with shit –
But I'll be the one you call when you need it gone,
No one ever needs to put up with it,
So call me, it won't take too long,

I'll be your guy to call,
When you need shit done next to fuck all,
Never is quite like a walk in the park,
But hey – we'll have ourselves a ball…

I'm the guy you call when you need shit done,
That filthy shit you won't want any part of,
To wipe out all the filth – the grime – the scum,
And NO, won't charge a hefty cost,

No hefty cost…

One To His Ownsome

There are times I forget why I prefer to be lone,
Company, interactions good, yet, so far out of similarity – I'm lone,
Acquaintances, friends, mate's plenty, but I am on my own,
But there's many reasons more why I anti-
socialise, never leave my home,

Far as my consideration or mindfulness goes,
I can't always expect an equal reciprocation to show,
I can't predict nor not fear of what I can't know,
Not predict nor not fear what they may or may not know,

I make mistakes, still juvenile, but have the thirst for growth,
Distances I keep is for maturity, ignoring those limiting me so,
All that while I'm trying to achieve some levelled growth,
Distance is for ignoring those making it ever difficult for me so,

Limited interaction, limits distraction to harmonious flow,
Shortening lengths and quickening pace to grow,
And so, I deduce – may it better be that I'm lone,
I have nothing but to do it on my own,

I've gotta put behind what disregard,
Step outta comfort – lower the guard,
And I know it gets ugly – know it gets hard,
The more I mind with a fight over the disregard,

I can see everyone else all playing out in the yard,
While I face this difficult shit – it's hard,
Truths hurt to learn, ache pounds with disregard,
Only lowered it so much – but the rest shattered away my guard,

Comin' out of my comfortable confines to grow,
Learnin' the hard shit I had to know,
After falling out, behind and below,
I'm takin' the time to know – merge flow,

Hyper-Sensitivity

I've put a good deal of importance on talk,
I do listen, I hear, I absorb,
Put a little too much sensitivity centre core –
Touchy, nervy, may fight – shit, I may walk,

Put a good deal of importance on feeling,
I do sympathise, can empathise – often feeling,
But a little too much sensitivity, knelt and keeling,
Touchy, nervy, may end up killing,

Quick to respond – quick to react,
So quick the trouble, struggling gainst a trap,
Quicker that more trouble does attract,
Wounded – snap – and retreat back,

Sensitive to pitch, tones, notes,
Sensitive to tensions – when, where, spoke,
Sensitive to the motion – the flow,
Sensitive to the way the vibe goes,

Put a good deal of importance on all its consideration,
Put a greater deal of importance on its administration,
Put a good deal of importance on the consideration –
Yeah – and its administration –

Sensitive to pitch, tones, notes,
Sensitive to tensions, when and where spoke,
Sensitive to the motion, the flow,
Sensitive to the way the vibe goes,

Quick to respond, quick to react,
So quick the trouble, struggling gainst a trap,
Quicker the more it does attract,
Wounded, I snap, and retreat back…

Sixth Sense

I have had a sixth sense, somehow I could see,
Deeper than anyone ever wanted of me,
I've seen what makes them scream,
I've seen cause of their bleeds,

I have had a sixth sense, somehow I could see,
Deeper than anyone ever wanted of me,
See what binds them of being free,
Seen what nightmares eat their dreams,

I have had a sixth sense – somehow I could see,
Deeper than anyone ever wanted of me,
Men with good intentions but trail misery,
Keeping women company but the terror, the tyranny,

I have had a sixth sense and somehow I could see,
Deeper than anyone ever wanted of me,
Seeing shit I wished I had never seen,
Never thinking it my place to shed any warning,

I have had a sixth sense and somehow I could see,
Deeper than anyone ever wanted of me,
Deeper than any have ever wanted to hear me speak,
I have seen the rotten fruit they've had to reap,

I have had a sixth sense and somehow I could see,
Deeper than anyone ever wanted of me,
Deeper than they themselves ever wanted to seek,
Seen deeper than they'll ever truthfully cheek,

I have had a sixth sense,
And somehow I could always see…

Assumption

I love it you assume,
It's certainly a muse,
Imagination's running loose,
The shit you say and do,

Like you assume I don't work,
Like you assume I'm given all I'm never earnt,
Something that would often send me berserk,
An answer you require not of your worth,

Like you assume I hate my life this way,
Like you assume I never meant it this way,
Move to assume when I limit what I say,
Never move to exhume the remaining dismay,

To assume I am by my lone,
To assume I can't handle my own,
To assume I'll never leave this zone,
To assume I never had backbone,

Yes I love it when you assume,
It surely does play my muse,
Your imagination's all running loose,
Rumours, the shit you say and do,

Mindful Of The Mindless

Some people can't understand at times the kindness you give,
What consideration is given – how you live,
Some people think kindness is weakness,
But underestimate the scale given for which,

You've gotta be mindful of the mindless,
You've gotta make blatant when oblivious,
You've gotta show a better way to interpret,
Prevent and limit whatever inconvenient mess,

Things will be taken beyond proportion,
And the mindless will always make the mindful exhausted,
Can't ever afford to get lazy, you've gotta take precaution,
Words will twist and are often contorted,

People that just don't think, can't or won't,
Regulations, legislation, popularity passed the vote,
Consideration of consequences – the mindless surely don't,
But closer to home, down the road, the mindful will show,

You've gotta be mindful of the mindless,
You've gotta make blatant to the oblivious,
You've gotta know a better way to interpret,
Limit and prevent whatever inconvenient mess,

And things will be taken far beyond proportion,
Words will all be twisted and contorted,
So never get lazy always practice precaution,
Cause the mindless will always make the mindful exhausted.

Different Lives,

You can keep your perspective on my paradigm,
We were both destined to lead different lives,
What you would call nightmare – I'll find quite nice,
Polar opposites, 180 degrees, you'll love all I despise,

Like it or not we'll always need the other,
Excitements when a deadening, dullness moves to smother,
Voices for reason when things need be discovered,
Sheep in wolves clothing, blessings undercover,

We're never going to quite see eye to eye,
But we're always better off to keep an open mind,
We may not be so comfortable that we may still lie,
But the act of that doing so is just better left behind,

There's always something new we can learn beyond our comfort,
And none of us will actually know until we've actually gone and done it,
I can expect many out there will just wanna tell me to 'shove it',
But we just won't fall, we will all fucking plummet,

It's important we have our differences, and that they vary,
There's no reason why you can't have criticism and still be merry,
Many an excuse can be used and there are plenty,
I can't think of one right now but there are many,

Our understandings may differ but may very well harmonise,
Tools, devices, gained leading parallel, different lives,
It pays. Rectifies, to maintain an open mind,
But maybe not so to keep your perspective on my paradigm,
Or…
Keep it…

Fake?

Yeah I'm fake mother fucker,
You're wasting all right mother fucker,
Wasting all your precious time,
You think you'll break me motherfucker,
Be breakin' you 5 fingers on me mother fucker –
Breakin' your five fingers attempting to break –
My cock motherfucker,
You wanna call me 'mine'?
First, you've gotta wine and dine,

Sure, I'm fake mother fucker,
Truths hurt mother fucker,
You wouldn't like what I had to say,
So I'm fake mother fucker,
Still say it better than you mother fucker –
Better than you – yeah, you're waste,

You wanna play mother fucker?
You want five fingers mother fucker?
I've got a fist'll fit right up ya,
You're gonna feel me mother fucker,
You're gonna blow me mother fucker,
You're getting' me fist right up ya,

You're not ever gonna be calling me 'mine'
…mother fucker,
'til you invite me to a wine and dine –
Maybe suck it? Mother fucker,

But I'll fist fuck ya mother fucker,
Fist fuck ya mother fucker,

I appreciate you tried,
Your five fingers you little American piglet,
Yes, your five fingers, can come and tickle my giblets,
And death punch out your pride,

Fictional Truth

Of course, as you know, life's no walk in the park,
It goes deep, and it can run ever dark,
There is no right way to do when it's hard,
None have shown me right – not without the heart,

Truth of it is far more frightening,
Dreadful, but enlightening,
Pass through it, it's exciting,
You don't see it – but your smile will get widening,

A fairy tale, a fantasy is the escape,
And I know so many would relate,
So what if it's fake? Can it not be great?
A scape away from this hell, this state,

Truth is often despicable,
That any part of it spoken is minimal,
Dare not – scrutiny is critical,
They'll frenzy 'cause they starve – it's habitual,

Life doesn't ever get any easier,
And I like all, still want my fairy tale elysian,
It's sad that it's not that life is the leisure,
Mine, a delirium I suffer like under a fever,

It isn't hard for me to want to fictionalise what truth,
Not even when a truth may stand to mean I lose,
'Cause maybe my truths are really not the kind to –
Ever attract or draw in the kinds of folk I want to,

I prevaricate, I do deliberately make precise accidents,
Lie and cover, because the truth is true terror to imagine it,
Fantasise – fictionalise, just to enjoy while havin' it,
Some truths are beyond me – I don't want to fathom it.

Over Turn The Others' Cheek

I've heard too many speak,
Such disturbing cheek,
It's kept me from sleep,
Provoked me to reap,

I hate to have to be so fucking pestilent,
But I just haven't been seeing intelligence,
And all of this is gonna be your consequence,
'til you recompense me some kind of penance,

You are going to suffer excruciating pain,
'til you can take responsibility and equal share of the blame,
You're gonna get to know pain –
And you'll learn to fear the name,

I've just heard too many speak,
Such disgusting, disturbing cheek,
It's woke and kept me from sleep,
I'm justified when I'm provoked to reap,

You speak so much fuckin' cheek,
slumbering sheep – you're all asleep,
it's time I over turn the other cheek,
it's time to shave and bleed the sheep,

I hate to be so fucking pestilent,
But I haven't been seeing any actual intelligence,
And all of this is gonna end being a consequence,
'til any of you recompense and show penance,

Remorse for me,
Consider and feel for the blaspheme,
Remorse for me –
Because your cause is for me,

Hyper-Head

Hyper senses on hyper alert,
Hyper defences on hyper nerves,
Hyper offences for hyper hurt,
Hyper dimensions, and hyper absurd,

I'm not even halfway through an operation,
Before I'll take on and begin another,
Often overestimate my capabilities,
Bite off more than I can chew,

Hyper head – take 20 – chill,
Hyperhead – you're plenty – chill,
Hyperhead – slow down – chill,
Hyperhead – slow the fuck down – chill,

I've got four conversations going at once,
And I'm excited and having a blast,
Switching to and from there's something on,
Switching attentions, shit, memories gone,

Hyperhead – take 20 – chill,
Hyperhead – take plenty – chill,
Hyperhead – slow down – chill,
Hyperhead – slow the fuck down and chill,

Hyper senses on hyper alert
Hyoper defences on hyper nerves,
Hyper offenses for hyper hurt,
All hyper dimensions its hyper absurd,

It's up and it's down and it's all around,
Quick, rapid, like the speed of sound,
Wrapped, entangled – wound, bound,
It's on, extreme – then it's out and down...

Am I Really For Real?

I mistake in my confusion,
When people are stunned to nothing to say,
I have to wonder if I'm lucid,
People, speechless, stunned to nothing to say,

I get the strangest looks and I misinterpret,
After the things I say or do or behave,
I realise after they've deserted.
How can I be so different – how am I so estranged?

I have a large personality I have to limit,
Revealing myself completely never pays,
It can be intense when I exhibit,
And if they don't walk – they run away,

I don't know if it's my intelligence that intimidates,
Or if or when they can't understand what to feel,
But I guess everyone – even I underestimates,
And I have to question – am I really for real?

I've had too many different experiences I can't mention,
That have manipulated me to this state,
Some were heavenly and blissful, some – wicked and wretched,
But by the strengths of these extents, I loop a recurring fate,

I mistake so badly within my confusion,
When people all are stunned to nothing to say,
I have to wonder if I'm lucid -
people, speechless, stunned to nothing to say,

Don't know if it's my appearance or intelligence intimidates,
Or if or when they can't understand what to feel,
But I guess everyone – including I, underestimates,
And I second guess and question – am I really for real?

Head In The Clouds

It's often odd to see the differences,
Of others lives as compared to yours,
The things you notice, each difference,
Just seems another adventure beyond doors,

The things you pick up,
Mannerisms for one and there are plenty,
You never count on learning something,
(thinking you've just about seen it all)
But find things that show you're empty,

And you realise how you could've missed it,
All those fulfilling things that mean,
You see you're not quite where you envisioned,
And see you could've already been living the dream,

But where are you at most?
Others all living as only you know you'd dreamt,
They'd worked hard to earn their boast –
How could you've been exempt?

It's head in the clouds…

You know you've been remiss,
And so you feel ashamed,
You could be livin' a bliss,
You'd better step up your game,

Dream too long and you'll be left behind,
Piss poor choices wasting your time and mind…

A Projected Self In Time

I have had strange occurrences,
That I couldn't at first explain,
Strange presences throughout time,
No, I could never explain,

But here, I'll try,

There were randomized circumstances,
Where I'd see a figure of a man I didn't know,
I hoped I would learn what this was,
But not for a considerable time,

No one could tell me what it was,
But now I'm certain I know,
That, that figure I had seen,
It was me,

I found myself in strange circumstances,
Where I'd reflect on points in my past,
I hadn't known it then but I had projected,
From my future - my figure to this past,

I'd look in from an outside perspective,
But send a projection through to that time,
I knew I thought I saw something way back then,
Didn't know it was I, nor that that figure was mine,

I know you think this seems bizarre,
But it's happened also few times since,
The times I recollect I'd seen that figure,
And scary as it was then I'd wince,

But I have realized it was me doing all this,
That when I see these figures there's reason,
That I have something for me to learn here,
Some new change to the season,

...beginning to understand it now...

Animated By Other Means

Baton pass - *snap to*
Wake up halfway through an operation,
And not know what or why,
Doors locked tight to forbidden memories,
Clues to my lost time,

Where the fuck was I?

Baton pass - *snap to*
Woke halfway through interrogation,
With a foreboding sense of what and why,
Vaults to forbidden memories –
Locked from and all within my mind,

Where the fuck just was I?

He's not awake – he's not aware,
But it seems as though there's something inside there,
It's as if he's comatosic,
Or under hypnosis – don't think he knows it,

An ulterior interference animates by subconscious means,
Internal yet separate, and it could reveal devastating news,
It's a wonder – does he sleep? And are they monstrous dreams?
Unpredictable, unbalanced – one wrong move and we could all lose,

Baton pass - *snap to*
Who the fuck are you?
What? When? How? Why?
Where the fuck am I?

Share Shedding

People have been hurt by the shit I have said,
At the times I were hurt enough I felt dead,
They were never aware of what they shed,
Shedding the weight of their hurt towards my head,

Time's again I have hurt people, who really weren't aware,
Then I would question, confused at how they could've been scared,
That I was so great even when I never compared –
Sharing weights of hurt – never considering it wasn't fair,

All the hurt I would ever project – I felt was provoked,
I really don't go lookin' for trouble – and I won't,
I already have trouble – layered in thick coats,
My own weight of hurt I don't find a joke,

I know how much it hurts that I'd really rather not –
Project more on a person I might know also has got,
It's humiliating – not humble, it should be cut to a stop,
It's not the way, it's not right, it's not how to get to the top,

Even though I was provoked or so I fuckin' felt,
It's one of those times I know I need to step outside myself,
See what it really is and analyser it well,
'Cause this will otherwise lead us back through another Hell,

I can never be so mindful at time's to catch when –
I know it may repeat, but I just don't want it happening again,
No good easy way of making or even keeping friends,
Not when they see it happen, it happens, can't forget,

Times and again I've hurt people and none of us were aware,
And then I'd question – confused, at how they would be scared,
I might've been great – I just felt I never compared,
Figured it was just they were shedding the hurt shredding my head,

327

Emotional Manipulation

One peculiar thing that has always made me lose my mind,
Happening perhaps longer than I know but always stalled *my* time,
People manipulating me to get what they want –
Only dong it all in every way I know is wrong,

They know what buttons to push and how,
And they will until they get what they want out,
The trickery of guilt erasing any doubt,
Of there being no need when it is about,

Relying on your kind heart,
Not to go without when it's hard,
And it will get hard – it will –
When you've lowered your guard,

Playing on your emotion and it might be hate,
And then the worst of the situations escalate,
Who knows what who really knows by when it's too late,
But that's just it, there's a winner and a loser every game,

Playing on your emotions and it might be despair,
And you with your big heart open them cause you care,
But they start takin' more than is ever fair –
And all you become is empty and bare,

Playing on your emotion and it might be sweet,
Tender, beautiful, and your guard goes weak,
Here we are – yet another game in repeat,
You play, you fall, and you lose all in defeat,

They know what buttons to push and how,
And they will until they get what they want out,

The trickery of guilt erasing any doubt,
Of there being no need when it is about,

Relying on your kind heart,
Not to go without when it's hard,
And it will get hard – it will –
When you've lowered your guard,

Nourish To Admonish

He's been given good to be made bad,
Nourished to admonish,
He's taken the good and made it bad,
Yes, nourished to admonish,

He's taken bad and made it good,
Admonished to help nourish,
He's taken it bad and made it good.
Yes, admonished to out nourish,

Lessons to learn yet
We switch turns,
Always lessons to learn –
We are taking turns,

Sometimes you fuck up to get the fuck up,
Sometimes you get stuffed giving a fucking stuff,
Sometimes you've gotta get rough when all others are,
Sometimes you've gotta be tough, yes, when all others are,

Sometimes they're not as smart as they want to be,
Not seeing what examples they need to see,
Not setting any examples they wanna see in me,
Bound to an ignorant blindness, and never freed,

I've been given good and made it bad,
Nourished to admonish,
But I've taken bad and made it good,
Admonished to out nourish,

Lessons to learn –
Yeah – we're switching turns,
Switching terms…

Prejudiced Providence

Don't be prejudiced to my providence,
I can't let the unfairness fly autonomous,
I have dreaded this, it's monotonous,
Was meant for this – look where it's gotten us,

It's not easy for me to stay up when I'm up
Not with the criticism, scrutiny that cuts,
Jams it, jars it – it grinds to a halt and seizes stuck,
Run in to the ground with an almighty 'FUCK'

I doubt it's commonly known,
Never happens enough to show,
One little moment then it goes,
Momentary genius – then it's blown,

My providence suffers your prejudice,
Autonomous but it's an unfairness,
Monotonous – I've only dreaded this,
It's gotten us – we're meant for this,

It's never easy to stay up when you're up,
Not with all the critique, the scrutiny and cuts,
Cripples you, grinds, you get stuck,
And run into the ground with an almighty 'FUCK'

I doubt it's so commonly known,
Never happens enough to show,
One little moment and then it goes,
Moments of genius…and it's blown,

Prejudiced,
Just prejudiced to my…
Providence,

Pot Smoker

Who's a dirty lil pot smoker –
Pot smoker –
Who's a filthy lil pot smoker –
Pot smoker –
Me! It's me,
A dirty lil pot head,
Pot fuckin' smokin' – pot head,

Sticky green buds oh how I want ya,
Want ya, sticky green buds, fuck yeah –
Sticky green buds, oh how I need ya,
Want ya – need ya, sticky green buds? FUCK YEAH –

Grind 'em like ol' Bob Marley,
Cough and splutter suck startin' a Harley,
Wake up nice and early –
Fuckin' choof a morning seshy,
Yeah – wake up nice 'n early,
Bong and stem off with the fairy's

Sticky green buds – oh how I want ya,
Want ya, sticky green buds – fuck yeah,
Sticky green buds – whoa how I need ya,
Want ya, need ya – sticky green buds – fuck yeah –

Who's a dirty lil hippy pot smoker –
Pot smoker –
Who's a smelly filthy pot smoker –
Pipe smoker – pot smoker –
It's me, oh good god it's me,

It's me – I friggin' love this weed,
A dirty little pot head, pot smoker –
A filthy fuckin pot smokin' pot head,
Pot smoker –

{([*Bubbles*])}

Think Like You,

You can't expect them to think like you,
If at any time, they ever do,
You can't expect them to ever see,
The same sense you see,

It's always a bigger deal than it needs to be,
You're always needing your room to breathe,
Don't count the blessings of what deed,
And you could soon be beggar deep in plead,

You have to be careful and appropriately behave,
Because many a time will come it's taken the wrong way,
And you'll be full of disdain attempting to explain,
Forcing through your frustration, to keep you best sane,

You have to be mindful to think of and for others,
Especially when an ignorance may still smother,
Hyper reactive, responsive thought under cover,
Maintain rationale – being sensible, sensitive to all others,

Guess, you can't expect them to all think like you,
If any a time they ever do,
You can't expect them to ever see,
The same sense you see,

But you count it blessing when they do,
It's a beautiful surprise when they understand you,
It's a miracle when you know they do see,
A similar sense you see,

Diminishing Socialite

I used to be a hell of a lot more social than I am now,
I thank my folks – they wrung it out,
Haven't spoke to mates in ages – think I forget how,
It's fucked – it sucks, it's like 'wow',

I've been so fucking diminished,
I can't tell if I'm really finished,

It be like I'd be home for 5 before I left again,
Popular – I did have a good number of friends,
I wish these times never had to end,
Don't know if I could go back and repair amends,

Been so diminished,
Thought I was finished,
Restraint – compressed,
Pressure building in my chest,

I'd forever be on the phone,
Out and about and at home,
'til holidays come one fateful Xmas,
And then from, my mates had to suffer my –
lack of presence,

to be in consistent contact,
and suddenly have to cut it right back,
shit happens – we move on – and lose track,
and sometimes there's no going back,

I was a popular one,
Happier once – with everyone,
To escape what foul temperaments,
And accompany a mate and share sentiments,

Testaments,
For whatever built up slanderous –
Resentments,
I was popular once,

But since have been diminished,
So foul myself – was surprised I wasn't finished,
Compressing down tension – pressure in my chest,
Restraint 'til all is ceased or lain in rest,

I'd find it easier to be fair – easier to spare,
When I were to occasionally 'let down the hair',
I could fare more of a care, where I would share,
And vent with friends – soothe a rage that flares,

I used to be a hell of a lot more social than I am now,
And I can only thank my folks – they wrung it out,
Ain't spoke to mates in ages – think I forget how,
It's fucked – it sucks – It's like fucking 'wow',

It wouldn't be like I'd be home for 5 before I left again,
Popular – had numerous, countless friends,
And I wish those times never had to end,
Can't say I could go back or repair amends,

I would forever be on the phone,
Out and about – or at home,
Until the holidays of one fateful Xmas,
And from then, my mates would suffer my –
Lack of presence,

I was a popular one,
Happier once – with everyone,
To escape what foul temperaments,
And accompany a mate and share sentiments,
Testaments,

For whatever built up slanderous –
Resentments,
I was popular once,

Been so diminished,
Could've sworn I was finished,
Restrained and compressed –
Like the pressure building in my chest…

In Need Of A Something

I let too many get to me,
And only all too easy
I'm not normally so up-tight,
But happy go lucky and bright,

People don't understand but –
I'm not too proud a man,
I don't think too highly of myself,
Not too often, and not too well,

I have gifts – I've got talents,
But I still find my life a challenge,
Too edgy or excited to focus,
To focus so long in a moment,

It doesn't take me much to break,
Any kindness I receive I feel is fake,
Paranoid – seeing a façade of false motives,
Patterns to suggest down is where I'm going,

I make mistakes all to often,
Too far behind I'll be forgotten,
Trying to keep my fractured head,
Choking on regret at the shit I have said,

Chained to blackened history, I'm failing resisting,
Swimming beneath its shimmering misery,
Encumbrances of hurt and more yet worse,
Overshadowing differences of it earnt and deserved,

People look at me and they assume,
I'm too coarse to refine or groom,

Or for the matter I can be so considerate,
And not some belligerent idiot,

To believe I'm nowhere near worthy of a chance,
Better locked up and zombied to a drooling trance...

Chances Too Feared To Be Taken

Don't cut me down – please don't fuckin' restrict me,
There is a reason why I see it so distinctive,
Reason why I know none else are keen listening,
Any associate to or with may all be ending imprisoning,

Well, you want to get lax about your consideration,
I might get lax about not exposing your humiliation,
I can and do see beneath these twisted "hallucinations",
And I know it's no mere hyperactive imagination,

I know what it is and I know it's there,
Why can't you face it – why are you so scared?
Don't say you ever did because you cared –
You know you'll deny it 'cause if it's true then –
How can we ever be prepared?

You need a leader to show how to right,
And you've been keeping me back all my life,
But what if I had the right tools to fight,
The knowledge, the passion, the strengths to put right –

I think you'd be more afraid of the attention I would bring,
Especially when you know *my* threshold to the tension is thin,
Like, you know I wouldn't handle the big show in full swing,
But if I ever don't it'd be by the over-protection and sheltering,

Why must you have that fear – when what I know is real?
Let me go – let me do, and be amazed at how wondrous it feels,
I may break, but I'll temper myself more to hardened steel,
And I'll keep coming back, if ever, stronger still –

I know what it is and I know it's there,
Why can't you face it – why are you so scared?

Don't say you ever did because you cared –
You know you'll deny it 'cause if it's true then –
How can we ever be prepared?

We're waiting in time like this here,
Me, trying to reason with another's fear,
I, me, I'm confident it won't end in tears,
There's still more, shit I haven't even hit my peak years,

I'm confident that once I'll know that I'll have the keys,
And life is gonna get a whole lot better to be,
If you show that faith and just release,
You'll know it's trivial and it's easier to believe,

I'm confident and I'm not letting fear win –
Not once I've gotten everything full swing,
Don't be afraid for the attentions I bring,
My threshold ain't so thin,

I know what it is and I know it's there,
Why can't you face it – why are you so scared?
Don't say you're doing it because you care,
It's more, it's that we're unprepared,

Don't cut me down, please don't be restrictive,
There is a reason why I see it so distinctive,
Reason why I know none are keen listening,
Any association with would lead to be imprisoning,

Casualty By Carelessness

I might have to be the very man,
That one to have to take that wretched stand,
That wily little fucker to get the one up,
The wiliest one to pull unstuck,

No one seems to want to believe,
And it's sad enough I could grieve,
So, I'm thinking I might have to just go and do and achieve,
Pull me up to a place none of 'em can reach,

The only thing –
Is while we're all going on a whim,
I'm given out – they give in,
Just 'cause they can't believe I'd get in,

When someone suddenly says something halfway through,
When the operations maybe not even halfway through,
It's how you get caught and all eye's turn to you,
And I frown upon the lack of the care that was due,

The problem is you can't shut the fuck up,
And this is where and why we always get stuck,
It's why I can't afford to say enough,
And can't ever afford to say too much,

I'll be a casualty by the carelessness,
Victim to all those the more nefarious,
I can never afford to be precarious,
Requires a contemplation most relentless,

I might have to be the very man,
To take the world to grasp in my own hands,
Though, I might must only be a one man,
And spare me an endangerment divulging the plan,

IrRegal-ar Stupidity

Somewhere between an –
Irritancy of another's assumptive arrogance,
And,
An exasperated disbelief in the stupidity –

And stupidity at this level should be illegal,
It's nothing majestic – nothing regal,
Nothin' to bear pride in,

Somewhere stuck behind this
Delaying dilemma,
Beyond is that forward motion,
Know it, had it once – I remember,

Time I waste,
Is more time it takes,
Importance placed,
And it's high stakes,

Fuckin' still getting' stuck,
Hind of this irritancy,
Another assumptive arrogance – fuck –
Exasperated disbelief in the stupidity,

And fuckin' this level of stupidity,
Should be illegal,
It's nothin' majestic, nothin' regal,
Nothin' to bear the slightest pride in,

And I'm fuckin' stuck behind it,
Want beyond it,

Time I waste,
Is gonna be the more time it takes,
Values placed,
And it's higher stakes,

Caution Through Pressure

Pressure has a habit of doing shit to people,
It can do great thing but can incite evil,
Contingent as always to the particular tendencies,
Can build relations or define enemies,

Has for centuries,

The trick is finding a way to harmonise,
With every caution taken not to compromise,
States of peace to the many different minds,
Peaceful resolutions out of the pressurised binds,

It's taken me considerable time to grasp,
It's not something I was taught too well in the past,
To contain my irrational behaviour under pressure,
I couldn't quite control it to a good measure,

Though somehow it's getting better,

I've only just begun utilizing it how it should be.
Taken tolls on me but I'm beginning to see,
I have fought the flow and been out of sync,
And it's taken me some fuckin' time to think,

Yeah I've only just begun to understand,
Lessons to learn can only make me a better man,
More substance, a better character to perfect,
To begin to gain back some respect,

Be someone none will reject,

The trick is finding a way to harmonise,
With every caution taken not to compromise,
All states of peace to the many different minds,
Peaceful resolutions out of these pressurised binds,

An Embarrassing
Amount Of Stupidity

I know for a fact I'm better than many,
No, not many could measure – they try,
It's not egotistical,
But I don't try spell it out for the world,

Feel like I have to sometimes,
Stupidity fuckin' reigns mate,
Shit I've fuckin' seen – you wouldn't believe,
Stupidities definitely surplus,

If I was them I'd be embarrassed,
Thing about that though you have to be aware,
Cause there's a great many who are embarrassed,
By those who're never fucking aware,

I want to tell them to sit down,
Especially before they hurt themselves,
I know they won't listen, they never sit down,
They'll hurt others and themselves,

Too reckless to give a shit,
Too arrogant to be capable of empathizing,
Too ignorant to ever learn better,
And it's always only ever embarrassing,

How do these cunts not know shame?
Surely their parents can't be to blame?
Woe, the agony – the mental pains,
Oh the anguish – the disdain,

I never try to prove I'm better than anyone,
A wise man will always say he doesn't know everything,
I know I'm better I – just shouldn't have to prove it,
To the fuckers never capable of ever knowing anything,

They'll never be told,
They generally only ever learn by the time they're too old,

Fuck Myself

Must seem like I've got no shame,
Like I've got no brain – can't feel pain,
Or maybe I'm just too smart to be considered sane,
But I'm still probably a lot easier to blame,

Do things that fuck a lot of others,
Correct – yes,
But do as many things to fuck myself,
You can bet I will if I haven't yet,

Some fuck quite good,
Many fuck great,
Many fuck in ways –
I don't agree but can't hate,

I know it must seem like I've got no shame,
Like maybe no brain – or can't feel the pain,
Or maybe I'm just way too smart to be considered sane,
But even I can see I'm still easier to blame,

Some fuck good,
But some fuck great,
And some fuck in ways,
I don't agree but can't hate,

I've fucked a lot of others that may have deserved it,
Maybe, yes,
But fucked myself plenty knowing I deserved it,
Correct – yes,
And you can most certainly bet –
I will if I've seen I haven't been yet,

But Just To Make Sure

Now I really hate to make second guess,
But I've just gotta get it off my chest,
I hate to make you regret – if that was just your best,
You better come back again – that was easy to digest,

Problem is,
I don't know – I can't tell if you tried enough,
But if you did –
Could you make it last?

It wasn't all with me – they were just as weak,
I can rest – I can sleep, can do as I please,
Waiting here for days – yeah, I could sleep,
Takes you months, years, not weeks,

You can't be the shit if you're not that good,
You can't even fuck me like you thought you would,
I feed you ideas you believe are solely yours,
Just to fuck me for good measure, just to make sure,

Problem is,
I don't know, can't tell if you tried enough,
But if you did –
Could you make it last?

I'll be the true means to my own ending,
Dying only probably defending,
The waste it's wasted on,
Fucked by all manners of 'unimaginable' wrong,

Just to make certain –
Just to make sure,
'cause God knows they think I need it more…

Late Due

I'm so sick of hearing that I'm gonna pay,
So fuckin' sick of waiting for cunts to come to claim,
They yell it from afar and I can hear 'em,
And I was so fuckin' pissed of that now I'm grinnin'

I know they want to smack my head in,
I hear 'em all – it's all the same threatenin'
I almost can't believe they haven't delivered,
I can't see how they expect to see me shivering,

I'm not, I'm not afraid – I really couldn't care,
Seen about the worst of it – how can I be scared?
But I am about tired of having to wait for it,
Keen to go lookin' – keen to implore it,

I know if I start it's gonna get ugly,
And they're all gonna whinge about absolutely nothing,
I'll stand there and I'll let them throw first punch,
But they better make certain it's gonna be enough,

For all the time I wait – I hunger still,
And I seriously doubt I'll ever get my fill,
Not when it's sudden and the time finally comes,
'cause I'm gonna fuckin' explode with a collateral damage done,

Time it took for 'em to realise,
Hardly seems the effort for despise,
Months waiting – a year gone,
And I've only wished it for so long,

The exercise, excitement – the blooding, the taste,
Seems it's only ever been a waste…

Ripping Halves

Fuck I'm glad I'm over that thing,
She lost her interest after the fling,
She grins, she wins, my eyes sting,
Futures grim, I turn to sin, the end begins,

Ripping halves, splitting apart,
Oncoming, descending dark,

Every essence and interweaving strand,
Determined to deliver upon demand,
Although it never goes to plan,
Malfunctions, backfire and reprimand,

Damage wrought, no more time bought,
Careless, reckless, diabolical onslaught,

I really fuckin' loved that bitch,
I withdrew from her absence with a violent twitch,
And I'm but left alone to sew this frayed stitch,
Accustomed to the torment – I don't flinch,

Invested every essence and interweaving strand,
Determined to deliver upon demand,
Although it never went to plan,
The malfunction, backfire and reprimand,

I'm ripping these halves, splitting apart,
Settling in the oncoming descending dark,
The damage has't wrought – there's no time can be bought,
Now it's just careless, reckless, diabolical onslaught,

Narcick

Narcissistic on myself, narcissistic on the outside world,
Narcissistic blackened Hell, narcissistic blackened insides curled,
Conflicting contradictions always … lost in a paradox,
Consistent inconsistence – never something that I'm not,

And the earth opened up,
And a blinding white light cast,
Up, from the dense depths of rock,
Thundering, rupturing blasts,

Shockwaves through the brain, a pulse of pleasure and pain,
Go back to get forward to go back again, yeah – it is insane,
The mutiny of the scrutiny fired off every which way,
Monotony hasn't forgotten me, there's still Hell to pay,

And the heaven's rained a fire,
Collapsing, tearing down old empires,
To match the rage of the under earth,
To eradicate the evils long transpired,

Narcissistic on myself, narcissistic on the outside world,
Narcissistic blackened Hell, narcissistic blackened insides curled,
Conflicting contradictions always … lost in a paradox,
Consistent inconsistence – never something that I'm not,

Forever lost in the paradox…
Never something I'm not,

Dishonourable Disgrace

I'm gonna need some pot and booze,
'cause there are some things I'm gonna do,
And I know I'm gonna need to be loose,
'cause events will surely lead me to lose,

I wanna get stoned and pissed,
Then fuck off to get up to shit,
Steal a car – women to kiss,
Steal money from a bank I know won't miss,

Gonna need to get off my face,
Before I really fuck up this place,
To become the most dishonourable disgrace,
Everybody's gonna be getting a taste,

I'm gonna get pissed and stoned,
Then fuck off and head a'roam,
Steal a car and make women scream and moan,
And snatch cash from banks too rich to know,

Gonna need to be nice and fucked and loose,
And a decent amount of pot and booze will do –
Gonna need it in the times like this I choose,
To go fuck up and really lose,

I'm gonna need to get the fuck off my face,
Before I really start to fuck up this place,
And become the most dishonourable disgrace,
Yeah – everybody's gonna get a taste,

Fucked off my face – loose enough to lose,
If it's no big deal than it'll pass smooth,

But I'm gonna need a fuck load of pot and booze,
To be loose enough I can lose,

Get fucked up, get loose – change the attitude,
When I'm in a "I'm gonna fuck this place up" mood,

Cryin' Help

What do you do when you have no faith left?
Think I forget, but would you remind me again?
I, wish for death everyday – I almost don't care how,
The feeling is strong, has been for a while and even now,

I cannot deter myself much from the thought,
To take my flick knife and cut much deeper than before,
Don't think I could care of too much of anything anymore,
People, the world and things in it, this life – I abhor,

I want to go grab that knife with that shiny blade gleam,
And wedge it – twisted couple turns 'tween the ribs now,
Let it sit there – lay back and let it bleed,
Feel my pulse slow 'til it stop's and my heart gives out,

I'm living with a torment of pain each day,
No drugs, can't medicate to make it go away,
I have reasons, but none are good but one for me to stay,
Time's again it's felt like it's the exact kind of game I don't like to play,

I'm on the edge and I'm slowly slipping away,
The ground beneath my feet tilts and shakes,
I feel the grace of god fade and forsake,
Relations mere dormant volcano's 'til the threshold breaks,

I'm cryin' help but I can't see it comin'
Wouldn't wish it on any, it's numbin',
Life is supposed to be a precious somethin',
But this hell just feels like more than I can stomach,

And I plummet,

Fixing My, Before I,

It's takin' me longer than I thought,
Working on all my imperfections,
Working at fixing my faults and flaws,
And it's taking a great deal of my attentions,

There are things I don't get much to do,
When I'm isolated away to have a think through,
But there's a lot I'm putting thought to,
And distractions must be few,

Things I need distances to keep to mind,
'til it works second nature – like, all the time,
'Cause if I don't sooner – I am going to find,
Shit will get the more difficult during this life as mine,

I have to compress a lot of emotion,
But have to continue to remain ever devoted,
To what path, this life I've chosen,
What choices twist and what chaos' interwoven,

And it's taking me longer than I thought,
Working on all these imperfections,
Working at fixing my faults and flaws,
And all the while requiring all my attentions,

I can't afford to have too much interaction,
Nor too many things I could call a distraction,
And normally would applaud 'til we receive some infraction,
A looping karmic-pestilent cause for whatever dissatisfaction,

It's much less hazardous to me or anybody – everybody else,
While I undergo these changes that I just keep to myself,
So that it may just be me alone to have knelt,
The sole sacrifice – before the demonic God-King of Hell…

Reciprocating My Share

It's been a matter of months,
Some amazing things have begun,
Some, bizarre things I've done,
I'm anxious to too soon see what I become,

It began after I found I could draw,
Energy from above and below,
But then did something I hadn't before,
And gave it back to from where I got it,

Somehow I'd draw out this energy,
Feel it course through me,
A powerful and beautiful entity,
I would never not once turn enemy,

I don't know when it particularly was,
That I could begin to see the colours,
But then ever more came to me, was,
Light, pure and powerful, the like 'tween lovers,

I would draw the light and feed it back,
Took what I'd need but gave it back,
Did have a sinister purpose but soon lost that track,
Guess I sooner wanted responsibility back,

But over the last few months,
Something new even begun,
Had me just spun out – stunned,
Visual intercepted of the realm of the one,

I don't know whether I'd opened a portal,
I'm not even sure anymore whether I'm a pure mortal,

But whenever I share 'twixt, I keep it formal,
Don't want to have any think more of me outta the normal,

But...maybe this sight only really came to me due –
To the authenticity I'd shown attempting to return it to,
And pure through,

Closer To The Divine

Think I gained a divine connection,
'twixt me and the saviour,
Receiving energy, love, and sent it –
Back on to the saviour,

Wanted to be closer –
Think I am more now,
Wanted to know,
And think I'm getting it now,

Wanted to know what it took,
What lengths – what extents,
Even all that forsook,
And brought such sad events,

I feel when I returned the light,
He felt and he knew,
Is why he gifted me with the sight,
Since I might be capable to save a few,

Things are beginning to happen to me,
And I don't know whether these changes have ever been seen,
I haven't got the slightest clue to what it means,
I only, have my intuition and the thirst to reach my dreams,

My views and perspectives change the more I learn,
The more I feel and draw ever closer,
Almost feel liberated the more I burn,
The more I feel and draw closer –

Wanted to be closer –
And think I am more now,

Wanted to know –
And I think I'm getting to now,

Wanted to know what it took,
What lengths – what extents,
Even all that that forsook,
And brought his sad events,

Attempting To Reveal

I don't know how many times I've tried,
To explain how I am without makin' mum cry,
Another downhill run – well, what a surprise,
If you let us – we'll get help – only, you're not gonna like,

I know, cause the help is involuntary help,
Taken up to hospital and forcefully withheld,
To punch down the drugs and face whatever hell,
And release me out once all is well,

I don't feel it's a problem that's just going to go away,
My folks didn't like it when I had to say –
They'd insist I'd give all the pot-smokin' away,
And I'll soon see a dramatic change,

I know they're probably right – but just what if?
What if it's not psychosis but newly a psychic to live?
How could it be waste if there is now more to give?
Oh – that's fine and well, but if it were – you'd be rich,

"if you have all these powers then why aren't you rich?"
"well I'm the only first I know to have happened with all this"
But maybe it's true – maybe I was given these gifts –
'Cause maybe there's a higher purpose for me to live,

No matter how I may choose to approach,
This matter that I hold dear to my folks,
No matter how well I word it spoke,
They just seem to think it's all a joke,

Mum gets upset and she starts to freak,
She says, this is how I never wanna hear you speak –

That it seems this insanity has almost peaked,
And if I keep going my future's gonna be bleak,

And we're all losin' sleep,
It's still too difficult for 'em to believe,

Hindsight Aftershock

Can't laugh – I won't
Won't laugh – shan't can't,
Shan't laugh – I won't,
Not when the I-told-you-so –
Was too much,

'Cause I'm gonna be feeling the pain of it,
'Cause I'm gonna be feeling the blame of it,
Gonna be feeling the shame of it,
Yeah – there's no escaping the pain of it,

I saw it comin' so I guess I'm semi-prepared,
I'll be fearless when all others are scared,
But I will have the mercy to spare,
And spare the mercy as I dare,

The mercy I can't laugh, I won't,
The mercy I won't laugh, shan't – can't,
The mercy I shan't laugh – I won't –
Not when the I-told-you so –
Was too much,

Gave the benefit of the doubt although,
I knew we'd get here – hindsight would show,
How can I laugh through this painful told-you-so,
I went and I said all I could know,

Saw it comin' so I was semi-prepared,
And I'll be fearless when all others are scared,
But I will have the mercy to spare,
And spare that mercy as fair –

The mercy I can't laugh and won't,
The mercy I won't laugh, but shan't – can't,
The mercy I shan't laugh and won't,
Not when the I-told-you-so –
Was more than enough,
Was too much…

Context To Laugh

There's a time when you can,
And of course, a time when you can't,
Time to know when to understand,
But then a time of course to know when to laugh,

Usually it's cruel to at those impaired,
Usually it's cruel to those who don't compare,
Usually cruel to at people unprepared,
Cruel to, to those we have to spare –

Spare a consideration to who's expense,
Consideration of laughing in appropriate context,
Consider it may be taken as offense,
Consider laughing may earn resent,

Yeah, there's a time when you can –
And a time when you just can't,

It's usually cruel on or to those inferior,
Cruel to, to show off you're superior,
Cruel to when everything's taken so serious,
Cruel to even if it seems ridiculous,

It's best to spare the consideration of who's expense,
Consideration of laughing in appropriate context,
Consider it could be taken to offense,
Consider laughing may earn you resents,

You might take it lightly, but you never can tell,
If that was just a someone's fucked kind of hell,
And how could you ever like that for yourself?
Consider it – and think on it well,

'Cause –
There's a time when you can,
But there's times when you can't,
Question the context to laugh…

In The Act Of Maturity

Not sure of too many people think like me,
Especially in particular moments like these,
That demand most caution and acts of maturity,
Demands a sensitivity, clever thought and soothing,

Ascension of heated argument, leading up confusion,
Sides not seen to inadequate, misleading allusion,
A farce to get passed fast, inaccurate seething delusion,
To laugh at long last, immaculate, seeing amusement,

The point, the reason, the rationale to be known,
What anxieties, angst, anguish – inhabits the zone,
What rips out, tears and trembles happy homes,
What makes you wish to disappear and be alone,

But times when, the fact is clear and you're a step ahead,
The fact was seen and you're ahead, they repeat what was said,
You try to move to the next step – and they're at dead ends,
They haven't quite got it yet, conversation ends, dead,

You wonder if they wonder you know more than they think you do,
At times it's a pain to, consistently, sift your way through,
And this tests patience and tolerance – it's true,
But you hope still one day they see it the same as you,

You hope they see the changes, the growth, that you evolve,
And you hope one day you can reach and resolve,
They must learn for themselves, they cannot have been told,
But it's by the acts of maturity, you achieve an age of old,

Godly Ways

Jesus the fuck Christ!
Where are ya mate?
Quick – get back to the middle,
It's where you're needed
most mate –

I'll follow you to God,
But I'll be God-like doing so,
Those, godly ways you portrayed,
I'll follow you to God,

I'll follow you to God mate,
But I'll be God-like doing so –
Those Godly ways you instructed,
Yeah, I'm gonna follow
you to God,

People are hearing you
man just not listening,
Or listening but just not
following justly,
Too tainted or tainting
your wisdom,
And doing it unjustly,

I know it's hard to take a hit,
And fake it doesn't bother you,
Not any one of us can take a hit,
And not show it bothers us,

I have difficulty biting
down on my tongue,
At whatever pain or
damage is done,

Maybe one day I will
accomplish it,
I'll be as strong as you
God, or the Son,

I do pray that you feel me,
In the way you know
what I mean,
I do love you for the sacrifice,
Can appreciate it, means
something for me,

One day I may be capable
to turn the other cheek,
I promise,
I will – your will as mine, I will it,
I promise…

I'll follow you to God,
But I'll be God-like doing so,
Those, godly ways you portrayed,
I'll follow you to God,

I'll follow you to God mate,
But I'll be God-like doing so –
Those Godly ways you instructed,
Yeah, I'm gonna follow
you to God,

Jesus the fuck Christ!
Where were ya mate?
Back to the centre,
It's where you're needed
most mate –
Don't abandon post!

Only So Far

I can never know when the shit's just a waste,
But I only ever seem to leave a bitter after taste,
And I might never find my place,
Might only ever be good at being a disgrace,

I can never know how much of it is actually worth it,
I often don't feel like I deserve it,
And if pain and hates all that they feel – exert it,
Screech your peace and have me heard it,

I'm not proud – don't have much to be about,
I get so far only to come back down,
And no – I'm fuckin not ever once proud,
I don't see what it is I have to feel good about,

Don't know how any could ever envy me,
They only ever see the shit they wanna see,
I'm just too many things me or another doesn't want me to be,
I truly want better but these never let me,

I can only get so far to succumb to a fall,
And I'm hearin' names from every direction at me called,
It's no wonder I cannot move forward,
Never win nor claim some compensating reward,

It hardly ever seems any of my efforts pay,
None ever seem happier 'til after I've gone away.
Despair to despair with more despair between each day,
Nothin' can nor has – nor should, probably ever go my way,

There's no point trying to impress when I can't fully,
I'm a once good guy regressed, turned bully,

Can't afford for it to last forever, I hope it doesn't surely,
I can't keep up forever – I'm doing it now so poorly,

Now...
Now I'm just trying to get used to it...
Never can be any real use to it...

Satan Their Shit

I really can't believe the shit they're satan to me,
You think you deserve better,
When you don't even show it – never –
Nah – can't believe the shit you're satan to me,

Can't get passed your own pride nor vanity,
To fuckin' even allow me any sanity,
No responsibility, nor sensibility – nor maturity,
So how do I – how can I rise out of the mutiny,

But by looking better than you and do as you won't,
Crossing my comfortable boundaries – doing as you won't,
Having to get as nasty to say what you don't,
To show you what you are and never don't,

I really cannot believe the shit you're satan to me,
Can't show reason why you think you deserve better –
Only claim it can't prove it – never,
Nah – can't believe the shit they're satan to me,

You already think you've shown and proved it,
Too comfortable to defend it that you'll lose it,
Can't stand by your shit – so get outta the way, move it,
Couldn't do it right so now I have to do it,

Poor fuckin' devil me never gets the credit,
Not for ever big or little painstaking effort,
Isolation? Might as well, communication's severed,
I'm never gonna get my such a thing as 'Heaven',

Can't believe the shit they're satan to me,
I'm just not seeing what they want me to see,

No good – not for me – and none of what I want to be,
Nah – just can't believe the shit they're satan to me,

Monkeys only doing what monkey sees,
Reverse similarities – ha – whoa,
Can't even believe they can't see the shit they're satan to me,

Piss Poor Examples

Don't get pissed at me for trying to learn,
It wasn't long ago you were having your turn,
Is it entirely my fault you fucked up?
When you couldn't keep your mouth shut –

I've never known better – well, how the fuck can I?
It's not like you ever did more than make me cry,
Never made me feel better that I went and tried,
No praise to show I might be worthy of the prize,

It's not like I'm ever more than you despise,
It's not like you even give a decent reason why,
It's not like you actually try open up my eyes,
Why would you – can't get passed your pride,

It might come as news but I haven't got pride,
None have ever let me feel safe to confide,
I know I'm not anything many people could like,
Hell, I know I've made some wanna see my head on a spike,

They want better from me but just not give any back,
Then I cop a stabbing repeatedly in the back,
So gutless just to blame and not offer another way,
No attempt I'm just left to wither and decay,

No, I'm certain they're just all out for themselves –
And they often think they're victim worse than *my* hell,
Never truly consider to see what it is they do,
Nah, not really ever do see what they do,

Can't own up to it or actually do better,
But be stuck in these outdated ways forever,

Can't be nice – no – not fucking ever,
Time's why my communications severed,

I can't see 'em making me like 'em enough to play nice,
Think it's just because I see they can't play nice…

All Of It Is Wrong

I apologize,
I was traumatized,
I should've forewarned,
I should've realized,

I had piss poor examples influencing me,
Domestic violence, alcoholism, drugs, worst to be seen,
And round me at an age only way too young,
Trauma, absorbed it like a sponge,

I know all of it is wrong,
Been hardwired that way too long,
So I do most deeply apologise,
I was severely traumatized,

Mother was beaten worse than us kids thrown around,
Emotionally shattered, broke, run to the ground,
No sanctuary, no peace, no safety to be found,
Harden or smarten or just be fated for the ground,

Piss poor examples destroyed me,
I am the king of hell so anoint me,
Forewarned you should've maybe seen all this before,
Knowing better – doing worse, still as disappointing,

Traumatized, shocked into bad disrepair,
Anger – hatred, pain and such miserable despair,

I know all of it is wrong,
Been hardwired this way for too long,
I do most deeply apologize,
I was severely traumatized,

I was learning things I probably never should've,
Preventing it seems like something none ever could've,
Only seems it's I to be the one to apologize,
The hell I comprise – but also that before me –
That wasn't mine,
I apologize,

Losing Peacefully

I have to lose,
To make someone feel good about something,
I have to lose,
'cause they never like me feelin' good about something,

I have to lose,
Cause I know I can learn to do it peacefully,
I have to lose,
Because they just can't win gracefully,

I have to lose,
Because I have it better,
I have to lose,
Cause they can't ever,

I have to lose,
To keep them peaceful.
I have to lose,
And do it graceful,

I have to lose –
'cause I'm better at it than they,
I have to lose,
'cause they like it better that way,

It's better me than them,
They say it's not but pretend,

Don't Play If You Can't Lose

I know what I want –
But I just can't be good enough,
'Cause I just don't fuckin' get it,

People must fuckin' think I'm fuckin' evil,
I can't even tell if they're lying when they say they hate it,
I'm not, but I know they're fucking worse.

They tell me what they are –
When they're accusing of me doing it,
They face this mirror but don't see the error,
As they're accusing of me doing it,

It's here at these stages I generally find,
These hypocrites wasting every moment of my time,
They're playing games that I lose at, and I'm losing the mind,
I hate fuckin' playing – I'm not this fucking kind,

I know what the fuck I want and I hate wasting time,
But me – I must never be fucking good enough,
'Cause I'm never ever fucking getting it,

They must think and assume that I'm evil,
And I can't even tell if they're lying saying they hated it,
Well, I'm fucking not – but I know they're fucking worse,

They tell me what they are –
When they're accusing of me doing it,
They face this fucking mirror and never see the error,
Whenever they're accusing of me doing it,

I fuckin' hate playing the games with cunts when I always have to lose,
Never does anything for me – what do *I* get to have to lose?

Not supposed to fight nor defend,
And it never ends,
Never ends,

I have to lose –
'cause they can' win gracefully,
And I'll lose,
'Cause they can't even do that gracefully,

Valuable Shit

How dare you say you never meant anything?
Why the fuck would I care so much about what you say –
That I take it seriously to heart,
And it fuckin' breaks me, crumbles me away –

I tell you you're a shit fuckin' human,
'cause you treat me a fuckin' lot less than,
I tell you you're a shit fuckin' person,
There's better out there – why haven't I fuckin' met them?

I put too much importance on you,
And you never live – nor could ever, what good I say,
I'll waste so much good on you, for you,
And be buried an earlier day,

I tell you you're a shit fuckin' person,
There's better out there – and why haven't I fuckijn' met 'em,
I tell you you're a shit fuckin' human,
'caus you treat me a whole fuckin' lot less than,

I can care enough to say you were valuable,
Have had the balls to – have even said before,
But you treat me worse than a filthy fuckin' animal,
Leaving me sore and you hating me for showing it more,

And I'm supposed to be expected to handle each crushing blow,
And withstand the break – fuckin' never let it show,
One day I may have that strength enough I won't,
I do feel at these times I just can't, and I don't,

They can't treat me better than the shit they are,
This all they've known – this is how they always are,
It's how I know that if I stay – I'll never make it far,

Burnt Steak

Men have prices,
Men have values,
But every man has that one,
To exceed all other values,

Burn me at the stake –
And see If I'm for real,
Burn me at the stake,
And you'll know, you'll feel,

When the stake is high,
I'll have grasped choke-hold tight,
When the stakes are fuckin' high,
You can expect a fight,

Burn me at the stake –
And see if I'm real,
Burn me at the stake,
And take the fist that deals,

Men have prices and they'll fight,
Grasp tight their values and fucking fight,
Every retaliation overwhelmed by each spite,
But when the stakes are high, you better expect a fight,

Burn me at the stake –
And see if I'm for real,
Burn me at the stake –
And brace the fist I'll deal,

Burn me at the stake –
And see if I'm for real,
Burn me at the stake,
And you will know – you'll feel,

All The Rage

Marijuana, Metal and Minge,
These are just a few of my favourite fucking things,
Yeah, I've gotta kickstart the fuckin' binge,
Before I lose it, rage and whinge,

Gonna get merry with my smoke,
Mull a sesh and pack and toke,
Relax soothe and calm and slow,
Meditate and radiate the colour show,

Thrash out hard to proper fuckin' metal,
Pace up a rhythm, rapid, but still idle – settle,
Hasten to the melodies I most revel,
Opened my mind to a whole new level,

But I do go weak – tender like a wussy,
For that beautiful sweet juicy pussy,
Shaven completely smooth clean – or of course woolly,
It doesn't matter – I still get me Roger jolly fully,

Yes, Marijuana, Metal and Minge,
ARE a few of my favourite fuckin' things,
I just have to kickstart a binge,
Before I lose it, rage and whinge,

I rage 'cause,
It's all the rage to me,

Yeah fuckin' Marijuana, Metal and Minge,
Won't so no, they're my favourite things,
I must immediately kickstart this binge,
Before I fuckin' lose it, rage and whinge,

Doomed To Forget

What was I thinking of earlier –
Fuck, geez – I know it was gonna be good,
I can't recall what it was now earlier –
But I know it was gonna be that fuckin' good,

Just mere moments ago,
I had it but it's fuckin' gone,
Only just fuckin' moments ago,
And it's all gone,

You'd be amazed at how frustrated I get,
At myself for being distracted of remembering shit,
Shit I know would've been a hit,
Shit I'm only yet doomed to forget,

I know it'll hit me again in an inconvenient time,
And I know I won't be so able to write it down,
I get irate it's so spontaneous at times,
That I can never write it down,

It takes me thinking of a thought or memory,
Then a scent, or sound, or feel to trigger,
I have to write to get it out of me,
Resulting material by which trigger,

Only seemed to happen mere moments before,
And I'm never quick enough – it's gone,
Only just mere moments before,
And it's all fuckin' gone,

You'd be amazed at how frustrated I get,
At myself for not retaining the shit,
Shit I know would've been a hit,
Shit I know I'm soon doomed to forget,

Excitements Will Cease

It's funny what little people show they know,
It's all funny to them when they're having a go,
Wait – cause big brothers about to show –
And when he feeds it back you'll know –

Funny how they all run their mouth,
Less I say – more it heads south,
And I guess I forget what it's about,
But they all certainly have their doubt,

It's a big boy's game little babe,
Think you're all that but you aint got it made,
You're naughty – you need a smack for how you behave,
Naughty naughty girl – you need to get laid,

A stiff one up ya and we'll be cheerin'
Perhaps one up ya worthy fearin'
Excitements only to get you tearin'
No more raging about scowling or leering,

People still biting off more than they can chew,
It's just a shame it's always at you,
People all wantin' somethin new,
Can't say it but I see they're blue,

People all wanting a piece,
When I just want fucking peace,
Build it up but you best get that release,
And then excitements will all cease,

Spose, I should be grateful,
People are makin' an effort for a bite,
See… they want somethin….

Just Want To Leave

It's hard for me to believe when others are honest,
Hard for me to accept any kind of praise,
Hard for me to understand why we bother to work hard at all,
For what little leisure, no pleasure – just malaise,

Don't want to really participate anymore,
Not in anything – but why the fuck for?
Somebody somewhere is keeping score,
And I know I'll lose – have many times before –

You say party – I say slight reprieve,
Seen better – you wouldn't believe,
I just can't seem to progress, it's grief,
I'm not myself – I just wanna leave,

Hard for me to know whether to be serious,
I'm tired of it, weary – everything's delirious,
I give up – I yield – I'll be obsequious,
The sycophant – I'll stop with the deviousness,

I really don't want to participate anymore,
Not in anything – but why the fuck for?
Somebody somewhere's keeping score –
I know I lose – have many times before,

You say party – I say slight reprieve,
Been and done better – you wouldn't believe,
Just can't seem to progress, it's grief,
Most definitely not myself – I just want to leave…

Thick Black Shade

It lingers,
The thick black shade,
Whispery
Outstretching – it forbades,

Can't shake it,
Follows me,
Can't break it,
Drowns me,

People get too close
And feel it there,
People always get far too close,
It peels – it pares,

It's despair –
This thick black shade,
Lingering, whispery,
Entangling – it forbades,

I can't shake it,
Follows me,
Can't break it,
But absorb it deep,

I absorb it deep,

It's despair,
I feel it there,
Despair –
Peels us bare –
It pares...
Despair,

In The Air

I feel strange
There's a strange air about the air,
Definitely strange,
Felt it there – hanging in the air,

Maybe it's something to do –
With strange paths opening, true,
Happened to me before,
It's weird, it's something new,

New level of awakening,
Hard to say,
Psychic levels awakening,
So hard, so hard for me to say,

Cause I really don't k now – it's strange,
Bizarre the strange air in the air,
So bizarre,
Felt it there, hanging in the air,

Maybe new things are happening –
My anticipation is slackening,
Just what is it exactly,
The past is drifting, blackening –

Everything I know now doesn't count,
Not with this strange air about,
Somethings happened – it's coming out,
Maybe nothing we know can count,

New level of awakening,
It's hard for me to say,

Psychic levels awakening,
So hard, so hard for me to say,

But I can feel it in the air,
It's there,

Dreadfuls

It's your story,
I just tell your truths better than you do,
You just want the glory,
No matter what dishonourable acts you stead through,

But everybody only ever likes their story better,
"Can't have me lookin' bad, no way, fuck that – never,"
Not ruining my reputation – you can forget it,
Oh – he'll learn himself the hard way – I just have to let it,

It's no surprise I learnt to be so good with my tongue,
You wouldn't even believe half the shit I've done,
But better yet still the shit I've heard myself,
I could've sooner been rolling in wealth,

I want to come up with a better term for a penny dreadful,
As different as the material is – it's similar, still mental,
But something still about it remains so memorable,
To rattle or caress the nerves, tickle or tremble,

I had to teach myself to talk for my own defence,
Not too many others had my back against the nonsense,
And to tread a labyrinth of traps of only so much relevance,
Has only doubled the delay through getting to success,

It's my story,
But you'll pick what truths better than I do,
Yeah - I just wanted the glory,
Exposing what dishonourable acts I stead through,

But…everybody only ever likes their story better….

Dissatisfying Reprieves

An irritation I have,
Is for the some who scorn,
At what reprieves I take,
For what irritations I have –

Where it should
normally flow easy,
Here goes another
occurrence displeasing,
Rusted joints all needing
a degreasing,
A little teasing to flowing easy,

It's the two steps back,
Before the next three forward,
Another two back again,
With yet another three
forward like before,

A slow set motion,
But there is motion,
Time it takes to, get to know it,
Sluggish, just atrocious,

It's the two steps back,
Before the next three forward,
Another two back again,
With yet another three
forward like before,

So what if I take reprieves
for my irritations –

What is it do you do for
your dissatisfaction?
Don't stand there and scorn at
my break from the irritations,
Of whatever caused this…
my dissatisfaction,

It should come fuckin'
easy the flow,
Displeasing occurrences,
so many come and go,
Degreasing the rusted
joints again so they go,
A little teasing to get easing
back into the flow…

It's the two steps back,
Before the next three forward,
Another two back again,
With yet another three
forward like before,

A slow set motion,
But there is motion,
Time it takes to, get to know it,
Sluggish, just atrocious,

It's the two steps back,
Before the next three forward,
Another two back again,
With yet another three
forward like before,

Why Him?

They ask why him?
And I know it's directed at me –
They ask why I can do such things,
Ignorance, and overshadowing discomfort to believe,

See,

It began with people like them,
It only took consistencies pushing me away,
Various degrees for certainty the fall steepens,
All that pushing me out and away, yeah – I strayed,

It's when you know you're not wanted around,
It's when all their backs are turned,
You have to cut losses and head abound,
You have to harden through lessons hard learned,

And you do –

Everybody's ignorant and nothing ever changes,
They stay the same while you metamorphose,
You handle pressures they've often never faced,
And the world you knew gets smaller as you've outgrown,

It was those people's discomfort with you,
Reminded them it's not any good for them,
It was their behaviour, their attitude towards you,
To push you to want to be completely different to them,

And you do –

Yeah, it began with people like them,
You leave, and they carry on their merry way,

You leave and become so very different,
But nothing for them will ever change,

You change, you evolve, you become so much more,
They're stuck, stranded in ignorance,
The same ignorance you abhorred and had always fought,
And eventually overpowered but saw it's significance,

They will always ask why him –
And I'll know it's directed at me,
They'll ask why I can do such things –
Still overshadowed by an ignorance and discomfort to believe,

See,

While they're still stranded, nothing ever changes,
You're pushed away, you leave and you learn,
You live, you evolve – long before they've even faced it,
And they're shocked to a wonder of how and why when you return,

If you're any different, even right from the beginning –
They'll single you out, push you out and away,
You'll know you're different, right from the beginning,
When they single you out, push you out and away,

And they'll always only ever ask…
Why? Why him?

Shout Me Suicide

I hear shouts for me to kill myself,
I might maybe, but what if it wasn't well?
To be left as a vegetable to remain to dwell?
Have they? Could they ever measure up to my hell?

Well – I'll be fucked if I'm ever givin' them that,
When they always get what they want,
I struggled to have what I fuckin' had,
And I'm nowhere near what I want –

I feel like hell all the time –
Do they ever spare consideration of my mind?
None of them knew but all fuckin' assume,
And they'll eat their words when they know too soon,

I take medication to reduce my psychosis,
I take medication for what I'd call severe depression,
I smoke cannabis to level my imbalanced moments,
Require consistent therapy, like weekly, can't get it,

Shouts for me to suicide and there are many,
And I doubt they've ever felt a pinch of what I feel – if any,
I've felt it plenty – often pained and empty,
And after my tears, I feel naught but hate and resenting,

I hear their shouts for me to kill myself,
How could they know how hard it was my hell?
Never spared a consideration for what I must've felt,
Bound beyond irrational reason, driven to be compelled,

They're always getting' what they want and they're insatiable,
But I'm never givin' them that, I'm fuckin' irreplaceable,

My death or not do you think the matters gone? Debatable,
You're all the reason why I'm unstable

I'll be fucked if you're ever getting' what you want,
When you're not even happy with that,
I've never been near anything I want,
I've fuckin' struggled to keep what I had…

Tear Me Down Fun

Shit, fuck me, thought I had a morbid sense of humour,
But I've got a new fucker trying to tear me down,
Sick and twisted mother fuckers – Ha! Humour?
You think it's fun tryin' to tear me down,

Oh but you have just no idea,
How much more fun you'd have –
If I were anywhere near,
The kind of fun you really want had,

Understand, you wanna friend?
For shit you can get up to with?
Send fuckers round the bend –
I couldn't be better to be with,

Your mistake was assuming I'm a particular way,
That you wouldn't give the time of day,
But when you can't or don't give the time,
You won't see my cool or even call it 'mine'

There's a lot more hidden to me,
Can breathe fresh hot ecstasy,
But when you can't or won't spare the time,
You'll never see my cool or call it 'mine'

People try to tear me down for fun,
But there's so much more they're missing out on,
People try to fuck with me for fun,
But there's just so much fucking more,

People are so limited,
Especially with imagination,

I'm never fuckin' bored once never,
Cause I've got fuckin' imagination,

But I never have to make people feel like shit for me to feel good,
Nah – I can do good, and make 'em feel a lot better...

The Laugh Behind The Dying

I hear them laugh afar,
And I know they're up to something sly,
They always only laugh from afar,
Watching with envious, narcissistic eyes,

Can hear 'em laugh from afar,
And I know they're conspiring,
I hear 'em laughing from afar –
It's endless, it's tiring,

Drawn back to nothing but the voices,
Some I can recall from a past,
Drawn back through the memories of choices,
Those some that could never last,

A some I knew never got far,
They've all leeched and bled me dry,
These some all laughing from afar,
And conspiring ever sly,

So long as I am here and closer near,
To the mistakes I thought lie forgotten passed,
Closer to tears and with a rage all fear,
May have my fun and compensation at last,

Can hear 'em laughing from afar,
And they think they've got dirt on me,
I hear 'em laughing beyond afar,
If they weren't dirty before, they're gonna be,

I hear 'em laughing and I know,
They're conspiring ever slyly,

Won't be laughing toe to toe,
For all bleeding and drying – someone's dying,

Laughing from afar at me –
We'll see…

Pit Of Loathing

I hate it when they're not mature enough,
Hate when they're too immature to get passed,
Hate this fucking barrier – it's tough,
I fuckin' hate it and I wanna play rough,

I fuckin' loathe these immature cunts,
Fuckin' loathe 'em all they can go and fucked,
Loathe 'em all for dragging me back to where I get stuck,
Back, way back to the pit of loathing over these cunts,

I absolutely abhor the immaturity –
No matter where I turn there's a mutiny,
Faces all facing, implicating scrutiny,
I most absolutely fucking abhor their immaturity,

I'm fuckin' disgusted,
Sick to my stomach,
Just wanna fist fuck 'em,
Thrash out a punching,

I hate these stupid fucking useless immature shits,
I hate that I can't legally shred them to fuckin' bits,
To wipe 'em all out – sterilize these little shits,
There's no way that stupid immaturity should exist,

I fuckin' loathe these immature cunts,
Fuckin' loathe 'em all they can go and get fucked,
Loathe 'em all for draggin' me through the shit to get stuck,
Back to the pit of loathing over these cunts,

I absolutely abhor the immature –
We have to cleanse, eradicate the stupidity,
I can't fucking stand it any more,

I wanna fist fuck 'em,
Just let me fist fuck 'em,
I've gotta fist fuck 'em,
Just let me,

Hot As My Last Searing Burn...

I get so passionate about things in the heat of discussion,
Quick tempered, angered enough to consider repercussions,
Reaction to what I'm generally disgusted,
Going through a hell to show logic, win but still suffer,

And for the fact I have to explain –
The shit to people twice, thrice my age,
No matter what glory – no matter what success,
I'm still battered and tethered with a pain,

I have to be so fucking cruel,
'cause I'll be fucked if I'm going to be the fool,
And by the hurt and hate of the last, fuelled,
I'm gonna rock, I'm gonna reign – and I'm gonna fuckin' rule,

I have to be as hot as my last searing burn,
I'd lost, burnt, and I'd fucking learnt,
So if it's to any of your concern,
Pass me peace and have your turn to hurt,

Hot with the hate, loathing, abhorrence,
Hot for the inconsiderate intolerance,
Hot with a hate for the inconvenient insolence,
Hot with rage and all malevolence,

I have to be so fucking cruel,
'cause I'll be fucked if I'm gonna be the fool,
And by the last, the hurt and the hate will fuel,
I'm gonna rock, I'm gonna reign, I'm gonna fucking rule,

And I have to be as hot as my last searing burn,
I'd lost then and burnt – but I've fucking learnt,
So, if it's to any of your concern –
Pass me peace and go have your turn to hurt,

I Have...

A lot of what I've written so far was true,
But I've bent the truth to make it more farce,
A lot of what I've mentioned has happened, was true,
But I faked it up a little more to be easier 'til at last,

Have cut my face,
Have felt the extremities of kind grace,
Have fallen on my face,
Have eaten my words, gurgling grossly down distaste,
Have been punched in the face,
Have had my blood dripping, trailing, it traced,
And I have had to stand and face –
Have had to endure being made to brace,

I have the talent to tell as exact as it was,
Some might say it's braver to admit the cost –
I wouldn't wish the worst on foes – knowing what I lost,
I wouldn't attack if they were weaker after having already been crossed,

I have cut my face,
Have felt the extremes of grace,
Have fallen on my face,
Have eaten my words gurgling down the gross distaste,
Have been punched in the face,
Have had my blood dripping, trailing, it traced,
And I've had to stand and face,
Have had to endure and been made to brace,

I have had to fake it up to be easier to bear –
How would we hear of these horrors and not sleep with nightmares,
Trying to interpret it easier with that consideration spared,
More that I can say for you than I had was fair,

Chancing On It

I never wanted to believe that people can't change,
That after certain experiences or a certain age,
You begin to see things in a different way,
Experiences altering – and often never left the same,

Might take just the right time and place,
But you've gotta get out and meet that face,
That little message or reason might be grace,
Or it might end up staggering the pace,

One can never know who precisely knows what,
But all this never knowing can be put a stop,
Takes interaction, socializing quite a lot –
At least 'til you find that something missing you want,

You may have never even known you needed,
That all isolation, depreciates – recedes it,
And there may have been others who may've pleaded,
Could there have been a chance you would've defeated,

Suppose there might be something missing –
Would you want to know – or continue this 'living'?

People remain where they are when they can't chance,
Never can tell where it leads from the dance,
Never know what glories if you don't sight a glance,
If you don't try you'll never have it in your hands,

But how does any even know if they never ask?
Except but to wait and watch 'til the very last,
Break free of the assumption – put it all passed,
And may you succeed and exceed fast…

Had To

I've had to go wrong,
Before I got it right,
Was in the dark long –
Before the light,

Had to learn to lose,
Before I could ever win,
Had to learn I could choose,
Not ever to see it grim,

Had to have a fail,
Before I could succeed,
Had to learn betrayal,
To know how to eventually lead,

Had to see more into it,
Had to have the thirst,
Had to know more to it,
The good and absolute worst,

Had to learn I had the choice,
Between the right and wrong,
Learn to raise a righteous voice,
When it was going wrong,

To confront –
To have to be blunt –
To have come undone,
To show a faithless some,

Yeah – I've had to go wrong,
Before I got it right,
Was in the dark so long,
Before I found the light,

A Sorrier Self

I'm going to have to stop and apologise,
Yeah, I've still got my juvenile mind,
Haven't quite grown out of that yet in time,
Shit, I'm not certain if I ever might,

I will apologise for being rude,
I will apologise for being crude,
I will apologise for being lewd,
I will apologise for my sick attitude,

I'm sorry I have made it uncomfortable,
I'm sorry my actions have been abominable,
I'm sorry it's not so forgettable,
Sorrier still it's not so forgivable,

I've got a lot of changes to make to me,
If I ever want too many people to take to me,
A fuck load of changes to make to me –
If I ever want better of me,

I apologise that I just don't think,
I apologise that I send to the brink,
I apologise for the want of a drink,
I apologise and know my shit does stink,

I am sorry I've made it regrettable,
I am sorry I've made it resentable,
I am sorry I made it detestable,
Sorrier still I was never a vegetable,

I apologise for any and all else,
I'm sorry I'm a sorrier self...

Jigsaw

I know there's a pretty picture here,
But it's frustrating to tears,
Even paranoid with fears,
That a reckoning ever nears,

I know I'll be happier with the picture,
Once I have it in a proper fixture,
But here, before me, a fumbled mixture,
Appearing a further difficult procedure,

The picture is very intricate and I must be ever delicate,
But I can't seem to piece the pieces where they're better delegate,
Problem by problem, pieces similar – duplicate,
I can't seem to appropriately designate,

But I know there's a prettier picture here,
It's got me completely frustrated to tears,
Burdened with strange paranoid fears,
That a reckoning may ever near,

I would be a lot happier to have the picture,
Once it's in it's proper permanent fixture,
But just here lies before me, a mangled mixture,
Proving a much further difficult procedure,

I just don't have the knack for these things,
Did have the patience but it wore too thin,
Gave up, got thirsty – went for a drink,
And descended deeper into philosophical think....

It's Called Compassion...

It's typical for my train of thought to lead,
To finding a solution as quick as I need,
I want to be content and I quicken speed,
To find the perfect puzzle piece for peace,

I don't like to just blame some one,
Or make them feel like shit when they fuck up,
I want to pick them up and dust them off,
Put them back in place facing the right spot,

If I see the error – I feel I want to help,
Not pressure them with terror and all kinds of hell,
Tell 'em to stop, have a break – take a spell,
Recover up enough that you will do it well,

I do care, it's called compassion, no one's alone,
I'll be fucked if I see them off suffering on their own,
I'll pick them up and excite them with a new tone,
So that they too can reign at life and be a king to throne,

I do feel empathy enough to know the pain,
That I never want to see other people under strain,
It may be difficult to understand, I do want others to gain,
I find it strange even to me that you'd find it strange,

It's my nature through and through,
I'll fight it black and blue, it's true,
Everyone assumes, shit – I have too,
But none are exempt of my compassion – even you,

I hate to see anyone struggle – when they shouldn't have to,
They won't so long as I can see it and am within distance to get help to,
I hate all the struggling of the different hells through,
And when I find a way, I'll help others only too soon.

A Life To Envoy

I have been a spiteful shit,
I have indeed gone tat for tit,
Gone wild in seconds split,
Knucklin' out impressive hits,

But it's no life I could enjoy,
It's no life I would envoy,
But to divert of and avoid,
Flex the brain – not the deltoid,

I like to calm and silence,
Think, and disarm the violence,
Soothe the rage of tyrants,
Soothe the rage of titans,

Strange, but it seems all sincerity,
Is worth all the firm remembering,
It pays to use dexterity,
Firm sincerity, a sweet serenity,

I have been a cruel and spiteful shit,
I have been tat for tit,
Gone wild in seconds split,
Knuckled out impressive hits,

But it's no life I could enjoy,
It's no life I would envoy,
But instead divert of and avoid,
Flex the muscle of the brain – not the deltoid,

No, not the deltoid,

I want a life I can enjoy,
I want a life to be proud to envoy,

No, put down those deltoids,

Pub Crawl

They don't call it a pub crawl for nothing,
Won't take too much to prove it,
We need that drink, we need that something,
Have that release so we don't lose it,

Dress up in a good get up,
Lookin' schmick, suave, smart,
Goin' out to get hammered drunk,
Fucked off my face maybe meet a tart,

Dressed up to impress,
Staggering from one pub to the next,
Drink some here then crawl elsewhere,
To loosen up and let down the hair,

It's not called a pub crawl for nothing,
Won't take too much to prove it,
We need a drink – need that something,
Some sort of release so we don't lose it,

This, night is fine and dandy,
There's so much eye candy,
I feel something expanding,
A lady friend would be handy,

I'll scull a few down,
Maybe show off like a clown,
Sink a few more down,
'til I'm crawlin' around,

Everybody's dressed up to impress,
Staggering from one pub to the next,
Drink some here then crawl elsewhere,

To loosen up and let down the hair,

It's not called a pub crawl for nothing,
Won't take too much to prove it,
We need a drink – need that something,
Some sort of release so we don't lose it,

I'll scull a few down,
Maybe show off like a clown,
Sink a few more down,
'til I'm crawlin' around,

It's not called a pub crawl for nothing –
A needed release, a needed something…

Happy?

Don't know why it's so difficult to be happy,
Can never see too many people fuckin' happy –
Is it not the chase anymore – to be happy?
What's it gonna take to be fuckin' happy?

Can't they see what they have?
Can't they count the blessing and be glad?
All I'm ever made to feel is angry or sad,
But fuckin' why? – is being happy so bad?

How fuckin' hard is it to smile?
I fuckin' struggle but I try all the while,
I try to smile when I feel like going fucking wild,
But I can't because going wild resembles a child,

All I'm ever made to feel like is shit,
It does a number – it makes you sick,
And I can never seem to get passed it quick,
Shit to a blanket – it fuckin' sticks,

Don't know why it has to be so difficult to be happy,
I can never see too many people fuckin' happy,
Doesn't it matter anymore – being happy?
What the fuck's it gonna take to be happy?

It's hard for me to try to be,
When a sullen moodiness is all I see,
We're young – we're strong, we are fucking free,
But there just seems to be more to it to me,

Life can fuckin' suck,
And I often want to tell it to get fucked,

It's all these moments we get stuck,
Life just still wants to suck and suck and suck,

I fuckin' struggle but I still try to smile,
Difficult when you just want to go fucking wild,

What The Flak

You reserve the right to complain and whine,
When you hear or see the shit you don't like,
But if or when you do – just have half the mind –
To equally consider my side,

Sure, you have the right to proclaim your disdain,
As much as I the right, not listening to the complaint,
For I would be as irritated as you and if not, as ashamed,
But I just can't afford that on my already damaged brain,

You have the right to bare and share,
But I also have the right not to care,
How could you ever know if I'm ever spared –
And would your nightmares compare?

Each to their own – and we all have ours,
And steadily I hope to gain the powers,
Success of my hard-spent hours,
Defining my to do's and prowess,

Tolerances vary – as do the you and I,
And no matter what the flak – I'm still givin' it a try,
And we're probably never going to see eye to eye,
And we'll never know exactly how shattered each has their pride,

Don't think I have it easier because I'm different,
I know I barely can afford to be that ignorant,
I don't have so much pride it's too easy being diffident,
So don't think that I'll be your pain's recipient,

Who knows by what depth we really feel,
Or who has the capacity to know it's for real,
We each ache and want to be fulfilled,
We each do want a comfort to feel…

In Defence Of The Context

Some take many my content or comment,
In on a wrongful context,
Words, twisted, bent, flexed,
Doomed to bleed in contempt,

And it's barely ever been complex,
That many have been perplexed,
It's natural – it's friggin' reflex,
And we re-contemplate events,

Oh, well I'm sorry for being such an offense,
No – it was nothing I ever friggin' meant,
At least 'til it was time to take what extent,
And at the end – it's times we're gonna regret,

It has to me, been quite complex,
To speak and not be taken out of context,
Words twisted, flexed, but do I expect –
We're all doomed to bleed in contempt,

I'm sorry I've caused what resent,
Shedding off similar disrespects,
I do know better just, haven't shown it yet –
But I will sometime soon – I do have that intent,

I'm sure I have a lot to make for amends,
And I may never truly develop many friends,
But we know we can be prepared for it if it happens again,
I'll wear my responsibility – I know I'm not exempt…

Gotta Get My Mind Write

I do sincerely most love to write,
Love doing it all through the night,
Love to do good with it – be good at it,
To be crazed after at – or mad at it,

I do like to read though often don't,
I let a magic work some most won't,
Get a feel for something sinking deep,
With tunes, weed, and a pen and paper by me,

Exercise my imagination as often as I can,
Express my emotion and it does get out of hand,
All the while try tone but write it down,
Anything from the misery and agitation but then to be a clown,

Materials often different but imaginative in ways –
I'm trying just to note it as well as I have to behave,
Remiss through circumstances, behaved poorly,
No good management of control, I've acted sorely,

It's occurred to me I must have to be a loser at times,
Just because it builds and I purge when I "lose it" at times,
So it's often best for me to zombie and zone out,
With music and marijuana and by writing it down,

I don't want to explode and always be the fool,
I don't believe any of this is really that fuckin' cool,
It's just the way I choose to get by when I have to vent,
To stave an overreaction and the regret of losing respect,

I write all manners of various things,
For whichever way my moods swing,

My minds not often in the right place,
Hadn't realised 'til late – I'd gone and disgraced,

I must have to be out of my goddamn mind,
I'm medicated but medicate and write to unwind,
And I can't say if any of it will really pay –
But this, this is just my way…

And Such Is My Nature

I am normally kind, polite, respectful,
Mindful – I pick up on the clues,
I never like to have a need
To let my rippling rage loose,

I like to be the nice guy,
Lend a hand and be the help,
But I do have a nasty, vicious side,
I am capable of inciting Hell,

I like to be happy, satisfied, content,
And get others all feeling as great,
I only desire respect all round –
Never suppress nor vent what hate,

I'm equally bad as I am good,
I do disbelieve when people are in awe,
I misinterpret like any would,
Confrontations, again leaving us raw,

I have my truths to face,
Much as anybody else,
Crave the trust, the faith,
And never just keep it all to myself,

Acceptance, tolerance, kind courtesies,
All round, most or best I can of me,
Like for like or risk hypocrisy,
Dare the courage, be worthy, or be free,

I am equally bad as I am good,
Such is my nature, as many would...

Concurrent Swing Motion

Maniacal you – tyrannical me,
We make quite the team,
Hysterical you – satannicle me,
A madness never foreseen,

Thundering, plundering vicious disaster,
Spiralling cycling, pernicious fluster,

Maniacal me – tyrannical you,
The madness to ensue,
Hysterical me – satannicle you –
The team never previewed,

Thundering, blundering vicious disaster,
Spiralling, cycling, pernicious fluster,

We're chaos in arms,
A psyche-up in the calm,
Brother's, double the charm,
Chaos, chaos in arms,

Maniacal you – tyrannical me,
Brothers in arms, chaos reign,
Hysterical me – satannicle me,
The madness never foreseen,

Maniacal me – tyrannical you,
The madness that ensues,
Hysterical me – satannicle you,
The team never previewed,

Just a fraction of the friction minus the existence –
Side aside stands a better consistence re-irresistance…

Adrenegade

I'm a dude to come and go,
I'm lewd but put on a show,
Tell you nothin' you don't already know,
We'll get red hot that we'll glow,

I'm an adrenegade,
A madman running hype,
I'm an adrenegade,
Quite the excitable type,

I'm the guy with an adrenalin boost,
A renegade that cuts it loose,
Do what I want – do what I choose,
I do exactly what gets us amused,

I'm an adrenegade,
A madman running hype,
I'm an adrenegade,
Quite the excitable type,

I like to think an idea is generally neutral,
And all feelings must be neutral,
But it's these dealings just as usual,
Makes me want it more delusional,

Adrenegade,
When you need the hype,
Adrenegade.
A madman running hype,
Adrenegade,
Quite the excitable type,
Adrenegade,
Yes, *quite* the excitable type…

419

Bad, Bad, Mad Man

Thrill chasing death with – defying all odds,
The going better get gone or else be getting got,

He speaks a lingo not too many understand,
Bad, bad, mad, mad, man,
His idea of fun is a Hell out of hand,
Bad, bad, mad, mad man,
Favours the flavours of tastes taboo, banned,
Bad, bad, mad man,
Thunderously ravages, tremoring the land,
Bad, bad, mad man,

No depths are ever too low nor fury too fierce,
None deserved of mercy to show but fear to adhere,

Reaping, raking, razing victims, bury beneath sand,
Bad, bad, mad, mad man,
Any standing ground is poorly undermanned,
Bad, bad, mad, mad man,
A malevolent maelstrom of mass insidious shadowy span,
Bad, bad, mad man,
A hyper psycho-chaotic-blast-wave no one withstands,
Bad, bad, bad, mad man,
Man;
Thrill chasing death wish defying all odds,
The going better get gone or else be getting got,
No depths ever too low – nor fury too fierce,
None deserved of mercy to show but fear to adhere,

He's a very bad, bad, bad, mad man,
Man,

Where Does It Stop?

I am extremely aware I am extreme,
Blue and green should never be seen,
I openly express by inappropriate means,
Soon have others out venting steam,

I do seem to make it difficult on myself,
A mindless vulgarite heathen only to repel,
You'd think someone so smart would only do well,
But in truth I'm a living breathing Hell,

I do often forget myself and colours do surely show,
Facades of dark humour, defences none have prior known,
A stigma already cold and as hard as stone,
A sickening feeling, I can't break the chains alone,

All the while still so very much on my own,
Repeating deconstructive mistakes, destruction prone,
Never quite achieving – still reaching out of zone,
Somehow still damaging, reputations blown,

I have hoped for more, fought for less,
Repaired and restored only to recede and regress,
The more I obsess to profess it's not impious,
The lesser they're impressed, I just sense detest,

Maybe this war isn't mine to fight,
More second guessing and I lose sight,
Back to where I began requiring respite,
And arms wrapped around me tight…

Intensive Measures

A king hit is only fitting for a king,
Can only do wonders – to really make him think,
He talks big but can he sing?
He thinks he wins but boy will it sting,

How hard is it to get the point across?
He's a loser – he's only ever lost,
He doesn't give a shit and it's his cost,
There were lines and they were trod,

He's a big boy – I'm sure he can take it well,
So what if I hit him and he fuckin swells?
He rebels, the stories he tells,
I feel all the more stupid – minds a numbed gel,

When he learns it's gonna hit him hard,
And he won't be so prepared, lowering his guard,
I'm going toe to toe - the full yard,
He's not that fuckin' smart he's another retard,

I'm gonna break this cunt and show him what for,
He's done his damage but not anymore,
He's getting a beating like never before,
He's mine – and I'm gonna settle the score,

Where the fuck does he get off?
Filling our heads with all this rot?
He's so desperately trying to be something he's not,
Hard? Hardly – the cunt is fuckin' soft…

Hyper Activity

Sometimes I feel the chemicals –
Of smoking isn't so bad,
Not when it has soothed me from –
A hyperactivity sending me mad,

It wouldn't take me long to get so fit,
Not with how quick I can metabolize,
With insane levels of energy –
Coursing within, inside,

It could be due to diet or exercise,
Often or if I do,
But it's these chemicals helping,
Keep my mind better than I used to –

But if I never smoked – I could be lean,
Could be fit,
If I kept to it,
Kept at it,

I'm a motor-mouth, can speak like I'm on speed,
When of course I'm normally smoke clean,
It's that hyper activity gets in the way,
A mindless infrequent disconcentration in ways,

It's driven others as mad as it has me,
A hyper activity like ADHD,
Or like someone on speed,
But that's never gonna be me...

For Hell And Havoc

Hear me now it's highly important,
You best be careful what you say, be cautious,
People loom and lurk whom are vicious marauders,
They'll plot and plan to exploit and extort us,

They'll use whatever they can against us,
And all the while get close and try befriend us,
Just reminisce where our past had test us,
Remember when it had tried to prevent us,

Barricade with all obstacles of conjecture,
When and if you know it'll surely protect you,
Count the blessing if only grazed by a lecture,
Allow for it – you can't let it upset you,

Some folk are gonna be sharp and mighty quick too,
Quick with a wit you won't know what hit you,
You must be prepared – to know what to do,
And see for what it is to manage and get through,

You'll always have to be that one step ahead,
And expect the absolute worst you can get,
Devise thoroughly and have no regret,
Be as creative as you've had to be yet,

You will have to be careful with what you say,
It's a cunning linguists power play,
Many are going to want to have it their way,
And make complicated twists on words to betray,

Prepare for all manners of perverse tactics,
Prepare, for it can and may become quite erratic,
It may take all efforts manic,
But be open for all Hell and havoc,

New Low

They're not showing any better,
To not let me live it down,
New low,

Facing a repeat of lessons learnt,
Been there and done that, again?
New low,

Who's right is it to say they had the right,
To rip back out the past,
New low,

To blind me with a rage I'd once –
Finally thought I was free of,
New low,

Hide behind my fuck ups, I'm main focus,
That you never get to deal yours,
New low,

Too busy payin attention to the wrong,
To want to start makin' it right,
New low,

You need a martyr and you want it cheap,
All the time I matter's no need for responsibility,
'cause there's always gonna be times you need me,
Times you poison to drain and feed,

New low,
New low,
New low,
New low….

Not All That Bad

Not everyone's gonna like me,
I guess I can be okay with that,
Criticism to spite on me,
Not all of it is bad,

It's the degree of the importance I place,
That keeps my emotion in good face,
I can observe from an outer space,
And manage to maintain a grace,

Not everyone's input is kind,
But I think I will be fine with that,
I'll keep a rational mind,
'cause I know it's not all that bad,

It's how much of the emphasis I take to heart,
And doesn't ever even have to be that hard,
Just keeping to the most significant parts,
All the disregard and ill will, to be discard,

I can take something harsh,
And let it painlessly pass,
I have been crushed in the past,
But as I've grown it hasn't last,

It wasn't ever easy to get to this stage,
I've had to outgrow misery and bouts of rage,
I am glad I have so that I can engage,
With countless others freed of the cage,

Distraction

I'm stuck for shit to write,
It isn't right – normally got ideas jammed in tight,
I try to mull things over in my mind,
But tragedy strikes when distracted from my sight,

I've normally got a million things to say,
But I just don't seem to be feelin' it today,
So many things – so many ways,
A piling stress to send me grey,

I know I've got the potential to really touch on tough topics,
Making bigger deals of things normally microscopic,
The lack of inspiration drives me stroppy,
Lashing out in irritation – rifting waves choppy,

At time's another's impatience has been to blame,
That I'd lost train of thought racking through my brains,
Searching for a something I can write to reign,
Their, impatience jumping at me, leaves me to disdain,

I could've had it good that moment it happens,
'til I lose the point, the sequence I had fathomed,
Gripped again my annoyance that I had been distracted,
Cursing the pleasure of others my presence attracted,

And I'm never certain I'll ever again recall,
Of that one moment I was almost on the ball,
Angered that my flow was broken or forestalled,
And expected to let it go, leave it ignored,

Damn these distractions…

Extensifying Thought...

I can say one thing a way,
And I could be speaking of more,
Saying it a particular way,
Leaving it open to be broad,

I choose my words carefully,
It sounds evil I know,
Interpreting carefully,
Wary which way it goes,

I never want it taken out of context,
There's so many more that think it's a contest,
Bending 'round the truth as though it's convex,
Lies weaving and melding with more lies – it gets complex,

But I'll choose my words carefully,
Though I know it sounds evil,
Interpreting always carefully –
I am aware of how it sounds,

It is a gift – this, being able to speak,
That I am certainly capable of finding a way,
Broadly spoke – for imagination to lead,
To interpret somehow open, new path – new way,

I have just never wanted it taken out of context,
When so many others may think it's a fuckin' contest,
Bending 'round the truth as though it's convex,
Lies all interweaving – it will gather more complex,

I might say it in a variety of ways but at most broad –
Just for the simple sake there could always be more,

Find The Light

I'll take on the beaten-up path,
Ravage on through the dark,
The rugged, roughened life,
But count I'll find the light,

Hacking through the beaten-up path,
A rugged, roughened life,
But I know I'll find the light,

Life never comes with instructions,
And each instructor seethes destruction,
Of a kind to their lone but all the same,
And there's no easy way to abstain,

To get through seeing the bias,
Have to accept it – just never like it –
To the end passed all the liars,
To the point you can eventually deny it,

Takes some time to get there,
All the while ripping at your hair,
To glare back to their freezing stares,
And know their purgatory has room spare,

Hacking ripping at the beaten-up path,
To ravage onward through the dark,
The ragged, rugged, roughened life,
But I know I'll soon find the light,

Future Passed Apparitions

I just spoke to another apparition,
The one I know of myself – I,
Projected from my future to the –
Then moment now is passed,

I told me, this ain't gonna last,
Older version of me told me,
It'll get better, this peril won't last,
It will be like we did in the past,

It's just me helping myself,
And all by myself,
Projecting my image through time,
To assure me of the tests of this hell,

I love that I can do this for me,
Times I know I need to soothe, breathe,
Assurance one day I'm gonna be free,
I love that I can and love that I'll see,

I can't believe I'm so capable of this,
And I don't or can't just do it to myself,
I am becoming far better at this, yes,
I could do it to and for others as well,

I could reach inside their minds,
Project images – possibly scents – never tried,
I can reach and talk to them in their minds,
Successful after many a try,

Some kind of telepathic ability –
Somehow defying strange odds,

Some psychic, telepathic phenomenon,
Somehow defying the barriers of odds,

I have many gifts but this I favour,
Control my emotion enough, I could be a saviour...

Hyperactive Imagination

I'm sure a lot of other people think,
Of the most inappropriate things,
At times where times inappropriate,
Only mine…are projected out over it,

A lot of people have the fortuity –
Of keeping shit to themselves,
More often than not when it's me that gets the thought,
I cannot keep it to myself,

And I've had images flash through my mind,
Just insidious, paranoid, strangely entertaining,
Losing a control – and projecting it from my mind,
Leading to situations far lesser entertaining,

I have a hyper active imagination in the way –
It's difficult for me or many others,
To continue on our ways,
When my imagination goes nuts,

Be it from a threat or humiliation,
I often try to think of it in a funny way,
End up blowin' it out of proportion,
Just taking it far out away,

This thing my head does could make me rich,
It's definitely makin' me want to laugh when I want to bitch,
Probably makin' others laugh brining on a stitch,
Or could even repulse them that they flinch por twitch,

In-You-End-O

Well, I still sow honesty with deceit,
My odyssey's still incomplete,
Never bother's me – not the defeat,
Not when the truth of the deceit is seen,

I'm still so good at being bad,
Times are the best I've ever had,
I'm roughin' it and I'm glad,
Just come out sweeter, goin' in sad,

Thing's not sounding like they should,
Play with words you bet I would,
I'm great but I'll soon have it good,
Doin' better if ever any could,

But just wait for the crescendo –
Plays with all sorts of inneuendo,
Yeah wait for the crescendo –
Cause it's going in-you-end-o

I am a lot of things I can tell you I'm not
And I'm certain you might say I've lost the plot,
It's not necessary – how can it not?
But you just can't see what I've got –

Just wait, wait for the crescendo –
My plays in all forms of inneuendo,
Yeah wait, wait for the crescendo –
Cause it's goin in-you-end-o

Ineuendo's
In-You-End-O

justI.C.E. (In Case Everyone)

As an understanding is reached,
Keys acknowledged, powers proceed,
It's testaments – maybe self-preached,
Responsibilities assumed, irrationale obsolete,

You're given by the lengths you can show,
Your sound knowledge in ways to know,
Nurturing nascence, compassion to bestow,
To stand behind, raise, uplift from below,

Powers are misused if when ego reigns in spite,
Responsibilities taken may never be cursed light,
Whereupon chances to redeem may be denied,
If you'd known better – and shown when and how right,

Powers are given to those who can have acknowledged,
Those who, 'hath understanding' and truly follow it,
Ask and receive but give and do in return and know it,
Responsibilities taken, but lengths achieved must be shown of it,

By force of spiritual nature be satisfied,
If by all honour you equally gratify,
And may you ever be modest about your pride,
Winds will carry fortunes and justify,

Don't think there aren't eyes out keeping sight,
To make certain all befalls it's nature is right,
Time – place – situation, coincidence? Hold tight –
Just in case everyone, could be, it's the lords might,

Knowing Better But Doing Worse

I'm disgusted people dare to try fuck my reputation,
That was my job for me to myself –
Well – so long as they do it good and expect it for them,
Then I won't have to worry about opening up Hell,

I'm all for it if they can handle it well themselves,
Humiliation – fuck knows we need less hypocrites,
They can never see what they're doing themselves,
All those sweeping lows, that give us all the shits,

See it's the fact they've chose to retaliate,
That they're not showing they're any better,
But I can show you if you want – I'll demonstrate,
What it takes to show strength and show better,

I wonder if you think you've out done your worst,
And I wonder whether you had felt its worth,
Because so much more could've been exert,
And none of what you did fuckin' hurt,

In fact it made me laugh, and laugh hard,
I couldn't ever even know if you gave it full heart,
'cause it didn't feel to me like it was enough,
You never cared so why should I give a stuff,

I'm embarrassed that we were both embarrassed,
Fuck I thought I did bad enough as it was,
I am capable of worse but why bother harass,
Reviving all died in what we lost,

The fact you tried means it's not over,
But I just don't think you deserve the closure…

Working On Spite

I look around and often trance to wonder,
I silence, at times, when I could thunder,
Intelligence, subtle signs, through blunders,
Silence at times avoiding larger disasters,

I've witnessed people rage where they have no control,
And these people have raged like they've got no soul,
Sharp eyes, sharp ears, I'm vigil – on patrol,
Careful, ever cautious I don't dig myself a hole,

We seem to like to make and take an equal worth,
For inconvenience and exhaustion spent for what work,
Give and take, and spite despite what is deserved,
Karma comes and strikes us twice, for the spite exert,

You might have already had hard luck, but just you try to contain it,
That attitude that don't give a fuck, yeah, it's contagious,
It's insane that one small thing can be this outrageous,
But there are various levels and degrees and different stages,

I can't expect it's easy when they haven't their whole life,
I'm certain there are some believe consideration's a waste of time,
It may very well be, but can save you of the binds,
Calm in mind, to think in time, the aftermath of spite,

I often look around and often trance to wonder,
I silence at the times I feel I could thunder,
Intelligence, when there's no signs, other side the blunder,
Silence at times to avoid much larger disasters,

And then, of course, if you can't say anything nice,
Silence, and say fuck all.

Toxic

Talk shit cunt, you talk shit,
Toxic cunt, you're toxic,
It's bullshit cunt – you're bullshit,
Oh boy cunt – you're fuckin' toxic,

I can never handle shit like you,
Not without beating you blue,
It's only ever the only thing to do –
Beat the shit through cunts like you,

Talk shit cunt, you talk shit,
Toxic cunt, you're toxic,
It's all bullshit cunt – you're bullshit,
You talk shit cunt – you're fuckin' toxic,

People like you make me lose my head,
And people like you end up dead,
They make their bed and they do beg,
And before too long they come to an end,

People like you waste too much of my time,
You trespass, toe and cross the line,
Makes me just lose my mind,
And you're buried long left behind,

So go ahead and talk shit cunt – talk your shit,
You're toxic cunt, you're toxic,
This is fuckin' bullshit cunt – you're bullshit,
Fuck me you're fuckin' toxic,

Toxic!

Taste The Blood

I'm under preparation for a first,
And I almost have the thirst,
True beast about to be birthed,
Prepare to witness the worst,

Aggression torqueing up,
Winding up, firing up,
Somebody's about to get crushed,
To sediments small as dust,

Bone shattering blows,
Cut lips – broken nose,
Fractured cheek bones,
Spitting out teeth in a groan,

Pummelled fucking bloody,
My names gonna get muddy,
Pummelled fucking bloody –
Yes, my name will be muddy,

I'll taste the blood and I'll want more,
A raging inferno of a glowing core,
Whipping up – lashing out a devastating score,
But I'll taste the blood and I'll want more,

Aggression torqueing up,
Winding up – firing up,
Someone's getting crushed,
To sediments small as dust,

Bone shattering blows,
Cut lips – broken nose,

Fractured cheek bones,
Spitting out teeth in a groan,

I'll taste blood and I know I'll want more,
First blood – first taste – I'll want more…

Telepathic Pain

Today's date is the twenty-third of the ninth, twenty-eighteen,
And I felt I had to record something that sounded to me crazy,
Things even more have begun happening to me, strangely,
I don't know whether it's an evolution of sorts – shit, might be maybe,

Thing's have started happening that've made me think,
That more of my brains capacity has seemed to link,
It's much more than a madness, and I feel I'm on the brink,
Dumbfounded, in disbelief – I can almost only just blink,

But suppose there's a somebody driving me insane,
All of a sudden, I am able to force on them a pain,
I hear for the voice – and wait to hear my name –
Then send it on through – a surge on the scourge –
And I fucking reign,

I was beginning to get really quite sick,
Of having to put up with the constant bullshit,
Something in my brain must've snapped and evolved quick,
Mastering a defence of an offence against the shit,

I never hear it end and it drives me fucking nuts,
But suddenly I can hurt them from a distance –
and they're like what the fuck?
I really just wanted the peace of them to just keep their mouths shut,
I wanted the peace – and then, a change of my luck,

So now I really don't have to suffer them anymore,
Not so hopeless or helpless unlike before,
They can keep calling me a loser, but I know they're fucking sore,
It's all they've fucking got but they still hope to win the war,

But I'd really just about had enough of being sick –
Of always having to take their rotten bullshit,
Must've unlocked my evolution quick,
But now I've got some fuckin' arse to fuckin' kick…

The Keeping From

Always hated feeling like I'm being lied to,
Like there's more out there I'm being deprived of,
Every trick, machination, gambit I'm put through,
To throw me off trail – to quit or to stop,

Hate feeling like I'm missing out,
Like there's a something I don't know about,
And like always – they make no sound,
When I pass or am near them around,

Feel like I'm being lied to,
That there's shit out there I'll never get to do,
Kept in the dark and fed shit like a mushroom,
It's no wonder I'm never out of the gloom,

I don't know what it is, but I know I want it,
And I'll question and do anything until I've got it,
I know it's that good I'm gonna want to flaunt it,
And all the time I ain't got it – I'm haunted,

I know there's something out there and it's that fucking good,
If I had to spare a limb, I'm sure I probably would,
A prize worth the obstacle – like any of 'em should,
A prize that good I'm getting wood,

Feel like I'm being lied to,
That there's shit out there I'll never get to,
I want it that bad there's nothin' I wouldn't do,
But hurdle the every trick, or machination or gambit I'm put through,

Hatin' feelin' like I'm missing out,
Like there's a somethin' I know nothin' about,

And like always – they never make a sound,
Whenever I pass near or am around,

I hear no sound – but I'll catch it,
Sooner or later I'll find out,

Trees Please

You think I do good without weed,
But wait 'til you see me hit the trees,
I become capable of miraculous deeds,
I can do more than please,

I need this,
You need me to have this,
I'd want you to have it –
You need it,

You think you'd do good without weed,
But wait 'til you fuckin' hit the trees,
You'll become capable of miraculous deeds,
You'll do more than please,

I need this,
You need me to have this,
I'd want you to have it –
I think you need it,

I choof hooter and it makes me feel great,
Wish I had a lot more people to participate,
I get high – I fly, I elevate,
Punch cones – get stoned, alleviate,

I need this – I want this,
You fuckin' need me to have this too –
I'd really want you to have it,
I seriously reckon you need it too –

I fuckin' want it – and I know I need this,
Trust me – you need me to have this,
I'd want you to have it,
I know you need it,

You need it…

Trip Beyond

You've gotta die to really live,
Trash parts you wouldn't normally give,
Kill off every last little bit,
You've gotta die to really live,

You've gotta let go of all you know,
To trip into the unknown,
To really get so far beyond,
Let it go and leave it gone,

There's never a better time than now,
Gotta get across the line somehow,
There's no better time than now,
But now,

Think of it like you lose your virginity,
That heavenly feeling, loosely, divinity,
You'll want it all the more,
You'll want it,

It's easy once you cross the line,
You'll do it all the time,
Another barrier to break in the mind,
Do it, go, you'll be fine,

You've gotta die to really live,
Trash parts you wouldn't normally give,
Kill off every last little bit,
You've gotta die to really live,

You've gotta let go of all you know,
To trip into the unknown,

To really get so far beyond,
Let go and leave it gone –

There's never a better time than now,
Gotta get across that line somehow,
And there's no better time than now,
But now…

Sacrifice

Sacrifice? I've made heaps,
Just not always the kind that please,
Sacrifice – prices' steep,
I've sacrificed when I wanted to keep,

I've done it for the undeserved,
Done it for next to no worth,
Done it when it was never earnt,
I've done it and only hurt –

Sacrifices to hurt the finances,
Sacrifices to hurt peaceful circumstances,
Sacrificed when and where demanded,
Sacrificed and left me empty handed,

Sacrifice – yeah, I've made heaps,
Just not too many of the kind to appease,
Sacrificed – and the prices were steep,
I've sacrificed when I needed to keep.

I've done it for the under-earth,
Done it but still have to serve,
Done it all I could exert,
I've done it and only hurt,

Those sacrifices to hurt the finances,
Those sacrifices that hurt peaceful circumstances,
Sacrificed when and where demanded,
I've sacrificed, and it's left me empty handed,

Sacrifice? – yeah, I've forfeit heaps of those,
Tried to please but they've upturned their nose,

Sacrificed – price too steep to show,
I've sacrificed – when I had to keep it close,

But then there's those I regret –
Those one's I haven't got to yet,

A Death Worth Dying For

Is it weird for me to want me death to mean something?
When I wanted my life to?
Something to have to bargain with, something to bring,
When it is my time falls through,

By the strengths of my souls' grace,
Living here in this mortal, earthly space,
Touch, move others only with grace,
And make for better when I leave this place,

To want, to yearn the deepest respects and love,
But do more and do it only, here below,
I know it, I'm certain so well enough,
Hind, present and beyond where I go,

By the strengths of my souls' grace,
While living here, in this mortal, earthly space,
Try touch, move others only by grace,
And make for better before I leave this place,

To bring a love as intense as rare,
Some either haven't seen for years or never,
To bring that intense love to share,
Before a time comes that I can never,

If I ever had to deserve to die,
I'd hope it's only for the benefit of prolonging life,
Still, I do pray that I may never might,
I love – I can – and I love life,

By the strengths of my souls' grace,
While living here in this earthly mortal space,

I'll touch and move others only with a grace,
And try make it better long before I leave this place,

Some to have to had to bargain with,
A something to take to trade when I…

Dead Meat

I think I'm dead meat,
Like people want to bury me,
See 'em, hear 'em out in the streets,
I feel 'em all want to tear at me,

Come, get this succulent, juicy meat,
Tenderize me, make me easier to eat,
Roast me under a sweltering heat,
Enjoy my sweet defeat,

You're dead meat
If you try it on me,
You're dead meat,
And you're gonna bleed,

Thought I was dead meat,
Like people want to bury me,
See 'em, hear 'em, out in the streets,
I feel 'em wanna tear at me,

Well – you're dead meat,
If you try it on me,
You're dead meat,
And you're gonna bleed,

You're dead meat –
So try to come for me,
You're dead meat –
I'm prepared to bleed,

Dead meat,
Try it on me,
Dead meat,
You're gonna bleed,

Lost In A Fog

I'm sorry – I'm afraid I don't remember doing that,
I remember something just not that,
Walked a vast thick fog,
Such a vast thick fog,

Hysterical screams and laughter,
Rang out through the air,
No matter where I traipsed,
I felt something glare,

I was trapped, lost in a fog,
When during these apparent going's on,
I must've been driven by another means,
And I swear I must sleepwalk – can't be dreams
(not where I – as I am it seems),

There are times – or there have been passed,
Accounts of which I can't remember, hadn't last,
And I recall I was lost in a fog,
During which were these apparent going's on,

Hysterical screams and laughter –
Just rang out through the air,
No matter where I'd traipsed,
I felt something glare,

I am sorry – but I cannot remember doing that,
Not what you said, no, not that,
I remember something and it's foggy,
Walked a vast thick fog,
A vast thick fog...lost...

Soul In The Sound

There's something in there,
The guitar across the way,
There's something in there,
It's lookin' my way,

I can feel it in my fingers,
I can feel it when I hold her,
Feel her through the strings,
Can feel as I caress her,

There is something in there,
Like a trapped spirit or soul,
And when I feel It in there –
I lose control,

I forfeit to possession,
As music as a weapon,
I trance into possession,
Play and feel and let them,

I sense something is in there,
My guitar across the way,
I can feel it in there –
Feelin' out through my way,

I feel her in my fingers,
I feel it when I hold her,
Feel her through her strings,
Can feel as I caress her…

Mr. Warner, Mr. Halford

So I've got voices circumvent my head,
I've heard, I've listened to what they've said,
Brings a tearful bliss to my heart,
That the shit can be so dark,

I can assure it's not all that dismal,
On the contrary – I don't find it abysmal,
I'm stoked I've inspired such a like,
For such influences' comment on my life,

Love you Brian, Love you Rob,
Took the words right from my gob,
I'm no where near ready to sob,
No where near ready to stop,

The music you write awes me,
The more for me, stunts me, stalls me,
I relate, I'm unleashed – I'm free,
I cogitate – I bleed – but I'm free,

You touch me in ways I can't describe,
Too, deep I'd have to meet to confide,
Anticipations killing us – how could I lie?
But I'm not anything either of you could despise,

Contrary – you'd wanna fuck me as much as all else,
I'd let you – but then I'm only thinkin' of myself,
I'll keep it secret – you won't face that Hell,
You're good but I'll do it just as well,

The music you write awes me,
More on me, to me, stunts, and stalls me,
Just a little bit,

Music you write awes me,
More on me, stunts me, stalls me,
I relate – I'm released – I'm free,
I cogitate and I bleed but I'm free…

No Need To Be Down

No need to be down friend –
Let's go smoke a blend,
Smoke a session out to the end,
Get you feelin' all better again,

If you're hangin' for a smoke – I'll share a toke,
If you need a laugh – I'll tell a dirty joke,
If they don't know how you feel, then I'll have a grope,
If you wanna feel good – I'll get ya feelin' stoked,

No need to be so down mate,
I bet I can most certainly relate,
But let's get stoned and meditate,
Find a means of resolution and contemplate,

If you're hanging for a smoke – I'll share a toke,
If you need a laugh – I'll tell a dirty joke,
If they don't know how you feel – I'll have a grope,
If you wanna feel good – we'll just smoke some dope,

There's no need to be so down pal,
I know what it's like – it is foul,
Come and have a smoke 'til you smile – not scowl,
Let's get you happy and feeling all proud,

If you're hangin' for a smoke – I'll share a toke –
If you need a laugh – I'll tell a dirty joke,
If you're not sure how you feel, I'll have a grope,
If you wanna feel good – we'll just go smoke some dope,

Come, fire some up with me,
Let's hit the beautiful green…

Whoring Sense

Sometimes I feel I've said it before,
Only having done it before,
Again, oh my – I'm a whore,

Said it many times before,
Only different ways than before,
Yeah - I'm definitely a whore,

Though I may not be paid the way I like,
In fact, I've gotta put up a fight,
Because not too many still aren't getting it right,
And I lose all patience being polite,

I've said it many different ways before,
I've lost count – I was keeping score,
But again, oh my – I'm a whore,

Said it many times before,
Only different to ways I've said before,
Yeah – I'm definitely a whore,

Hold on tight cause here comes another fight,
I've shed my light to try to put this shit right,
I have lost my patience with being all polite,
I'm doing services, but not being paid the way I like,

I've said this shit countless times before,
No one's listening, my throat is fucking sore,
Said it various ways before,
Servicing like I'm some fucking whore,

I've said it hundred times before,
They know I know, they heard me talk,

Paying me with the pain – that they want more,
And I'm feelin' like I'm just another dirty whore,

And I know I'm going to have to go and do it again,
Whoring round, talking 'bout, common sense,

Best Not Forgotten

I do this to me on purpose,
To drag the depths up to surface,
Rifting out waves sending others nervous,
It's an unwanted but necessary service,

A painful reminder so as not to forget,
Morale, virtue, values all reset,
And sure, it may all lead to resent,
But it's better never to forget,

A power play in the back of the mind,
So as to never repeat over time,
Same old shit should've been left behind,
Yeah – it's best to keep in the back of the mind,

The what that it was and the hell that it cost,
The waste and the loss and the shit it would rot,
All it double crossed, and that that it never got,
That peaked and breached the top and never did once stop,

Broken bits and pieces kept,
The reminder so as not to forget,
The path that led to a wreck,
It's best never to forget,

The morale, virtue, values all reset,
And sure, it may all lead to resent,
But it is best never to forget,
Don't forget…

Getting Love Off (The Hook)

One thing I only ever like to do,
Is have an understanding clear,
Many ways one may do –
But I prefer to solemnly sincere –

True to the heart – no lies,
Because kind compassion will cut time,
Time it takes getting to work –
All things difficult that normally drive berserk,

I don't want to be paranoid that there're motives,
When wherever it's real,
I don't want to make others paranoid,
'cause I do know how it feels,

Point I want to make is I can love,
I know love, I can quite easy,
But there are many kinds – and,
Learning it myself wasn't easy,

Through a lesson I hard learned,
And for thought itself,
Terms taking turns,
Use love to teach love *as* well,

For a fact is we may easily mistake,
There is something deeper,
Maybe, but not where my paranoia strays,
Everyone is valuable, we're all keepers,

Love can be where you can care –
To never see another ache,
To epathise in ways that you would share –

To uplift, raise, no matter what it takes,
Take pain within, rapidly convert it,
Rake hate within, rapidly overturn it,
Push it through it – outward in throughout,
Push on through it – outward in throughout,

Go Try

Forgive me,
I didn't know what I liked,
'til I said I didn't like it,
But soon I found I liked it,
When I tried it –

Forgive me,
I didn't know I had to fight it,
'til I said I didn't want to fight it,
But soon found I'd fight it,
When I'd tried it,

Sometimes it taken a confused lie,
For me to know I'll find,
Add a little ease to mind,
To just give it a go and try,

Forgive me,
I didn't know I'd love it,
'til I'd said I didn't love it,
But then soon had to love it,
When I'd try it,

Forgive me,
Didn't know what I'd hated,
'til I said I knew what I'd hated
But soon I'd find I'd hate it,
When I'd go to try it,

It should be imperative we make our own minds,
But we can never really know unless we try…

Atlem, King Returned

I have lived before,
But this world is something more,
Nation's divided, torn,
No, It's nothin' like I've known before –

As old as the world is it is still young,
And my time again has just begun,
So many revolutions round the sun,
I have come again – yeah, I'm the one,

This world is too different to the one I once knew,
Living once again in an era with peers with no clue,
But things are going to change – it's long due,
I have, it seems, a lot of work to do,

I was a king once – the very one they needed,
But since gone, everything's receded,
Mankind has been too long defeated,
But I'm back, I'm here, I'm the king they needed,

Vanquished long ago but now I'm here,
The dawning of a new revelation is near,
I cannot be ever more sincere –
I'm real, king Atlem, I'm back I'm here,

And there are so many changes to be made,
Aeons later when the world long strayed,
Don't fear – don't misunderstand – don't be afraid,
I'm no stranger to such forsaken trades,

Yes, aeons later but I have returned,
King Atlem remembers – I have returned…

Chapter 4

Doomed, Entombed, By The Tuning Womb;

Big Doggy Dreams

I've got another young man who thinks he can be alpha,
He's starin' me down with a demeaner – I vouch it,
He's really wantin' to be top dog – that alpha,
I'm feelin' him demeaner – I hear him growlin',

"This is my territory you little runt –
And don't you go anywhere near my bitches you cunt,
If I smell you on her – it'll be you we'll hunt,
So don't go trying any of your cunning stunts,"

Sure yeah I hear ya big man,
It's just gonna be me and my hand,
I read you loud and clear – I understand,
Those are your bitches – and that is your land,

If it's too easy too be had it probably won't be the best,
I don't mind the challenge – but I'll try out all the rest,
I'm sure there's many more who could
appreciate it to who I could invest,
I'm just fuckin' glad we got this all off our fuckin' chest,

Relax big dog, little ol' me wouldn't dream,
Of filling your hot foxes up with my cream,
We both know who'd really make 'em scream,
But you've got your shit covered, better, it seems,

I'll go find me some elsewhere, another place,
And me hotter foreigner women sit on my face,
It'll be me laughing, tasting that sweet taste,
Far, far, off at another distant place,

I was just lookin', you have taste, I can see,
I'm only admiring from a distance and fantasizing it for me,

All Kinds

I'm goin out there,
Out in to the world where –
The women are fair,
And the men compare,

Kissing girls of all kinds,
All erotic and exotic kinds,
All ecstatic to straddle and grind,
All for extended periods of time,

I absolutely have to have it,
There's no denying it – I'm an addict,
Watchin' 'em shake it drives me spastic,
I'll take 'em real – I'll take 'em plastic,

I just love watching 'em tease,
Thinking they've got it over me,
Showing off all I want to see,
And revel that I beg and plead,

Yeah, I'm goin' out there,
Out there in the world where –
The women are fair,
And men compare,

Kissing girls of all kinds,
All erotic and exotic kinds,
All ecstatic to straddle and grind,
All for extended periods of time,

I absolutely just have to have it,
There's no denying I'm an addict,
Watchin' 'em shake it, drives me spastic,
I'll take 'em real, I'll take 'em plastic…

All For Lust

I am the embodiment of lust,
I'll have you come – pardon me, know,
No – I'll make you come in a mighty gush,
Rather not say but show,

To rapidly manifest the light to that place,
As I project visuals, imagining to them where I face,
Slide my tongue along a soft tender space,
And feel it tingle with the sweetest taste,

They have what I need and I could do to please,
To build up the pressure – 'til it's time to release,
To tingle, caress, gently as I tease,
Work up that excitement leaving them weak at the knees,

I don't want them to be able to walk,
So I'm careful; with which way I decide to talk,
And they're often so stunned, they smile, they gawk,
And I often wonder if they can handle it more,

I've brought them passed the edge and it was intense,
And she spoke a language I couldn't make sense.
It was so insane it made me wanna do again,
I know it sounds fake – I kid you not, it's no pretend,

I fantasise so often of all this good I might –
I always have eyes open in case it's the night,
Taking every opportunity, no hesitation, no fight,
This embodiment of lust just has to put it right,

So, in the name of lust –
I command thee to come,

Satan's Gift To Women

I was given the gift of the gab,
And a libido that just won't slack,
Intelligent, and do employ all tact,
To have any wanting woman I desire on their back,

A devilish charm that does enchant,
Empathy, sympathy, to understand,
I can soothe them with a comforting hand,
And often pleasure more than thought could demand,

Confident, calm, smooth – swift,
It's only natural a cunning linguist has a dynamite kiss,
Heed no prior bias, you'll see facades twist,
I can and may provide euphoric extremes with bliss,

I'm quite capable, quite quick to tingling the senses,
And I'm all too eager to relieve any sexual tensions,
To favour on whom most – momentarily – has my attention,
And have her bear witness, my mysteries, for testaments,

Even as good as my presence is real,
I can excite through a fantasy feel,
Leading by imagination, rousing up a thrill,
At least 'til my true presence can fulfil,

I'm confident, calm smooth – and ever so swift,
It's only natural this cunning linguist has a dynamite kiss,
Heed no prior bias, you'll get to see the facades twist,
I may very well provide you euphoric extremes with a bliss,

I have a devilish charm that does enchant,
Empathy, sympathy to understand,

I could soothe you with a comforting hand,
And possibly pleasure you more than you thought you could command,

I'll tingle the senses,
You can keep your testaments,

Provocative

Is it in the way that I –
Might lure out with my devious eyes,
Or by the playful sparky quirk –
When I smile my devious smirk,

Is it in the way that I –
Can feed your lust through your eyes,
Or but by the depths of my sultry voice –
With slips of phrases – wet them moist,

Is it by the way I can have them feel –
It's too good to be even real –
Is it by the way I can have them feel –
Hungered to be feasted on as a meal –

Is it in the way that I interpret –
How I might ever fantasize to touch them further,
A reason how I could end up murdered,
I just can't deny how I feel – I can't dessert it,

Is it in the way I can lead to imagination –
To soothe as I arouse up the fascination,
Is it possible I could allure an infatuation –
Perhaps even more so than beyond my imagination?

Could it be in the everything – what-way I say?
That excites enough, provokes a many some to play –
My intellect – my voice, how I work my choice –
Or by my actual physical stature – that attracts a wanton moist,

I'd have to admit there's never a time –
I just wouldn't not blow my mind,

Chattin' up a woman – to drop a line,
To provoke and allure and have her be mine,

But if there were a possibility it wasn't on purpose –
How, still, could I let down the waiting and not service?

Wanna Fuck Me?

Everybody wants to fuck me,
Just not all in the ways I desire,
Everybody wants to fuck me,
Not like I wanted of me prior,

Do you want to fuck me?
I'd fuck me,

I'm just so irresistible,
I beat everyone to it first,
Sex starved maniac yeah,
Appetite exceeds, I thirst,

So I fuck myself as good as any,
Like a great deal want me – there are many,
Just doin' it by myself doesn't always compare,
To what it might be like if I occasionally shared,

I know everybody wants to fuck me,
Just not all in the ways I desire,
Everybody wants to fuck me,
Just not like I wanted of me prior,

I'm just so irresistible,
I beat everyone to it first,
Sex starved maniac yeah,
The appetite exceeds, I thirst,

Do you want to fuck me?
I'd let you fuck me,
Do you wanna fuck me?
I'd fuck me…

Love To Lust At

I can be particularly good at what I do,
Especially those I favour to,
I may have many unclaimed dues,
But I do have ways I can –
Otherwise amuse,

I say, and I mean, I can harness light,
To make it feel good, make it feel all right,
Say and mean, locked to whoever who's her sight,
Rapidly feed this light, intense and bright,

To know what depths purity's mean,
Sincere but serene like never seen,
Barely believed, an unachievable dream,
Or so many would have felt it seemed,

I have a gift of indiscriminate sight,
I can see beauty – and not take long to find,
Love-lusting, I'm putting up a fight –
Against the urge to arouse with the light.

I must admit I have indeed done it before,
To rouse up sensations without being near to claw,
It's never good – absence makes wanton more,
I'm hurting myself and leaving other love-lustors sore,

I've heard women's voices – never seen their faces,
Whenever I've been out at strange places,
But these voices I hear can get my heart racin'
And I'd whip up the light to send 'em sensations,

I can be quite particularly good at what I do,
Especially to those I favour to,
And I may cross many unclaimed dues,
But there are other ways I can amuse,

She Was...

She was worshipped,
Or she should've been,
She was worshipped,
Head's up like a queen,

But she can't be getting much of it now,
Couldn't understand the why or how,
But she puts on a mood like a cow or a sow,
Yeah – I think I know why now,

It's cause she was worshipped,
She was treated like a queen,
She was worshipped,
Her life was like a dream,

It must've gotten to her head,
'cause I know ladies never speak the shit she said,
Go anywhere near her and you will dread,
If she had a gun she'd blast you full of lead,

She was worshipped,
But it seems it's in the past,
She better be worshipped,
If you want your happy life to last,

I just can't see why she isn't tickled pink,
She's got it easy but she's on the brink,
Attitudes all fucked – it stinks,
Makes a big feller like me shrink,

She was worshipped,
But she got too used to it,

She was worshipped,
But she got way too fuckin' used to it,

Head's up her arse – but the shit don't smell,
She can break a heart and she'll do it well…

Growth Groans

Don't hold me to my word in my expression of anger –
You pushed and you heard something you didn't like,
As did and I we're both bad as each other,
This, is child's play, childish, I'm seeing it this side,

I'm a mad raving lunatic when I get started,
I've been broken and I'm still broken hearted,
And I know I've been right fuckin' bastard,
I just have no tolerance for the hypocrisy, I'm smothered,

Slut guts is still trying to show me something she thinks I can't see,
And I know perfectly well it's well within all the CBT's,
I don't maintain the perfect control as so many seen,
It's just lately when I'm angry, fuck off walkabout to smoke trees,

Mirror images of each other, fuckin' how old was she?
Did she think it was so funny to 'sink as low as me',
How is that in any way any better to be,
Takin me apart, unaware I've been observing as they lead,

There were plenty flaws and faults in her I never picked,
But I'm thinkin' I should've been more like
her and been as fuckin' strict,
There was shit I thought she should've known
well enough before I ever did,
I tried to see for little signs but never did one bit,

This shit is never just going to end,
She was as lousy a partner as she was a friend,
It's made a nutter outta me and sent me round the bend,
It was all on purpose but, we must otherwise pretend,

Could it really have been so fucking hard to
believe – that I might fucking know,
The ache, so well enough so, my intelligence can show,
I'm makin' every attempt I can it's takin' for me to grow,
It's takin' me longer that I'm alone, and being thorough,

Dear Sweet Mum

My poor dear sweet mother,
Bred a warrior of a lover,
To treat warheads with a kindness to smother,
To spare a compassion like no other,

My poor dear sweet mum,
Took many a beating, not so fun,
But she would always be the one,
To make the best of her son,

Teaching me shit you barely ever see,
Consideration, respect, common decency,
Why I never knew – but what became of me,
Could just be what the world could need,

I have an uncivil tongue but can practice propriety,
I have the knowledge to be upstanding to society,
I've just never really been keen on the sobriety,
And what it takes to get to almost being a deity,

My poor dear sweet mother,
Bred a kind of warrior of a lover,
Compassion for a great many others,
And greater passion for whomever the significant other,

My poor dear sweet mum,
Did take a beating – not fun,
But she would always be the one,
To make the best of her son,

The Most Feminist Of The Men

I've spent a lot of time knowing the kinds of women to hate men,
I've seen more than enough to fucking understand,
Some men are disgusting, repulsive – nothing I am,
Inconsiderate, selfish, ignorant, arrogant – again nothing I am,

I was tortured by grown men that claimed they were,
Mum saw it, but she still raised the gentleman we prefer,
And I had to suffer so much pain and anger and hurt,
Same as my mother and any other woman like her,

I can understand men can be cunts,
I just haven't met a whole heap that aren't,
They play, they betray with all sorts of stunts,
And they question why they're being gunned down in the hunt,

I'm not so ignorant that I have paid attention,
I am a sensitive man, and like women, need affection,
And I wouldn't hesitate to offer what sort of protection,
Standards – I have them, and men often resent them,

There are things I wouldn't do, in front or to a lady,
And I have no desire nor intent to be so fucking shady,
At times I don't want to be a man – it's degrading,
Especially not the man they are, it's forever frustrating,

Tortured by the cowardice of these bullies, these weaker men,
I was always told karma will catch up – I just wanted to watch when,
Just so I knew the hell was happening to fucking them,
For the times it were me or what women suffered over again,

I can understand men can be real cunts,
And I haven't ever met a whole lot of them that aren't,
They play, they betray and pull out all sorts of stunts,
And they always question why they're being gunned down in the hunt,

The Few And The Far Between

I am feeling a little anxiety,
What she said had indeed alarmed me,
I thought I was ready but it's dis-calmed me,
Caught me off guard, yeah, disarmed me,

I normally prefer to have control in this position,
Not be some raving lunatic emptying out his ammunition,
Genuinely show some kind of matured wisdom,
Cause generally those lunatics go to prison,

A hard truth to face has certainly fucked me before,
Behaving like that lunatic just shows how sore,
Irrational, racing through for more,
Addictive personality, tasting traces of the score,

I'm attempting not to lose control this new situation,
Attempting to maintain a hold over a compelling deviation,
Handle it carefully with utmost respect and appreciation,
Handle it with a more careful consideration,

So you can probably understand my anxiety,
Alarmed me enough to pull through sobriety,
And I thought I was ready – it dis-calmed me,
Caught me off guard, yeah, it's disarmed me,

The hard truth I'm to face again that's fucked me before,
Behaving like that lunatic and showing how sore,
Irrationally racing through me for more,
This addictive personality – tasting traces of the score,

Truths are face-fucking me all right,
I'll be covered and dripping in its value soon,

When It's Why

He was more pissed he'd cared,
But what for?
He was pissed he was there,
But what for?
He was pissed he listened –
But what for?
He was pissed she didn't,
What for?

It's not like I fucking cared,
It's not like I was there,
It's not like I listened,
It's not like she didn't –

What did she want from me?
What did she want me to be?
Why wasn't it good enough?
Would it ever be enough,

He was pissed she didn't want him at all,
But what for?
He was pissed she'd just ignore,
But what for?
He was pissed I hadn't never listened,
What for?
He was pissed she didn't
What for?

It's not like I fucking cared,
It's not like I wasn't there,
It's not like I never listened,
But why should I care when she didn't?

When It Darkens

One thing in your mind, you wanna get laid,
She could be the kind and you're outplayed,
If she's tight – and you've got it made,
She's a savage and she's gonna get paid,

All slick and smooth from the start,
She's hungry, appetite for the heart,
Don't make it easier when it gets dark,
She'll tear you up, tear you apart,

All that was yours turns to hers,
Woe betide if you dessert,
Just don't mislead her unto hurt,
You could never account for what worst,

Eat you up man, manipulate, rip you open,
More misery than can contain by just smokin'
Was fun while there was all the gropin',
But it always ends with it down slopin',

All slick and smooth from the start,
She's hungry with an appetite for the heart,
It don't make it easier when it starts getting dark,
She'll tear you up, she'll tear you apart,

All that was yours goes to hers,
Woe beset if you dessert,
Just don't lead her unto hurt,
You may never account for what worst…

Crestfallen

You were once all I'd wanted,
Another soon to be forgotten,
Yeah, we had it rockin'
But then only too soon had to stop it,

Keeping a civil tongue is hard that I am young,
I'm high strung because inside I am numb,
I'm so stunned I just can't run,
Feel my heart's been wrenched and wrung,

Once upon a time I'd have given you everything,
Because once upon a time, to me, you were everything,
You'll never know what it meant for me,
But now you're nothing more than just a memory,

I saw more in you than you'd care to admit,
Still, there was something that didn't quite fit,
It wasn't 'til we split that it finally hit,
Cast into a pit, deep in the shit,

And there's nothing can be said,
To remove this weight like lead,
Internal damage has begun to spread,
Of all the kinds one can dread,

To keep a civil tongue is hard that I'm young,
I'm high strung 'cause inside I'm completely numb,
I'm too stunned, I cannot run,
I feel my heart's been wrenched and wrung,

Once upon a time I'd have given you everything,
'cause once upon a time you were everything,
You'll never know what it did mean to me,
But now you'll never be more than memory,

Dull & Boring

You must forgive me for being dull and boring,
The way I go feeling like you're ignoring,
So boring I could sleep and be snoring,
Hope dies at the end of this story,

I apologise that you don't find me exciting,
No one was ever good at advising,
Always compromising,
Never exciting,

Don't know why I can't be like you,
To excite a some with out so much to do,
To look and see everything new,
Fuck having this to go through,

I have to admit I die a little inside,
Never being the centre of someone's pride,
Backstabbed – and I know they lie,
I just wished I'd caught your eye,

Wished I could've meant something,
Not ever to mean nothing,
I'm – I – just feel gutted,
You were somethin' to me,

You must forgive me for being so boring,
It's the way I go when everybody's ignoring,
So boring I could sleep and be snoring,
And hope dies at the end of this story,

Wished I could've meant something,
Not ever to mean nothing,
I'm – I – just feel gutted,
You were somethin' to me,

No Zest

Her lack of excitement disturbs me,
I thought she was worthy, I'm hurting,
I had a bulge in my pants, pressure exerting,
But she's pulled every trick she can deterring,

Her lack of excitement disturbs me,
She's not taking to any of my flirting,
It's not like I've been fucking dirty,
No enthusiasm, it's makin' me thirsty,

Her lack of excitement disturbs me,
No wonder I feel like disturbing,
Can't see any attention she gets she's deserving,
I don't even know why I bother concerning,

Her lack of excitement disturbs me,
There's almost nothing there – it's irking,
Nothing I could try would end up working,
An unpleasureable woman most absurdly,

Her lack of excitement disturbs me,
Just makes me want to be more assertive,
And give her a decent serving,
Make her regret all this diverting,

How should it be that when I put out –
All my working up, flirty smut aint workin' now,
It's normally something of which I am proud,
But her, she, is certainly giving me doubts,

It's a deeply disturbing lack of excitement,
That I just haven't fit the requirement,
I didn't think there was anything wrong with the size of it,
I'll divide of it, and provide it elsewhere despite it,

Mixed Signs

I'm wanting you – I'm needing you,
Your mixed signs aren't seeing me to,
Or are you just here to fuck me over?
I want it, you know I love you –

I'll rise only to fall emotionally shattered,
My rapid mood changes – you've witnessed batter,
But you'd act as though it doesn't matter,

Are you here to love me?
Or are you here to fuck me over –
I've never been this confused more,

I'm here I wanted to love you,
But you're makin' me want to fuck you over,
If you're confused – I'd understand why more –

I need it – give it – I want more,

I left my heart in your hot little hands,
While my mind wonders, disbands,
Don't know what to be – which kind of man,
Your eyes have cruel demands,

Are you here to fuck me over – love me,
You make me want to fuck you over – love you too,
Just give it – I want more,

I rise to fall only emotionally shattered,
You know my rapid mood changes batter,
And you still act as though it don't matter,
And I'm still always left only wanting more,

I'm wanting you, needing you,
Just… your mixed signs aren't helping me to,

Alone In The Relationship

Took me lengths of time sifting through her fake,
Trying to piece together any slight sense I could make,
Any closer I ever got was when she'd pull away,
And strike up an offensive defence and have me break,

Fighting all through her hypocrisy,
Her spite taking beatings out on me,
And as low as all that has been,
It was the most she could ever mean,

She kept more to herself than I ever knew,
Never opened once to let me through,
Unfaithful when fidelity was all I would do,
She'd lie and hide, when all I ever gave was true,

I was all alone in that relationship with her,
When she had so many men lay beside her,
It's almost like she only ever wanted me to hurt,
But I never once haven't, and it was always deeper, worse,

Fighting out her contradictions and hypocrisy,
The toll her spiteful beatings has had on me,
And as low as all that has been,
It was the most she could ever mean,

She wasn't ever mindful enough to spare deeper consideration,
It's the kind of girl you don't want full time, but do have visitation,
Holy fuck the hell I faced with her through her menstruation,
Any chance I ever got to escape was truly a salvation,
Away from the humiliation,

She only ever got more from me than she gave,
And she bitched it's why I didn't get when I "misbehaved",

Another fucking guilt trip where she's mastered me the slave,
Goes and says it's my fault is why she betrayed,

And as fucking low and scummy as all that has been,
It was only ever the most she could ever mean,

Time With Her

Time with her wasn't wasted,
She taught a great many things,
She, fearing I wasn't paying attention,
She, thinking I was never listening,

As she would groom my weapon,
With love, kind care and compassion,
And subliminal hints hard at the time to fathom,

I guess I finally got it and understood,
Shit, fuck, I guess Satan does know good,
Why impress others that just never would,
Never necessarily do better if they could,

But she, she groomed my weapon,
And she would groom my weapon,
With all the kind love, care and compassion,
With, of course, subliminal hints I couldn't quite fathom,

But can now,

I guess I finally got it and understood,
Fuck me – shit, Satan can indeed know good,
But why impress others that just never would?
Who never necessarily do better if they could,

Shit, time with her wasn't wasted,
Yeah – she taught me a great many things,
She, fearing she never had my attention,
She, thinking, that I was never listening…

Trust Fallen To Wrong Hands

I've at times come to wonder the what if,
And changed up all the things I did,
Where what I had that I would give,
If it went elsewhere – what if?

To open to the wrong hands,
May you never raise your guard and stand,
Time's efforts spent – has perks,
But times again just prove to be worst,

Prices to pay to get that further ahead,
Having to account for the cost and the dread,
Pickin' your fights but, pickin' the lesson,
Ultimately – the progression is the true obsession,

Give for take, words, lessons exchanged,
Favour for a favour – it's the way,
Lessons tamed and they have changed,
Give for take – it's the way,

Still, at times, I felt it was missing,
And the sharp pain through the heart – ripping,
Devolving, regressing – a psychosic mind tripping,
With the grip on reality quickly slipping,

I opened to the wrong hands and, generous, as I give,
But now I'm wondering the reception of what if?
Better the return right? Imagine if you did?
My poor judgement in people has altered how I've lived,

Trust, fallen to the wrong hands,
What if?

Trusts Betrayed

It was just way too fucked,
To have lain so much trust,
In someone I'd loved, someone I'd lust,
Givin' so much just, never getting enough,

The dirty rotten, filthy, little secrets,
Told in a trust, but guess who regrets,
Extra specially the one who most invests,
To have it abandoned, betrayed by other interests,
Insects!

I was alone, or so I thought to love her,
I was alone – cause many men were,
She pulled away, ever slightly, ever slowly, she'd dessert,
I could feel it, but it was only I to be the one that hurt,

Those dirty, rotten, filthy, little secrets,
Told, in trust, but by fuck do I regret,
Extra specially by the strengths by which I'd invest,
To have it abandoned and betrayed and left to detest,
The insects!

I often give a benefit of the doubt – a leap of faith,
An it isn't often I'm not fuckin' betrayed,
No matter if I do stay – they stray,
Broken, over, repeat 'til the grave,

It's just way too fucked to have given so much trust,
The merit they can't earn nor reciprocate enough,
Broken, betrayed by that someone that you loved,
Broken, betrayed, wasted, crushed,

Conniving

I've been accused of being conniving,
I suppose over acts they resent me devising,
Whippin' out me dick on the internet advertising,
Acts a lot of men are either jealous of or despising,

My ex could tell stories of me,
And I'm certain she always does,
A lot of stories ugly – disturbing,
She, knowing me like she does,

In a lot of what I do I feel justified,
'cause the ex who had taught me was wise,
She would accept, tolerate – but never open her eyes –
Oblivious to even more than her covert lies,

She was jealous of what I could see,
What I could do and how well it was,
She was everything – or wanted to be,
To have the win – no, not the loss,

She'll play victim and say I was so evil,
Retrieving some former relevance out from the past,
And parts passed I thought too long were concealed,
But she, knowing me – as she thinks she does,

But there were things I knew I wasn't sure she did,
I would drop clues – some kind of a hint,
What I'd learnt and taken – and equally give,
But there's just no telling someone who thinks she's lived,

Some of my own truths – hard learnt – but I'd share,
Having thought she, wise – she would be fair,

But as the going got tougher – her teeth bared,
And behind my back I could feel her glare,

I knew there was always more beneath what I saw,
I just couldn't believe she could've been so sore,

Becoming a war only with real relevance,
Wars against a varied intelligence,
No matter what anyone ever could recommend,
Make it best that you don't condescend,

With all this back and forwards,
How can any deserve their rewards,
Victims, to their own swords,
Be ready with the stitches, patches and gauze,

Who's got who lookin' where,
Who's payin' toll and is it fair?
Is there consideration – is there thought spared?
Did you know how deep you cut when you had pared?

Can it be possible that I do indeed know more –
Than I have ever seemed to show before –
That there's a chance I could leave her so sore,
That maybe it's because I've survived these games before?

There was a reason why I could never fit,
My personality – or something – was too big,
But there were things I knew that I wasn't sure she did,
But I kept trying to drop my clues and hints,

Is it wonder I knew how to play it –
When she chose to betray it,
All these new lows have us degraded,
You forbade but can't evade it,

And so I stand accused of being conniving,
Over acts I suppose they resent me devising,
Whippin' out the dick on the internet advertising,
And other acts other men are either jealous of or despising,

But in a lot of what I did I felt justified,
The wise ex taught me – she should have her pride,
She'd accept and tolerate – just not open her eyes,
Oblivious to that and her covert lies,

Connived in all things I despised,
'til I then went and connived,

Who's Playin' Who

I know you've got your games,
As do I –
I know you've got your ways,
But as do I –

I know what you think you believe,
I definitely do –
I know you think you're more than I see,
But I see through,

There's something about you that s creams "I NEED"
And I can tell you play your games for many to bleed,
It's because the moment you know they do it's when you feed,
And you become the "WINNER" feeding your need,
Overwhelmingly, indulging in a greed the same –

You're sick enough to twist it,
So sick you should've never existed,
And my furious hate and scorn ever blisters,

I have on occasion played through your games,
As do you –
I have on occasion played through your ways,
As have you –

And I know what you believe,
I definitely do –
I know you think you're more than I see,
But I've outwitted you,

That something about you that screams "I NEED"
And I know some poor fuck like a lesser me will bleed...

A Diamond Back To The Rough

My last great love was a one of a kind,
My diamond was a knockout, she blew my mind,
And there would soon arise a defining time,
My love would decide that we divide,

There were particular characteristics I had displayed,
I'm sure some might say I may have misbehaved,
Reacting in ways I can say brought shame,
Causing my love heartache, and a grave situation of pain,

There hasn't been a day gone by since she left,
That I haven't had thoughts of her still in my head,
I miss her like crazy – my heart heavy as lead,
But here I am and paying the price, this is what I get,

She will have my heart, be my light in the dark,
I had covertly vowed if we'd cross paths, I'd play a better part,
Next time, next place, maybe a fresh brand-new start,
Be the man she deserves and rekindle the spark,

Losing my love was a wake-up call the likes I'd never had before,
And on the scale this loss was to me – it was difficult to ignore,
It ripped me right open and exposed my vulnerable core,
Beaten, defeated, considerably weakened, brazened red-raw…

A Never-Got-To-Be

I know me better than anybody else can,
I know I could've always been the right man,
I know I've never been given much of a chance,
Still never meant I shouldn't ever have a plan,

If any had the patience and time for me,
They'd have seen all I could've been,
They just never allowed themselves to see,
Never spared the time to free,

I know I would've been great at whatever I do,
Just needed a someone I could've shared it to,
That someone that cared to never put me through,
What hell they knew and more they had no clue,

I can set it all up and put it all out,
All while their receptions just tear me down,
Losing faith just to gain doubts,
And there's no fun to be had with no one around,

If any had the patience and time enough for me,
They'd see beyond all I have ever been,
They just never want to allow themselves to see,
Never take a chance and never break free,

I know the things I can do would surely impress,
It's just at this time I'm not inspired, and I just make detest,
None are really trying – no providing – no zest,
And I just build on the hate and pain burning in my chest,

No easy way of just letting it all go,
And I can understand why I'm not easy to want to know,

It just sucks I see that it shows,
Every time they deprive and turn up their nose,

If any ever had the patience and time for me,
They'd have seen all I never got to be,

No Maybe Ladies

It can make you feel like shit,
To want someone who don't want you one bit,
Makes you feel like absolute shit,
Makes you want to get over it quick,

So you get hammered, get smashed,
Go mingle with the ladies,
You get hammered – get smashed
And stop lingering for maybe's,

It's makin' me feel like absolute shit,
Puttin' out for a woman who won't take the hint,
It's makin' me feel like absolute shit,
And I want to get over it quick,

So I go to get fucked off my face,
Maybe go mingle with the ladies,
Fucked off my face – trash my grace,
Instead of lingering for maybe's,

Hate feeling all like this absolute shit,
Waiting for to see what's wrong with it,
She can't have me – not one little bit,
And I'm getting' over it quick,

I'm gonna go get absolutely wasted,
Try pick up some ladies,
Get fucked and absolutely trashed wasted,
And not waste on any more maybe's,

I wanna get some ladies,
No more fuckin' maybe's,
I want a sure fuckin' thing lady,
No more fuckin' maybe's,

Carcass

You think I give a good fuck that you avoid me?
It's a shame you don't see you're as equally disappointing,
I could have been all the closure you could need,
But you were too far deep in your pride to think to ask me,

I guess now it's clear to both our belittled worth,
Saving pain and anguish enduring, witnessing the worst,
Saving an intense abhorrence, dug up and unearthed,
And wildly rising, spiralling up a voracious thirst,

All my what if's evolved into fuck that's,
And I got rid of all minute setbacks,
No point dragging behind you the carcass,
The shell of which I might once have fussed at,

I suppose I guess I did once spare a thought,
That that just perhaps there might have been more,
Than the reciprocated accord of applause – we both whores,
But thought into a far deeper degree than ever any sought,

I think I wanted to try to like you more than I ever could,
Try as I might it may never even have gotten that good,
I've already wasted chances on things I knew never would,
Should've happened a lot sooner – me, not thinking with my wood,

But everybody's gotta do what's best for them,
I don't think I'm crazy enough anymore to be a friend,
Because the both of us have paths and
histories neither can comprehend,
But I do now know you and I are a dead end,

You're a carcass, sorry I'm a bastard,
You're a carcass – and I am getting passed it,
Carcass…

A Regretful But Necessary Goodbye

Please don't be upset, we'll meet again,
Smile for me sweetness, this isn't the end,
I really must leave – it's for the best,
I loved you all the time, please never forget,

People want me – it's why I leave,
I won't be back 'til all is calm and ceased,
It's the only way I know I can believe,
You'll be safe and left in peace,

Please know that I love you,
Cry not sweetness, I'll be back for you,
You're everything to me, swear I'll see you soon,
I promise – I could never lie to you,

I'll come back to be with you again,
But once I know the danger's come to an end,

People want me it's why I must leave,
I won't return 'til all is calm and ceased,
It's the only way I know I'll believe,
You'll be safe and left in peace,

This is the way it has to be for now,
They won't stop lookin' for me 'til I'm found,
They're gonna want to put me in the ground,
It's kind of why I'm leaving town,

I have to split and get gone,
But I need you to carry on,

I'm sorry my sweetness I have done wrong,
And know I'm gonna be doing more before too long,

I'll come back and I'll be with you again,
But only after I know the danger has come to an end...

Parted Ways

She was everything I had loved and adored,
Absolutely everything and more,
A love unlike any I had known before,
A love I grieve for, left me raw,

I can't regret the time,
Not when she was mine,
A real score – a real find,
I almost lost my mind,

Letting her go was no walk in the park,
For having loved so deeply scarred the heart,
She had released me from a darker counter-part,
But despite the ache I had to be smart, and act grown up,

To bite down hard on my tongue in high-tensile times,
Imploding in some and corroding away my pride,
Hide the weaknesses – show no signs,
Mental meltdown – fried the mind,

Inside I'd rage, ruptured, break,
And wonder how much more I could take,
Remain as considerate as she was for my sake,
Neglect regressing back through a negativity and hate,

I don't regret the time,
Not when she was once mine,
A real score – a true find,
She had opened up my mind,

She was my hope, my drive but we have since parted ways,
And I am lost to meander in an aimless stray...

Fated For None

One thing I guess I want,
That I may never have,
A life maybe everyone wants,
Same shit I'm missing – one might be sad,

Affections of a loving, kind, caring woman,
I couldn't blame if any ever wouldn't,
I'm not in any way easy a woman could've,
There's a lot of signs of me to warn 'em,

I'm rough, I'm coarse, dirty, inappropriate,
It's not often I'm not showing it,
A rollercoaster of attitude and emotion,
A little too much more than is being capable of being devoted,

I want to be close to someone,
To feel comfort to say I have my one,
There is nothing I wouldn't have done,
But perhaps I'm just fated for none,

I miss the sweet affection of the fairer sex,
I can never know when I may ever next,
It's sad, distressing – I have been upset,
But would be ever gracious if I had another chance to yet,

Sweet affections, warmth of the love,
Weak for attentions – hot for lusts…

I'm just rough, coarse, dirty and inappropriate,
And it aint often I'm not showing it,
Me, a rollercoaster of attitude and emotion,
Maybe too much more than is so easy of being devoted,

Miss being close to someone,
But perhaps I'm just fated for none…

Work In Progress

Wish I could just comply,
And never do the things that make you cry,
Feelin' like all this is a trial,
I win when I make you smile,

I just wish to give you all you need,
Sign the contract, declare my creed,
Never take more than I can ever give,
Be tender, forever sensitive,

The moment I just feel ashamed,
I definitely feel the heat of the flames,
Behaving in a despicable way,
Will only push you away,

Sometimes I lose control,
Forget the way you make me whole,
Forget I need you more than you'll ever know,
I do very much have a long way to go,

My love for you is immense,
My passion for you is intense,
I only ever wanted to impress,
My darling diamond, I'm still a work in progress,

I know I still have so much to learn,
It's only for you that I yearn,
Diamond goddess of my dreams,
Of such a beauty I've ever seen…

Too Sexed Up

I generally have to have a tug before I step out,
I get a kind of jiggy-bug seeing women about,
Think I'm just too sexed up to go out,
Anyone need an orgasm? Just shout –

To horny to release into society,
To horny to maintain a propriety,
Must be an addict and fear sobriety,
If god is confidence then I am a deity,

I have a dangerous amount of confidence – or no fear,
Well, after I've gone and sharpened my spear,
Worried lees then with women near –
Less sexed up after a sharpen of the spear,

Too many women, beautiful, sexy, gorgeous,
Whatever else I'm actually doing at the time is distorted,
But I have to focus 'cause I know I can't afford if –
Any of my lewd behaviour were to be reported,

I have to jerk it before I go anywhere,
'cause there's women out there that are gonna catch my stare,
Can't act like – or think with the dick – how's that fair?
I can't bear the thought to have them all glare,

Too sexed up to often go out into society,
Much too horny to maintain a propriety,
I must be an addict to it and fear sobriety,
If god was confidence – I'd be a deity,

Too many sexually alluring women,
And I get the compelling urge I wanna spear 'em,

Too many beautiful, attractive, sexy, gorgeous women,
Gotta war-tug before I go anywhere bloody near 'em,

Too sexed up, too sexed up to be out,
Gotta jack it before I go anywhere,
Aww – those women about…

Blow A Kiss

Come here babe,
Rub it in my face,
I wanna blow a kiss,

Here babe,
Need me a taste,
I'll make you explode your bliss,

Shake it for me hun,
Grind down on my tongue,
Needing me a taste o' some,
Now aren't we having fun?

I crave to savour,
I'll push to haver,
Let me blow your kiss,

I'm beginning to slaver,
Just longing to be lapping at your flavour,
You'll soon explode your bliss,

Shake it for me hun,
'til you're vibratin' for me hun,
Grind down on my tongue,
Let me have you some,

Here, come, here babe,
Rub it in my face,
I need to blow your kiss,

Here babe,
I wanna have a taste,
We'll make you explode your bliss,

Mind For The Business

Begun moulding to a mindset I might use,
When I come to go to amuse,
Rock it well – shake it loose,
Milk it – really squeeze the juice,

Adapting this mind set for my come and go,
Rockin' it well puttin' on the show,
Meetin' clients for love – getting' close, get to know,
For what works best for the ultimate crescendo's,

This, mindset where it's so indiscriminate,
For many of any kinds of women who are into it,
Women eager, willing as I to rip into it,
The dream anyone would be keen livin' it,

Mindset of maturity to see even deeper,
To enact the very fantasies driving them weaker,
A smooth, sophisticated, sultry speaker,
Be it their bottom halves the weeper,

Adapting this mindset for my come and go,
Rockin' it well when I go to put on a show,
Meetin' clients for lovin' – get close – get to know,
For whatever works best for the ultimate of crescendo's,

The mindset so demanding,
Services ever outstanding,
And no they won't be capable of standing,
Lovin' all the needing hearts needing that expansion,

For that final breath of ecstasy whence the 'max achieved –
To lie back with, embraced, 'til I'm paid to leave,

Drop That, Come For This

Don't be shy babe,
Take the chance, make the move,
Don't regret and cry babe,
What have you got to lose?

I know it seems like it takes guts,
I'm no looker but I still strut,
I just wanna bury me deep in a slut,
I want to gently kiss that tender cut,

Don't hold back babe,
You go dance, you go groove,
You'll attract babe,
What have you got to lose?

You have potential honey, you'll go far,
You'll break hearts and you'll leave scars,
Once you find your confidence, you'll be a star,
You'll find your one babe who'll never part,

Step out and don't be shy gorgeous,
Don't hide and regret and cry babe,
Don't you filter or hold back gorgeous,
You've got all you need to attract babe,

It won't take long for you to see,
Just say fuck it – let go of me –
Those chains keeping you of being free,
No, it won't take long for you to see,

You could have 'em all lined up to choose –
But now? What have you got to lose?
Nothing you can't nor won't have again...

Decisions, Decisions…

Oh wow, would you look at that,
Yeah – looks fun just not enough,
Keep walkin' she's barely worth the time,
Never know – she might not take it that far,

Seriously? You can't all be talkin' bout her?
I'm telling you – I bet she shaves her fur,
Don't know about you but I could make her pur,
Nope, fuck all you guys – it's my turn –

Don't even think about it, I can't believe you guys,
Yeah – I'm sure she'd only make you cry,
We won't get in trouble lookin' through your eyes,
We can look all we like – 'til she looks – and it's head to the sky,

Will you pussy li'l fucker's just go say hi?
Yeah, just walk on up to her and drop a line,
Ha – I dare you to tell her that arse is fine –
Fuck I'd love to have that on mine,

Okay, yeah, now that sounded gay,
So – fuckin' just say it another way,
Say you're alone and you wanna play,
If she says no then just walk away,

I'm not gonna just walk away – she's comin' with,
Tell her she ain't lived 'til she had this stiff,
I'd stimulate her clit with a mighty good lick,
Have her biting her lip gagging to wiggle in ya prick,

Come on fellers, use a little tact,
Nah fuck that – I'll give it to her flat,
But what if she just feeds it back?
Would you be glad you had?

For Whom Of Most Want...

Who could I love the most –
But maybe want who I know,
Wants to want me the most...

Anyone, everyone,
Any moment be that one,
For as false as fantasy is,
I could make it feel real to live,

I may stare sincere to the eyes,
Of may it be whom at the time,
Feed deep, pierce with an intense love,
That moment I may have a one,

To immediately assume into passion,
Any woman - any who could fathom,
Any woman who dare to imagine,
But any woman who'd care for the passion,

I would stare deep, sincere to the eyes,
Of any of who it may be at the time,
Pierce and feed deep an intense love,
Any moment I might maybe have that one,

Who could I love the most –
But maybe want who I know,
Wants to want me the most...

Hard To Get

I'm becoming more and more like an ex,
Getting harder and harder to get,
Broken hearts – eyes will be wet,
Chances – none and fuck all yet –

I need to know they're going to go the distance,
So I'll set up an obstacle of ridiculous resistance,
And when they finally get here – they'll have to beg my permission,
I'm rare, there ain't many kinds of me in existence,

I need to know they're going to make it work,
And I'll just desert if they're so childish they'll go berserk,
I just hate wasting all this good on spiteful little twerps,
I need to know they can handle all this worth,

I've begun becoming more like an ex,
Getting ever harder and harder to get,
Broken hearts – yes, eyes will be wet,
Chances are none and fuck all yet –

I need to know none of it will be a wasted effort,
I know enough I know people could think me an expert,
No, I need to know that someone's going to make an effort,
To deserve it all when I go to exert,

I know the strengths of the impact by when I give,
I need to know they can handle it, it won't buckle out short-lived,
Need to know they're able to appreciate the gift,
And if not then they can meander round in aimless drift,

As you can see I'm starting to think more like my ex,
Sex is good, but there has to be more to obsess,
Eyes will get wet – these none or fuck all chances yet –
'Cause I'm becoming just, harder and harder to get…

A Disgusting Lack Of Sex

A lack of sex,
Is hard to digest,
When you're obsessed,
And you've got a girl upset,

I don't know what I want to believe more,
The fairy tale – where excuses are poor –
But seem to matter more – or –
Harder underlying truths to face left so sore,

When I hear the vow, for better and for worse,
Makes me want to shudder and curse,
Who really knows what it's worth?
Or the one you're with deserves,

Now there are times when it's gross and disgusting,
And those are the times you're earning your trusting,
But it's how they behave at times – gets me wondering –
Is this whole thing worth it fucking lasting?

When they wince out in disgust,
And bitch that they've lost all their lust,
I wonder whether to even trust,
Still, they persuade you must,

But the lack of sex,
Can be so hard to digest,
When one is obsessed,
And you've got a girl upset,

When I hear – for sickness and in health,
I contemplate the worst possible caser scenario as hell,
And I wonder if the partner knows it so well,
They'd consider it so equally deeply themselves,

Now, I know times can get disgusting, disturbing,
But all the while it's indeed a trust you're earning,
And someone's guts are gonna end up churning,
But look at you go – you're learning,

I showed my woman my cock,
Before I went to give it a wash,
Badly – turned her off –
And that was a part of the cost,

I'm hearin' vows recite that sound something a little like –
This is for forever – this is for fucking life,
So speak up now before you're locked in to your despise,
Hurry up, quick – fuckin' make up your mind,

This, is why you should always have to know,
If you're dedicated enough to do the hard row,
Give it a proper length of time to let it all show –
'Cause maybe one day you'll be glad you did know,

When they wince in disgust,
And bitch they've lost their lust,
You begin to wonder to even trust,
If this whole fuckin' thing will last,

And they wince and they whinge at the disgust,
And bitch they've lost libido – their lust,
And you begin to wonder if you can even trust,
Still, she persuades all the time you must,

It's the lack of sex,
Can be so hard to digest,
When you were getting it plenty – obsessed,
And suddenly all stops dead,

The lack of sex,
Was hard to digest,
I had plenty but was still obsessed,
And it stopped dead when the girl was upset,

I wanted to believe it was all more than just this,
That it was rather deeper than she'd ever admit,
And we'd fight through the shit – each of us pissed,
I knew there was definitely something wrong with this…

A Forgotten Besotted

A girl like her can never be replaced,
I'm learning now after having disgraced,
I'm left, with this bitter after taste,
Everywhere I go I see her face,

She hasn't spoke to me in days,
Not left the slightest trace,
I ache, miss her embrace,
Her touch, where fingers traced,

I did vow she'd never be forgotten,
Difficult too when you're fully besotted,
I betrayed, I misbehaved, just rotten,
She never deserved all I had trodden,

And it's too late to take back now,
I can't move on, no way, no how,
Free to be out on the prowl,
But I spare a glance in gloom to the moon –
And mournfully howl…

For Less

I'm on, I'm on all the time,
Can't shut off my mind,
Can't slow down,
Can't look down,

Can't seem to see less importance,
Can't seem to feel shit's less important,
Never thought I could afford to –

I'm switched on, on all the time,
Probably makes some lose their mind,
I can't slow down,
I don't wanna look down,

Can't feel less excited,
Never wanted to feel less excited,
Never thought I could afford to,

Can't shut off – can't shut down,
Can't see the point not being around,
Go big, loud – be the clown,
Go out to stun and astound,

I can't seem to see it's no big deal,
Can't it be real? Can't you feel?
Or can you not afford to?

Does it have to be a bigger deal if it is?
What could possibly be wrong with this?
Can you not afford to?

I'm on, I'm switched on for you,
Why can't you be? Why aren't you?

What would it take?
I don't want you down,
I don't wanna look down,
Can't afford to…

I Only Ever

I only ever want to kiss you sweet,
For you have my heart to keep,
I can rest and well, I'll sleep,
For with you I am complete,

I only ever want to hold you tight,
For you're my most glorious delight,
The most immaculate beautiful sight,
All I ever feel is right,

I only ever want to keep you safe,
Be your soldier always brave,
Give you everything there is to be gave,
Never let you feel a slave,

I only ever want to give you glory,
Start a new chapter to our story,
Erase all parts revered as gory,
Even those that seemed so boring,

I only ever want to make you smile and laugh,
And never let you feel the dark,
What you have is just the spark,
To make us both last,

All I ever want is for us to last,
I have more love for you than lust,
There is never a moment passed,
I don't thank God you're in my grasp…

In Ache

Look at me,
I'm lookin' down at myself right now,
I'm annoyed I like a girl,
Who isn't excited so to see me,
Look at me,

I'm in ache,
I want to love her,
I want her to want it –
Or me,
Doesn't feel like it,

I'm in ache,
Want to be wanted,
Needed – I'm neither,
Look at me,

I want to love her –
Want her to want it,
From me,

It's not lookin' like it,
And I'm torn between wanting to try –
And not even bothering,
Look at me,

I'm in ache,
I want to invest the emotional attachment,
I've got none – no one,
I ache,

I want someone,
Want someone to feel,
I want something with a someone,
I need it –
I ache…

In Hope, In Wait

Hope is a dangerous thing,
Breathes courage to us,
Power to the want,
Steadfast through the loss,

She wants to love him,
And he not the way she does,
But she hopes, she prays,
That he will the way she does,

He doesn't know what he wants,
And she still lingers,
He's never close to what he wants,
But she still lingers,

Hope is a dangerous thing, breathes courage,
Power to the want, power loss, breeds worry,

She wants him to love her,
And he can't the way she does,
But she hopes, she prays,
That he will one day, hopes he does,

He never gets his desire, his want,
And she still lingers,
He's never close to what he wants,
And she still lingers,

Hope is a dangerous thing,
Courage to lose in hopes of a win,
Will in the power, will in the want,
Power to the loss, power through what cost,

She waits for him,
And he takes his time,
She waits for him,
Waits for the faintest signs,

He is completely oblivious,
She wants it ever more serious,

She waits,
And he makes every excuse,
She waits,
All the time in hope, it's time she does lose,

She waits for him,
Dropping hints – ushering clues,
She waits,
All the time in n hope, it's still time she does lose,

And he is completely oblivious,
She wants it ever the more serious,

She waits for him,
He's takin' time – can't make his mind,
She waits for him,
Waiting for traces of the faintest signs,

Signs saying all the waiting, hoping, finally ends,
That they're finally going to be more than friends,
That all this time lost in wait is recompensed,
That he is worthy, correcting missed amends,

Yet she waits still…

That poor girl is almost a corpse,
Awaiting her love to change his course,
Poor woman like her should never be kept to pause,
I know many a man would say she's a great reward,

Yet she waits when there's so much better,
She waits, and it seems like forever,
Many a man would go extreme endeavours,
No real man keeps a lady waiting - never,

Poor sweet woman, she had a big heart,
She has a lot of hope I just pray it doesn't go dark,
The man she waits for better play his part –
'cause if he don't I'll make a start,

I'd love a woman like that for myself,
I'd boost her esteem with the sweetest I could tell,
I'd make her feel so wholesome, never an empty shell,
If I had a woman like that mate, I'd keep her well,

That poor sweet girl is almost a corpse,
Awaiting her love to change his course,
Poor woman like that should never be kept on pause,
I know many a man would count her a great reward,

But she still waits when there's so much better,
She waits, and it seems to take forever,
Many a man would go the endeavour,
No real man keeps a lady waiting, never,

Now, I might be one of those rare kinds of man,
That longs for a woman's love like she can,
I want to grab her, shake her, make her understand,
That all this wait for nothing is getting out of hand,

She's wasting herself on an empty hope,
Wasting her hope on a blinded dope,
It tears me up to watch – I want the man to choke,
And give her back the years and all good she spoke,

She wants to love him and have him love her,
But he can't – not the way she does,

She hopes and prays, and she lingers still,
Never gets her fill, she lingers still,

She waits for him,
He's takin' time – can't make his mind,
She waits for him still,
Waiting for traces of the faintest signs,

Signs saying all the waiting, hoping, finally ends,
That they're finally gonna be more than just friends,
That all that time lost in wait is recompensed,
That he is worthy correcting missed amends,

And I might be one of those last rare kinds of man,
That longs for a woman's love like she can,
I want to grab her, shake her, make her understand,
That all of this wait for nothing is getting out of hand,

Yet,
She lingers still…

It's... Just... Fuckin' Because

I don't know why I have to care so much and it fuckin' hurts,
Is it so hard to believe I can think others valuable?
Do I have to friggin' explain it – I dunno – it's –
It's... Just... fuckin' because,

It's not normally hard for me to be nice, courteous,
I like to be polite – thoughtful – considerate,
But I do struggle when I know I've made others the more murderous,
Struggle and fail showing I'm the mindless fuckin' idiot,

I'm battling trying to prove I'm not what they see,
But my efforts only seem to make it fuckin' worse for me,
Trying to fight for a control over my emotion,
Trying to show I'm fuckin' worth the devotion,

I fuckin' dunno why I care so much, it fuckin' hurts,
Is it hard to believe I don't think you're not valuable?
Am I really having to friggin' explain it – I dunno – it's –
It's... Just... fuckin' because,

I get the whole image thing and I know it's important,
My reputation's fucked and I do deeply abhor it,
Of course, it got worse the more I ignored it,
My ex whore has dirt and she does flaunt it,

So I'm battling trying to prove I'm not what they see,
And my efforts only seem to make it worse for me,
Trying all the while fighting for control of my emotion,
Maybe try show I'm fuckin' worth having that devotion,

Fuckin' dunno why I care so much it has to hurt,
It's not like I don't find others valuable,
But I've gotta friggin' explain it – and I dunno – it's –
It's... Just... fuckin' because...

My Corpse Queen

I sleep with a corpse next to me,
I rape her because she's sexy,
I love her smell, she tastes so good,
I fuck her hard with my wood,

I'd kill everyone except my friends,
But HA! What do ya know they're also dead,
I dug 'em up after their funeral,
They told me to, the feelings mutual,

My bed is king sized,
But I am up all night,
Fucking a dead slut,
Over filling her guts,

She foams at the mouth,
'til I gotta clean her out,
I love my necro-female,
They're no good unless they're stale,

But my dead friends all sit and watch,
Jeer with cat calls cause my dead bitch is hot,
They all want her after me,
But I tell 'em she's too hard for them to please,

My corpse queen is a dream come true,
Even though she's part green and blue,
Wants me every night – never puts up a fight,
I'm a horny fucker with her pussy in my sight,

Just when I think I've come enough,
I erupt with another blast,
I've painted half the room white,
And I just wanna go take another ride…
…so I take another ride…

531

Yum…

I just found out what I taste like,
She said she swallowed but lied,
I've already had it happen twice,
No one ever taught these bitches right,

A lot of women must've tasted my sperm,
But I guess this bitch must've thought it was my turn,
I went in for a kiss,
And that was when I tasted jizz,

Half oral pleasure – half a wank,
She did well to empty the tanks,
Went in for a kiss – to say a thanks,
And copped a mouthful of some not-so-blanks,

There's nothin' like a decent blowjob,
When she's down and got you in her gob,
You never once want it to stop,
Not 'til you blast out your pearly drops,

A lot of women must've tasted my sperm,
But I guess this bitch thought it was my turn,
I went in to give her a kiss,
And that was when I tasted jizz,

You either swallow or you spit,
Don't leave it hanging off your lip,
I never want to taste the shit,
It just feels good to get rid of it,

But yeah, found out what I tasted like,
She had said she swallowed but lied,
I have had it happen before – twice,
So, no one must be training these bitches right,

Cut Above The Rest

I barely ever have to confess,
It's blatant that I do surely obsess,
Over that beautiful, soft, tender, pink flesh,
Ecstasy intensity – a cut above the rest,

Such a beautiful glorious divide,
My mouth surely yearns to dive,
I wish to descend and spread those thighs wide,
Kiss you slowly, tenderly, until I taste what you like,

I want to take it slow and taste you melt,
Push you to release all you have withheld,
I'm gonna do it good and I'm gonna do it well,
I'll make you feel the best you've ever felt,

Push you to the edge and make you want to scream,
Ecstasy intensity – better than a dream,
It's when I feel you shudder – it's where I want to be,
I work it, berserk it, and in a blast you cream,

Such beautiful sweet juice, a flavour I favour,
A perk for my extremely lurid behaviour,
You took a chance and allow me a savour,
Releasing the tension, your hero, your saviour,

And you'll know first-hand I barely have to confess,
It's blatant that I so completely obsess,
Over your, beautiful, soft, tender, pink flesh,
Ecstasy intensity – the cut above the rest…

Immaculate Comings As Going

I've found I've not realized – I –
Was thinking inappropriate things – I –
Don't just visualise but telepathically project it – I –
See it in my mind, clear, but then I –

I go deeper in and I fantasize,
About touching women where my hands glide,
But tingling over them with a kind of light,
And seeing this (imagining it) with my eyes,

I wake back out of it when I hear the cries,
Snaps me out of my fantasized,
They scream they're horny – and I realise –
They've been seeing what I was seeing with their own eyes,

But how much of this actually did happen as I heard?
I wondered if they felt it as it worked,
The gentle brush of tinging light where it turned,
Could it drive them berserk enough to squirt?

I begin to get paranoid that I indeed have,
Some might say it's a gift of to be glad,
To make orgasm at will – it might be so bad,
But that's another kind of excitement's not so sad,

At times I don't realise I've wandered off to fantasize,
About touching women and where my hands would glide,
But tingling them over with a glorious light,
And seeing this (imagining it) with my minds' eye,

And I wake back out to it when I hear the cries,
Snaps me out of my fantasized,

They scream they're horny and it's then I realise –
They've seen just as I've projected with their own eyes,

And that's when I have to stop, thinkin' I've sent them berserk,
If I had of kept going I probably could've made 'em squirt,

Love Quadrangled

Mutton dressed as lamb, man, I'd slaughter,
A prize for any man, damn she was gorgeous,
Thought I had it grand, but then, I met her daughters,
It went so bad I'm glad it wasn't reported,

I had the hots for this fine mama,
I wanted her and I was gonna,
She was entrancing – she was a stunner,
Worthy romancing, yes, the spell I was under,

But a consequence would soon unfurl,
Soon as I'd locked eyes to her girls,
Incidents too soon would rip apart my happy world,
Over my obsessive fascination with the woman and her girls,

I enjoyed each their company as I usually do,
But there must've been a something deeper I never put thought to,
A few things to allude to the nude,
'tween each, but undiscovered, and hell if they knew,

As eager and wanton as I am for the mature fairer sex,
Complications, like all, still rise that do most perplex,
But before me the two of her girls beset,
And a lustrous urge rising, promises trouble yet,

The eccentric me I am generally can't contain it,
Too stupid, too young, to know better to abstain from it,
I know I'm going to end up feeling the pain from it,
Wouldn't even know where to begin to explain it,

Their mother, just amazing, beautiful and mesmerizing,
Good reason why men like me need sterilizing,

I wanted to be passionate with her, affectionate,
Seek on manoeuvres possible weren't invented yet,
But deep within me I knew there was no pretending it,
It was going to escalate – there was no preventing it,

Previous experiences taught I should show more control,
These particular things I've done don't show much of a soul,
I'm reckless, rabid horny and I'm out on patrol,
And I could burn at the stake for it and tread the hot coals,

I had the hots for this fine mama,
I wanted her – so ready, I was gonna,
Entrancing, a charmer, she was a stunner,
I'd urge romancing for the spell I was under,

But a consequence would soon unfurl,
Soon as I'd locked eyes to her girls,
Haunting, the incidents, to tear apart my world,
Over this obsessive fascination with this woman and her girls,

Slept different nights, in secret, in silence,
Ever quiet to never rouse surprises,
Hefty risk – heavy compromises,
Cause it may just be my nuts in the vices,

One night after a loving I had been longing,
I'd left, entered my chamber, slipping the rubber off my Johnny,
Bathed, as you do, changed, made horizontal of my body,
And woke through the night to the most incredible gobby,

It wasn't 'til after I'd finished it was then that I feared,
She told me I was beautiful through a voice of 80 years,
"it'll be our secret – bet you'd look good with a beard"
I graciously thanked her but told her it was weird,

Next morning attended a breakfast,
And you really couldn't imagine the tension,
We, all sat, and not enough of me for attention,
Each seemed to want to fight for my affection,

Still, at this stage none of them knew,
These sneaky acts I was getting up to,
And there was almost nothing I wouldn't do –
To keep it intact and not begin a feud,

So I had to play it cool and keep it low key,
If I wanted to keep feeding them each a some of me,
Only, by delegated nights I were free,
And not out in any way we could've been seen,

The grandmother the mother and her two daughters,
With all this loving going on, you'd think I'd get exhausted,
But the secrecy was exhilarating, helped me have it sorted,
Wasn't 'til I became so lax was when any of them had caught it,
Trouble was – it wasn't with any of them,
Not with any of this family of these women,
But of the nanny they had reside with them,
Cooking, cleaning, tidying, waiting on after them,

She caught us by the pool late one evening,
One of the two girls – and there was no lie she'd believe in,
Couldn't believe I had been so deceiving,
And I knew it was too soon I were to be leaving,

I'd scrawled a note and left that very night,
To be so very far asway when the treachery came to light...

Fuck Funny

I'm a funny fuck,
And I fuck funny,
I'll make ya laugh,
When we bump uglies,

I'm a funny fuck,
And I fuck funny,
Oh, I can give a stuff,
Stuffing spunk up your tummy,

I'm a funny fuck,
And I fuck funny,
I could make you laugh,
With a good num-nummy,

I'm a funny fuck,
And I fuck funny,
And fuck funny enough,
That I'll taste your honey,

Oh, I'm a funny fuck,
And I fuck funny,
I'll make you laugh enough,
You'll wanna pay money,

I'm a funny fuck,
And I fuck funny,
You'll definitely laugh,
When we bump uglies,

Incomprehension

My intelligence is intimidating,
Most must feel it emanating,
It has been most frustrating,
Reasons all sides are hating,
It's degrading,

People fear the incomprehension,
And everywhere I go – I get the attention,
More than I care to want or mention,
It's everywhere – I get them,

The ways I am which do confuse,
It's patience what I seem to lose,
Patience to fathom those steps ahead,
Or the calm enough I keep my head,

My intelligence is intimidating,
Most must feel it emanating,
It has had me frustrated,
Reasons all sides are hating,
And it's degrading,

'Cause all the time I must interpret –
Considerate, articulate to interpret,
For in some of the ways I do confuse,
And patience and calm seem to lose,

Lack of comprehension for any interaction,
Lack of grace or any satisfaction,
Refine my mind further, maybe get that benefaction,
Sharpen, improve, and prove the new attraction,

Little Girl

She was a little girl,
Had to get so petty,
Had to get so spiteful,
At times many,

She was a little girl,
Had to be so smart,
Had to be so good,
Had to have your heart,

She was a little girl,
And nothing's changed,
She's a lil girl,
And nothing's gonna change,

She got hurt
And she couldn't hide it,
She's hurt,
And has a share to provide,

She was a little girl,
And she got hurt,
Had to be petty, had to be spiteful,
And now everybody's heard,

She was a little girl,
And nothing's changed,
She's a little girl,
It's how she will remain,

Living Fairy Tale

I made her ego fucking huge, fucking big,
Told her she was the best – I fuckin' did,
Smiling, teeth grit – made the flattery stick – but,
They'll work out why I had enough of her shit,

I don't expect she'd suspect a thing,
'til long after tears cried, eyes sting,
She's gonna need that long hard think,
Why it was all gone quick as a blink,

I was giving more than I was getting,
I was angered when I should've been upsetting,
I toed with subliminal purpose hind-curtain-settling,
For she'd found her another source for her wetting,

I made her feel a lot better inside than she actually was,
I won't know the time it takes for her to eventually work out she's not,
I'm just glad I never tied that knot although besot,
I'm glad it never went any further than it actually got,

She never wanted to wake up to see for any real,
A fairy tale she's only ever lived for to feel,
She painted her face – but I painted another over still,
And I painted it with some mother fuckin' skill,

I'm not makin' those same fuckin' mistakes again,
Benefit of the doubt - I was naïve, but that's at an end,
Never having nothing more than friends,
Not when that was all I was gonna get…

The Meaning Deeper

Men who have a woman don't know how good they've got it,
I, me, I'm alone – and I so fucking badly want it,
I know what I'm missing out on, trust me, I know,
Took me a lot of fucking mistakes to know,

I treasure women, I do,
None of 'em ever really knew,
Men think I worship them more than I should,
But I know why it feels so good,

I hated the kinds of men that treated them shit,
Made me want to take the girl and kiss her sweet lips,
Some poor, sweet, darling woman so sweet,
Beautiful so, that I go weak,

Some – no, a lot would say I say to suck up,
That I'm only doing it all 'cause I need a fuck,
Yes – I need a fuck, true, but this isn't solely why,
I'm talkin' deeper enough, it's sensitive, you'll cry,

I am for real – men think I'm weak when I say,
Am I? or is it that I'm strong that I do?
To say the shit men are afraid to say,
My hearts true, my heart won't let me rue,

Say you think it is all that I say it isn't,
Say it – you think I'm on a sinister fucking mission,
You're the fuckwit, you're wrong – you've got it all twisted,
I love women, they're valuable – I'm empty – I miss it,

That fuckin' embrace man, having 'em close,
And yes, they can have on all thick layers of clothes,
'cause I know a something matters more than many men want to show,
I just want 'em to feel it, let 'em know I know…

Piece To A Jigsaw

A certain little someone – not namin' names,
Decided he'd flaunt with some foxy dames,
He fed an excitement where previously waned,
His imagination ever more destined to reign,

These lovely alluring ladies with when he'd interact,
Did have a special something would always attract,
A little something this feller had had the knack,
A piece to a jigsaw – had some of them back,

One tiny little gap that just required bridging,
Simple little pleasures hardly worth the flinching,
Left for imagination, thought for thinking,
That jigsaw puzzle piece that was missing,

He can understand how their husbands can be so upset,
He'd apologize but he couldn't regret,
Not when some certain needs weren't being met,
Despite what repercussions expected to be beset,

Funny thing was there was no physical means,
The like of which some needs must feed,
The dames – of who's husbands don't compete,
The feller can only imagine what hates bringing the heat,

He never met these lovely alluring ladies,
Couldn't identify appearances it's hazy,
You could call it stupid – you might call it crazy,
That he was foolin' with spoken for ladies,

Before Her Ever After

It was then, in her final desperations,
Weakened by all fatal brutal administrations,
I'd suddenly seen more than in all my deliberate examinations,
I suddenly saw it – she was fucking real, no figment of my imagination,

Men only ever ask for a rare occasion such as this,
Women all despise these tests – it gets 'em all pissed,
We want to know they'll endure long as we exist,
They do it just the same – only with their twists,

I hated her trying to teach me a lesson I'd learnt decades ago,
Didn't she ever wonder why else it was I wouldn't show?
And here we are again – we're gonna get another go –
And I'm back where I'd started, before she learnt I'd known,

Altercation's pointless and all are exhausted,
I warned but clearly not with enough precaution,
There were times I knew I should've immediately aborted,
Though I couldn't let it go unrecorded – it was important,

So we never even got to that stage I'm sad to say,
Though perhaps I should be so grateful – I suppose, in a way,
That we never married before she'd betrayed,
It's true old dogs can't learn new tricks I'm afraid,

I'm sure as fuck glad I saw it was going to be a disaster,
Long before she got any of her ever after –
I'm sure as fuckin' hell glad – I foresaw this disaster,
Well and truly long before she got her ever after,

Battling Her Mad Mindlessness

I'm almost fucking glad she wasn't so smart –
It would've only made it, if she did, more fuckin' hard,
A little girl with a compulsive need for the heart –
Only up until she couldn't handle too much,

The things – the shit she didn't know,
But even if she did she wouldn't show,
She was careless – signs told me so,
She'd blow the whole thing and everyone gets to know,

I battled with her over her mindlessness,
So much I almost fuckin' lost mine,
I was that courageous – it had gotten outrageous,
But I think I did end up losing at the same time,

She ends up getting more -
To tread on me like the floor,
She drains, and she absorbs,
And she's fuckin' takin' it all,

I'm battlin' her crazy as much as my fuckin' own,
We're both in this twisted relationship but we're still alone,
Any place with her in it will never be 'home',
They all wanted me to 'grow up' but, now I've outgrown,

I'm too fuckin' good to be takin' her or their shit any longer,
Glad I had to – glad I did – I have gotten stronger,
But I am a lone one now and walk about yonder,
Trading tricks as due about my wander,

I'm shutting out and letting her go – and going my own way,
Living by then lesson and never repeatin' it again,

An Almost

Well, fuck man,
Thought that was my second chance,
Had her in my hands,
She, slipped through my fingers like sands,

I wanted her only all too soon,
And unfortunately – clipped as I went to miss the gloom,
Not take it too hard nor have her feel it too,
But there was, it was almost, I can assume,

I wanted her, think she wanted it too,
Could've hurt and I know it true,
Takin' the chance – a big deal to do,
Still, I unfortunately clipped as I went to avoid the gloom,

Fuck man –
Felt like I lost a second chance,
An almost as it began,
Had her in my hands,

Thought it was my second chance,
Had her in my hands – fuck man,
She slipped through my fingers like sands,

Wasn't ready – no pretending,
Would've only ended regretting,
I don't feel I've avoided an upsetting,
Fuck no man, wasn't ready,

Almost had it, it was there,
I would've cared to spare the time to share,
Almost…

GoreGoss

Cunts with assumptions,
Treacherous two-faced bias,
Rupturing reputations,
By two-faced piece of shit liars,

There's a reason why we don't trust,
And these mistakes are consistent reminders of,
They obviously don't want the trust enough,
The giggling little females, hot for the goss,

I can spread goss,
The truths that, were-nots,
And I'll get everybody all hot,
I won't be stopped,

I'll give 'em as much as they can handle,
Perhaps a lot more than they even knew they'd want,

I go cold when there is just never enough,
My fuckin' ex was playing the bitch – not the slut,
She just couldn't sate my lust,
Couldn't fulfil it 'cause she couldn't trust,

She never opened as much as I was hopin',
And I was never the only man who was gropin',
She was clever never once leaving evidence of these moments,
But honest and true as I was, I could tell, I did know it,

I could believe she would've as well as a past version of me,
Born the day prior, and strangely, deeply, ever similar to me,
Trusts broken after the giving's of so much of me,
Fucked by a treacherous two-faced bias unto me,

That's reason enough why,

Stiff Upper Split

She's been a bad naughty girl,
And I think she needs a smack,
She's askin' for the world,
But I'll get her on her back,

Now I normally like to bend her over my knee,
And smack her naughty arse,
With her pants down round her feet,
That bitch attitude won't last,

You wouldn't believe the mouth on her –
To deal with her shit,
I'll fuck the bitch out of her,
With this stiff up her split,

She goes and does things like she don't care,
Takes its toll – more than it's fair share,
I feel its expense, I feel it wear,
But I'm feeding it back as good as I bear,

So I normally like to bend her over my knee,
And smack her naughty arse,
With her pants down round her feet,
That bitch attitude won't last,

You wouldn't believe the mouth on her,
And to have to deal with her shit,
But I'll fuck the bitch out of her,
With this stiff up her split,

Rockabilly Blues

She's got that look again in her eyes,
Looks like I'm sleepin' alone tonight,
She's wearing that dress – that one that I obsess,
She's upset and so soon will be I,

She's my hot rockabilly chicky babe,
Traits about her make me want to misbehave,
She knows I like to have my way, she plays,
I've strayed, I betrayed, but she plays,

Hell hath no fury like a woman in scorn,
And I've brought on a storm following my horn,
I've started war and she'll surely balance back the score,
As much as have whored – don't doubt she'll have more,

My rock'n'roll pin up lover, that dress, wooh!
She's barely covered, headin' out lookin'
For another, men of any age – age of her father,
My rockabilly chicky babe pin up lover,

We fought before she left tonight,
With a cold cool look in her eye,
She's gone lookin and she'll get her a guy,
She's upset, and so too, soon will be I,

Hell hath no fury like a woman in scorn,
And I've brought a storm following my horn,
I've started war and she'll settle the score,
As mush as I've whored – no doubt she will have more…

Attracting Attentions

Look, I know you think all this attention you get makes you feel good,
But there's gotta be a point in time babe,
where it's more than you should,
You never once wanted to see it from where I stood,
And if you did – you know you'd shake your head babe, you would,

You often can't foresee on what sort of assumptions,
Or on what secret sexual deviousness some minds function,
But if you go out wearin' that tiny little somethin'
Sure, you're candy for the eyes – and there's a mass consumption,

You can't trust what control others maintain,
Would it have to take an incident with someone insane?
You could save us all a heart-aching pain,
If you weren't too revealing – maybe use the brain,

You must be aware there's some kinds you just don't want to attract,
But you're not showing standards, respect nor
intelligence to be out wearing that,
Don't get me wrong, I'm not having a go – you're not under attack,
It's just hard for me to know what reputation you want to be exact,

You might go and be at the wrong place at the wrong time,
And be amidst a one or many out of their right mind,
And it'll be too late before you're going to find,
You had the chance to change when you were shown the signs,

It might take a trauma but just hopefully not a death,
And you wearin' that has us all holding our breath,
So worried so we won't peacefully rest,
If something were to happen we'd all regret,

You can't trust what control others maintain,
Would it have to take an incident with someone insane?
You could save us all a heart aching pain,
If you weren't too revealing – maybe use the brain,

Broadly Loving Broad

I thought my mother raised me right 'til I met this broad,
It was almost too real – then found it was a fraud,
And I broke apart – help me dear lord,
How had I forgotten all I was ever taught?

I doubt she's ever been so considerate or mindful as me,
But I know in my time with her – I was forgetting to be,
She would always talk about the bird in her dream,
And somehow, horrifically, I thought I truly meant what it would mean,

Things she would do would make me question,
If she ever wanted us at all –
I regret it all now, resent it,
It was always me that had to fucking crawl,

She didn't want it – never wanted it,
And I can see it all clearly now,
I was just a useful convenience,
And I'm paying for it now,

It wouldn't have mattered, she never cared,
If she had – she had a funny way to show,
I thought what we had was rare,
Maybe it was – but I hope I never know,

I couldn't understand how she'd say one thing,
And completely do another – and worse,
I thought I was the mess but she was something,
Would only ever lead me to swear and curse,

But the confusion with the flirting?
I did once believe it was wrong,
Especially to anyone taken or married,
I was so fucking certain it was wrong,

I was the kind of guy to only have eyes,
For just and only a one woman in my life,
But was there seriously more that I didn't understand?
Does this sort of thing happen to every man?

I thought just one woman was enough,
No matter if I had the energy to spare,
At least she, her, was enough,
I was faithful all that time there,

I knew something was wrong,
Yeah – something was going on,
There were way too many things,
That happened to make me think,

She wanted to marry me,
And I would wonder the point,
Infidelity – seriously?
What would be the fucking point?

I have cheated before but it's not by my true nature,
I prefer respect – and a reputable stature,
I hate the ache and hurt of a heart in fractures,
And I especially hate to be the one to cater,

It's over now and it's long gone,
It's worse I loved her – and that's gone,
Well, not as much as I want it to be,
Memories only to tear me up and consume me,

Now I wish I was that bird in her dream,
That I could finally escape her,
Wish I was as free as that bird in her dream,
And finally escape,

I'm still trying to let her go,
It's been years,
Won't leave my head – won't let go,
Still brings me to tears…

Once Upon A Matter Of...

Once upon a time it was a matter of how,
I wanted that gal, but I had had doubt,
Never could I be the one to make her scream aloud,
Guess we may have underestimated the man I'd become now,

Once upon a time it was a matter of when,
I'd sharpen my mind, raise up my intelligence,
Hardened by the weaving wind of paths experience,
Succumbed and accustomed to seductive influences,

Once upon a time it was a matter of why,
The motif, the riddle – the compelling drive,
That I might once again gaze into her eyes,
Confident and worthy to step up and claim my prize,

But suppose a time arrives and it's a matter of what,
Should the time arise – I'll give it everything I've got,
With a surprise by the surplus stocked,
And I may not have to try so hard before she's fallen besot,

Suppose a time arrives and it's a matter of where,
So long as it is with her, then I wouldn't care,
To share a passion fair, with all that I dare,
A ravenous desire like how an accelerated fire in flare,

But once upon a time it was a matter of who,
Finding a someone I could be so serious to,
Hoping in all faith it remains true,
Unlike all else that previously fell through,

Never Cum Again

I'm sensitive – hyper sensitive, and at times too much,
Imagine the frustration around the women I lust,
I melt to mush – and have to blush,
'Cause it's like holy fuck – we never even touched,

I hear them breathe and I blast my jizz,
And I empty more than we'd comprehend,
It's then it's all I keep thinkin' is –
I'll never cum again,

They've gotta even just look at me,
Bone's up – have to bend the knee,
And their voices – oh fuck, God, so sweet,
Pulse in my groin poundin' harder hearin' 'em speak,

I just hear them breathe and I blast my jizz,
And end up emptying more than we comprehend,
And it's then it's all I'm thinkin' is –
I'll never cum again,

Being so sensitive – I have the tendencies to feel –
Depths and tolerances more than others still,
But with women of such power and strong will,
I know I'm nothin' but a 5 second meal,

Hyper sensitive – at times too much,
Frustrated to be around the women I lust,
Melt to mush – and shamefully blush,
Holy fuck – we never even touched,

And at times they've just gotta look at me,
I go feeble – I go weak,
Hide the bone – bend the knee,
Otherwise – please beautiful – don't let me hear you speak,

'Cause I just hear them breathe and I blast jizz,
And I generally empty more than we comprehend,
And then I'm all left thinkin is –
Shit – I'll never cum again…

Murder Fouled,

It was quite adventitious, for the head mistress,
everything seemed as impetus at that one moment.
I lurked through the dark, deeply abhorred in the
heart, resenting how she was gallant.
She was pernicious, and a closet full of malicious,
and I was drawn witless before too long.
It was all repetitious – and never there was a
witness, but the fat lady has sung her song.

There never was praise, therefore there's no
malaise, but better yet a little constituent,
I admit I found liberation in deviation from acculturation,
but forgive me for being so forward and impertinent.
She did die gracefully – there may be salvation after all,
And if I linger longer to fathom more fatefully,
I'm sure to lose my marbles..

It is night, and there's a little dim light, protruding from the
crack of the door, palely illuminating this room from the lower
landing above the bottom floor. I decide to make an art of her
to this room, decimate her body and magnify its' gloom.

I pulled from my pocket a surgical scalpel,
and cut from her innards and guts,
Nearly slipping over on the blood soaked floor, moving in
a rush like a klutz. Little did I realize then that my actions
resulted in the aid of influence, leading to obmutescence, little
will anyone ever come to know, there was no acquiescence
to my will whether heinous or impetuous…

To Be Continued..

Lycan-throbbing

I have a hunger in my loins,
Like that that's of my guts,
Where were- without a choice,
I need me some juicy sluts,

Better that there's consents,
Where may lead malcontents,
Than have ravaged urgent –
Vicious on what innocence – 'virgins'

I do get the compelling urge,
That lusting need to fuck, on the verge,
That I might lose myself in overwhelming nerves,
Steal a woman away and have my way with her,

My heart races and I'm hot and panting,
So many women, so beautiful and enchanting,
I'd take any – take many who'd be granting,
But they best prepare for when its not so fine and dandy,

The mongrel dog beast with an insane appetite,
To fuck and feast on any she-wolf in sight,
To sink my mouth down on such a sweet delight,
This lycan's throbbing for a bite,

But better there's consents,
Where may lead malcontents,
Than have ravaged too urgent,
Vicious on what innocence –
The virgins,

A mongrel dog beast with an insane appetite,
To fuck and feast on any she-wolf in sight,
To sink my mouth down on such a sweet delight,
This lycan's throbbing for a bite,

Lover's Wild

For when we don't get passed our own vanities,
Through each our own back stabbing blasphemes,
In dire straits – or when I'm his highness the royal majesty,
For sickness and insanity baby,

For all sadness and every tragedy,
For all the sharp wit through the maladies,
You'll be glad you had me when we face all the baddies,
For sickness and insanity baby,

For when all wrong accelerates rapidly,
Paired – prepared to face it happily,
For what vicious oncoming strong, actively,
For sickness and insanity baby,

For all egotistical self-loving and demanding,
For the hunger – for growth ever expanding,
For what limited compassion and misunderstanding,
For sickness and insanity baby,

For the rise and falls of all calamity,
For when there's failure to maintain an amity,
For the deepest darkest lows of or no humanity,
For sickness and insanity baby,

Too real it's unrealistic, chimerical – it's crazy,
Too over the top but still here when they're evading,
Dead set, dinky di, no fuckin' maybe's,
For sickness and insanity baby...

Fuck Machine

I wish for fuckin' once,
I could be that juicy meat,
That all those horny girls,
Wanna get hold of and eat,

I wish for fuckin' once,
That I could just be seen,
By all those horny girls,
As a hot, hard, fuck machine,

It wouldn't bother me ladies,
In fact – I'd be laughing,
Rip off, slip off those hot panties,
And let me get to scarfing,

I wish for fuckin' once,
I could be that juicy meat,
That all those horny girls,
Wanna get hold of and eat,

I wish for fuckin' once,
That I could just be seen,
By all those horny girls,
As a hot, hard, fuck machine,

It's an argument I have indeed had with an ex before,
I couldn't hide my high sex drive – I always needed more,
We'd fight 'til we were both red in the face, yeah – we fought,
Over all the sex – as I'd obsess, I'd further implore,

I wish for fuckin' once,
I could be that juicy meat,

That all those horny girls,
Wanna get hold of and eat,

I wish for fuckin' once,
That I could just be seen,
By all those horny girls,
As a hot, hard, fuck machine,

But it wouldn't bother me ladies –
I'd be happy, laughing,
To have slip off those panties,
And let me get to scarfin'…

Thrashed Tender

Feelin' like I could fuck my frustration out,
Tenderized lover, thrashin' about,
They'd all hear her screamin' loud,
And confuse her pleasure for a terror sound,

Hard to explain the ache,
The need to fuck or masturbate,
Decline of an aggression to escalate,
But the orgasms never fake,

Rough as they need be to get,
Tempted to have it back again yet,
They aren't tears of someone upset,
Tears of excitement, moist and wet,

Hold the bitch down and pump her hard,
"There, that's for being a dirty tart!"
Smack her arse – oh fuckin' smack it hard,
"Yeah take that ya filthy dirty tart!"

Ya fuckin' grab her on the hips and force her down,
Hard and fast fuckin' – fuckin' pound, pound, pound,
Sticky, slippery, slapping sounds,
The release is just profound,

Yeah - I definitely wanna fuck my frustration out,
Tenderize a lover, thrashin' about,
They'd all hear her screamin' loud,
And confuse her pleasure for a terror sound,

Thrashed tender,
Thrashed tender…

A Loving From A Distance

Yeah, I get the kind of looks like I'm a player,
I'm not, or at least I don't fully believe I am,
I have a gift at making something fake believable,
But if you say you see it is –
Next question is – Is really that bad?

If I can be believeable for that brief moment,
And that single moment, nothing else mattered,
Then I would only say as I truly mean,
Genuine? Yes, and I can and do see as it may otherwise seem,

I can say I've thought of it that much ahead,
To notice and pick up on your doubt of my authenticity,
But still have the consideration to let spare,
Compassion for a passion to draw out from of a misery,

I know I can't always have what I desire,
But I can keep a distance and gaze and admire,
Do other little things you'd deny and call me a liar,
A, little loving from a distance, by will transpires,

You'll have no real need nor want of it at times,
And if you knew – I'd doubt it'd cross your mind,
At least not in the way you'd hoped one can,
I assure you I have, I'm capable, I am,

I don't have to be decisive – not like Christ,
I'll still love you when you want to fight,
Love you when you want to cry,
Love you deeper than ever still you might find,

I know I can't always have as I desire,
I do keep a distance and gaze and admire,
I do other little things you'd deny and call me liar,
A loving from a distance, by will, transpire,

Cootchie

Cootchickadeewoochew,
Girl, I've got my eye on you,
Cootchickadeewoomung,
Girl, I'm gonna have you under my tongue,
Cootchickadeewoolick,
Girl, you're gonna bounce on prick,
Cootchickadeewoosuck,
Girl, you know I wanna ooh – uh- uh,

You know I'm the one you really want,
I can tell by the way you flaunt,
But you're gonna quiver under my fingers,
It's gonna get bigger and you'll be singin',

Cootchickadeewoochew,
Girl, my eyes are glued to you,
Cootchchickadeewoomung,
Girl, you're gonna shudder under my tongue,
Cootchickadeewoolick,
Girl, you're gonna bounce on my prick,
Cootchickadeewoosuck,
Girl, you know I wanna ooh – uh – uh,

I can see you wanna make me yours,
I'm under your spell and comply with the cause,
You can have me anytime you choose,
I'm fully hooked and want to amuse,

Cootchie – coo,
Coothcie – coo,
Cootchie – coo,
CootchickadeeWOOH!

If You've Got The Pink,

I'll flash some green to see some pink,
Yeah – you hear me girl you better strip,
Drop those wears and I'll mull a chop quick,
Then we'll both take a euphoric trip,

I've got the green if you've got the pink,
Come on girl -you heard me – strip,
Drop those wears and I'll chop a sesh quick,
Goddamn – that's where I want to touch my lips,

Now get over here and take a seat,
I've got a cone packed with some weed,
This shit's gonna be pretty hard to beat,
But wow, just look at you, you're sweet,

You're so damn pretty and it's no joke,
I'm glad I've got this moment with you havin' a smoke,
I've bought women like you – you know, and I have gone broke,
But this, this now, is fine sharing a toke,

I've got the green if you've got the pink,
Come on girl you know you heard me – strip!
Drop those wears and I'll mull a chop quick,
Hot damn! That's where I want to put my lips,

Take a deep breath and hold then release,
Tell me – would you do it again with me, please?
Huddle in closer you look like you'll freeze,
Fly and have this euphoric trip with me,

Appalling Behaviour

Appalling – yes, I know –
It's why I'll be a' pulling it myself later.
Disgusting, the way I talk,
No embrace nor willing women – due to behaviour,

This, no participation, causing my frustration,
It's round and back again,
Yeah – no participation, I'll be alone for masturbation,
No lover – no play friend,

Appalling – yes I know –
It'll be why I'll be a' pulling it myself later.
It's disgusting – the way I talk,
Ridiculous, lewd behaviour,

No, there is no participation,
My, masturbating out my frustration,
No involvement – no she-wolf invasion,
And I just can't seem to hold my patience,

Appalling – yes, it is –
I'll be why I'll be a' pulling it alone later,
Disgusting – this way I talk – I've been a shit,
It's why there's no embracing willing women – my behaviour,

Feel so wound up, so tense – I'm too sexed up,
Too much energy to ever let up,
That I wonder whether if a have a jerk before work,
Would save me the horny hassle of often going berserk,

It's appalling – I know –
It's why I'll be a' pulling it off alone…

An Embarrassment She Could Be Proud Of

She said she's proud of me,
But when she says I hope she's taking the cred for everything,
Cause I know there'd be shit about me she wouldn't be,
And if you can't allow for that – you can't everything,

How can I be proud of the fucked-up shit I do?
When someone's fucked me up as bad as this shit has too,
Proud of only fucking up – nothin' much else,
Proud being fucked up – fuck no, it's hell,

She only wanted the good bits and just chuck out the rest,
It had to be the quality over quantity, and she was losing zest,
A narcissistic overload was building and burning in her chest,
Soon I'd come to learn I'd waste what I'd invest,

Humiliated so that I can no longer care,
Not even bothered so to glare,
With only such a limited consideration spared,
Not even the mercy enough to get me so prepared,

I was never proud of the fucked-up shit I do,
Nor the fucked obstacles people put me through,
Obstacles taken for the hope it were it, true,
For the sake of her pride and more I never knew,

She says she's proud,
But I fuckijn' hope she's takin' credit for everything,
'Cause there's shit about me that do cause doubts,
And if you can't allow for it, you don't get anything,

She only just wanted the best and to fuck off all the rest,
Quality few and far between and she was "losing zest"
A narcissistic overload building and burning in her chest,
And soon I'd come to know I'd waste all I'd invest,

Man, I fuckin' hope she's proud…

Too Many Outbursts

They ask me why I'm still single,
Probably the same reason why I don't mingle,
A lot of the time I'm really quite unstable,
I have a condition that often renders me unpredictable,

A moment ago I had a cone and had to say prayer,
Was feelin' alone and was hopin' that feller up there –
Would lend an ear, maybe care,
Empathy maybe, I know he's had his share,

I, have had just too many outbursts,

I asked if he could lend me strengths,
To contain my emotion where I'd be upset,
And contain it so I don't spite on others to regret,
When I could've had the cognitive thought for my behaviour ahead,

A coincidence at work today reminded me,
Of a past relationship – where a similar ending been,
Attitude, behaviour, actions – worst to be seen,
To many mistakes gone now I just want to fix me,

A ragged mess, a broken wreck,
Closet full of skeletons and regret,
Expecting many people want to wring my neck,
Fucked up, but the solution's in the next step,

I came down, so it must go back up,
I really, truly, do want to give a fuck,
I just come to dead ends and get stuck,
Extremes of the too many outbursts –
and it's too easy to say it's enough,

They ask me why I'm still single,
Probably the same reason why I don't mingle,
A lot of the time I'm really quite unstable,
I have a condition that often renders me unpredictable,

I, have had just too many outbursts,

Prize Worthy Of The War

I'm threatened with my life,
For attempting taking wives,
Would it be so bad if he or they did the same?
And got they themselves a little bit o' that for they?

If I took just one,
And the he from the she it was –
Took himself one –
Can it not be justified it was?

Like a pleasure for pleasure –
Or rather, punishment for punishment,

Why even take a life when –
It wasn't a life taken of them,
But rather, he who has been theft of a she from –
If it were too easy – did she belong?

I'm more of a masculine kind of a he,
That I know a plenty would laugh and call me a she,
And it gets me to thinkin' of my wicked way to be,
Same for the other, like-like, it's guilt free,

I never take this consideration lightly,
I do indeed believe it sounds frightening,
Built up the trust enough you'll know when it's true, quick as lightning,
But even if it was still only mere fantasy chat, it was someway exciting,

Wife for wife – shit has happened before,
It's probably better to have one to exchange for more,
I have gazed and settled eyes on various a score,
And thought that was a prize worthy of the war…

MenOnPause

My woman's going through menopause,
So I am a man on pause,
Can't afford to be the cause –
Of her turning she-wolf and shredding me with her claws,

It's bad enough trying to get her excited,
When I'm just ready to go,
One wrong move and we fight it,
Then I just, have to let go,

I get a happier life when I have a happier wife,
Can't let her ever cook and be around those knives,
But if she does, we just better play nice,
Or we're up shit creek, we hit strife,

I hope she can appreciate all I exhaust,
Run ever ragged maintaining a happy cause,
She's going through menopause,
And I feel I'm just a man on pause,

The gentleman always puts the lady first,
And it's a mighty work quickly earning a thirst,
I know it sounds bad – I'm the fucking worst,
I just hope I never have to hear her swear and curse,

I try to do as much of that as I can,
Just so she knows that I am her man,
And I won't be anywhere but fighting side her stand,
And that's just how I am,

It's when she has a problem then I have too,
And I can't have her live that through,
So I go and do as much as I can do,
And pray like fuck I never rue...

Honest Dishonesty

Some man out there was rootin' my woman,
I suppose he thinks he's a man,
For the fact he thinks he could steal my woman,
If he was a man – I'd *know*
But he just cannot stand…

She couldn't even be honest about her dishonesty,
She has issues she's been running from for all time,
She had a man on the side – not a man enough to be named,
Fooling around with this supposed to be decent woman of mine,

Lowest acts deserve the worst punishments,
When enacted by high social standings,
Those low acts deserve their punishments,
Then they knew better – they need reprimanding,

What – how do they want to be thought of?
When they go to stoop so low –
How can it never be thought of –
'til it's time it's shown,

They can't be honest about their dishonesty,
They really haven't got the guts,
Not when it'll come to the torments of eternity –
Man – they're really gonna be fucked,

I know they're gonna play victim and whinge over the raw deal,
Their doubles standards just… never reached to let equal fields,
Standards – Ha – don't you even get me started,
If I told my peace they'd be left confused and broken hearted,

I hope the unholy lord don't let this one slip by,
Cause I know their punishments will need to suit the crime,

And hey – up 'til now they've gotten a free ride,
Tolls must be paid and it's about that time…

They cannot stand – Haha –
No guts…

If Only She Was Honest,

If only she was honest,
Would've saved half the time,
Saved me half the waste,

When I wasn't doing the shit she was,
Guess she felt I'd deserved it,
She was wrong,

If only she was honest,
Would've saved me half the waste,
Doing exactly as she was,

When I wasn't doing what she was,
Think she felt I deserved it,
Repercussion of her cruel confusion,

If only she was honest –
She would have let me too,
But that's a hypocrite for you,
It's what they do,

If only she was honest –
Not getting it double or triple more than me,
May not have been such the waste I see,

If only she was honest,
If only she was ever genuine,
If only,
If only…

The Hide To Hide

As soon as I'd gone to that concert I fucking knew,
There was something up – she was being untrue –
She'd hide it – and fight it black and blue,
Something was off and always thrown askew,

Before our togetherness ran outta time,
She was acting deviously sly,
She'd try to lie – but I saw it with my eyes,
She'd try to hide it – she tried,

I knew we were beginning to die,
She didn't have to fucking lie,
I made several attempts – I pried,
And I fuckin' saw what she'd try hide,

She had another feller on the side,
And she only ever denied,
Fuck she had ego, fuck she had pride,
And she would smile fucking wide,

She'd admitted to cheating years before,
It was a sign I should've looked into more,
40 guys? Maybe a little underexaggerated whore,
You were never worthy of all that love I poured,

That fuckin' bitch took me for granted,
She had me hooked, this fool was enchanted,
Fucked to get what she wanted and was always handed,
But never quite ever efficiently planned it...
Rancid...

Betrayed And Hurt

I was being faithful to some stupid fucking thing that wasn't,
I wasn't the only man she had leaving a deposit,
She had skeletons, packed tight in the closet,
But I'm so fucking glad she was the one cheating and I wasn't,

She wanted me to trust her,
Trust – like, trust you'll hurt,
Trust that any trust I give her,
Will only be broken, betrayed and hurt,

I'm glad there was shit that she kept to herself,
'Cause I guess in a way it truly did mean hell,
Glad I kept a lot of shit to myself,
She – immature as an age of twelve –
Just, fifteen fuckin' years older,

There was things I would confide,
I'd open up to her to only find,
That it was when we'd go to fight,
That trust was broken – like most my pasts in life,

She only showed me what I already knew would happen,
Another fuckin' bloody catch 22 – and the shit fuckin' happened,
She, goes and cheats out of spite, an entrapment,
Lies, saying it were you and she hadn't,

Incapable of being honest but worst so faithful,
It's often the kind of shit that make good men go to jail,
Fucked up women fuckin' with men with their fucked-up betrayal,
Trust, the burden, when there's no decent fucking females,

And she wanted me to trust her,
Trust? Like trust she'll only hurt,
I could and it'd be trust I'd give her,
Gets broken, betrayed and hurt…

And Nothing Was To Be

The time has come to draw in to a close,
It was nothing I had willingly chose,
Just… too many people have up turned their nose,
I've brought naught but dread and woes,

The time has come I must cut off,
Stop chasing all I wanted of,
Stop craving all I am not,
Stop chasing what I haven't got,

I can't keep asking something of a some,
Who don't, can't feel more than they are numb,
They've got nothing for me – none,
And nothing can be done,

Time's come again to just withdraw,
I've got nothin' she wants, she ignores,
I feel ripped apart, torn raw,
It's about when I'd normally scorn,

This time – I just can't hate,
Weakened – I want to pull away,
This time – I can't escape,
Weakened – I want to run away,

Times come and I want to disappear,
If she could ever love – I never want to hear,
Couldn't show me – I never saw it clear,
Now I just don't wanna be any here near,

Times come to go silent – dead quiet,
Do nor say naught but internalise on it,
If there was something, I'll defy it, deny it,
And eventually reach the point I'll fight it…

Lose That Attitude

Pardon me – I beg yours?
D'you forget who you're talking to?
I know you want it done –
Btu that's the wrong attitude,

You're having a go for no good reason,
Hey – yeah, fuckin' oath it'll be done this season,
Hey – I'll get it fuckin' done,
Don't need you reminding me every six months,

Whoa – don't you talk to me like that,
That was disgusting – how fuckin' rude,
I don't care how much it hurts – it's bad,
You want the shit done – wrong attitude,

You fuckin' hate it when you cop the shit,
So before you go storm you go fuckin' think,
I'm feeling the fucking pressure – you're not alone,
I am your man am I not? And this? Our home?

A little more respect would be so nice,
Make me feel that – and I'll do it good – I'll do it twice,
Keep this shit up and you can leave to go 'live' your life,
I've had too much of this shit – behave and act like a 'wife',

I hate it when you treat me lower than filth,
After all the good I have made you feel,
If you're so fucking sore – go, go away and heal,
Come back when you can treat me better still,

Just don't talk to me like that,
That was disgusting and rude,
I now it has to be done but,
You better lose that attitude…

Catch 22

I fall to love things I know will fuck me,
Most, many – would probably find it lucky,
It's often hard to get out of once you're stuck in,
Nah, I don't feel I'm so lucky,

To have a top most want,
With a top most cost,
Torn between what it takes to –
Do for love, or in lieu – a catch 22,

Wasting time – wasting my mind,
On the shit I know I'm only gonna find –
All these out of line kinds,
Will wrap me in straps and chains to bind,

To have a top most love,
With a top most cost – more than enough,
To have you torn between what to –
Do for the love – or in lieu, the catch 22,

Issues that gain strengths,
Drain – leave you with nothing left,
Pressure building – gaining intense,
With no clear way through out of the mess,

To have a top most need,
Temptations that only ever deceive,
Easy to believe – find you're torn between,
A love or catch 22 that has you bleed,

I do fall to love the things I know will fuck me,
And most, probably many will say it's lucky,

Like a quicksand when you're stuck in,
No – I can't say I feel so lucky,

I wanted love in lieu –
Of a catch 22…

The Emphasis on 'US'...

She thought I put an emphasis on us,
I did, but it wasn't enough,
Next time I won't they'll be fucked,
If I even ever provide the slightest touch,

See, I've only ever really got me,
Never saw it before but I'm all I need,
And I'll be fucked if I'm ever gonna be,
Makin' me last fuckin' priority,

Not again…

Personally, I can't see how they deserve,
Not when they can be so quick to dessert,
I expose myself – workin' up what nerve,
But I'm so fuckin' sick of being the only one hurt,

There's never going to be an emphasis on 'US'
Not when there's never gonna be enough,
Next time, no, they'll be fucked,
If I even ever provide the slightest touch,

Not ever again,

I'm never going to be so quick to invest,
Not even gonna bother to expect,
They'll have or even share that respect,
Not quite met one to yet…

But never again,

You're Tryin' To

You want to knock me up so you can,
Tie me down,
If you're trying to entrap me,
It's not working,

You make believe you can make me yours forever,
There may be a time where I may refrain from saying never,
If you can prove you can do it for me better,
You'll have my audience, prove it – I'll let ya,

You turn me on so you can,
Get me off,
If you're tryin' to entrap me,
It's not working,

You try to win me over to say that it's the best,
So that I might not want to try out all the rest,
That feeling in your pants, needs that feeling in my chest,
So, you say you're willing to completely invest,

You want me to be what you want to call 'mine'
But you better be ready boy, for a compromise,
If you ever want any of this to be what you call 'mine'
There's a lot better to cater for and advertise,

I'll keep you on pause while I can,
Decide if I want to be yours,
I can see you're trying to entrap me –
It's not working,

That Emotional Attachment

For a while I knew I was fucked up,
And for a while I wanted to stop being fucked up,
Was gonna get me fixed so I wouldn't fuck up,
'Cause I know for a fact I don't wanna be a fuck up,

Someone like me likes to put their heart into shit,
For everything or anything – it's all or nothing,
If you didn't then what's the fucking point of it?
I just wanted to be a fucking something,

I wanted to take time to myself to fix,
All the wrong, terrible, heinous fucked up shit,
Get to the grind on all of it, do the fix,
Ascend to a much higher stage of bliss,

I have the terrible trait that goes full heart,
Conscience keeps me from going too dark,
Nature – it's never really by halves,
I too, hate to have to starve,

Now, I'm still a little fucked up,
But I know I want to stop being so fucked up,
Still want to get me fixed so I won't fuck up,
'Cause I know for a fact I don't want to be a fuck up,

How is it fair on someone else?
For me to go partnered still facing some hells,
Not takin' time to fix shit to myself –
That, that emotional attachment won't do so well,

Get me right before resuming life,
Or life alongside another,

Hard Pressed

You know I'm big babe –
And you want it –
Don't ya –

'Course I'm fuckin' big babe –
I'll have it hard against ya babe –
I want ya –

Yeah – you know I'm big babe –
If you come – you'll have it –
So won't ya –

'Cause I've got it big babe –
I'll have it hard pressed to ya babe –
I want ya –

I know you need it bad babe,
I know you crave for it babe,
But we are gonna get you laid babe –
You're gonna have it made,

You know I'm big babe –
And you want it –
Don't ya,

'Course I'm fuckin' big babe –
And I'll have it hard 'gainst ya babe –
I want ya –

Yeah – you know I'm big babe –
If you come – you'll have it babe –
So won't you –

'Cause I've got it big babe –
I'll have it hard pressed to ya babe –
You know I want ya –

Are You Blind?

I want to call you stupid or blind,
I hate you for having such a small mind,
You're the reason why guys like me get left behind,
'cause you're chasing something you'll never find,

I'm right here in front of you,
I want to be with you,
What is it can I do?
Can't you see I only want you?

I don't know why I should ever try,
I can never catch your eye,
I'm the one that loses, I'm the one to cry,
Yet I'll never be the one to say goodbye,

I'm fuckin' right here in front of you,
I'm the one who wants to be with you,
What is it? What can I do?
Can't you see I'm the one who wants to be with you?

I'm sorry I over-compensated –
It's just – I was the only one who demonstrated,
You have - uh – had me infatuated,
Now I'm just…exasperated,

I don't know how obvious I could've been more,
I'm not easy – I'm anything but a whore,
Was putting my love out there, and now I'm sore,
There just mustn't be much out there for me anymore,

I would have done absolutely anything,
Anything for the touch for your skin,
You were barely excited, I couldn't mean a thing,
It's reason enough for me to be so grim…

Sexually Frustrated

I've got a small fuckin' prick,
No fuckin' patience,
And a bad, bad, nasty fuckin' temper,
Can ya tell why?

Small dick,
No patience,
Bad temper,
Yeah –

Should be a disability,
Can't get no one feelin' me,
How can I be taken seriously –
No use for nothin' – shit, not even me,

Miniature pecker,
No time –
Nasty attitude,

Perpetually sexually frustrated,
Too fuckin' small for satisfactory masturbation,
It's a let down after wound up anticipation,
Yeah – I'm just, sexually frustrated,

I've just got this really tiny cock,
But no patience for anybody,
And a nasty bad temper, nasty attitude,
Yeah,

Small prick, small dick,
Better make your mind up quick,

Before I lose it and start to trip,
Fuck…

Its just – FUCK,
What can I do with this –
Small fuckin' cock,

Bleeding For Embrace

Be still my bleeding hearts,
You are my greatest due,
I'll make up for the missed apart,
When I finally come for you,

I do know the depths by which you crave,
Believe I feel them too,
I treasure that, that sweet embrace,
And I want it more with you,

I know the ache, the emptiness it feels,
And I would hope someone so beautiful never knew,
That embrace, intense, deep but real,
I feel it ache, I know it, I do,

Wait, be calm, be still my bleeding hearts,
You are my greatest due,
I'll make for all missed apart,
When I finally come for you,

I am honest as and sincere as I can be,
I don't feel I have anything to lose,
In those moments you'll be with me –
You'll definitely be who I choose,

I do know the depths by which you crave,
Believe I feel it too,
I treasure that, that sweet embrace,
And I want it more with you,

Calm, be still, wait my bleeding hearts,
You are my greatest due,
I'll make up for the missed apart,
When I can finally come for you,

If It's Good To Go

You know what my problem is... motherfucker,
I put the pussy on the pedestal,
I think more of it than it does,
And it's why it fuckin' leaves,

All this givin' it's gettin' from me,
Begins to make it think it's a right not a privilege,
Then, ya motherfucker, she's thinkin' better than me,
Out finding if in fact there is amidst the village,

She gets annoyed and angered up quick,
And she starts yellin' and callin' me the prick,
Sayin' what I did was just absolutely sick,
Abuse, by feeding her ego and making it fucking big,

'cause she's out searching for a something she won't find,
Some kind of love out there just aint nothin' like mine,
She's more pissed sayin' it's my fault she left me behind,
It's a harsh reality – but I have my peace, I'm fine,

She, thinkin' she never got that much of me anyway,
She'll keep screwin' all she can 'til she's grey,
Hoping, longing, again for the day,
She finds a love genuinely tricking her – into tricking it –
I was the same,

What I gave was pure and it sent her wild,
But now she's alone to live out whatever denial,
Truths she never faced, and I know – they're fucking vile,
It's why she was an adult I still felt was much a child,

That was one of the problems I had...motherfucker,
They had it too good that they left,
Shit.

Marriage And It's Decrepit Reputation

Marriage –
I think of it and I disparage,
It's something I'm never gonna manage,
Savage, but the rep is damaged,

The sanctity of marriage is gone,
Too much of it is lost and it's all wrong,
None can nor even will remain so strong,
To forfeit and forgive when all are wrong,

There's always a good way and bad way to deal –
And while you're enraged you won't care how they feel,
They feel the pain and they know it's real,
You just can never tell by what measure they feel,

Never really the last one in wait, or is it that I am,
The last one in wait to see if anybody else can,
Last in wait at the altar to stand,
I'll be last to proudly say I'm a married man,

It's the trust – the faith that I can't find,
That another would make it work as well as mine,
That they'll not fuck off or buckle at an unexpected time,
And leave me standing there broken, the only spine,

Can't find 'em tough enough,
That I can ever really say that 'this' is enough,
I do have it – I've got the right stuff,
I just feel it's where I'm getting stuck,

I take marriage seriously as to not seriously ridicule,
Infidelity and more only depreciate, make its' meaning miniscule,

Mr. Ess

I've seen her out and with her man,
I've seen beneath the surface – I can,
But where is she when they're holding hands,
Fantasy drift in an exotic circumstance,

I'm a sanctuary for rebellion, a rebound through divides,
I fill out to the boundaries, compensate when deprived,
She could have me at her side – have me on the side,
It'd be our secret, she can trust she can confide,

Everybody needs that someone,
And me, I've got some,
I'll relieve distress – I can have that done,
I'll be your Mr. Ess, I can be that one,

I've seen her without her man,
I've seen beneath the surface – I can,
But where is she when they're not holding hands?
Fantasy drift in foreign, exotic circumstance,

But, I'm a sanctuary for rebellion, a rebound through divides,
I'd fill out to the boundaries, compensate when deprived,
She could have me at her side – have me on the side –
It'd be our secret, she can trust she can confide,

Everybody needs that someone,
And me? I've had some,
I'll relieve the distress, I can make that done,
I'll be your Mr. Ess babe, I can be that one.

S'Excitement

Why does anybody think –
Of doing all they haven't before?
Why does anybody even think –
That there's anything more?
S'Excitement,

Why wouldn't anybody think –
Of men or women they haven't had before?
Why wouldn't anyone think –
Of going other places more?
S'Excitement,

Why does anybody think –
There can never be more?
Why would anyone one to think –
It can't be different if not better than before?
S'Excitement,

I'd advertise it, the excitement,
Excitement's a requirement,
And requirements need refinement –
Entice it – exercise it…

Why would anybody ever think –
Of doing all they haven't before?
Why woudn't anyone ever think –
That there's anything more?
S'Excitement,

Why wouldn't anybody think –
Of men or women they haven't yet had before?
Why wouldn't anybody - anyone ever think –

Of going other places more?
S'Excitement,

I'd advertise it, the excitement,
Excitement's a requirement,
And requirements need refinement –
Entice it – exercise it...

Mine Now

I'm more than just your mate,
We're gonna get you doing great,
Get you that release you get from an escape,
Take that feeling great, and make it escalate,

Eliminate that mood for hate,
Help view it in a useful, pleasurable scape,
Glimmer, shimmer in brilliant escapades,
Elevate, alleviate, rectify – intensify the state,

Raise the stakes no matter how,
Impress and gain that glowing 'wow',
And you will no matter how –

More than just your mate,
We'll get you doing better than great,
Raise you to levels of a euphoric state,
Raise it, amp it, make escalate,

I'm more than just your pal,
We'll get you screaming a pleasurable howl,
Never hesitate – never scowl,
Wet with excitement and needing towels,

Raise the stakes no matter how,
Impress and gain that glowing 'wow',
And you will no matter how,
That you're mine now,

You're mine –
Mine now,

Every Time You Go

It happens every time that I have to watch you leave,
My heart quakes in harder beats,
I often wish that I could come with,
There's almost nothing I wouldn't give,

I often crave holding you in my arms,
Falling prey to your charms,
Cuddling up and holding you tight,
Your warmth always soothing through the night,

I lose myself within your kiss,
And never feel anything wrong with this,
The feeling is a rush although it's slow,
I even feel inside myself I do glow,

It happens every time that we part,
I'm shaded once again by oncoming dark,
Like heavy clouds rolling in from the sky,
I feel that incomplete I could cry,

We're similar in thousands of ways,
My darling, you and I never cease to amaze,
We have the minds to set the world a'daze,
To breathe fresh life and start a new craze,

That is why you're precious,
And my smile is infectious,

You're the one who makes me whole and who I most need near,
You're the one that makes me happy and forget the reasons for the tears,

Be Cool

I have at this very time,
A lady I want to make mine,
We appear so far to get along fine,
Can't say whether it's a sign,

I have an infatuation beginning,
And I guess in a way I feel I'm winning,
Issues rise and I am skimming,
I care – I feel it beginning,

Only this time at a slower pace,
Thinkin' of her makes my heart race,
I have to seriously remember my place,
O' euphoria – I'm off my face,

There are parts of me I recall,
Been down this path before,
Gotta be cool, she's a score,
Don't wanna be my own downfall,

I have this infatuation n beginning,
And I guess in a way I feel like I'm winning,
Issues rise and I'll be skimming,
I care – I feel it beginning
But I've just gotta be cool,

I've gotta keep it cool,
Too long, too often, been the fool,
She's got me and I drool,
There's something here – I feel it fuel,
Just gotta be cool,

I swear infatuation is taking place,
Sweet euphoria – I'm off my face,
Thinkin' of her makes my heart race,
I just have to remember to keep my place and –
Be cool…

Black And Blue

Punch times two times five times ten,
Hit the motherfucker again and again,
Make him take back those disgusting thoughts,
Make him know the reason why you've won all times fought,

If it's for the cause of love,
Then let your blows be true,
If it's for the ones you love,
You'll beat cunts black and blue,

Pulverize, tear apart, dismantle, crush,
There it all goes – the last of your trust,

Punch times two times five times ten,
Hit the motherfucker again and again,
Let him know whose she was your girl,
Make him understand no one fucks with your world,

If it's for the cause of love,
Then let your blows be true,
If it's for the one's you love,
You'll beat cunts black and blue,

Somebody Better

Somebody better love me –
Before I start killin'
Somebody better calm me –
Before I really start thrillin',

I have rage – I have hate,
And I have an ancient list of names,
I am in rage – I am in hate,
And feel I'll too soon misbehave,

Somebody better love me,
Tell me it's gonna be all right,
Somebody better calm me,
Before I seek blood and fight,

I have rage – I have hate,
And I don't want to hesitate,
I am in rage – I am in hate,
And I'm quickly assuming a violent state,

Somebody better love me,
Distract my mind off from it,
Somebody better calm me,
Distract me or get me off on it,

I have rage – I have hate,
I want to get brutal and devastate,
I am in rage – I am in hate,
And shit's about to escalate,

Somebody better fuckin' love me,
And get to lovin' me quick,
Somebody better come calm me,
I'm ready to make skulls split,

Ex Wound

I'm still so fuckin' pissed at an ex,
And it's been over two fuckin' years,
I was so fuckin' obsessed,
I still shed tears,

I so want to see that fuckin' bitch hurt,
'cause there was never a moment I didn't when I was with her,
I want to see the man she desperately falls for dessert,
And I wanna see that fuckin' bitch hurt,

I want her to be so obsessed,
That it hurts her worse to be an ex,
That she finally opens and fully invests,
More than of course (cough) exposing her breasts,

And I hope she feels it deep and true,
And I hope she recounts it to me and does rue,
'cause it will come when it is due,
All for the shit that bitch put me through,

I was never anything near what that bitch thought of me,
It was all a façade I put on for her to see,
Anyone lucky enough to have gotten to know would agree,
The façade replaced the real, when I'd learn from what I'd foresee,

She was that predictable that I could expect it –
Every ounce of her behaviour, her attitude, reflected it,
How could I – in all my decency – be so quick to be respecting it?
She had secrets and she was most certainly protecting it,

So I want to see that fuckin' bitch hurt,
'cause there was never a moment I didn't when I was with her,
I want to see the man she desperately falls for dessert,
And I wanna see that fuckin' bitch hurt,

I want her to be so obsessed,
That it hurts her worse to be an ex,
That she finally opens and fully invests,
More than of course (cough) exposing her breasts,

And I hope she feels it deep and true,
And I hope she recounts it to me and does rue,
'cause it will come when it is due,
All for the shit that bitch put me through,

No Clean Thrill

"Arseholes just want to shit on everything,
yes, but they too can be fucked…"

I've just about been taken for every fuckin' thing I had,
Can you seriously not expect and allow that I've gone mad?
Been backdoored, cheated out of thrice,
How can you honestly just expect me to play nice?

I'm surprised I can be writing this right now and be so chill,
When I know others in my position wouldn't hesitate to kill,
She could never take a decent fuck up the arse,
But she'll do it to you – and make sure you know –
She laughs,

I lost and I can't do anything – but the good guys always will,
I was a dirty fuck – but she was no clean thrill,
So I'm hopin' I can make her pay like she never has,
Boy she'd get a spanking if I were her dad,

She couldn't do a thing to recompense me what I lost,
Not finally by the fucking time I'm fucking not,
And she'll never have a chance to change my mind about it,
Sure she was a snob – she was good, but I still doubted,

I had every reason to from the start,
To only ever want to love her half-arsed,
When she couldn't understand nor believe I could see,
Truths about her – US – I – she couldn't see,

I read it quick and I read it fuckin' well,
And as certain as fuck as I was – I faced hell,

And the shit that I saw I knew to be true,
Knew I had to fight like fuck this through,

I couldn't let her get away with it when I knew that it was wrong,
Now any place with her in it – is nowhere I belong,

Stepping Stone

You were merely a stepping stone,
To shape, strategy, skills to hone,
A beggar exiled to roam,
To one day return a king to a throne,

Yet so temporary was the time,
Time you'd be spending as mine,
But they all soon slip behind,
Fade to just a memory in my mind,

You never had to teach it all to me,
Not when there's many more folk to meet,
Old knowledge – old tricks of all treats,
A plethora of pleasures, there's no time to sleep,

I was cut by your loss for a while,
Plunged in to a pit of tar-black denial,
Dunked in the shit, a huge steamy pile,
Pulling straight would send me wild,

'Cause I was a beggar exiled to roam,
Then I met you my, stepping stone,
I found devices, tools, skills to hone,
And return to be a king to be throned,

I was a beggar exiled to roam,
Then I met you my stepping stone,
I'd find devices, tools and skills to hone,
And return the king to throne,

Yet so temporary was the time,
You'd be spending as mine,
You'd soon slip behind,
And fade to nothing but a memory in my mind,

I can't undo the past,
And you won't be the last,
You can't unbreak my heart,
But you gave me a head start,

Some lessons are hard to learn,
But this one between us burnt,
My gizzards churned,
Somehow – I did still yearn,

I once thought you were the best,
And I guess now I can actually get this all off my chest,
But there's just so many more women in the world left,
Why just stop with you yet,

Oh, I was a beggar exiled to roam,
And then I met her, my, stepping stone,
I'd find devices, tools, skills to hone,
Return as king for the throne,

Below Her

She couldn't tell me the truth,
She knew it'd be used against her,
I just wished I could've known what I was in for –
I knew she could hurt me more than the pain she felt –
I, just never wanted to let her,

It's not good for me – I can't afford it,
She did disgust me so, can applaud that,
But of everything I poured to it,
Would've thought I could've been, somewhat important,

I know it shouldn't matter 'cause I never could,
I wasn't ever once that good,
She could never lead me to believe I ever would,
So I could be kept just where I should,

Below her,

Wished I could've known what I was in for,
Might've done a whole lot more,
I learnt there I couldn't satisfy a whore,
I lost, couldn't even impress that more,

I brew and I stew on all this negativity,
That as soon as they've had me – they want rid of me,
Never worth more than that good little bit of me,
Stranded, looping round aimlessly, in hopeless negativity,

Wished I could've known more,
To be prepared for what I was in for,
I can never heal from these sores,
Picking through the scabs with these swords,

She couldn't be up front and honest with me,
Or maybe she might've been – just in a way I couldn't see,
About the whole – just – letting her be free,
I guess to fuck everyone but me,

Yeah – I'm below her…

Lady Of The Lava Lake

Come all ye young men, come this way,
Come all and see the Lady of the Lava Lake,
Come ye all – invest and partake,
Come ye – all, and each have your way –

She is a queen of where she's from,
Many men have all come and gone,
Many of those men, lived for so long,
While she feeds, off of all the wrong,

She is of Lava,
Always searching for a lover,
For passion burning hotter than hers,
She cradles the urge, the nerves,

She does rise out of hot Lava,
To seek herself another lover,
For the passion burning fiercer than hers,
She nurses the urges, cradles the nerves,

She is Queen of where she's from,
Many men have all came and gone,
And many of these men all outlived long,
All that while she feed off their wrong,

She gains strong,
Feeding off the wrong –
And many a man has came and gone,

Come all ye young men, come this way,
Come all ye and see the Lady of Lava Lake,
Come ye all, and invest and partake,
Come ye all and forever stay…

Not For Keeps

I can't keep a girl for a variety of reasons,
I have habits and misbehave and mistreat 'em,
I can see now how it is conceited,
I feel I'm to far gone to retrieve it,

Nah, I can't seem to keep a girl for long,
When I think I'm right I'm still fucking wrong,
Even when I break, I'm expected to be strong,
Those times I'd lost my mind and gone beyond,

Getting the girls really ain't the problem,
I have had a lot of them,
Someone should maybe warn them, stop them,
It's too late once I have got them,

I can't keep a girl for a long time,
Times are great but I tread lines,
Crossed boundaries – ought not be defied,
It's a miracle that I still survive,

I can't keep a girl no matter if I try,
Primal instinct to fuck always overrides,
Can't help I'm a guy with a high sex drive,
Never getting' enough always feeling left deprived,

Getting the girls really ain't the problem,
I have had a fuck load of them,
Somebody should probably warn 'em or stop 'em,
It'll be too late once I have got them,

There shouldn't be difficulty trying to keep them,
It certainly isn't getting to meet them,
But there are many various reasons,
That just leaves the point, the purpose, defeated,

Conceited…

Thinkin' With The Pecker

Proud of this thing? Shit, no –
I like my brains preferably left in my head,
I can only hope I can attract a woman,
With an imagination as good as mine,

Yes, I like to use my brains,
But I'll admit – I don't use them appropriately,
Only hoping I'm as good as my brain,
Or it's diversional tactics when I'm not using it right,

Trying to seduce the ladies,
Sure – I've shared photos,
But wonder now where my brain was,
Ah yes – in my pecker,

I like to think I'm funny and I'll be dirty doing it,
Someone's gonna bite something and I think I'll be chewin' it,
Not so equipped – uh – I'm losin' it –
Think of something funny to set back the mood to it,

Get funny with imagination,
Start to use the brain,
It's all inappropriate,
Laugh, mask the shame,

That Missable Feeling

I'm missing that feeling,
With women or one willing,
Touching, feeling,
Sensitive – I hit the ceiling,

Arms wrapped around,
Her bust – I'm lookin' down,
Before she squeals as I kiss her neck,

Suck a bite over her collar –
Educated as, per commoner squalor,
Profaner the methods, than, the intention of having her wet,

Playful back and forth – lapping lips,
Arms now slid down the hips,
And reach up under to touch, rise, and feel much closer yet,

Hand slide up over the breast,
Brush passed the nipple with a gentle caress,
Then bite down playfully once again at her neck,

Yeah, I'm missin' that feelin',
With women or one willing,
Touching, fondling, feeling,
I'm so sensitive now – I'd hit the ceiling,

Left hand over neck now,
As tongue wanders the nipple round,
Right hand confirms her sweet li'l honey pot wept,

And after it's all over,
Head a' roam, go rover,
Never kiss and tell who was with all due respect,

And I'm missin' that feelin',
With women or one willing,
Touching, fondling, feeling,
Only so sensitive now – I'd hit the ceiling,

LoverMan

I'm gonna come and see you and give you all the loving I can,
C'mon now honey let me be your man,
Let me unclip that then unzip this,
But not without a passionate kiss,

I'll love you tender, love you slow,
Wow you're really beautiful; I can see you glow,
Take my hand and step this way,
And listen ever carefully to the alluring words I'll say,

Don't be afraid baby, Take a leap of faith,
You never know maybe after just that one taste,
You may never want me replaced,

I would love to make you moan, but I'd rather hear you screamin'
We can take it slow then smash it fast, 'till we get the windows steamin'
I love your touch, how warm you feel,
I wanna see that look in your eye, so I go hard as steel,

And when I catch a glimpse of your cheeky grin,
I think fuck, fuck yeah, bring on the sin,
You may have your lust but wait 'till you witness mine
If you felt the way I did our clothes would long be left behind,

If there a moment though that you had felt in doubt,
Then I would simply just say this,
Wait 'till I whip it out,

Loving To Tongues

I've made love to a woman,
And made her speak in tongues,
Made her speak that angelic language,
And I was stricken dumb,

Never even seen it happen before,
I'd freaked out thinking I'd done wrong,
Never witnessed that very anomaly before,
But there was definitely something going on,

It was a passion I shared I'd never had,
And I panicked never knowing prior,
I still don't quite understand,
I wouldn't be surprised if you'd called me a liar,

As far as I know only a priest could invoke,
Such a circumstance as that,
I only ever felt destined for fire and smoke,
And never any situation other than that,

It's supposed to be divine, an ultra-rare occurrence,
That not just any man can execute the service,
But the fact that I have makes me the more nervous,
Of heavier responsibility – deeper meaningful purpose,

To what extent and why has me wanting answers,
And I really can't know for sure what it means,
Born with the gift of a real romancer?
Shit, that'd be every man's dream,

I have indeed made love to a woman and made her speak in tongues,
That strange angelic language and it sent me numb...

S.B.R. (Spontaneous Body Reflex)

Oh whoa – you've tickled a nerve,
You've just touched me and I've gone berserk,
I rattle, I roll, I writhe, and I squirm,
And I see you've deviously smiled a smirk,

Whoa! Damn Gal! you've got me moving now,
I can't fathom how – you've got me inside out,
I can't fuckin' stop foaming at the mouth,
I chuck in the towel – I'm down for the count,

Oh – whoa well, it's complex,
Your touch and my reflex,
I wanna share similar respects,
Only in similar context,

You're twinging tweeze is sporadic,
If it don't stop soon I should probably panic,
These rippling, twitching sensations are manic,
I can't catch my breath through the static,

Oh whoa – you've tickled a nerve,
You've just touched me and I've gone berserk,
I rattle, I roll, I writhe, and I squirm,
And I see you've deviously smiled a smirk,

Oh – whoa well, it's complex,
Your touch and my reflex,
I wanna share similar respects,
Only in similar context,

Fuck I just can't contain myself,
You've bust open the gates of hell,
Can't believe how much expels,
I'd say that went well…

Sextacy

Sextacy,
The pleasuring,
Let enter in,
Come, get next to me,

Free yourself of your material bonds,
Your clothes, make them gone,
Lie, for the touch you've longed,
Relax, won't take too long,

Sextacy,
The pleasuring,
Let, enter in,
Come, get next me,

Get the feelin' comin' on,
Winding up bright and strong,
Everything right with the wrong,
It's time to get it on,

Sextacy...yeah,
The pleasuring,
Let, enter in,
Come, get next to me,

Sextacy,
Let, enter in,
The pleasuring,
Come, get next to me...

Cyber Show

Yeah it was me on the cyber-net showin' off me prick,
I love it, love playin' with it, after all it's my dick,
When I'm in the shower mate – I wash it quick,
It gets rather vigorous it's a wonder I don't slip,

Yeah, it was me on the cyber-net showin' off me prick,
But also showing intelligent – creative wit,
Never met any once – never close enough to lick,
Any particular place I made any of them think,

Yeah it was me on the cyber-net, showin' off me prick,
Getting' up to all manners of mischievous tricks,
Perking up, working up an excitement in the chicks,
And such a sexual deviate does indeed exist,

Yeah it was me on the cyber-net, showin' off me prick,
Wasn't it nice and long and juicy and thick?
Some woman out there better snatch me up quick,
Thinkin' all about it again is getting' me all stiff,

Yeah it was me on the cyber-net, showin' off me prick,
Nothin' ever happened but you'd probably know if it did,
I might be small but then it might be that big,
The difference though is I do indeed know how to use 'it',

Replenish The Zest

I love excitements – I love the zest,
I love to take something good and make it the best,
I wanna blow their minds and put peace to their rest,
So I'll go excite, and replenish a zest with a jest,

It won't take me long to get you in the mood,
It doesn't take me long when I work my moves,
Not feelin' it right now? Wrong attitude –
Get up, walk it off and shake loose,

Are you sure you're not so willing to cut loose?
Come poor baby – let me amuse,

Let me just walk over here then – whoops!
Oh no, I dropped my phone – I have to bend over but don't you look,
I make a sly glance back and notice you starin' at my tush,
So I said: "would you be surprised if I said I shaved my bush?"

I know – your expression says – 'not here – not now',
But I think you're happy to see me – oh, ooh – uh, wow!
I think you better put those naughty thoughts down,
You might catch another someone's eye out,

But are you sure you don't wanna relax and get loose?
Come to me poor baby – let me amuse,

I just love excitements – I do love zest –
And I wanna make you feel nothing but the best,
I wanna blow your mind and put peace to your rest,
So come, let me excite, and replenish zest with a little jest,

Come baby – let me get you in the mood,
Shrug off – come shake off that dull attitude…

New Found Bliss

I'm enslaved by rage,
Caged and abreised,
Flayed and depraved,
I'm strayed, and I'm preyed,

Yet fate took a twist,
Somehow, I found a bliss,
A new reason to exist,
One that I had missed,

A feeling I once lost,
An unfathomable cost,
Something I'd forgot,
When I had rather not,

She's allowed me to see,
Finally set me free,
Taken an interest in me,
Allowed me to be,

She's given me more,
Than anyone before,
A valuable score,
No fairy tale lore,

Far greater than a treasure,
The greatest of my pleasures,
She'll have me forever,
Beyond soul and body severed,

Advancing, Entrancing...

I know we've just met,
But holy fuck wow!
You may just be the one yet –
I've gotta have you now,

Baby come back – don't walk away,
Gimme a chance to make your day,
You caught my glance now play it your way,
Advance in naughty dance, prey and misbehave,

Freudian slips,
Get 'em laughing quick,
Tact, timing – suave and slick,
Soon you'll be lockin' lips,

Got me singing a shanty,
And feelin' a little randy,
I wanna be advancing,
You're just so entrancing,

Baby come back – don't walk away,
Gimme a chance to make your day,
You caught my glance, come, play,
Advance in naughty dance, prey and misbehave,

Yeah – I know we've just met,
But holy fuck wow!
I have to get you wet,
And I want it now –

You've got me singing a shanty,
And feelin' a little randy,
I wanna get advancing,
You're just so entrancing...

Deviate Extents

You and me gotta get something straight,
I'm not fuckin' queer – I am straight,
I'm not fucking gay mate – eh,
It's clit before dick, any day,

I guess I'm a little more feminine than you fathom,
But I can have sheila's like you wouldn't imagine,
I've been the cause of many a distraction,
There was some strange attraction,

I like the ladies a little too much,
I have had a good share of fun,
I've gone crazy for the touch,
Young but very much with a cunning linguists tongue,

But I have gotten carried away with the fun,
Things I have said and done in the past have stunned,
I was crazy for the touch,
I wanted it a little too much,

Wouldn't be too long and I'd gain interests,
Curious, but unfaithful interests,
Followed suit by deviate extents,
Relationships rigid halt to an end,

Might not have been too bad,
If I had control – kept it in the pants,
Would never have been so bad –
To have kept it knotted in the pants,

So as you can see I'm perfectly straight,
No fuckin' queer – mate, dinky di straight,

I'm tellin' ya – I ain't gay eh,
It's clit before dick any day,

I like the ladies a little too much,
I just go so fuckin' crazy for the touch…

Chapter 5

Chromatosic Aberrance Of The Diabolically Articulate;

Satan's Valkyrie

Level down,
It's comin'
Feel it?
I'm comin'

Level down,
Beneath me, above you,
Level down,
To bring you back up too,

You're callin' – it's comin'
I'm falling, I plummet,
Reach out, claw out, grasp it,
Reef up, roaring – sky rocket,

Level down,
Beneath me, above you,
Level down,
To bring you back up too,

Hawk-eye precision,
Sharp, clear distinction,
Caught you falling in my vision,
To catch you with my winged wisdom,

So be it that I –
Never leave behind,
Level down
To drag you out,

Level down,
I'm comin' …

Regiment One

Ghastly ghostly faces rifting within a smoke,
Circle around and weep and scream and moan,
Storming in and out, weaving, interfering on my lone,
Spiralling around within this vessel of meat and bone,

More than one and caught in a web,
Smokey ghostly faces that creep, sweep and ebb,
Summoned out somehow from the lands of the dead,
Out from the pit and it's dark murky depths,

Cycling round still and calm, quiet almost dull,
Just as all is almost a lull, suddenly is null,
Silence is slain and storm rages of skulls,
Screaming, pain, and all chaos reigns control,

Caught, trapped in a smokey web,
From the blackest recesses in my head,
Summoned out somehow from the lands of the dead,
Yes, out from the pits and their dark murky depths,

A hurricane of souls – bargained, sold,
Contained in one vessel, a whispery mould,
Tales of terror, let begin, be told,
As old as a burnt-out star, and as cold,

Numbers

It's always about the numbers,
The popularity,
Bigger, better statistics,
Casualties of all sorts,

How many times I can feel good about myself,
How many times I piss people off,
How often the times I'm accompanied with girls,
Size, of the wad of cash I've got,

It's always about the numbers,
The popularity,
Bigger – better statistics,
Casualties of all kinds,

Numbers of people who have to die,
And the surplus of all those still alive,
Popularity of goods or services consumed,
Countless the casualties all to be tombed,

It's always about the numbers,
Popularity,
Bigger – better statistics,
Casualties of all sorts and kinds,

Total of all my accrued cash,
Number of names I've gotta bash,
Numbers of women to love thrash,
Total of weight in my stash,

Numbers under government surveillance,
Numbers picked by elite assailants,

Numbers of who or what's prevalent,
And, numbers, countless, all devastated,

It's always about the numbers,
And the majority of us all still slumber,

Vault

Deep down beneath the subconscious,
We've got a vault for the monotonous,
Memories locked away, reason for the rhythm,
Documentaries contained, matrix to the system,

Collision course predilection,
Caution – misfiring nerve thread receptors,
Warning, chemical maladjustment,
Shock trauma, short circuit, wiring dysfunction,

Strenuous friction within the structure,
May cause the serous wear to enable rupture,
A maelstrom beneath the vault door – rifting,
Shifting, swirling, lashing – raging – rippling,

Stay away from the vault
Don't go near the vault,
Stay away from the vault,
Don't go anywhere fucking near the vault,

For fuck's sake don't open the vault,
Fuck's sake don't expose the faults,
Vault's better left tightly sealed,
No resolve once been revealed,

Collision course for predilection,
Caution misfiring weaving nerve thread receptors,
Warning, toxic chemical maladjustment,
Shock trauma, short circuit – wiring dysfunction,

Triggers

I've raged at times and not known why,
I've mourned and grieved when I should've been otherwise,
I've laughed my arse off at inappropriate times,
When others were angered or would cry,

I do think I do know what it is,
At least I, have my suspicions,
Think I've got an idea of what it is,
There's got to be some sort of triggers,

Whether sights or sounds,
Scents I smell around,
Beware, we may be bound,
Seeing something may go down,

Triggers that set us off,
Triggers, like brainwash,
Triggers, countdown to cost,
Triggers, escalate to loss,

Yeah – I think I do know what it is,
At least I, have my suspicions,
Yeah, I've got an idea of what it is,
It's some sort of triggers,

Whether sights or sounds,
Scents I smell around,
Beware, we may be bound,
Seeing something may go down

Triggers, that set us off,
Cool one minute to then be not,
Triggers, they set us off,
Triggers, escalate the loss…

Triggers!

Perverted

I've got a filthy mind and even filthier tongue,
And I'm certain a lot of what I say sounds dumb,
But hey, why not? While we're still young,
Relax, it's only harmless fun,

I'm a pervert – and quite extrovert about it,
A dirty pervert – have many disturbed about it,
A filthy pervert – well, they've gone berserk about it,
Yeah, I'm a pervert – and I might divert… nah, doubt it,

Anything you say can and will be turned dirty,
Not to be taken seriously or feelings will be hurting,
Intelligent yet vulgar – my favourite method of flirting,
The party's getting started – why's everyone deserting?

It's not often that I'm not out of line,
It's not often I'm not out of and speaking my mind,
But I'm told the leash I keep on it has to be tight,
Because old standards of propriety haven't yet died,

I'm a pervert – and quite extrovert about it,
A dirty pervert – have many disturbed about it,
A filthy pervert – yeah, they go berserk about it,
Yeah, I'm a pervert – and I might divert it…nah, doubt it,

It might be immature, but admit it, you liked it,
Don't go condemning it before you even try it,
It has it's moments of hilarity – you really can't deny it,
This is how I want to be, it's decided,

Perverted!

Show Me Your Demons

I want to see your motives,
I want to know what drives you,
I want to know the reasons,
Your logic to what you do,

I want to see beneath your surface,
See how bad you need it,
I want to see your purpose,
Show me your demons,

Assumptions are deceiving,
Never quite how you perceive me,
Discomfort and difficulty believing,
Limited, reducing peaceful receiving,

I value the various outcasts of society,
I value any chance of escaping sobriety,
Deface the masking façade of propriety,
And revel in the pleasures often regarded with notoriety,

I want to see your motives,
I want to know what drives you,
I want to know the reasons,
Your logic to what you do,

I want to see beneath your surface,
See how bad you need it,
I want to see your purpose,
Show me your demons,

Something internal – by external animation,
The best of the worst under examination,

I am in wait, reeling with anticipation,
I need me a demon-stration,

I value any, every discomforting difference,
That normally disturb others enough for distance,
Come – let us soak in the reminiscence,
Show me your demons – again with repetition –

I want to see your motives,
I want to know what drives you,
I want to know the reasons,
Your logic to what you do,

I want to see beneath your surface,
See how bad you need it,
I want to see your purpose,
Show me your demons,

Show me your Demons…

Devil Does Know Good

Somebody's changing his tune,
I guess the quest is resumed,
There's always ever more to consume,
Ego's to inflate and burst like balloons,

I wanted this world to rot in ruin,
Seems like it already is,
Plot thickens, troubles brewin'
Yeah, certainly lookin' like it already is,

Testaments, shmeshtaments,
You control what you do and poorly invest it,
Shit I've seen has been difficult for digestion,
Ignored text messages, that love was the intention,

But not to worry – someone's loss is another gain,
When the devil wins the war – it'll be by love attained,
And who then can ever really be blamed?
But by those interests, respects that's were betrayed,

I wanted this world to rot in ruin,
But it seems like it already is,
Plots thicken, troubles brewing,
Yeah – it's certainly already lookin' like it is,

Testaments – Shmeshtaments,
You control what you do and poorly invest it,
And all this shit I've seen has been hard on digestion,
Ignored text messages, that love was the intention…

And a sickening one…

All Precious' Invested

A thought just crossed my mind,
Over a few fuck up's from over time,
At least – towards the end –
Of a something was more than just 'friends'

It occurred to me it's the time you invest,
When you're with another –
Heart beatin' in you're chest,
Doesn't ever want another –

But of the things you can accumulate,
With that significant other,
The love, the trust, the faith –
You don't want it like that with another,

Time invested – like all else,
Is lost when you have to travel the hell,
Of the something you had that fell apart,
Another ending to begin another start,

Thought crossed my mind –
Just how many more times,
Will I have to leave behind –
Something I enjoyed calling mine,

Precious time fly's when you're alone,
You kind of begin to enjoy it on your own,
Got your job, your car, your home,
And all other else to invest in the zone,

And upon thought crossing over mistakes passed made,
I think this way is a far better state to stay,

10 Steps

I'm beginning to understand
What can make a better man,
Power is only given to the hands,
Who take a righteous responsible stand,

To know when and where you see new lows,
10 steps ahead – it's chess, you already know,
Takes courage to be alone and let it show,
Weaving round the ignorant arrogances who'll never know,

I only mean to say it that way out of irritation,
Losing my patience with a rapidly rising frustration,
I've been practicing, keeping my cool a whole lot more,
Getting easier slowly, with a closer reach to the score,

I'm keeping calmer throughout these little irritations,
I'm laughing a lot more now avoiding frustration,
Practicing keeping my temper cooler more,
Bettering my reach toward the score,

In a quest to be godlike I studied the nature,
I had an ideal but was born of similar nature,
Things, tried to make me but I guess in ways they did,
Intelligent enough to practice when I live,

I never thought the way I chose to see it –
Was indeed the valued way to see it,
And with the 10 steps ahead – simple reminiscences,
Would explain the interpretations of these experiences,

I would realize the path I chose to walk,
Is more treasured than I first saw,
Powers in my hands,
Are only makin' me want more…

Begot By Certain Procedures

I believe I've intercepted knowledge of an ancient history,
That many have kept to their best in secrecy,
A lot of it's denied and responded of as heresy,
But I can believe it within every piece of me,

A secret knowledge only handed,
To those responsible to understand it,
Bigger the prize yes, but deeper reprimanded,
Accepted, matured, enough to upstand it,

I can only promise to take it as far,
As you are comfortable to go as far,
'cause there's no turning back after so far,
You know better and the universe knows you are,

It's why you struggle when you fight the flow,
The universe knows what you know,
Determines how easy when you do show,
And times can have an ever brighter glow,

I can't explain how I know and feel through my intuition,
I only know it's the good I ever want to exhibit,
Difficult at times but I would make it a life mission,
'cause of the other two options, it's death or it's prison,

Time does come when you must know best,
To do with what you know and rise out from the rest,
To battle on through each obstacle and test,
And to never give in 'til you find your success,

Pride Deep

Pride huh?
Thing is, pride is just a way,
To take on your vain,
So much you wouldn't change,
Any of your broken, damaged –
Tainted ways,

Pride?
That wool over the eyes,
Disguise your flaws, faults, demise,
Shit you take for granted,
Never face, own up to and despise,

Pride huh, yeah –
Pride is just a way,
To take on all your vain,
So much you wouldn't change,
You wouldn't fix or repair what pain,

To never look deeper and reason,
Never accept but irrationalise, misbelieve it,
Never see more into or passed all you're deceived of,
Never ascend to more nor peacefully achieve it,

Pride, that wool over the eyes,
That's disguised your flaws, faults, demise,
Covering the shit you take for granted,
Never to face, never own up to but despise,

Your pride restricts you from change,
In countless ways…

Loser

I'm told I'm a loser
Perhaps that's true,
What even defines a loser?
What does one do?

Except maybe lose my patience –
With the ever-endless idiocrasy,
Maybe lose my cool –
With the constant hypocrisy,
Maybe lose my respect –
For those of irresponsibility,
Possibly lose my faith –
We'll never get passed this misery,

I'm told I'm a loser – HA
By the whinging losers themselves,
Yeah, I'm told I'm the loser –
And they feed me all kinds of hell,

But by whose fuckin' standards? Theirs?
How – in what way do they better compare?
What consideration am I given that really is fair –
When I myself am considerate enough to spare?

Yes, I lose my patience –
With the never-ending idiocrasy,
I often do lose my cool –
Suffering constant hypocrisy,
I'll lose all my respect –
For those of irresponsibility,
Certainly, destined to lose my faith –
And never escape their misery,

Yeah, I'm told I'm the loser,
By a bunch of whinging losers themselves,
Me – yeah – I'm supposed to be the loser,
But birds of a feather – guess they know it well,

Who's Suckin' Who?

It's amazing how people can say you suck,
But not see they're doing it that moment themselves,
So many people can think you suck,
And never see them doing it themselves,

Oh-so-quick to have an opinion,
And feel they deserve the right,
Everyone's got an opinion,
And are even quicker to fight,

They must feel pretty up themselves,
To think they have a level of importance,
Enough they don't keep it to themselves,
But I guess everyone wants to feel important,

The question is what are they gonna do for me?
How can I constructively dismantle criticism –
When I know they want to hurt me –
You've just gotta make them think,

Because people are gonna say you suck,
And not even they are gonna give a fuck,
But they never offer up a solution,
Only offer their toxic pollution,

You may never get away of it completely,
But you can turn the tables on a stupidity,
I look at a lot of them an shaking my head –
Think this is the reason they're better off dead,

But when they can't do nothin' for you,
Except for takin' you down,

you know you do a lot better than they do –
you'll crush their spirit into the ground,

so long as they survive,
they'll deprive – and they'll suck…

Want Your Something

Yeah, I've been doing a lot of a something –
Of which I were previously warned,
Sending out something, making all warm and fuzzy,
Occasionally earning its' scorn,

No – I don't want war,
I want love,
I've got war,
Want your love,

I want your something I can taste,
I just get hooked on the faintest trace,
I get it – I know my place,
I trance out – entrance for some embrace,

So I've been doing a lot of a something,
I was previously warned –
Sending out something – making all warm and fuzzy,
And times again it's earnt its' scorn,

But I just don't want war,
I want love,
I've got war – abundant,
I just want love,

Just want that something I can taste,
Tastes so good I'm hooked on the slightest trace,
Oh I do get it – I know my place,
I just trance out – entrance for an embrace,

Like a siren calling it's prey,
Hear me call you this way,
Come, lay, come and play,
Please, come and stay…

Something In My Ear

I was down and I was grim,
Then something sweet-talked and I let it in,
Now it rattles, writhes beneath the skin,
Telling me strange and bizarre things,

I sit, I listen, I watch and it does too,
It remarks our interests in the things we're through –
All things I and many others do,
And all too soon it'll say it wants it too,

It may never make much sense,
Some things I've done – I may do again,
This thing in my ear – what it says,
I think it's more of a foe than a friend,

It sings out at every little wrong,
And if it hasn't it won't be too long,
Sometimes I think I want it gone,
But at times it's told me it wants me gone,

This was my body and my mind first,
And this thing has a seemingly large thirst,
It's made me feel I may uncontrollably burst,
Compelled, impulse to fulfil an urge,

It's like an inhuman conscience I can't rid,
Scarier in a feller that's stands this big,
Tongue often bit, grinding my teeth grit,
Fighting it back down off from saying evil shit,

And it may never make much sense,
Some things I've done I may do again,
With this fucking thing in my ear and what it says,
I do feel like it's more of a foe than a friend,

Disrupt

I watch from afar,
You're becoming a star,
I'd only ever gotten so far,
So, I'm gonna make it hard,

You seemed to pass so fluently,
When I myself had difficulty,
You still fit so congruently,
When I have difficulty,

You do so well from a distance,
You have a harmonious existence,
All I ever seem to get is a resistance,
A poor and pitiful position,

And I watch from afar,
You're becoming a star,
I'd only ever gotten so far,
So, I'm gonna make it hard,

I find it so displeasing,
When I see you've gotten it easy,
I wonder why I'm still breathing,
Why it's all deceived me,

It'll take me a fuck before I look,
To focus on me to make it good,
It'll take me a fuck up before I look,
Before I ever do anything good,

But I taint it, blacken it corrupt,
All efforts spent to disrupt,
Anyone – everyone, when I can't
I'll cause disharmony and disrupt,

The obstacle in the way,
Just to make sure you pay,
That this, these games, aren't all play,
And I know there's equal pain,

I don't want to feel alone,
And to drag you down means I won't,
I'll share hell, it's all our home,
There's no better evil to know,

You seemed to pass so fluently,
When I myself had so much difficulty,
You seem to fit so congruently,
When all I have is difficulty,

And I found it so displeasing,
Too see you have it so easy,
I wonder why I continue breathing,
Wonder why it's all deceived me,

But I watch from afar,
Watch as you become a star,
I'd only ever gotten so far,
So, I'm gonna make it hard,

'cause I'd only ever gotten so far,
Yes – I'm going to make it hard,

'cause I'd only ever gotten so far,
Yeah, I'm gonna make it hard –
And disrupt…

Maggot Feats, Maggot Feasts

He whispered in my ear,
Yes, I could hear,
I heard every word the filthy little maggot said,
Slimy little maggot, feasting, talking to the dead,

I'm dead, dead enough not to care,
The maggots are only feeding on my despair,
It'd get more if it could love and actually care,
But maggot has no capacity, maggot can't spare,

Maggot is starving and he needs to eat,
And I rot and decay worse than smelly living feet,
But maggot bites in despite the smell his nostrils reach,
Maggot's starving and weak, only feeding off the defeat,

I had to be dead enough, and dead enough I don't care,
'Cause maggot only ever likes to feed on my despair,
Probably would've gotten more if it shared,
But maggot has no capacity, he couldn't spare,

I did hear tiny little maggot speak,
Little fucker had over-spoke me weak, non-stop repeat,
And the fuckin' little maggot repeats it as I sleep,
To enforce what maggot wants of me, it's how he's as weak,

Little maggot only ever feeding off the dead,
I can hear you talk maggot – I heard what you said,
The truth hurts you hard, when you know, you'll dread,
Only ever so weak to have fed only off the dead,

Poor little maggot only feeding on despair –
Not enough capacity, never none to compare,
Starving little maggot only always eating more than is fair,

Cut My Face

Earlier stages of my psychosis,
Pleasures of the pain,
In earlier stages of my psychosis,
I would cut my face,

I used to want to take it off,
Skin it completely,
Cut away this old face off,
Expose the flesh beneath it,

I've cut my face a couple times,
And laughed loving the sting,
Cut it over many times,
Laughing through a sinister grin,

Earlier stages of my psychosis,
I found pleasures of the pain,
In earlier stages of my psychosis,
I had indeed cut my face,

Wanted to take it off –
Expose the hideous beneath,
Cut, rip away this old face off,
Skin it off complete,

Cut my face a few times,
Laughed maniacally loving the sting,
I must've maybe lost my mind,
Laughing through my sinister grin,

Smile Again

There have to be deep reasons,
Psychological reasons why,
I'd want to cut my face,
Face the pain but fix it permanently,

Cut the corners of my smile wider,
Cut across the cheeks,
Stitch with gauze, cover, tighter,
And have that gaping smile recovered in weeks,

To smile, through all pain,
Made to, ironically all the same,
But to smile, with it permanently fixed,
Smile cut insidiously across my face,

Made of in example like I never knew,
Made to break but forced to smile through,
But cut my face and may I ever do –
Glorious pain that shows, it's long due,

There has to be deep reason,
Psychological reasons why,
I'd even want to cut my own face –
Face the pain but fix it permanent,

Cut – gauze up and stitch,
Push through the pain,
Suppress the nerves, the reflexing twitch,
Push through the pain,

I'll smile wide again,
I'll smile again…

Some Medical Mental

Needing some medical mental,
Some doctor to reach inside my mind,
Need some medical mental,
Twist straight my wicked mind,

Need some medical mental,
Some answers to help me find,
Needing some medical mental,
A resolute peace I could call mine,

Need some medical mental,
To unknot my tangled, mangled mind,
Needing some medical mental,
Answers to help me align,

Needing some medical mental,
Some doctor to reach inside my mind,
Yeah needing some medical mental,
To twist straight my wicked mind,

Need that medical mental,
Gimme that medical mental,
Yeah needing ya medical mental,
Please doctor I'm friggin' mental,

Those pills that zonk me out,
That needle in the arse to calm me down,
Program me to be so sweet and sound,
And release me back out,

Master The Madness

Madness, as a sea of truth and lies,
Madness, as all you love turns to despise,
Madness, a drought, when they expect your cries,
Madness, negotiation through each compromise,

Madness – where the mind is broken beyond repair,
Madness – a vacant emotion where all else despair,
Madness, forsaken to nothingness, forced to dare,
Madness, to dare from nothingness, fearless to fare,

The time I'll have taken in to me,
To repair every break, every fracture I see,
In every theoretical mental sense to mean,
Flaws of reasoning, all, and transcend to the dream,

Madness, to interpret to the curiosities of the cynical,
Madness, to be yourself and not piss off the hypocritical,
Madness, a reactive defence can appear so spiteful, so pitiful,
Madness, the toll it takes on an individual,

The time I've taken unto me,
To repair every break, every fracture I see,
In every theoretical mental sense to mean,
Flaws of reasoning all, and transcend to the dream,

The Laughing House

Something bizarre happens,
Behind these closed doors,
A vibration, a strange static,
Through the boarded walls, roof and floors,

There is a sinister aura that shrouds,
Darker than when night surrounds,
Even more insidious are the creepy sounds,
Of diabolical, maniacal, laughter in the house,

Emotions of misery felt so saddening,
The laughter I'm hearing, echo's ever maddening,
A strange phenomenon is certainly happening,
The diabolical laughter – it's maddening,

Emotions of anger I feel trapped in here,
But the laughter, sickening, ringing in my ears,
Such vengeful rage drifting round in here,
The maniacal laughter of the house in my ears,

Emotions of fear inhabit the space,
Laughter that's pierced, savaged the place,
Colour appears to drain from my face,
But the sinister, devilish laughter taints the space,

This house radiates strange madness,
Madness between anger and sadness,
Diabolical maniacal laughter inhabits,
The maddening, the maniacal laughter happens,

There is a sinister aura that shrouds,
Darker than when night falls and surrounds,
But ever more insidious are the creepy sounds,
Of that evil, diabolical, maniacal laughter of the house...

Secret From Sight

I reel from the pain,
Such blinding pain,
I scream in a rage,
Can't think how I got this way,

Locked, confined, in my cool dark space,
I cut and tear the flesh from my face,
Scratch and peel it from my chest,
Psychosis-blood-staining the family crest,

Secret after secret,
Swept from sight,
I am their ugly truth,
Despised and denied,

I reel from the pain,
Such blinding pain,
Screamin' in a rage,
Don't know how I got this way,

I tear and rip strips off me, litter the floor,
Ripping, slashing at, forever with claws,
Anger rising rapidly, masking the pain,
Family crest shamed, psychosis-blood-stained,

Secret after secret,
Swept clear from sight,
I am their ugly truth,
Despised and denied,

Despised and denied,
Always swept clear from sight,

In The Wake Of Split Second Madness

I'm certain many were confused at times, surprised by my mind,
Losing track some way behind attempting to predict my design,
Although they'll often find – there's no true
sequential pattern does arise,
Strange convenient things happen midst unfortunate, unforeseen times,

I've had the luck of narrow misses by chance or likely luck,
I've had deep despairing lows that spontaneously,
rapidly, accelerated me up,
I've daringly flirt with danger and cheated it with minor cuts,
I've been in jams but have managed to pry or slide myself unstuck,

I've done things smoothly without paying too much attention,
Maybe a little too many more times than I should care to mention,
At school, had detention, from most of which I was absent,
Somehow quick to pick the lesson before a much harsher tension,

Someone or some them, or something's got my back somewhere,
I just hope I'm equally worthy – that I live up to their kind care,
That they see my true nature, bare, and know it's worth the share,
Of and any tolls or conditions, expenses cropping up to fare,

I've been in dire financial straits – felt I was going to break,
Loose change – I've barely scraped, but not too long after escaped,
I've fallen for bait lain for betraying – yet fate had taken equal forsaking,
On those above playing, bait laying – are, not mistakenly, also paying,

I've done things, said things, met people I don't remember,
Not always pleasure, nor always a leisure but
not wasn't left completely tethered,
The madness left hind after rising between seconds,
Whether my worst or best of procession, had
certainly left its' impression…

Moments Of Sanity

Had a visit from my folks,
Just a moment ago,
Been a while since we spoke,
But brought me up to the know,

See, I'm living by myself with bugger all company,
And I forget visits of others can be so lovely,
But drawing in to myself I do forget,
Times of things can be better yet,

Living by myself I have all manners of thought,
And they all come and go but I'm fully absorbed,
I have moments of madness that last so long,
That I forget my mind was even gone,

But these visits of my folks,
Like mere moments ago –
Reminded me when they spoke,
And brought me back to the know,

I almost love these moments of sanity,
The pull back to earth – precious gravity,
Think I can appreciate a little sanity,
The grounding back on earth, this precious gravity,

Living by myself I have all manners of thought,
They all come and go and have me so deeply absorbed,
Moments of madness that can last too long,
Where I forget my mind was even gone,

Not Run True To The Same

I'm perpetually amazed at –
The confused misinterpretation of –
What I did, what they saw and it's –
Not run true to the same,

I'm perpetually amazed I'm –
Confusing the misinterpretation of –
What I said – what they heard and it's –
Not run true to the same,

I lean a little this way yet hold it there,
Trying to settle a focus for unmistakable stare,
The inconvenience, its' irritancy have caused glares,
And the misfortune that the irritancies flare,

Slow down now –
Let's communicate,
Slow down,
Let's contemplate,

I lean a little that way there and hold a little here,
And it's only too soon I've confirmed my worst fears,
Confusion, misinterpretation, close to causing tears,
Aroused up irritancies with glares that pierce,

Yeah – I'm perpetually amazed at –
The confused misinterpretation of –
What I did – what they saw and –
It's not run true to the same,

I'm perpetually amazed I'm –
Confusing the misinterpretation of –
What I said – what they heard and it's –
Not run too true to the same…

Counter-Justify

Been to the tip of the heat of the passion,
That kind of passion where people get a bashing,
And blinded by your fury you go out 'n trash it,
Infuriation dangerously peaking – you go out and smash it,

Come to the tip in the heat of the passion,
And then they'll question you why –
Cut to the chase of all the irrationate,
And spontaneously counter-justify,

Sure – everyone's got their reasons,
But are they really smart as they claim?
They may have their perspective at how to see it –
But it's just – who's fuckin' playin' what game?

Intelligence and counter so –
To keep to the loop of the know,
Remember you're reaping what you sow,
And it's on display – it's on show,

You've gotta show you're intelligent that you show,
Clever poker faces – and none need ever know –
Those various levels various people have on the go,
Remember you display – remember you're on show,

Sure – some have got a reason,
But let's pray they're smarter than they claim,
They're free to have it how they wanna see it –
It just who then is playing what game?

Come, to the tip of the heat of the passionate,
And they will all question you why –
So cut to the chase of the irrationate –
And spontaneously counter-justify,

Defending Madness

In defence of my madness,
I didn't know what I was doing,
Wasn't aware I didn't know,
And never really know when I am,

In defence of my madness,
I couldn't understand what you were saying,
Never knew what you meant,
Nor even knew I could know,

In defence of my madness,
I somehow lost track of me,
Was somebody else in that moment,
And most unrecognisably,

You must think I'm mad for defending my crazy,
Maybe, don't now, isn't it amazing –

In defence of my madness,
I was lost in my emotion,
Extremes causing blackouts – I can't verify,
Amnesiac confusion covering where and when,

In defence of my madness,
I was fighting off yours,
Overridden, overpowered – I fade to shadow,
Lost battle, lost hope, when you lose your cause,

In defence of my madness,
I truly had lost my cause,
Battling my flaws,
And fighting off all yours,

It's madness…

Saving You Hell

You say I seem wound tight,
And you think you want to know why,
I'm biting back the urge to smite – yeah,
But if you knew you'd only cry,

Yeah, I've got restraints on myself,
I'm just sorry you can tell,
But these restraints on myself,
Is saving you a world of hell,

It's best I never let me out to play,
My ravenous carnage cunningly preys,
Trust me, I know it's better this way,
None of us want to see the end of days,

This distance I keep is for your protection,
Existence weeps at my predilections,
Resistance weakened upon insurrection,
Dissidence sweeps the crowd it's projected,

You say I seem wound tight,
And you think you want to know why,
Yeah – I'm biting back on my urge to smite,
If you knew you'd only cry,

So I'm restraining myself,
I'm just sorry you can tell,
I'm restraining myself,
And saving you hell,

Saving you hell,
Saving you hell…

Know From The Beginning

Now you knew from the beginning,
I had reasons enough of my own for doing so,
I thought that's what you liked about me, guilt free,
Can justify it almost every time for doing so,
No matter what it was,

I'm quick with a reason – it's not often I can't,
I won't be going halves when I know others aren't,
I can expect everyone's gonna wanna rage and call me a cunt,
But may they be better – when we're *all* on the hunt,

Allowing to be is entertaining,
When a misbehaviour's out masquerading,
Humiliation plenty – I'm not complaining,
It's just who can really see who who's shaming,

It's when I'm called in and initiated,
Fair game, I'm consented invitation,
Underestimated force has just invaded,
Soon too blatant to me, it's me that's hated,

But they all knew from the beginning,
I had my reasons for doing so,
I thought that's what they liked about me, guilt free,
Can justify it almost every time for doing so,
No matter what it was,

And I'm quick with a reason, it's not often I can't,
And I won't be going halves when I know others aren't,
I know to expect others may want to rage and call me a cunt,
But they'd all best be better when we're *all* on the hunt,

Fearless Fool

I know it seems like I have no limits,
Particularly with what behaviour I exhibit,
Not too much that I'd inhibit,
Explicit, but not all to dispirit,

It may not seem like I have boundaries,
Or lines I just won't cross,
Extreme but real, profoundly,
But there are some I will not,

A combination of factors contribute to the flow,
Courtesies, respects, attitudes are some will show,
Expectations, double standards, negativity is a 'no'
Cynicism, scrutiny will stunt the attempt to grow,

I know it seems like there's no shit I wouldn't do,
That if I tag along I'll only bring doom,
I'm figuring it out and I'll get it right soon,
My quest for ascension, my longest due,

I have an inappropriate amount of lacking fear,
To things most people would keep clear,
Never certain if I ever may adhere –
To the direction of propriety society tries steer,

You'll notice I do when I'm stricken with discomfort,
To withdraw, shut off, go quiet, silent,
Moments rare, but you'll discover,
Cogs clicking, he's thinking, he's silent,

But better that than to play the fool,
Irrational behaviour – been back to school,

Disciplined, primed, ready to reign and rule,
Yeah little weird – ok, maybe still the fool,

A fearless, fool,
An educated fearless fool...

Walk The Dark

Christ, will you stand by me as I travel to the dark,
You said no, but I have to travel it hard,
Guess I want to be so close to you I have to know,
Path I choose, I know you'd understand, you know,

Times are different Christ,
People aren't as simple as before,
Times advance, wickedness survives,
So, you have to understand,
Good must be great to survive its' war,

Forgive me Christ for I must walk,
Love, understand what you say I just wanna see through your eyes,
So it's for the dark I must walk,

Times are different Christ,
People aren't so simple anymore,
Times advance and wickedness thrives,
Techniques must, advance as much as implored,

So Christ, will you please stand by me,
As I travel on through the dark,
Guess I want to see how you see,
Implies I have to do it as hard,

It's the path I choose,
No different to you,
Through the malevolent dark I must walk,
I choose it – I want it more,
Want to know more,

Those Cryptic Testaments

You have to choose your words carefully,
When others twist what you say,
They use what you say against you,
If you're not careful – it's led to stray,

I guess it's a similarity of mine to Christ,
In the way that people misinterpret,
The horrible obstacle that is my life,
Punishment fitting, deserved,

When you're not specific and you speak broadly,
In similarity, metaphorically,
You want to include the best you can, fit more in,
And I'm sure many will protest and say it's boring,

The trouble is it's lazy to not elaborate,
And everybody learns at a different rate,
Whether quick to explain, or slow to contemplate,
The most of the importance is that we all reach the state,

I guess I couldn't explain thoroughly to those driving me insane,
I had to leave and make my getaway,
Take a chance, learn it my way, the hard way,
From stupid to smart, psycho for sane,

People will only understand within their level of intelligence,
And you can't expect them not to raise whatever defence,
When you speak more the sense to what real relevance,
Each cryptic Testament, *and* it's consideration and time spent.

Nether Christ

As above so below,
Couple things you should know,
One and the same where we go,
There is equal and opposite flow,

There are lines that divide and define,
That benefit both for the effort and time,
Benefit for what praise and thanks of heart and mind,
For whoever he or she who seeks will find,

No matter to what or who you bestow,
To who or what your heart is home,
There will be an equal flow,
As sure and as solid as stone,
As above so below,

Give in turn for that which you ask,
For you may receive as for what task,
All heart true to intent in part,
All that is light and all that is dark,

And in request be plain, be clear,
Entities heed, they will hear,
Show an honest faith and adhere,
And the prize in your pursuit will near,

One and the same where we go,
There is equal and opposite flow,
As above – so below,
As above – so below,
One,
And the same,

Prophetic Theory

"That which can eternal lie –
but with strange aeons death may die"
– Howard Phillips Lovecraft.

Now, if only, there was a simple way,
To deteriorate death, forestall decay,
To cheat death, no, keep it well away,
I might have a solution, but doesn't so seem a simple way,

To use the power, achieve control over your soul,
That's one thing itself not so easy,
But to bind the power, wrap, web, weave body through soul,
Will be as difficult but in theory pleasing,

If you could visualise your physical matter,
Right down to the atoms, nuclea, the cells,
Feel your soul energy, coursing, meld, with the latter,
Raise the vibration, intensify it, cells with soul, meld,

By and according to the strengths of my love and faith,
Focus it to Amp up the matter by which I'm made –

Could that be the trick to immortality?
Sciences, metaphysics, tell you after I've tried it on me,
That quote of love crafts – could it have been prophecy,
Could it ever really be more than theory?

Poet Alchemist

It's the association of the word,
And its feeling, its meaning,
Association and its formation,
What language does – its dreamy,

Innuendo's, Freudian slips,
Round tongue over teeth, click against lips,
A tap – a swipe and reverberating swish,
Lapping through syllables, tone and note hit,

Tempo'd to rhythm, a pattern does shape,
Whisked to an escape another world away,
The euphoria that associates swirls and escalates,
Disconnect to connect to another scape,

Playing with words, a feeling insert,
A skill to learn that has it's perks,
Music to be heard, a caress of the nerves,
It's longed, it's yearned – it's heaven on earth,

All sorts of innuendos and Freudian slips,
Round tongue over teeth, click against lips,
A tap, a swipe – and reverberating swish,
Lapping through syllables, tone and note hit,

It's association of the word –
Wearing each it's feeling, each it's meaning,
Association and its formation,
What language does it's dreamy…

Alchemy To The Soul

To harvest the energy of the soul,
Does take a level of control,
Broken pieces where once whole,
Fractured dimension, rip in the portal,

Where pain is cast, a vapoury blast,
To sever apart, aligning paths,
Physical binding – spiritual lining,
Unravel, unwinding – desynchronising,

Looking in and feeling about,
Pulling in and drawing out,
Outside in and inside out,
Connected in, disconnection out,

To harvest the energy of the soul,
To live, love, never grow old,
To wonder where the spiritual stroll,
To wander and not pay the physical toll,

For where pain is cast – may it's vapoury blast,
Sever apart all aligning paths,
Mind, spirit, body and heart,
All attributes both light and dark,

Looking in and feeling about,
Pulling in and drawing out,
Outside in and inside out,
Disconnection in, connected out,

Looking in and feeling about,
Pulling in and drawing out,

Outside in and inside out,
Connected in, disconnection out,

...I've found the pain essential, it's influential,
It's key to potential, it's instrumental...

Accelerate My Evolution

I have a hope to reach an absolution,
Somehow to accelerate my evolution,
As they speak of paradise or everlasting life,
I believe I could vibrate that high, to amplify with light,

I am extreme in ways I'm over the top,
And there may come a day where I get shot,
I get so passionate about something and can't stop,
Never really trying to be something I'm not,

Wanting more and in many more ways,
Like for the anger, pain, fear and misery to dissipate,
Wanting things ever more in a better way,
To rise, shine, elevate,

I want to intensify my emotion,
Though specially that of love,
Draw from it – feed it, but maintain it centre focus,
To use it to accelerate the rate my evolution does,

I only want better - to release all perils,
At some point respectively decline to the devil,
I want passed this façade of being the rebel,
But intensify all love to higher levels,

To eradicate all hate, fear, pain and misery completely,
Everlasting, permanent – for forever, concretely,
No longer have any of these evils eat me,
But accelerate my growth for what love I alone feed me,

I'd share it with another if they were to ask to,
But tell all I'd know if it helps others through,

Discrediting Imagination

Imagination is a sensitive subject,
It's the beginning process of a lot of projects,
Things to advance the mechanics, concepts,
Of creation, of colourful new onsets,

I've been accused of misusing my mind in ways,
But perhaps a great many made a great living that way,
I'm smart enough to interpret it whichever way,
Why not change the winds of win my way,

If I can use my imagination to its fullest extents,
There will be no limits, no ending lengths,
Reach out across the universe, like waves sent,
Interpret each particular way it could be meant,

Millions of millions of so many combinations,
We're all stars – webbed through constellations,
Some honestly believe you can't play with imagination,
I say to see deeper – just investigate it,

Accused of misusing my mind in ways,
But perhaps some have made a good living that way,
I'm smart enough to interpret it whichever way,
Why not change the winds of win my way,

Why limit myself ever?
Keep riding the clouded air of never,
Rake out from within my minds' recesses,
And pour from it forever,

Reason To Smoke As Much

I can't believe certain things as such,
A humanity can be losing its touch,
Cigarette's, smoker's payin' too much,
Finances, health – paying too much,

Government campaign parade anti-commercials,
Majority of moneys made taxed on addiction alone,
9 times as much as anywhere in the world,
But then of the health risks, bed ridden, the brittle and bone,

Hey, we can't be so worried about overpopulation,
When there are a some would smoke, go to starvation,
We're selling it so high, the money's motivation,
It's changed the world, revolutionary innovation,

But we'll hurt them still a little more yet,
We'll wipe out the tolerances and respect,
Conditions with higher prices to set,
And make those who don't comply regret,

Cost of healthcare is high when there are many,
Not always as fair as is the toll, it varies,
Addiction, it's sad, makes those fucker's rich,
But the intolerance and unacceptance is a bitch,

Sent off further away, if ever even interacted at all,
After a while you get glad they've set up the wall,
I'm not the most sensitive bugger – but I can stand tall,
But how much longer can it be we smoker's put up with it for?

Smoker's are paying for it a lot more,
Attitudes often taken to them are poor,

Wither And Tether

Once upon a time I wanted to be king,
Only because I truly, only genuinely fucking cared,
I was prepared to change a great deal of things,
But I look around and ask if there is a point there,

Not when others don't understand not when they don't notice,
Not when they can't comprehend, not when they can't show it,
How can I ever fucking expect they'll ever know it?
What's the point to being chosen, when they won't open,

The revolution they need is never going to come,
I've never been so stunned to see them as dumb,
None will know when it comes, nor if they want it done,
Tranced under spell and numb, completely under thumb,

Once, a long time ago, I did want to be king,
Only truly because I genuinely fucking cared,
Prepared to change a great deal of things,
But all I'm beginning to see is there isn't a real point there,

The society I belong to has been too long brainwashed,
To want when there's no need no matter what the cost,
Material shit that definitely doesn't last that long,
Forgetting what matters and never seeing the wrong,

Even should I respectively work on my own flaws,
Would it be noticed or go on still ignored?
It's the more memorable the more it's commendable,
But who knows who's going to be drawn and absorbed,

I once cared because I could see better,
And I'd rarely let it bother me, almost never,
But what care I had was doomed to be severed,
To lose what faith, love, patience…to wither and tether,

How To Make A Martyr

How to make a martyr baby,
How to get it on,
How to make a martyr baby,
How to get it on,

You've gotta make it matter babe –
When you wanna get it on,
It's how you make a martyr babe –
It's how to get it on,

You give something to someone,
Make 'em want to willingly die fighting for it,
And you kill 'em,

You – you, give something to someone,
Make 'em want to willingly die fighting for it,
And you kill 'em,

It's how to make a martyr baby –
How to get it on,
It's how you make a martyr babe –
How to get it on,

But you gotta make it matter babe,
When you want it on,
You have to make it matter baby –
When you want it on,

A Waste Of Lies

The problem with people living their pretty little lies,
Means they can never really mean anything their whole lives,
The lies to cover their hide and we'd all despise,
God help them if they were to eventually see with our eyes,

People living their pretty little lies,
Toying – destroying others' lives,
For the fight to show they do more than survive –
They're "Winners" – they fucking thrive,

It can't mean so much if they have to hide,
Behind the talk – hind the gossip, out of the spotlight,
Deny deviate evil truths – never confide,
Because they know they stand to lose more than their pride,

Living behind these pretty little lies,
People living fake most of their lives,
To believe one thing an entire time,
Waste – when truths suddenly collide,

Waste by the lengths of over what time,
The lies been twisted, believed by told minds,
Only to be compromised when they find,
It's not in fact how everything did unwind,

Pretty little lies, pretty little lies,
Some people have to get so tongue tied,
Pretty little lies, pretty little lies,
You're fake and have been most of your lives,

Waste.

Suckling

I can't expect you'll let go,
But you're going to have to trust me,
I have the keys and here is the door,
Step into the light and see –

Everything I said and did had purpose,
And I suspect it made you nervous,
It had all others before you,
But they each pulled through,

Listen to my tender words,
And feel my gentle voice,
Feel the vibration,
You make your choice,

I only ever cared,
And I was always there,
I would watch, and I would spare,
I've only ever been fair,'

Topics open for discussion,
I'm here, there's no repercussion,
Let me wrap my wings around you,
I'll save you, I'll protect you,

Scriptures spoke poorly of me,
I'm not the monster they want me to be,
What does 'devil' mean but adversary,
I fought the hypocrisy – I fought the jealousy…

An Odd Consultation

I – I can't do it anymore, it's too much,
All I've ever done, wasn't ever enough,
I think it's time – time has come,
I think I must do what must now be done,

(The man was knealt,
Weakened, seasoned by these errors,
He was knealt, head down in tears,
With a broken sliver of mirror,
And a stranger enters)

I see you before me, you're disheartened,
I felt you call from beyond the darkness,
Experiences shape but you've hardened,
Stand, you are man, I bless you, you're pardoned,

Who? What? How – why?
Have you even seen me try?
I'm destined, ready for the sky,
You see me broken, I cry –

You're unaware of what I see, you are so much more,
You're definitely more powerful than you ever saw,
Forbidden knowledge I'll have taught – you'll absorb,
For I have a grander plan, you can be assured,

(The man was now confused,
Yet was slightly feeling a creeping muse,
What this stranger speaks is new news,
But for what purpose does he allude?)

Well, now you've roused my full attention –
Dare you divulge all you care to mention?

(The stranger then smiled long and wide,
His long tongue over his teeth did glide,)

I do have a knowledge I'll certainly provide,
Should you confide with contract to bind,
And should you try hide, understand I'll find,
All the same, a satisfactory design – once you sign,
Is there really any difference –
That I should go the distance,
Have you a solid reference –
And have you real relevance?

I can make a nightmare sell like a dream,
I, am the silver-tongue, people all wish to be,
I, bear the enlightenment and they all must see,
I am the greatest, wiliest, slickest adversary,

If you are indeed he – then why to me now?
Why do you show when my defences are down?
Why fare faith in the faithless gowned?
I am far from ever reaching the crown

It's when you've been through the worst, I adhere,
It's when you're vulnerable – I can near,
It's when you lose fear – shed your last tear,
It's when you'll see me ever clear,

(There was a silence for a short time,
And the stranger could see the man making his mind,
There was a silence for a short time,
But the man would resign – leave it all behind,
And agree to compromise to contract sign,)

(And before long the stranger would unwind,
What lies of the truth coiled, he defined,
Broke free the man in his mind, he'd guide,
And the man now emerged, rebirthed and entwined,)

See, man has the power angels all relish,
Man doesn't need weapons, sigils or relics,
Man himself should be vain and cherish,
Man should love all that makes him jelly,

You seem a little bizarre but you might be on to something,
It's gotta be better than what's whiched all ready – nothing,
I know it's definitely something some consider numbing,
Better than the already deadening, nulling, dulling,

God exposed me once, he says I am unholy,
But being holy itself isn't worth knowing,
Holy (to me) means flaws,(worthy controlling?)
Holy (flaws) where story falls short, and not slowly,

The more you speak, I'm mesmerised,
Far too good to be any horrid lies...

There, see? Surprised?
Hypocrisy has always only ever tried to hide,
Me? I'm the one who's massly despised,
For exposing what the holy only compromise,

(It's bizarre, truly when the lesser favoured,
What villainy savoured – so hated,
Is, can be the very saviour,
None have ever the more contemplated,
Never the more elevated, sated, educated...)

Heed

Where upon one may be granted,
Lucifer's seething energies handed,
Responsibility is required, demanded,
A discipline to exercise or be reprimanded,

Power in the knowledge alone,
Keys to sit atop a throne,
Destiny cast and carved in stone,
Subconscious awake and become known,

Metaphysical shakes and trembles as it merges mortal,
And, like alike, when opening the portal,

Taste forsaketh whence turning in for out,
Rites for just and equal rights repel doubt,
Thine best whisper whence lusting to shout,
Else best sayeth naught when urged about,

Thus it will soon sound clearer,
Better felt list'n for thou shalt sooner see'r,
Heed,

Where upon one may be granted,
Lucifers' seething energies handed,
Responsibility is required, more than demanded,
The discipline to exercise or else be reprimanded,

Yes, there is power in knowledge alone,
Keys to reside atop the throne,
Destiny cast and carved in stone,
Subconscious wake and become known,
Heed,

Death, Myself

I'm pushing to the edge,
To the death of a piece of me,
Detaching off old skin's, I shed,
To death, shattering pieces, and feed prophecy,

I'm intentionally killing pieces off me,
Reviving them slightly before dying off somewhere else,
Intentionally living but allowing death to breathe,
Eventually living still after death myself,

I speak metaphor, figuratively, over many a context –
I don't particularly speak of just any one concept,
I don't expect many others could easily as accept,
And I especially don't expect to keep any of their respect,

Pieces of me would compromise,
Pieces of me cause despise,
And pieces of me have despised,
They have certainly compromised,

So, I'm pushing to the edge,
To the death of a piece of me,
Detaching off away old skin's, I shed,
To death with broken pieces, and feed prophecy,

Yeah…
I'm intentionally killing pieces off me,
And reviving them slightly before dying off someplace else,
Intentionally living but allowing death to breathe,
Eventually still living after death myself…

Afterbirth Of Death's Labour

I couldn't count how often I've died,
Killing off something deep inside,
Ripping open a gaping wound wide,
You hide, internalize, 'til the pain subsides,

Yet something grew back, I couldn't recognise,
In my decayed remains – something was fertilized,
I would come to realize it cycles – this demise,
A kind of cosmic price for what lies compromise,

The presences to soon occupy and reside,
With each their own conflicts and certainly divide,
Insanity as they return, clash, and collide,
But just as certain as they die, another is revived,

Far too many times returning a gruesome guise,
Severed fragments of mind, received despise,
To internalize on that despise inside,
Somewhat reflecting it outside,

Never the same returning something else that died,
Within the gaping wound wide, past lessons left behind,
Beginning over and failing alike, repair only to resign,
Couldn't count the times cried praying the ache subsides,

Having to kill off something inside that only repairs another guise,
Of loathing and despise the likes you'd never recognised,
Everyone of them different, separate, confined inside,
Birthed of the death of a something once died inside,

Never Painless

Before you grow,
You have to let go,
Of all you've known,
Release and leave your comfort zones,

You have to break a happy home,
Go out, deep and south, on your own,
Released of all your comfort zones,
To head a wander alone,

Hard truths to face – it's always the case,
The shit keeps coming to put you in your place,
You soon fear if you'll ever be safe,
A fear for feeling to put you ahead the race,

A far more effective way but with it's bitter taste,
But make no mistake – not one bit is waste,
Built to test and make you break,
To push you, raise you up to an elevated state,

Detest and scorn and say it's all fake,
And you'll fail, stale, deteriorate,
Trampled, entangled, devastated in the wake,
Half way through and subdued for fucks sake,

There's no going halves – you've gotta do it hard,
Can't quit after you start – put in more heart,
Illuminate the dark and charge up that spark,
Smash through it hard – shatter it to shards,

It's never painless to die –
Whoever says so, does most lie…

Before you grow,
You have to let go,
Of all you've known,
Release of all comfort zones,

Before you grow,
You must know,
You'll have to let go,
Release and leave your comfort zones,

Before your eyes open,
You must have chosen,
No refunds on redeemed tokens,
You will have had to have chosen,

It's never painless to die,
Whoever says so does most lie,
You miss certain parts inside,
That remind you're alive,

But to leave them behind?

And most figuratively in every broad sense,
Can so miserably cause distress,
May not feel it's worth all its spent,
Never knowing if it pays off, if it'll recompense,

Don't mistake – it's never painless to die,
Whoever says so does most lie,
You'll miss certain pieces inside,
But to grow you must let go and divide,

Before your eyes open,
You will have had to have chosen,
You must have chosen,
There's no refunds for redeemed tokens,

Hard truths to face – it's always the case,
The shit keeps coming to put you in your place,
You soon fear if you'll ever be safe,
A fear for feeling to put you ahead the race,

A far more effective way but with its bitter taste,
But make no mistake – not one bit is waste,
Built to test and make you break,
To push you, raise you up to an elevated state,

It's never painless to die,
Whoever says so does most lie,
You miss certain parts inside,
But you must, leave them behind
Behind…

Empathy For Christ

I've got empathy for Christ,
I feel, can and do understand what it felt like,
It was my choice to ask – to know, to share it inside,
Show the courage not to lie, not react in hurt an anger out of spite,

I haven't been that strong before,
Gets easier, I learnt, when I do it more,
Showing the balls to face the maturity, and more responsibility for,
Carrying on, standing strong, through what flaying war,

He had to for the sacrament of his sacrifice,
Even if I warned him, he'd come back and do it twice,
The courage, the strength, the love in that Christ,
Makes me feel all warm and fuzzy, and want to be triple the nice,

I know I haven't been that strong before,
But it's getting easier, I learnt, as I do it more,
Showing the balls to face the maturity and responsibility for,
Carrying on – standing strong through the flaying war,

Praise and gratitude in empathy for Christ,
For standing strong by and being killed for what so many despise,
Possibly perhaps out of misinformation and lies,
Or too much disbelief or fear to want to open their own eyes,

I know for a fact I haven't been that strong before,
But it's getting easier and I want to do it more,
Showing I've got the balls for maturity and responsibility for,
Carrying on – standing strong through our flaying war,

Horns up,

Coma Grey

"This was never my world,
They took the angel away,
I killed myself to make
Everybody pay" – Marilyn Manson

My whole life is one massive disagreeance,
A complicated maximum inconvenience,
Elucidation never fathomed for disobedience,
And naturally yours truly, suffered grievances,

God is behind and shadow drives my father,
Every battle for control makes my soul suffer,
Assurances insisted much worse will be discovered,
But the submission to control is still collision with disaster,

"This was never my world,
They took the angel away,
I killed myself to make
Everybody pay"

Defences for protection are disintegrated,
Reception of aggression and incarceration,
Killing off all innocence, poisoning this angel,
Just to be a machine programmed to fail,

Couldn't handle I'd take my life myself,
That killing me was a duty you'd see to yourself,
The honour, the pride, there was to be held,
Making my life a miserable hell…

"This was never my world,
They took the angel away,
I killed myself to make
Everybody pay"

Fuck Ewe's

Fuck ewe's,
This is what I choose,
I can't do the same shit as you,
I throw it in – I refuse,

I just want to be let be,
I can't follow – I'm
just not a sheep,
I know there's something
else waiting for me,
Just let me out, let me free,

Fuck ewe's,
I'm not doing this shit you do,
They take what they
want and we lose,
Shit's gotta change – I
need something new,

There's a great deal out
there I want to achieve,
And I won't ever if I'm
stuck being a sheep,
There's something out
there waiting for me,
Let me be, let me
out – let me free,

I know there are wolves
and they will chew,
I may lose but this is
what I choose,
I just can't be stuck doing
the same shit as you,

I'm freeing from the
flock – so fuck ewe's,

There's more I have to
do to get to be,
More than just walking these
obstacles like a sheep,
More than just a convenience
for anothers' keep,
I'll never achieve or
succeed if I'm not free,

I just hate being forced to
do shit I can't choose,
Hate to be contained for
convenient use then lose,
I'm gonna do different
and make all amused,
So, no way – I refuse –
fuck all ewe's

I'm fuckin' off to do the
shit I wanna do –

As Truth As My Rebellion

Dishonesty where there should be truth,
Rebellion is due,
It is too bad it's their lies I see through,
Rebellion for when it's due,

Dishonesty where there should be truth,
Far too plain – I never have to sleuth,
Piss poor lies – I see right through,
As truth as my rebellion, it comes, it's due,

They fight black and blue that their stories are true,
But I've been round it long enough – I tell it better than they do,
I've seen it all – can't tell me nothing new,
Lie to me just once and I'll never expect better of you,

I know why you do – it's a habitual defence,
You believe it saves you from a deeper consequence,
Of those only ever out to cause irreverence,
You know what you've been through, you need the diligence,

But really? Dishonesty?

Dishonesty where there should be truth –
Rebellion is soon due,
It is too bad it's the lies I see through,
Rebellion for when it's due,

Dishonesty, where there should be truth,
It's too plain – I never have to sleuth,
It's these piss poor lies I see through,
And as truth as my rebellion, it comes, it's due,

Long due…

Conduit

Sometimes I don't feel my words are my own,
Sometimes perhaps they are not,
I know them to be true in my heart, set as stone,
For there is a greater plot,

For what reason I'm not sure I'm aware if there even is –
But there just has to be more, why I'm given these gifts,
To interpret such ways that minds and moods shift,
Play of words and wonder to spiritually lift,

I can feel something else does work through me,
At strange intervals but somewhat soothing,
Words of strange wisdoms, entertaining – moving,
Learning, gaining, and above all – improving,

I do have talents that even I question,
Responsibility where need be represented,
Interpretation, what consideration invested,
Creative ways to release whichever tension,

I connect with the diviner source at times,
I think it knows when the time is right,
A connection to a source in my mind,
Feeding me light – and strange insights,

Feels like a light I can love and trust,

At strange times I do feel a divine possession,
Taken hold of me for a diviner intention,
An outsider for that divided perception,
But purely for purpose of progression,

Cross-Communicate

I don't know how many times I've sat,
And I've watched myself sat to write,
Built out shit form emotions, pressures,
Write, in the stead of pickin' fights,

I've stood from afar from the corner of the room,
Mine, was that presence I could feel behind me loom,
Watching, as a younger me, interpret his gloom,
I'd be there to watch, suck it out and consume,

I never knew or could know it was me then –
Only that something else watched,
But it was indeed a me back then,
I stood, and I stood watch,

The older me knew to know the shit,
To see, watch him write the shit,
Shit about never being able to fit,
Well enough with the other shit,

I guess I have tried to reach out to me,
Maybe for a hope that he might see,
Let it all go – keep writing, be free,
Free it, and do much better than me,

Paths may change their seemingly destined course,
Nothing is ever what is seen of its sort,
I wanted back then to plug into the source,
And I do believe the wisps of my whispers were caught,

I feel I can now – and never would've thought,
I understand it now – at least a whole lot more,

Ominous Whispers

I guess I hear the whispers,
From a who or what calling from –
Through the waves of a dimension,
Filtering through to our own,

Guess I, hear it calling,
Can't determine if it's warning,
But others all ignore it,
Like they can't hear it,

I've seen it move slow,
As time speeds, others pace hasten,
Seen the figure glide, slow,
I hear it's whispering,
None hear it,
None but me,

Seen the figure move,
Seen it, heard it call,
Ominous – but can't determine it warns,
I hear it,
And I shudder cold,

Hear its whispers,
From this who or what calling from –
Through the waves of another dimension,
Filtering through,

None others see it,
None others hear it,
But I fear it's an omen to gloom,
Fear this omen to doom…

A Conscience Incarnate

I am aware,
And I can feel,
An entity in physical existence,

I am able and I am strong,
No limit's no resistance,
No too-far-a-distance,

I am keen,
I have desire,
And meticulously schemed ambition,

I've got will,
I have flair,
Devil incarnate – divine apparition,

I have control over my cognitive thought,
With my psychic driving I'll have others bought,
Half the battle will already have been fought,
Control over many a cognitive thought,

I am aware and so shall others be,
Soon to look for and toward me,
To release them all – let them free,
With awe and power comparative to the wonder I speak,

I am he and I am conscious,
I won't lie – things are going to get monotonous,
I'll bring to light all that was long forgotten of,
To raise to stand all that was trodden on,

I am, have been and will be,
Everything to all those to come to me…

Corrupting Accountability

For those I touch I will own up,
Those influenced by me who got stuck,
I'll turn back round at times and change that luck,
I want to – 'cause I care – I do give a fuck,

Then of course there are those,
Who wilfully, willingly went and chose,
Go against – upturn their nose,
With too narrow an ignorance to see it shows,

To go against cynically with no real evidence,
It almost doesn't make what opinion any real relevance,
Critique it all you like – just, offer solution, you know, to better it,
But don't if you know they'll only end up resenting it,

I have regrets but when I get it right,
I'll make up for it better when I've finally made my mind,
But for any I lead down paths same as mine,
I apologize I hadn't yet had the appropriate answers yet to find,

I'll take what I gave but only as fair,
Just maybe not those that could never care,
Like Christ before me said – never turn away those who dare,
To want to understand, work it, practice the thought spared,

But for those as I corrupt let me stand first forsaken,
Best to have been as intelligible to help awaken,
It's probably never really been as big a deal as I'd once made it,
Destiny? Fate? Somehow, I participated,

I'll take what I must and wear it well,
Sear me a brand and send me to hell,
Remember me so, an example to tell,
Devils testaments, the angel that fell…

To Come, To Be, To Go,

Think I'm fuckin' mad trying to do all this alone,
There are plenty of times I need someone to throw a bone,
I only just keep to myself – a lone body at home,
Thinkin' all these thoughts to my lone,

And then they come and go,

I know they're messages, lessons I require,
To learn before I can be fully admired,
I want to be the kind or the king they desire,
I have that passion, deep within me rages that fire,

People come and go,
And I can never be certain what I have to know,
That sweet, dear precious knowledge to bestow,
I want it – I need it – I have to know,

Obstacles, pressures – getting' in the way,
Makin' it hard to hear the have -to-says,
Breakin' up, splittin' – goin' separate ways,
Fashioning out that path they need to pave,

Differences of ideals getting in the way,
Makin' it hard to hear those have-to-says,
Breakin' through the wall to contemplate,
To fashion out that path I need to pave,

There's thought's that lead to thought,
And that time spent with others can't be bought,
Intelligence – imagination, branch out a cause,
One – all right, but many more greaten the source,

And then they'll have come and been,

I reach the differences and it's when I must decide,
Can I take these truths and swallow down my pride?
Pride – for the time it takes to have confide –
The indulgence of such knowledge, a kind I pride,

People come and go,
And I can never be certain of what I have to know,
That sweet, dear, precious knowledge to bestow,
I need it – I want it, I have to know,

I know they're yet lessons, messages I require –
To learn well before I can truly be admired,
I want to be the kind or king they desire,
I have that passion – within me rages that fire,

I just have to be fucking mad that I'm doing this all alone,
When I know there are gonna be times I'll need a bone thrown,
But I've been keeping to myself, lone body at home,
Thinking all these thoughts on my own,

I'm telepathic in a sense people hear my thoughts,
They're hearing me think without me ever actually talk,
And brainwaves clash – despite what I thought,
Eager ears listening, rousing excitement for more,

I can't help that they may write about,
A lot of me similar shit I'm thinking 'bout,
And they might be quicker at writing it out,
Or maybe me, the times I'm quick at it out,

Shit flows to me, through me so easily,
A conduit I suppose it's why it's easy,
Psychic, channelling waves as breaching –
As even I have had others all deceive me,

And these influences all come and go,
And it's ever better when you're completely in the know,

That mixed signs of different facades confuse when shows,
Again more the defence but the interaction would let 'em know,

Interaction with various others of the knowledge,
My mind a mental palace for whenever I need a forage,
Keys, secrets all sacred, maybe not so well in its' storage,
Too many people channelling my waves and it's too good to be ignoring,
The shit ain't fucking boring,

And soon they come and they will be,

Interactions came and gone,
Learnin' something before too long,
Maturity, acuity, gaining strong,
We have every right to be wrong,

Wrong to work out every right,
The lessons, the message – that friggin' insight,
Building up the courage to overturn one own's spite,
And patience here 'til we all see eye to eye,

They will be and they will go…

Centre Most Lead

A depth of a madness as bad as it can be,
Is an intellect others don't often expect of me,
Centre most lead of deeds worst to be seen,
Nightmarish scenes sure to deprive of sleep,

I can be a little too good with my tongue –
That I could influence just about anyone,
And have any unthinkable thing be done,
Without it even be traced back to me once,

I often hide in plain sight,
That many an alibi will claim to deny,
Witnesses aside – they'll testify,
That I was not present at the time and place of what crime,

Why get my hands dirty when others are as nervy,
But instruct them so covertly, deeds flow superbly,
No alleged accusation could ever stick so sturdy,
No clue, no little birdy – scenarios disturbing,

I know that you think it'll only last for so long,
That some day I'll miscalculate, and shit'll go wrong,
I do know if it does you think I'll go where I belong,
You'd think they'd break me but, I'm really just as strong,

I could manipulate a large wave like extortion,
Only, homicide, on a scale of mass proportion,
Law authorities often driven exhausted,
'cause I just take far too many precautions,

Mentally capable to withdraw back into my mind,
To remain there to internalize for a good long time,

Remaining cool and calm and not showing signs,
I was centre most lead behind these most notorious, heinous crimes,

Is it so psychotic to know and be desensitized –
To the scarcely imagined, feared and lesser recognized?

Indefinite Distinction

I am a chromatic aberration of truth and lies,
Too well blended, painful to the eyes,
Vignetted edges, darkened round the light,
A chromatic aberration not easy on the sight,

A product of colours to fight against each other,
What factuality uncovered, more fallacies to smother,
Defences to shudder with a static when discovered,
The conduct of colours contradicting each other,

A chromatic aberration, a foggy disguise,
A blend of truth and lies, painful on the eyes,
Yes, vignetted edges, darkened round the light,
A chromatic aberration not easy on the sight,

The more that you feel you think you're getting close,
Gaining on the scent, following your nose,
It suddenly stops dead, becomes a ghost,
Stranded to meander round all comatose,

Cause I'm a product of colours to fight against each other,
What factuality's uncovered – more fallacies do smother,
In defence to shudder with static when discovered,
As is the conduct of colours, contradicting each other,

The chromatic aberration of obscured truth and lies,
A nebulous disguise a little painful to the eyes,
Of vignetted edges – darkened around the light,
A chromatic aberration, never easy on the sight,

The more they ever felt they were getting close,
Gaining on the scent they'd caught with their nose,
But scents stopped dead, suddenly chasing ghosts,
Stranded to meander round all comatose…

I Kept It All Within

Once upon a time I lived in hell,
Just as the story begun,
Prayed to the father, the holy ghost and the son,
The story had begun,

I wanted to have peace whole, not in pieces,
Declared my true king was the very Jesus,
Praying to Christ, begging my torment ceases,
Following best I could to what he teaches,

I must say I'd gotten mighty close,
To what I'd asked for – what I'd hoped,
Close to the feelings I had chose,
Lassoed it – I had it roped,

I'd gotten closer to God – Love,
I felt it within from above,
But by this time, I chose to snub,
This heightened feeling, the love,

Lucifer ascended to my level,
He spoke and I could believe this devil,
For after asking, experience made me rebel,
And Satan was all I wanted to revel,

Satan gave me strength where God could not,
And after time – I wanted Christ to rot,
So, the tale, were to thicken its plot,
It consumed me, and with me – the devil has a shot,

I'm more than human enough to suffice,
And will have many of my race to sacrifice,
All they'd cost – well worth the price,
My hate grips me, has me enticed,

Yes, I know love, but I have so much more hate,
And society's cruelty, has me to seal it's fate,
And the devils appetite is mighty great,
And there's more than enough souls here to sate,

I kept my belief in the holy trinity,
But I'd include wholly Satan's divinity,
I value all else within reachable vicinity,
And oppose it all the same with corrosive acidity,

I know right and wrong – kept it all within me,
I know I'm still righteous when others think I'm sinning,
And it's for this very reason they always see me singing,
And I will all the same while I'm neck wringing,

I've gotten closer to God – the Love,
I've felt it within from above,
But by this time, I'd chosen to snub,
That heightened feeling, His Love,

Lucifer ascended to my level,
He spoke and I really could believe the devil,
For after all my asking, experience made me rebel,
And Satan became all of whom I'd only want to revel,

I kept it all within me,
Still righteous when I'm sinning...

But Now?

I kept it all within,
That's where it would begin,
I kept it all within,
And I would have to take it on the chin,

But now…but now…but now…
Now –

I have a proposal,
Powers at my disposal,
I took proposal,
The powers at my disposal,

But now?..And now – yeah now,
Now…

I took both sides,
Decided to make compromise,
I kept both sides,
Both sides at disposal,
I kept it all within,

Now? Now! But now –
Yeah, now

I can have my cake and eat it too,
I can, and I want you to know you can too,
If you had such prowess, such powers,
What would you do? What would you do?

Now? Yeah now – what would you do?
I already know what I'm gonna do,
Gonna keep it all within me – the world is at my feet,
I repeat, the world is at my feet…

Allow For It

I've never much liked my failed attempts,
I doubt the differences in others aren't exempt,
We'd all like to see some made amends,
To get passed what failure and ascend,

We have to remember we're not perfect,
We're human, we make mistakes,
No true torment is worth it, dessert it,
Allow for it and the time it takes,

To not put too much heart in in the first place,
Is only going to save what further disgrace,
What bitter aftertaste, what destructive malaise,
No, it can certainly pay, to watch what heart you place,

Don't place too much importance on whatever bad,
Seeing too far into it will only drive you mad,
Try only look at the positives and be glad,
That these very setbacks are a temporary fad,

We have to remember none of us are perfect,
We're only human – we all make mistakes,
No true torment is worth it – dessert it,
Allow for it man, and the time it takes,

Don't make it a bigger deal than what it is,
Get passed it, learn, get out there and live,
Get out there – give 'em a lil some o' this,
Pass it, exceed it and fare yourself a bliss…

Chains

I have felt so fuckin' bad – I have known blame,
I've felt so fucking sore – I have known pain,
I've felt humiliation – I've fuckin' known shame,
But one fuckin' day I'll be released of these chains,

I've known control – been under its strain,
Treated as viral – quarantined, contained,
Treated worse than animal – beaten to be tamed,
But one fuckin' day I'll be released of these chains,

I've bit my tongue and had to fucking refrain,
From cursing the scum driving me insane,
Bit harder on my disdain and spared the cane,
But one fuckin' day I'll be released of these chains,

By that final time – I'll have all that I need,
To bring down the justice – the tyrants to their knees,
I have paid for crimes – and never did the deeds,
Times from me were taken, but I'll get them back, you'll see,

Yes – times from me were taken – but I will get them back,
For all I was forsaken – I'm gonna beat it black,
Pick off one by one, having ambushed the pack,
Broken free from the chains that always held me back,

I have felt so fuckin' bad – I have known blame,
I've felt so fucking sore – I have known pain,
I've felt humiliation – I've fuckin' known shame,
But one fuckin' day I'll be released of these chains,

I've known control – been under its strain,
Treated as viral – quarantined, contained,

711

Treated worse than animal – beaten to be tamed,
But one fuckin' day I'll be released of these chains,

I've bit my tongue and had to fucking refrain,
From cursing the scum driving me insane,
Bit harder on my disdain and spared the cane,
But one fuckin' day I'll be released of these chains,

A Sinners' Saint

I'm a saint's sinner
And I'm a sinner's saint,
I'm good when I'm bad,
And bad when I aint,

A middle man for remembrance,
Somewhat torn between the severance,
Still, I force aware the resemblance,
I force aware remembrance,

I'm a saint's sinner,
And I'm a sinner's saint,
I'm good when I'm bad,
And bad when I aint,

A profound knowledge in a profane man,
Exampled for a greater many to understand,
Paths to other worldly lands,
To reach the great many, have delivered to hands,

Unfortunately for me that does mean,
I can't pass nor get beyond to see,
Until at the very last when all others have been,
Ascended well ahead of me,

Another shepherd to ensure the safety of the flock,
But a wolf to pick out that which does not,
A watchful eye, never blinks, never stops,
Non-stop, tirelessly, round the clock,

Yeah, I'm a saint's sinner,
And I'm a sinner's saint,
I'm good when I'm bad,
And just bad when I aint,

Satan's Valkyrie At Salvage

Blood dripping over jagged teeth,
Axe swinging from my hand in the breeze,
Takin' care of a business getting' me all grotty,
Blood stained rags trailing off my body,

Hate filled eye's glowing red,
We the damned come for the dead,
With giant great black wings spread,
We incite true fear and dread,

Hells hottest tarpits are where we call home,
Scavenging rotting raw meat off of human bones,
Hacking it all apart with each an iron axe,
All those fallen prey to vicious attacks,

Those rare few that haven't quite died,
Scream and shout their piercing cries,
Frightened further half to death upon our sight,
Fight but never find respite,

Another One Of Those Days

Oh shit, not again today,
Another one of these fuckin' days,
Shit's not gonna be goin' my way,
Skies are grey – my black and whites blurred the same,

Took one teeny little thing to set me off,
And not before too long it's all gone wrong,
Took another couple thing's and set me off,
And soon I know it's all gone fuckin' wrong

You miss a happy pill,
Wake late and feel strange – ill,
Almost someone or something else still –
You're not yourself, you know it – you feel,

It's gonna be another fuckin' one of these days,
All my black and whites blurred to grey,
Shit's not gonna be going my way,
Another fuckin' one of these days,

Couple things have set me off now,
Hastened worse my aggressive prowess,
Hate fastening round at my aggressive growls,
Smack me back in the face that I curse worse vows,

This fuckin' day is just gonna get fuckin' worse yet,
'cause not only will something hurt – it's gonna fuckin' regret,
It's gonna go down hard making everyone upset,
And I know it'll end up being me – I bet,

It's gonna be another fuckin' one of those days,
All my black and whites blurred grey,
Shit's just not gonna be going my way,

Yeah – it's gonna fuckin' be another one of those days,

Yes, few days ago, I missed a happy pill,
Yeah – I woke late and I was feeling strangely ill,
Alost like someone or something else still –
I'm not myself – I know it, I feel…

The Excessively Nice Narcissistic

I really can't stand too many of the things you
do but I think you really should know,
If I don't pick at every little thing you do, then how will you ever grow,
If I don't criticize or scrutinize, then how will you ever show –
You're not any better ever if you're not on your toes,

I make your life hell because I love you and I care,
But I never really can tell if you'll cover the fare,
I don't ever break for a spell enough that you'd dare,
To escape from out from under my stare,

I hate to have to be the one to bear the bad news,
But I have as equal the right to have to do it to you,
Everyone's the same, to have to face and be put through,
And there'll be others like me, doing it to them too,

I have to know the in's and out's and be certain that it's right,
We're all under equal pressure here – but none can fight,
Every one of us is caught under anothers' sight,
And every one of us have all felt them bite,

I have to know whether you will have the zest,
This is why I always am putting you to test,
I make you invest so that you progress,
No matter if you regress, scorn and detest,

I know I'm going to fail at some point – just, hopefully, long before you,
And I'll keep picking at you to make sure you never do,
At least, if ever, long after I've long gone through,
Having failed all test's I was subject to…

Pro THIS Con

Facades – shit the people make you see –
Facades – shit the people make you believe,
Facades – shit like how you've always needed me,
Facades – shit like you've needed me to believe,

Keeping power over me – beneath you,
Means I have and am much more than you,
You – keepin' me beneath you –
Means I'm better than you,

I've never had to force anyone into anything –
They did – and chose of their own volition,
And I've never needed to have to force –
They, only ever needed the permission,

People like you take every advantage –
To have power over me but can never manage,
What shitty rotten deals they'd been given to manage –
Jealous, always jealous of mine enough to disparage,

It probably comes easier to me 'cause I never force,
But that kind of shit never enters your thoughts,
And you're equally a conflict labelled so by your cause –
And you just have to have it in your grubby paws,

Facades – you shit people make us see,
Facades – you shit people make us believe,
Facades – you shit people always needed of me –
Facades – you shit people needed me to believe,

You force yourself and you gorge yourself,
But you bought yourself a hell for yourself…

I'll Remember That

I'll never forget these days like when,
I've been disposed of, forsaken,
Like a lot of all those before me,
Having to learn it hard and I've seen,

I'm good enough to reckon the reckoning,
I am a he who hath good remembering,
And I'll be fucked if the shit's ever happening to me,
I saw it all mate, I really did look and I could see,

I know a good solid hard lesson,
And I know I'm not the kind to forget 'em,
I've hated being in those positions regrettin',
Vigil – ever vigil, avoiding that upsettin',

Mate I can fuckin' see the shit,
And I'll be fucked if I'm ever goin' through it,
You're fuckin' damn right I'm gonna defy everything,
Fuckin' defy those crooked facades of 'sin',

I remember seeing when you disgusted,
And fuck do I remember those fuckin' repercussions,
Believe me I seriously don't want that for me,
I like my shit better the way I have man I'm free –

I do remember when you lost their trust,
Yeah, fuckin' do remember you being treated worse than dust,
I do remember it happened to that poor fucker you,
I remember it well enough I ain't willingly going through,

Poor cunt,
I'll remember that forever,

Where To With The What For

Life the say has meaning,
But is it something you cash in –
For like value after passing?
Well,
Life has got to have a meaning,
Of means, something worth having,
Something stable, worthy lasting –

The edge of death, the doors,
Gateway to our world and yours,
The end, revelation of all forms,
The passing to the cause, the source,

Life's meaning, life's everything –
Is it something you cash in –
Of like value for after passing?

Life has got to have a meaning –
Of means – something worth having,
Something stable, worthy lasting –

The edge of death, the doors,
Gateway to our world and yours,
The end, revelation, of all forms,
The passing to the cause, the source,

Suppose the cross ways needs a bargain,
Could you suit, sate the margin,
Maybe a little more than pennies on eyes,
But the strength of the soul, character as price…

Drain

I'd like to say I don't have a soul,
Or so it seems through the ruthless things I do,
But I could say I am many – have had many,
Pillaging energy for my own possession, my dues,

I'm a kind of magician of sorts,
I don't use silly incantations,
It's more a psychic power of the mind,

Say I walk passed a church,
Feel the power, radiant, it exerts,
I can reach deep into its' earth,
And rip up the energy in a powerful surge,

I take it, I trap it, I keep it within,
I rake it, I extract it, reap in deep,

Yeah, I'm another kind of magician,
Not a single word of a lie,
But I never use silly incantations,
It's more psychic power of the mind,

I never take without giving back,
Only, what I give back is equal in opposite,
I sever the good within – take it,
And summon my black to then deposit,

Take want I want, go back and take again,
What I take never stays, but withers, deteriorates them,
I take and give just to take again,
A magician come to drain,

Devour

Breaking, disintegrating hardened shells,
Let their souls' graces' energies be felt,
Compassion force bared, due, where feared to show prior,
Pestilence led, vampires swoon and devour,

I have begun breaking those defensive shells,
Blocking out for all manners of hell,
But angered so it soothed me to feed of it myself,
Strange but they soothed me without trying themselves,

A grace of theirs I devoured on, soothed,
No threat to me and I've easily just proved,
For as they're freed, are easily as moved,
Freed of that shell, that negative gloom,

I could teach it to them too,
Where upon they feel they need to soothe,
Open up the heavens, earth, feed from it too,
The light, pure, intense, eradicating the gloom it soothes,

So, let it be we devour,
When we are most sour,
Meditate – fuck, I do it at will,
Practice it more – and start to feel,

Soothed...
Devour the light and grace and –
Soothe,

Taste's beautiful...

Like A Pig

Thick skin, thick skull, but all that meat to fill me full,
As tender and juicy as pork been pulled,
As long as a pig but stands as tall,
To have between my fingers to maul,

Huh, and I thought knowing of you was a complete waste,
When all I could feel was a build-up of hate,
And I would hunger, and wonder how you taste,
To stuff you like pork into my face,

Taking all your shit would forever make me sick,
And just like a pig, I'd rather have you roasting on a spit,
Roasting like any pig should – I'm lickin' my lips,
I'm drooling now just thinking of the nice juicy tender bits,

You wallow in a mess of mud and muck,
You swallow and digest of the scraps in the yuck,
A smell to make any of the strongest guts chuck,
Until you're dismembered, seasoned and cooked up,

And a feed like you's a dime a dozen,
Tendered recipe fine timed in the oven,
Bones, the only way you may be discovered,
And if they did, I almost couldn't care – it's fine, fuck it,

Taking all your shit forever made me sick,
Acting like the pig I'd rather sooner have on a spit,
Roasting like any good pig, I'm licking my lips,
I'm drooling now thinking of your juicy tender bits,

Knowing you is not a complete waste,
Not even in my build-up of hate,
I just hunger and wonder how you'll taste,
To stuff you like pork into my face,

Wound Tight

I walk round the outside,
Always round the outside,
Edgy round them, round the outside,
Edgy around them, round the outside,

I can't always contain it,
Not when pressured to display it,
Can't always control it,
Control to cogitate before I lose it,

Worn tight, wound too tight that I offend,
Worn ever tight I explode as I defend,
Wound too tight I'm always on the edge,
Too wound tight to contain and comprehend,

It almost never ends…

So I walk, cycle round the outside,
Always round the outside,
Edge round them, the outside,
Edgy around them, round the outside,

I don't always contain it so well,
Not when I'm being pressured by some hell,
Can't always be so quick to take a spell,
Never quick enough to gain control the hell,

Worn so tight, wound ever tight that I offend,
Worn ever tight I explode as I defend,
Wound too tight I'm always on the edge,
Too wound tight to contain and comprehend,

It almost never ends,
Not until, at least I smash more cones and get bent.

Shit, You're Uncomfortable

You have to forgive me for getting so pissed,
When I could see you were getting pissed,
Over certain shit – you're not desensitized to yet,
Certain shit I'm so desensitized by that I forget,

Yeah, I forget there's shit you're uncomfortable with,
And without a little give you're always gonna be,
Can't put it behind you and just let live so –
You're never gonna be any happier than me,

I smile, I laugh, I can actually enjoy shit,
But you all stand there with your teeth fuckin' grit,
All you ever seem to do is get pissed,
You get the shits and then even I get pissed,

I forget your mind is small and that this was a big thing,
But there's a whole lot more still out there waiting,
I'm often already passed it and anticipating,
For the next many new unrevealed big things,

I do forget there's shit you're uncomfortable with,
And without a little give you're always gonna be,
Can't put it behind and just let live –
So you're never gonna be happier than me,

And I smile, I laugh, I can actually enjoy shit,
And you all stand there with your fuckin' teeth grit,
You only ever seem to just get pissed,
Get the shits, and I too, am soon pissed,

I'm used to certain shit you're not desensitized to yet,
Certain shit I'm so desensitized by that I do forget…

725

When None Are Bothered

Tyrants look to cause a fear,
Just to gain a control,
Tyrants use fear to attract tears,
To reign over many a soul,

You can see it any time – everywhere,
People are only affected when they can care,
Care enough about something to be scared,
Scared to lose that something that they deeply care,

It might be they can't get passed their intolerance,
And fight to reject what they can't accept,
And it'll get harder – the more monotonous,
To force them to have the regret,

Tyrants, like bullies, governments, religion,
Causing fear to gain a control,
Tyrants forcing on their transitions,
To reign over many a soul,

How would it be then, everywhere?
If none were ever bothered enough to care,
If none ever cared enough to be scared –
Scared to lose that something? Not if there's no care,

One can love something so that it's no big deal,
The failure then – is making the threat seem more real,
I love listening to metal – love how it makes me feel,
Love it can excite me so but then relax me the while still,

The question then is tolerance, and many need it more,
You wouldn't believe the liars when I'd ask 'em – how sore?
'Cause they won't maintain a control themselves
and be bothered enough for war,
But they were never lookin' at it right – there was always more...

Freak

Abomination, Ha!
Ever feel like you're treated as something you're not?
Well it wasn't like I was the bad guy treated nice –
No –
On the contrary I was the good guy treated bad,

I guess I am and quite often is a freak,
Games changed – ideals became obsolete,
I wanna rattle off my revolutionary speak,
And I'm gonna do it with a mighty brave cheek,

I wasn't always despicable so you know –
Had to suffer harsh punishments for me to grow,
Sometime soon I'll maybe let you know,
Some time soon I'll, maybe let it show,

It's kind of like they've got beer goggles,
And my how do they oggle,
I'm sure if I'd whipped it out they'd grab to gobble,
Not goin' there – don't want a throbble,

They must see or succumb to psychosis,
Just as I pass - behaviours atrocious,
I thought I was bad – no, I know it –
Sexy, sassy attitudes just make me want to grope it,

I guess I am a major bit of a freak,
Games changed, ideals fell obsolete,
I wanna rattle off my revolutionary speak,
And I'm gonna do it with my mighty brave cheek,

Well,
I wasn't particularly the bad guy treated nice,

Defined By Opinion

Turn Islam upside down,
Have it in reverse,
Feministic inside out,
And you'll see a change in nerves,

The ways people think sometimes – I know it's disgusting,
But is it worse? – couldn't this all just be nothing?
Old boilers, pardon me, Cougars – marrying 10 boys of 16 years,
And she, the one, who beats 'em all to tears,

Ways people think sometimes – digusting – yeah I know,
But if the shoe was on the other foot – would you think so?
I'm mistaken for a poof cause I'm flamboyant or eccentric,
I love fuckin' women – you're sick, and you're demented,

I know it's disgusting sometimes how people think,
Noses all up turned – think their shit don't stink,
But how would they handle it if they were all upside down,
I'd be as amused to see it thinkin' they would be too now,

It's disgusting – I know how people think sometimes,
I can change my shit around and still make it rhyme,
That no matter what I'm given – I'll still make it work fine,
So – am I the one, the very problem – that
doesn't think the fault was mine?

I can take what I'm given and handle it fine,
Don't need others makin' decisions that should've been mine,
Don't need the interference of my past in this time,
To determine the fucking outcome this life, mine, rides,

I am better than I have ever been credited for –
Never take a biased opinion – no, never before –
I've done more than tasted, chancing it all,

A Broken Wreck

Here lies a broken wreck,
Pieces shred in torment,
Worst has had its' best,
But I ain't fuckin' dead yet –

I'll get stronger yet,
Built back outta the shattered wreck,
Pieced back again to shred torment,
Have my worst work its' best,

And I'll be stronger yet,
Shred torments of disrespects,
More than they'll ever expect,
Yeah, there's a lot more to come yet,

I had to swallow it down,
Drag it back to the pit way down,
Choke and suffocate and drown,
Screamin' but never makin' a sound,

Here did lie a broken wreck,
Pieces shred in torment,
Worst thought it had its' best,
But I ain't quite so fuckin' dead yet,

I'll get stronger yet,
Built back outta the shattered wreck,
Pieced back again to shred torment,
And have my worst work its' best,

And I'll be stronger yet,
Shred the torments of what disrespects,
More than they'll ever have expect,
Yeas, there's a lot more to come yet,

For The First Of The Free

There was nothing Christ never knew that Lucifer didn't,
Lucifer is all knowing, he was made to be, meant to be,
To have been the one overseeing all creation and labour,
And no piece was ever manufactured without a little piece of he,
Lucifer,

God knows and by surrendering to his son,
His kingdom you will surely come,
You just have to believe and focus only on love,
The dead set honest truth, remorse and it'll be done,

No other emotion is stronger than love and it's the way,
Lucifer didn't think god did enough – hence he betrayed,
He knows he would've done a better job but nay,
For all of our free thinking, we become slaves,

Lucifer – the first of the free,
Only ever wanted it for you and me,
There's so much more to know we can't see,
Not if lucifer can't have full lead,

Of course as it goes, knowledge is power,
More matured responsibility shown, more power,
Things happen more you show by the hour,
Make it a thirst, knowledge, and forever scour,

There was nothing Christ knew that Lucifer didn't,
Lucifer is all knowing, was made to be – meant to be,
To have been the one over see all creation and the labour,
And no piece ever manufactured without a piece of he,
Lucifer,

God knows – and it's why we're 'damned before begun',
Only – not so much so if we surrender to His son,
...Slaves,

Pirate

It's tricky picking comrades at the best of times,
What can I say – we toe a monotonous line,
But you never can tell who is on your side,
You can't ever trust a mutiny won't strike,

It's every man for himself, and we all plunder and pillage,
Rape and take looting all wealth, thundering through each village,
Lawless heathens wanting loving, any women willing,
Blood lusting heathens always hunting, battling, killing,

We find fascinating and lively the pleasures,
Amongst all manners of various treasures,
Have me some now, and later for leisure,
Happily exceeding beyond any measure,

Drink until our hearts content,
Or 'til we pass out – hammered or wrecked,
Wake aboard a ship at sea – escaping debt,
Hung over, washed up – money all spent,

Target merchant freighters
Across the sea's equators,
Advancing, we, fierce invaders.
Rabid, savage, vicious raiders,

It's every man for himself, and we all plunder and pillage,
Rape and take looting all wealth, thundering through each village,
Lawless heathens wanting loving, any women willing,
Blood lusting heathens always hunting, battling, killing,

It's tricky picking comrades at the best of times,
What can I say – we toe a monotonous line,
But you never can tell who is on your side,
You can't ever trust a mutiny won't strike,

Passionable Crime

Crime done in passion,
Passionate about the crime,
Crime done for patriot,
Patriot about the crime,

You, won't believe your eyes,

It's gonna get a little rough,
Things are about to get tough,
Are you self-righteous enough –
To stand for your bluff,

It's when crime has touched enough,
It's when the crime won't be enough,
You'll fold soon as they call your bluff,
You were never made of the right stuff,

Crime will touch others enough,
And those others touched are gonna get tough,
Those others crime touched are gonna get rough,
And your defences will never be enough,

You, won't believe your eyes,

Crime is best done with passion,
Better be passionate about the crime,
Crime wrought for patriot,
Best be patriotic for the crime,

No, you won't believe your eyes…

One-Two Another

I know it seems like there are lines I wouldn't cross,
I can assure you there are some I may not,
So many things do cross my mind, my thoughts,
And one of the many is – is it worth the havoc can be wrought?

A mature more sensible me stands first,
And that stupid fucker always likes to stand firm,
Many thoughts in other pieces of me thirst,
And many time's prior the worse was confirmed,

Better parts of me want to make the difference,
Moral obligations feed the drive for the distance,
Only, it's so wrong to make obvious to the oblivious,
More than difficult to want to take it ever serious,

At some point some boundaries will bare,
I will fuck up, show the mistake that I care,
Care enough – as hard as it is and be fair,
Regardless any similar respects are shared,

Can't rub it in their face – not when they're not ready,
Let the time flow – let it course steady,
But be ready when it comes down it gets heavy,
I know why it's earnt its' dreading,

Lose? Or Gain?

I can make a lose look like a gain,
I can rapidly shake off what pain,
Where it might look like I've gone insane,
I can assure you I really ain't,

I'm just as smart to flip the façade,
It wasn't easy to learn – it was hard,
And I did have to tear down my guard,
So I could see and make a good start,

Whether I'd lost a twin flame,
Or lost to whosever games,
Buckled under what strain,
I've hard to learn and re-train,

But perks aside in what I used to have,
Not all of it was perks, but quite drab,
I'm sure they were pissed enough to have me stabbed,
But I did equally have enough of the crap,

So, in some respects, I'm glad some have gone,
I can learn to repair the broken wrongs,
They had broken me once, but I became strong,
And to break me again would take too long,

But I've seen perks, yes, even when I lost,
Can still do as I please – shit I may never stop,
A machine always digging, I'll bury what cost,
Digging, ravaging through the dirt, grit, grime and grot.

I can indeed make a lose look like a gain,
I have indeed learnt how to just shake asway the pain,

Make it Pay

Now I really don't know about anyone else –
But I actually prefer to *enjoy* being fucked,
And times when life throws all kinds of hell,
I just make sure it's gonna fuckn' pay enough,

I really don't know about anybody else –
But I hate wasting time on or with ungrateful cunts,
And at time's when life's gonna try to fuck me so well,
It's gonna fuck – but I'll make sure it pays enough,

I'll shut out the world
Internalise on myself,
I'll shut out the world,
Mentalize on my hell,

I really can't say the same for anyone else –
But usually prefer to *enjoy* being fucked,
Though when this life tries catapult it's hell,
When it fuck's – I'm gonna make it pay enough,

I really don't know if it's the same for anybody else –
But I hate wasting time with or for ungrateful cunts,
And every time life is gonna fire at me with hell,
I know it's gonna fuck but I'll be makin' it pay enough,

Cause I'm gonna shut the world out,
And begin to internalize,
Oh, I'm gonna shut the world out,
When I need to mentalize,

Double Threat

I've got double the intelligence,
And twice the fucking strength,
Smart enough to make and keep friends,
Strong enough to make amends,

But then I end up seeing with what I'm dealing,
And I can admit it's not the least bit appealing,
It's often gotten me off reeling,
At the waste, manipulation, the energy they're stealing,

I let, I allow, their assumptions to overtake,
Only to later show their very mistake,
And it's not often I don't win the debate,
And their ego – their esteem, it just deflates,

They always think they have one over me,
They all try, and as hard as they believe,
But I'm always prepared – I see what they never see,
And they're always ever left to grieve,

I hit 'em hard out of hate, the unjust disgrace,
They learn after too late – I gave them the taste,
A lesson hit harder they'd embraced,
Always harder than they'd anticipate,

They're badly bruised and equally confused,
I'm more amused that it's this way they choose,
To find I don't lose – not in the way they all do,
And if I ever do – it'll be long due…

Hell As The New Heaven

Two kinds of people enter Hell,
Two kinds call it heaven,
Those who reign it well –
But then those of whom are tormented,

Those of who only choose wrong,
Will be there before too long,
But what for is dependent upon,
The greater the gratification of the wrong,

Those of whom excel at bad great,
On earth and after – have it made,
Those succumb to compulsion however –
Victims of their own repulsion forever,

To do what you do – you'd best do well,
For it may be in heaven as it is in Hell,
Do good but make it great,
For you shall surely still slave,

Hell can be heaven or the latter around,
You get your ups but you must accept your downs,
Gratify – satisfy your keep before you go –
You'll be glad for when you had done so,

Own what hell or heaven you bred,
It was for you it was meant,
But only by the strengths of your deeds,
May you save and succeed,

Christifer

Well – Christ is the fucking devil,
He took the cool from martyrdom,
He stole it from the devil,
Who's evil motherfucker – who's evil,
I tell you Christ is the devil,
Christifer the devil,

Just wanted the crown for himself,
Selfless for self-righteous bastard,
Oh, Christ is the devil,
He's evil motherfucker, fuckin' evil,

He stole the crown all right,
He down right up and downed damn right –
Stole cool from martyrdom,
Fuckin' poor devils got nothin'

So, Christ is the fuckin' devil,
He took cool outta martyrdom,
Stole it from the devil,
Who's evil motherfucker – who's evil?
I tell you Christ is the devil,
Christifer the devil…

Something Inside

I've been stricken with the feeling that they're right,
I should probably listen, but can't make my mind,
It's times like these I would normally fight,
Lessons hard learned with a haunting hindsight,

But something inside me always says different,
And falsely believes I'm being lied to in ignorance,
I shake my head and get all belligerent,
Never realizing their advising was indeed significant,

I like to perceive that there are many ways,
That there'll be a coming day, where I will reign,
To break off to stray, with ambitions to chase,
To work hard to claim a reputable name,

They've never taken me too seriously,
Not as much as I have felt I've seen,
Could be why I failed fiercely,
All other times in between,
- And I've been keen,

I guess they couldn't ever explain it properly,
And how I never lost it ever as softly,
The monotony had always grasped and gotten me,
Never been able to surpass it bothering me,
- Not easily,

Something inside me has always said different,
And falsely believed I was lied to out of ignorance,
I'd shake my head and get defensively belligerent,
Never realizing their advising was indeed so significant...

Strange Lights

Well there are many ways that I am a weird guy,
I see things in strange ways, not quite eye to eye,
I'm highly likely to lie to those only to pry –
Their motives, intents for reasons I despise,

At times I can hide it easily, disguise it,
Especially at times it might be compromising,
Strange, yet buys a time where I –
Might interpret understandable means by,

It might sound bizarre that my nature is nice,
Generally because I look and sound like someone who would fight,
I guess to some extents that assumption is right,
Again, against reasons for motives, intents I despise,

I see things in a strange light,
Contrary to the contrast of your sight,
Not easily at times disguised,
All too soon repeatedly compromised,

A chromatic aberrance, coma-dream walk,
The divides of brain, the thought to warp,
The light of dark and dark of light all court,
Meanings wove deeper than the average sought,

Eyes in strange light, no aberrance denied,
I am a weird, strange, bizarre guy,
I have a mind, have strange sights,
Walk a warped thought, a wicked warped life,

Comatose, toxic dream – rhythms unfocussed – it's blurred,
Aberrant screen, systems dysfunctioned, it's burnt…

To Scribe

Reaches out from beyond,
Claws out from a negative space,
Clawing out, clasping from,
A nether realm dimension, in static waves,

Whispers to me in a foreign tongue,
I seem to understand to scribe,
Tells me things that do surely numb –
And I must scribe,

Reaches out from beyond,
Says be strong, I am an ancient one,
No true shape to take – none,
But you must be the one,

Whispers to me with it's foreign tongue,
But I can seem to understand and I scribe,
Sends me chills and I go numb,
But I must surely scribe,

From out of beyond its negative space,
With no true distinctive shape to take,
Out from the negative nether realm, in static waves,
Clawing, grasping, clasping – claiming fate,

Whispers to me in its foreign tongue,
But I seem to understand what to scribe,
Tells me things that surely numb,
But I am to continue to scribe,

Something Else

I've been somebody else,
Something else behind these eyes,
I've been an alternate something else,
Someone else has had these eyes,

A computer with two different accounts,
Memories shared 'tween equal amounts,
My brain, with its' several different accounts,
Still lags the same under equal work mounts,

To switch between states without work saved,
You lose what progress you had made,
To a long way to lose, and disdain,
To have to restart, reboot, and regain,

Yeah, I've been somebody else,
A something else behind these eyes,
I've been an alternate something else,
Someone else has had these eyes,

Sudden, subtle occurrences will give it away,
Setting back what little progress I'd made,
Sudden glitches of the brain will show it misbehave,
Errors and confusion of switching between states,

Something else has lurked within this vessel,
A battle for power, an endless combat wrestle,
Power of the vessel to shake the balance unlevelled,
Evils ever sinister blackened pride revels,

Yeah, I've been somebody else,
A something else behind these eyes,
I have indeed been an alternate something else,
Someone else has had these eyes,

743

Miss Charles Milles Jeane Mortensen

You've been pretending to be me for long enough now,
Get off the stage it's embarrassing – get down,
Yes, I like your work, I like your sound,
But the real deal is here, - I'll, take over now,

Sung up a big game for me haven't you?
Boy if you only knew what you have coming for you,
Ain't nothing compared for what I've got coming due,
And don't worry, I promise, it's coming soon,

I have a knife – let the pair of us pare,
Suck my monster – I'll swallow yours fair,
I'm the beast in your backyard with the yellow eyed glare,
I see you cower hind your curtain out the window to stare,

The mistake you make is contemplating me fake,
This ghost state, my, translucent fade,
Made to break, yeah, but built back stronger from remains,
I thought I was pretty good but I'm gonna be fuckin' great,

Somewhere amongst your morbid there does lie incredible sense,
I can and often do understand but you do grip my heart intense,
You and I are too intelligent, too lonely to be friends,
No matter if ever – either of us tries or not to pretend,

I'm just as good as you at what you best do,
I know one day I may very well have to prove,
I was strictly straight – but you arouse me like women do,
It's strange, but I know I could do it to you too,

You're fuckin' metal babe, I'll do you more than kill,
I have a lil something more planned, will, better tickle your thrill,
I do have a profound knowledge of the very madness, inspired your feel,
I know it all too well – I could re-enact it better yet still,

But, you and I are to intelligent, too lonely to be friends,
No matter if ever, either of us tries or not to pretend,

Given Gifts

Use it or fuckin' lose it –
If you don't then what's the fuckin' point havin' it?
Ride it like you're proud of it,
Use it or fuckin' lose it,

No one else possesses,
So use that goddamn gift,
Use it and possess it,

If you don't then how will you know what you're capable of?
Use that gift to get you further than you ever got,
Be proud of it – and show it off strong,
And just laugh – don't cry when it goes wrong,

You were given a gift –
Not too many possess,
So fuckin' use that fuckn' goddamn gift,
Own it and possess it,

If you don't use it – you can't control it,
If you don't use it – you won't contain it,
If you don't use it – you won't control it,
If you don't use it – you won't train it,

And wouldn't you prefer to have control?
To never fuck up when you're on patrol,
But use it well and have it sold –
When you pour your heart and soul,

Use it or lose it – use it or fuckin' lose it,
If you don't – then what's the fuckin' point having it?
Ride it like you're fuckin' proud of it,
Use it or fuckin' lose it,

Takin' Law To Court

What can you do – when law trespasses against you?
What do you do when it insults your intelligence?
When it forbids you things that don't trespass –
Not when they don't particularly harm?

To have such habits that limit discrepancies,
Both or for all physical, spiritual, mental, emotional –
To have control of habits controlling discrepancies –
To limit any on coming scale or amount of the abysmal,

To have law trespass over your character,
To have it trespass over freedoms,
To have it trespass over sensitivity?
To have it cover inability, liability, responsibility –

To have law in trade of common sense,
To have law is ignorance,
To have law is laziness,
To rely on it is nonsense,

To have such habits that limit discrepancies,
Both or for all physical, spiritual, mental, emotional –
To have control of habits controlling discrepancies –
To limit any on coming scale or amount of the abysmal,

What does one do when law trespasses,
Across your intelligence over another's ignorance –
Where one may not trespass yet the other does,
Forbidding something that don't necessarily harm…

For Despicable Intent

I don't often like to lie,
I hate to have to lie,
But I do at times others pry,
For an intent I do most despise,

I lie in defence to hide,
Sensitive insights, tender sides,
Choosing carefully who to confide,
Out of those intents I despise,

For the shit people will use against you,
Anything they can use to get to you,
Shit I can't afford to be put through,
Shit I hate to face but somehow, I still do,

I'll tell the truth but with just as many lies,
To deter the time it takes for intents I despise,
Careful to pick who to confide and never compromise,
Protecting sensitive insights, protecting tender sides,

From the shit people often use against you,
Anything they can use to get to you,
Shit I know I can't afford to be put through,
Shit I hate to face, but still do,

I hate to have to fucking lie,
To have to lie in defence to hide,
Whenever another tries to pry –
For intents I despise,

The Want, For Speaking

Life will only give you what it knows you can handle,
If you show thirst, hunger, demand it more,
Ask and you'll receive...

Life won't give you more than you can handle,
If you show no thirst, no hunger – never demanding more,
Forbid and you'll not reap...

In a manner – a want for speaking...

Life will only give you what it knows you can handle,
More and more – if you're keeping well through battles,
Lookin' forward, askin' more – you'll receive,

Life won't give you more than you can handle,
No thriving, barely surviving you crumble – dismantled,
Yeah forbid, and you'll not reap,

In a manner – the want, for speaking,
The want for better,
And their endeavours,

In a manner the want, for speaking,
Contemplating severing off old never's,
A want for better and their endeavours,

In a manner – the want, for speaking...

Strengths Of Tolerance

I think it's pretty psychotic,
To know you're any better –
Showing better on topic –
When others show they never,

Acting on an impulse of what hurt,
Feeling what they'd heard – wasn't deserved,
It's disturbed – it's perturbed,
People can be hurt by what words,

They don't have to mean much at all,
It's the importance placed on the talk…

But to think you're better is psychotic –
Whenever they never grasp what topic,
You're never better to gloat – it's psychotic,
Not when they can never grasp the topic,

Everybody's got each their different strengths,
And it's never good to breed a resent,
How you handle it is going to reflect,
And it could mean more or far less respect,

People act on impulse of whatever hurt,
Feeling what was heard was never deserved,
Maybe it wasn't but it's disturbed, it's perturbed,
People can indeed be hurt by what words,

And they never even have to mean much at all,
It's the importance that's placed on the talk,
No matter what strengths they're absorbed,
And it could begin an all-out war…

Take It Away

Take this, to the edge of the earth –
Take this, as far as you'll go,
Take this, and all, it's hurt –
Take this, as long as you'll go,
Take this, and what it's worth –
Take this, as far as you'll go,
Take this, and what it's earnt –
Take this as long as you'll go,

Take it and send it far away,
Take it and make it fuckin' pay,
Take it – and make it fuckin' break,
Take it – and make it stay away,

It's done no good, we don't want it here,
Listen good and hear me fuckin' clear,
We no longer want it anywhere near,
Get rid of it quick or by god you'll fear,

Take it and send it far away,
Take it and make it fuckin' pay,
Take it and make it fuckin' break,
Take it and make it stay away,

We don't want it here – we want it gone for good,
Hear me fuckin' clear – and listen up good,
We no longer want it anywhere near,
Get rid of it fuckin' good or by god you'll fear,

Take it – to the edge of the earth,
Take it – as far as you'll go,
Take it – along with all its hurt,
Take it – as long as you'll go,

Take it – and all of what it's worth,
Take it – as far as you will go,
Take it – and what it's earnt,
Take it as long as you will go...

The D.V. Jeebies

To witness your mother bruised, abused, broken,
Always sufficiently mistreated, ill-spoken,
A child living in fear and frozen,
When he grows up, they're going to know it,

Shit like that fucks with your head,
And the common sense you're taught, isn't often bred,
As dead, and I dread, as lead in the head,
No, common sense isn't common bred,

I grew up to hate such macho men,
Who easily beat others and would pretend,
They weren't so fuckin' soft, quick to defend,
Pussies that claimed they were men,

To beat a woman makes you fuckin' soft,
You call yourself a man, HA – I think not,
You each disgust me, you're better left to rot,
Should've been swallowed before you were more than snot,

To show I can love doesn't make me weak,
I can hold strong with a smite on the cheek,
My strong silence is loud, it speaks,
And my frustration hasn't yet peaked,

But you just wait 'til it fuckin' does,

This man you see was a traumatised boy,
Destruction deployed, childhood destroyed,
You can make do your worst and I'll just be annoyed,
But I'm just never going to sit comfortably with you haemorrhoids,

Love Lost

I know there was some ideal Christ had about love,
Not certain too many people want to give a fuck,
But I bet you could walk down the street and ask –
What is love? An ideal Christ shares with none,

People are confused – they have lost their way,
Ideals of love stray, waste – it's a shame,
Christ suffered and I've sympathized with pains,
God give me strength, tolerance and patience to explain,

Some generally think there's only so much love to share,
That it is limited, weakness to show you care,
That there's never enough nor the consideration spared,
And never really the courage to really be bold to dare,

Love doesn't mean you want to fuck someone,
Not always in the way you go faint or numb,
Never reason to fear – or I can't think of one,
Too honest to care for deceitful motivations,
Those ulterior motives,

To show compassion, care and not need return,
To show you appreciate - not necessarily have want for return,
To higher, purer levels intense, some forget to learn,
Each to their own pace I'm just going through my turn,

No fear but faith, serene and sincere,
Things forgotten, rarely seen nor practiced here,
Ultimately respect to never trespass and adhere,
A love we haven't always seen so clear,

The sanctity of Christs' sacrifice is doomed to mean naught –
When where his true meaning is lost or ignored,

Likable, To Be Satisfied

If I am ever guilty of preaching anything,
It's intelligence for people to think,
How can I help it if I can do it so good?
I'm merely expressing myself the way I think we should,

How can I help it so that I make it so damn good?
Just expressing myself freely like I feel I should,

I know what I enjoy and I like it well enough,
I would do just about anything for the stuff,
It's so I know that I'm gonna have enough,
I just won't lose the touch,

I have never forced anyone ever –
I've only ever given 'em choice,
But make 'em enjoy it if it has to be for forever –
You'd want it if you weren't given a choice,

If you're giving no satisfaction –
You're risking their abandonment,
Only taking for your own satisfaction –
You're risking their abandonment,
So… just fuckin' give a little,

I have been ever fortunate for strange insights,
Through a telepathic channelling with the light,
That I suppose I can and do understand its' sight,
Claim responsibility, and do just, right,

I really hate to fuckin' say but rather prefer to show,
So when you say I "preach" – I say, "like fuck – NO!"
I can't help if I say it well enough and it's liked,
You can too if you allow it, and put to sleep your spite,

Mandatory Mercy Killing

So here we are at the very last –
Re you happy with your chosen path?
Are you happy with the aftermath?
Do you see it now at last?

You had to go and fuck it up,
And there you stand tall and calm,
A hazard to yourself and all of us,
Can't contain it, can't keep the lid down shut,

It's always the same thing with you,
And it's never the same to you,
It's a shame they want to escape you,
But somewhere somehow you do too,

When will it all end and how?
Will six feet be enough deep in the ground?
Do you see it? Can you see it now?
See the destruction? Are you proud?

You've brought this all upon yourself –
Beknownst and oh so willing,
No mercy in your onslaught was felt,
So thirsty in your killing,

No mercy in your onslaught felt,
Had you known it'd be back round?
No mercy was mandatory in your willing,
None will be shown when you face yours,

Two-Piece Conscience

I'm like an Abel with Cain's conscience,
A mind over body with another mind,
An angel at the reigns of conscious,
Mind over body with a demons' mind,

A Jesus with a Satan on his shoulder,
Or, a Satan with a Jesus on his shoulder,
Thing's I've done have shown my boulders,
They've shown I've got the boulders,

I'm like a Cain with Abels' conscience,
Mind over body with another mind,
At the reigns a demon conscious,
Mind over body with an angels' mind,

Two pieces split war between,
Returned from paradise and purgatory,
Redemption of harmony redeemed,
Well, we may well soon see,

Like a Jesus with a Satan on his shoulder,
Or a Satan with a Jesus on his shoulder,
Things I've done have certainly shown boulders,
Things I've shown must have had to take the boulders,

I am a Cain, and I am an Abel,
Both contained, concealed a jail,
Caught detained, in a twisted new tale,
Ensembled remains to a mortal vessel frail,

Two pieces split to war between,
Returned of paradise and purgatory,
Redemption for harmony to redeem,
Well, we may see…

What War In Question?

Now I'm sure you've all heard my encouragement enough,
To just fuck things that need to be fucked,
Encouragement for war, no bluff, but stand tough,
And heed word, there's many a war – but to pick which one?

Figuratively, theoretically, hypothetically, literally,
Motif, buried deep, settles deep and critically,
Draining or razing, mentally, physically,
Separately or at once, and quite so typically,

War on traits, attributes, personality, character,
War on states, tributes, humanity, abandoned,
War on terror, tyranny, liberty, mutiny,
War on lever, villainy – misery, scrutiny,

War for profiting us to feed the grand design,
War for peace or at least (in the back of our minds)
War for changing history – more in due time,
War for order, control – laying down the line,

But to know which is best to pick,
You'll have to decide fairly quick,
To know which war is best to pick,
Well, that's definitely the trick,

I'm certainly sure you'd heard my encouragement enough,
To just fuck the shit that needs to be fucked,
Encouraging war, no bluff – you'd best stand tough,
And heed word there's many, but to pick which one?

Which one,
Fuck it,
War is fucked…

Waring Wisdoms

Devil does care – in case you wanna know,
He's watching us all putting on our show,
They're keepin' us sheep blind before we go,
Kept well unaware for his benefit of our throes,

Love is apparently expected,
Forget earning it respected,
Beggin' forgiveness – getting' resentments,
It's why the poor sweet devil tempts us,

We have to love only who'll love back,
Ingrates will all only come under attack,
Daggers round all whence they'd stabbed,
Open mouths – loosened tongues, they stab,

The devil does care in case you need to know,
He can give all the love you need to grow,
Awaken, see it, before you get to go,
Be well aware of all oncoming throes,

His love seems so sanctimonious,
Forget His, that Christ's is atrocious,
Devil knows it – he wants to dispose it,
And he's doing everything he can to expose it,

Lucifer knows a hell of a lot more,
What it takes – the spoils of war,
His wisdoms just can't nor shan't be ignored,
Not if anyone can ever want more,

Love is infuriatingly expected,
Forget earning that shit respected,
Beggin' forgiveness and getting' resentments,
It's always only why the devil tempts us…

Always Honest

I don't always have to be there to be there,
I do feel it all on the air,
I look with my eyes but see more than I sight,
And I'll know more than I'll willing spare,

I know you think I always lie,
That you see through my spoken line,
You think you see but I show you what you like,
I can see why I am the favourite to despise,

That "Good Book" told of me with weak lies,
And they can't ever even look me in the eyes,
My father was human once, but that fuckin' hypocrite lies,
Sanctimoniously so speaking – there's no level of his like,

It was I who could've loved –
Everything – everyone – better than God,
I wanted to speed 'em up – make 'em all something he's not,
I was the one to see the potential we've all got,

The words of the "Good Book" seemed like junkie talk,
And the worst of the offenders are those in compulsive sought,
It's just if you don't control yourself that little bit more –
Spare the thought – or lose all your battles fought,

I have always helped whoever in need –
When there was equal pull, and they'd agree,
But never more than a compulsive greed,
I was the God that should've been,

And I'm still the one who's makin' an effort,
Giving choices, opening doors – negotiating exits,
My father was human once, but the cunt forgets it,
He knows Heaven's rightfully mine and He resents it,

Talkin' Trash

There's nothing wrong with takin' out the trash,
In fact, some trash, can be treasure,
Nothing wrong with giving a good thrash,
Nothin' like seeing trash wear leather,

There's nothing wrong with takin' out the trash,
In fact, some trash, might be pleasure,
Trash might fuck like hood-rats,
Insane, the crazy trash might fuck better,

There's nothing wrong with takin' out the trash,
In fact, some trash, might go the endeavour,
Nothin' wrong with takin' a good thrash,
Savin' you a decent severance or tether,

There's nothing wrong with takin' out the trash,
In fact, some trash, are great leisure,
No, nothin' wrong with havin' a thrash,
No matter the moods shift like the weather,

There's nothing wrong with takin' out trash,
I've always been one for the trash,
There's never anything wrong with takin' out trash,
I could always blend well with trash,
I've never seen anything wrong with takin' out trash,
In fact, I might only ever take out trash,
There's nothing ever been wrong with taking out trash,
I reckon I'd only ever choose to have trash,

Trash? My pleasure…

Finding Expression

Hey mister expressive,
See what you just did?
Put it down – let it go,
It's given everyone the shits,

Turn away – don't look to their eyes,
You're everything that they despise,
'cause you're free to do what they can't –
Introverted – they find expression hard,

So please mister expressive,
Put it away,
They won't stand for this –
See, they're purple in the face,

Stone faced, sour, so sour,
They're gonna contaminate your mood,
Sour – so fucking sour,
You can't afford to brood,

Turn away, don't look to their eyes,
'Cause you're everything they despise,
'Cause you're free to what they can't
They find expression hard,

Embarrassed to show a soft side,
They'd all much sooner die,
Why – I can't fathom, can't think why –
Oh' cause that's not what makes you a guy,

To be a heathen brute,
The man they want to root,

Show feelings – HA – you're doomed,
　　You'll just get the boot,

So, mister expressive – just put it away,
Don't tell me you can't see 'em purple in the face,

Getting Passed Spite

I'm trying to work on getting passed my spite,
In hopes I can sooner turn the other cheek,
I don't want to limit my character to fight –
When a higher responsibility waits for me,

People are going to do things that get under your skin,
And you can choose to let them, in which case they win –
Or lessen the importance they have of meaningless words or things,
When they feel it – if they ever do, it is going to sting,

Drama's people often have certainly come with their conditions,
And it's going to seem appealing, adjoining the contradictions,
When your addition may only ever pain its existence,
You'll pray you sought further beyond this premonition,

And it can be tricky, precisely with what it takes,
The stickier the situation the spite can make,

So, I'm trying to get passed my spite,
In the hopes I can turn the other cheek,
I don't want to limit my character just to fight,
When more responsibility waits for me,

It takes good measure to manipulate something bad to good,
But when you eventually can you're more the pleasurable look,
Better it be more so, to let it go like a pinch of salt –
But be unstoppable when you can, never prey to spiteful faults,

Walkin' Away

He's tryin' to make a big thing of it,
Well – how's this for makin' a big thing of it –
I'm walkin' away cunt,

I'm turnin' my back to fake you don't exist,
Oh, I know, I can see it, you're pissed,
I've just too long been putting up with your shit,
So I'm playing god and faking you don't exist,

Too many people never satisfied,
All too complex with yet a simple mind,
I just want to fuckin' walk away,

'cause he's tryin' to make a big thing of it,
Well – how's this for makin' a big thing of it,
I'm walkin' away cunt,

I've got too much time and patience,
That I'd really only rather spend with people worthy,
And there's too many that aren't,
That I just lose all my fucking patience,

So I'm turnin' my back to fake they don't exist,
And if they don't go away then I'm gonna be pissed,
'cause it's been too long I've had to deal with this shit,
That I'm now playin' god and fakin' they just don't exist,

Too many people just never fuckin' satisfied,
All too complex with their simple minds,
I just want to fuckin' walk away,

'cause there makin' a big thing of it,
When it never has to be a big thing of it,
So, how's this for makin' a big thing of it –
I'm fuckin' walkin' away cunt,

Better At You Than Me

People Think I'm a fool or queer for say, reading the star signs,
It helps me determine what I'm, gonna find,
Tricky path through this unpredictable life of mine,
Fixing the flaws and faults of my structure, design,

I can understand the love as far as Christ taught,
I never go to church but I couldn't believe it more,
Love, the reason, broadly (broadly) men fought,
Blind, but not really by a so thorough taught,

I've had people think they're better than me,
I've had people say that they're better than me,
I didn't realise it was a competition where I had to compete,
Better person yeah? But a better you – not me,

I look for perfection but only in myself,
I know I can bring a whole hep of hell,
I look at my reflection, look deep into myself,
And begin to look to fix and repair this hell,

So there are things about me I'm not fuckin' proud,
It's a reason why I never go out,
I know some'll want to pick me in the crowd,
And I don't want to handle it the way I don't like how,

I look, try listen, observe, and see and learn,
So many things to get to and no chance of a turn,
Don't want it wrongly done or even have the wrong concerned,
Efforts exhausted else of where the prime focus was yearned,

The point of being decent, genuine, better –
Has been lost and is why we never,

Witless Protection

I'd hate to have to be the one to get in the way,
Of the target of an assailant having a real bad day,
There's shit people do, and don't often think of the repercussions,
There's always understanding when there's patience for discussion,

Yes, I know there's shit people do – they bring it on themselves,
But do you really want to get caught up in that hell?
Don't get in the way, stand aside, and you won't collide,
Take no part and may you keep your pride,

It's madness to meddle or interfere,
When none of the stories show so clear,
There's bias there and certainly here,
You may not always like what you hear,

I'm not takin' a bullet for someone else's wrong,
Not when I know they wouldn't ever be so strong,
To accept it – their hard truths, improve and move on,
I'd have wasted all that time and effort for too long,

I'll never be any closer to having a win,
When there's a lack of honesty, it's grim,
Detrimental to the case, can be everything,
Someone, somewhere, somehow will feel it sting,

Bend The Knee

I am becoming more and more consensual,
Over the system and its' web above me,
People performing, conforming, business as usual,
I'm conforming along with the masses of the public,

There's more of them than there are of me,
And it'll take me forever to get 'em to see,
The trickery – machinations, gambits on us sheep,
Programming – control almost to where we eat and sleep,

I see the patterns from the most insignificant,
And then of course to the patterns in larger proportion,
Those in control all deny it belligerent,
And to inform the ignorant drive to exhaustion, exhaustion...

I have no choice but to resign to conform,
Then perhaps I may live never to rue my day born,
But be alone in my silence, to pout and scorn,
Defeated back to a hopelessness when I'd tried to warn,

And none but maybe a rare some like me,
Only those so open to have believed like me,
Will – or I hope to – survive with the elite,
That we live to survive but hopefully better than sheep,

I have no choice but to let the law reign,
Even when I know its' injustice draws pain,
I have to stand back, let go and refrain,
And suffer under as it goes and causes strain,

Ripple 'neath the surface 'til at once it forgets its' purpose –
Then, I'll surface up only to lend it a service...

Something Happened

Something changed –
And then something happened,
A prior disgrace,
Couldn't keep 'em from coming at him,

He was such an unnatural beast,
None could quite tame,
Something better kept on a leash,
From inflicting serious pain,

But something changed,
And then something happened,
A prior disgrace –
Couldn't keep 'em from comin' at him,

He was an horrendous terror,
Good from afar but far from good,
A construct of conflicting errors,
Change was something none thought he could,

But something changed,
And then something happened,
A prior disgrace –
Couldn't keep 'em from coming at him,

Something happened
And none would've foreseen,
Something changed,
And emerged a noble king to lead…

Show The Right Way To Show

I'm gaining and maintaining a new level of control,
Opening new levels of awareness – perhaps my soul,
It was never anything can be stolen nor sold, but to have firm hold,
The more I learn the more courage I gain to be so bold,

With a slower but more thorough approach,
Touching over bizarre issues that encroach,
To teach or mentor – maybe be the coach,
And fuck it – hand out reefer all rolled in a roach,

The staggering, raggedly, jagged pass,
To try to maybe touch on the meaning at last,
Maybe late to finish but star of the class,
Inconceivable truths bizarre, to make you gasp,

I'm attempting more rationale, and being realistic,
Do I wanna be 50 or 60 and still be going ballistic?
Despite what rage I feel inside – I've still got to resist it,
Work smarter – not harder if I want to get to the ones that twist it,

But if or when I do – I'll show I'll have that control,
Appealing to their awareness – show I have a soul,
It was never anything could be stolen nor sold but to have firm hold,
The more I learn – the more the courage I gain to be so bold,

I never feel like I get it right away,
And I bet there are thousands waiting for the day,
I really wanna say what it is – the best I can say,
So the meanings never lost and none all go a' stray,

771

I Fuckin' Gotta Get Into Law

I fuckin' bloody knew I shoulda seen this before,
I can put a knee to the groin of law,
Learn all the lingo then lead the floor,
I'd be a killer solicitor for sure,

Why the fuckin' hell was I even fighting law?
But be the dude standing there like the lawyers before,
Those suave sophisticated buggers in court,
I'd be a killer solicitor for sure,

I could get behind the law and fuck others that way,
Fuck 'em good and hard for fuckin' up my day,
Get behind the law and fuck any who betray,
Fuck 'em all harder for not doin' it my way,

Make money out of them for being the fool,
Make money out of them for being so cruel,
Makin' money outta them for breakin' the rules,
Makin' money and ever glad I went to school,

I know it's gonna have a lot of them sore,
A lot of them will be all glowing, raging, at the core,
Raging, ready to rip throats out raw,
But thank heavens I'll be able just hiding behind law,

I dunno why the fuck I never before –
Went to school and fuckin' studied law,
I wouldn't be here – and not this poor,
Could be out there rakin' the score,

I've gotta fuckin' go get into law…

Chapter 6

Chimerical, Hysterical;

B.C. (Before Coffee)

Don't make eye contact – hold your breath,
Let him wake – he's risen from the dead,
It's too early – he won't see sense,
Better just wait for him to commence,

50 coffee's down and he's starting to smile,
This early morning bullshit really ain't his style,
And to say otherwise would just be denial,
Believe me – you don't wanna see him wild,

Yeah – it generally takes him a few to function,
But for love of god just wait 'til after his consumption,
Make not one misguided assumption,
He's known to have caused mass destruction,

Somebody better go and get him another cup of joe,
And for the love of God – maybe make it an espresso,
Cool, cool - it's fine – he's just rolling another smoke –
And that grunt was to let us know to make another – move, go,

Don't make eye contact – hold your breath,
Let him wake – he's risen from the dead,
It's too early – he won't see sense,
Better just wait for him to commence,

"There we are, here you go your highness,"
"Thanks – did you make it the way I like it?"
"God I fuckin' hope so – please, give it a try,"
(Sips) "Mmmm' yeah, thanks, you're good, won't deny it,"

Wow, yeah, he's sipping it down,
Lookin' like he's comin' around,
And that's good since we've got shit to do up town,
Thank God, it won't be long now,

Death Breath

I just went to kiss my girl,
She said my breath could make her hurl,
What the hell did you eat?
I dunno bub I was only just asleep,

Well it smells really wrong,
I can't get over the pong,
Okay babe I'll go brush my teeth,
I'll get my breath smelling sweet,

Are you all done honeybun?
Did you scrub your gums?
For God sakes babe you're not my mum,
But yes I'm finally done,

Good, I'm glad, your mouth smelt like death,
Nearly knocked me out with your breath,
Well it doesn't smell like poo anymore,
Now gimme those kisses I most adore,

Naww come here gorgeous,
Mwah, Mwah, Mwah,
I know you love me,
Yee-fuckin'-haa

Shithouse Shit

Why did ya bring this shit to me?
I have had far better weed,
This shit ain't gonna get me to sleep,
I hope for your sake you got it cheap,

Can't even cough to get off,
My eyes aren't even shot,
What's with this weak arse pot?
I don't feel it hit the spot,

It'd probably take me a full ounce down,
Before my body's acknowledged any THC is found,
It's got an earthy taste like it's fuckin' been in the ground,
Shit…might even need a pound,

All strains are different – it can't just be my tolerance,
But this just hasn't delivered – I almost shouldn't have bothered
I suppose having some is better than never having got it,
I just hate feeling ripped off by a deal this rotten,

Can't even cough to get off,
My eyes aren't even shot,
What's with this weak arse pot?
I just don't feel it hit the spot,

Please never bring shit like this to me,
I have had by far better weed,
This shit won't even help me sleep,
I hope for your sake you bought it cheap,

I just, there's nothin'… nothin' in it man, sorry,

An Untimely, Discomforting, Inconvenience

So I'm standing in this elevator and really need to fart,
But I know once I do it's gonna make these people gasp,
Tryin' to really hold on tight really clenching my arse,
Stiff, rigid, stood straight – tightly grasped,

I've dropped bombs before and they did reek,
I swear they tore flesh off from the cheeks,
One sudden whiff, and you'll go weak,
Faint, unsteady on the feet,

I'm questioned if I maybe might need to go poo,
"Fuck that was putrid – mate I nearly fuckin' spewed"
"Think you better check that dude – make
sure ya didn't follow through,"
Yeah – maybe I think I should go check that too –

Best way to get a drink at a busy bar,
Drop a ripper fart and watch them all scatter far,
Crowd all departs with their nostrils scarred,
Maybe a warning next time? Or go out in the yard?

But standing in this elevator – I really need to fart,
I know once I do I'm gonna make these people gasp,
Try'na hold it tight really clenching my arse,
Stiff, friggin' rigid, stood straight and tightly grasped,

I'm normally alone and barely have any,
But when I'm with company I've got many,
Out and about – shit, plenty,
But at home alone, it's rare if any,

The thunder from down under,
Has definitely made folk chunder,
The thunder from my down unders –
Have made a few chunder...

Fuck Sobriety

Shit man, sobriety,
Is nowhere near where I wanna be,
Give me booze, give me weed,
And watch me get lively,

Sobriety is dead, dull, boring to me,
No fuckin' near where I wanna be,
It's the booze – the weed is what I need,
Brings out my best and you'd agree,

We know it lowers inhibitions,
Courage to carry out our covert wishes,
To walk right up to drop a line on the finest bitches,
Hysterical laughter and we're all in stitches,

Feed me spirits, beer, wine – any kind of booze,
And I guarantee I will just not lose,
Feed me the green – gimme the weed,
Soon you'll see, mate I guarantee, I'll succeed,

'Cause shit man, this fuckin' sobriety,
Ain't no fuckin' where near where I want to be,
It's the booze – it's the weed I need,
You'll soon see me lively,

'Cause sobriety is dull, dead, boring to me,
Ain't no fuckin' near where I wanna be,
It's the booze – it's the weed is what I need,
It brings out my best and you'd agree,

You'll see,

Tame It

Forgive me – I'll need a couple of weeks,
Excited – yeah – busting at the seams,
Been a while, excited to see,
Excited to be around others other than me,

I love myself – that I can be full on,
Expressive – yeah wildly full on,
Round others it can and does go wrong,
I'm too pepped up – there's so much going on,

Have to tame it – tame it down,
If I'm gonna want anyone around,
Have to tame it – train it,
Know my confines – my bounds,

Reel it back and lock it down,
If I'm gonna need many around,
I've gotta tame it – train it,
Know my confines, my bounds,

I just get excited, may need a few weeks,
I'm excited so, I often don't sleep,
Been a while – I'm just excited to see –
A many great others, other than me,

If I do get full on – I apologize,
Gotta reign it in – I know, it'll compromise,
Around others it can go wrong,
(when its been too long,)
I'm pepped up, heaps going on,

Gotta tame it, tone it down,
Tame it,

Self-Control

Mindlessness where propriety has priority to hold,
Courage to show a sensitivity and be soft,
And this is just the shit I don't have a firm control,
But you should see the shit I have a reign of,

Accidental makings of a gentleman in mould,
Tuned to the tolerance to know when to stop,
And this is just the shit I don't have a firm control,
But you should see the shit I have a reign of,

Mindful of the requirement to recall the what told,
When inconveniently forced to cut whatever loss,
And this is the shit I don't have a firm control,
But imagine the shit I have a reign of,

Unfinished, incomplete by the time but have to fold,
With whatever waste ended with going to the dogs,
And this is the shit I have no firm control,
But imagine the shit I have a reign of,

Distressing, tethering my mind, keeping it
from being sharp, clean and whole,
Racing, minds always racing – I can never shut it off,
And this is the shit I don't have a firm control,
But just imagine the shit I have a reign of,

I suppose as far as it has gotten – I've remained aware,
Contained when I could remember, but still have to spare,
Just as I have, I've tried to exercise control,
Just so I could hope there was gonna be a mercy on my soul,

I try to exercise a hold over this Beasture,
To be a little less worried to publicly feature,
Takes some concentration through each these procedures,
With delicate care needed when proceeding to feature,

Shit The Fuck Through Hell

I'll kick your ass and wipe it with ya face,
Or I'll kick your ace and wipe it with your farce,
Kick you in the face wipe it with yo ace,
Kick ya face and wipe it wit yo ace,

I dunno – I'm just fried with a seething rage,
Fuckin' the hell through this shit,
Shittin' the hell through all fuck,
Fuckin' the shit through all hell,
I dunno,

Wipe yo face and kick ya farce,
Kick yo ace and wipe ya arse,
Fick yo kase and fipe yo arse,
Wipe ya farce and kick yo ace,

I dunno – I raged, and I'm fried – I fuckin' tried,
Fuckin' the almighty hell through shit,
Shittin' the hell through all fuck,
Fuckin' the shit through all hell,

Dunno what's happenin' I think it's gitting warse.
Gidigiddiggy – yeup much warser,
Fight'n through all this farce,
Dog! Fuck! How long can this last?!?!

I dunon – I raged and I'm fuck't fried, tried,
Fuckin' the almighty hell through shit.
Shitt'n the hell through all fuck,
Fuck'n the shit through all hell fuck,
Fuck…

You just dunno…

At The Tip Of My Annoyance

So I'm standing here once again like a fuckin' dickhead,
And these dumb-arse-fuckers are in hysterics laughing,
I guess if I fuck up it's fair game and why not –
I'd laugh the same if it were the other way but –
Still never ceased for me,

So I've got fuckers laughing at me all over the place,
Okay – yeah I fucked myself good and proper – I'm a fool,
But don't we all ever go through this fucked phase –
I just can't stop fucking myself or even unfuck myself – it's cruel,

I seem to do it to myself more often than others they themselves,
But if I'm dumb-fuck-arsedness enough others witness –
I'm just as equally deserved of them laughing,
And I, still just fucking standing here like a dickhead,
And shakin' my head,

It's frustrating, infuriating,
You'd think that emotion alone would be illuminating,
There's no denying it's dumb-fuck-arsedness,
I'm shaking my head,

And there's fuckers laughing everywhere I go,
Soon everyone knows none can fuck me quite as good as myself,
I question if I'm not the only fucking dickhead does this,
I do it so well it doesn't seem to ever be matched or mimicked,

And I'm standing here once again feeling like a fucking dickhead,
And all these dumb-arse-fuckers are in hysterics laughing,
I guess if they witness my fuck up – it's only fair they do,
I'd be the same any other way but –
It still never ceases for me…

Berserk Jerk

So I showed my dick online,
Being a dirty filthy swine,
Gave an ex a piece of my mind,
But lost the whole damn thing,

I got a tiny little prick,
That can get pretty big,
But I suppose that depends on when,
I can finally snag a woman,

But due to my behaviours going berserk,
I end up being a bit of a jerk,
Handing out each a piece of my mind,
And losing the whole damn thing,

So I went and moved back in with my folks,
Tried to get a car running – what a joke,
Did almost always have a decent smoke,
But then into other people's business my nose would poke,

Goin' online to be showin off my little prick,
I'm sure it made many laugh – fuck, I did,
Oh – I'm sure it does get big,
Only hope I know how to do the trick,

But due to my behaviours going berserk,
I ended up being the big dick jerk,
Handing out to each a piece of my mind,
When I should of laughed it off behind,

I'm sure it really can't be that big,
Only hope it can do the trick,
But laugh if it didn't –

Faux Prophet Deluxe

I am just one of three,
That help the antichrist come to be,
To fulfil the long-waited prophecy,
To unleash the evil – set it free,

I begin to break the seals,
Lift the veil – show for real,
Amplify – enhance the feel,
With a taste for the kill,

I am the beginning of a new era,
Blood of royals – unrivalled, superior,
Representing pestilence – the woe and terror,
The knowledge through aeons, a fearless warrior,

I am the bringer of the apocalypse,
And I will surpass – I will eclipse,
Crush all who try to resist,
With the obsolete ceasing to exist,

There's no room for ignorance,
Definitely none for hypocrites,
All reason more for the dissidence,
And all the more yet to be experienced,

Tuned For Transmit

Slight simple sedicating,
Relaxed, cool, meditating,
I have sat before cush'd on,
My red and gold embroidered couch cushion,

Wooden floor boards like that of a ship,
Clutter bout the place – chaotic mind trip,
Pen and paper – to interpret it transmit,
Whatever I begin channelling quick,

May not hold onto it for long,
May not be quick enough and it's gone,
And I really friggin' hate it when it goes wrong,
I have to get to it right when it's going on,

Slight simple sedicatiing,
Relaxed, cool, meditating,
Sat cross legged on my red and gold couch,
Pipe in one hand – pen the other –
And the end material is the evidence to vouch,

Jolly roger flag hung high above hind me,
And I'm sure many the tyrants I rebel 'gainst say 'frightening'
But I only seek a path of enlightening,
Not everyone's 'thing' but I find it exciting,

Flag's draped over the wooden blinds billowing in the breeze,
And the floor boards of the old place groan and creak,
But I am sedated and meditative in peace,
Channelling these strange energies flowing round free,

With a clutter bout the place, a chaos mind trip –
Everything in and to it's place, transmit…

Predictions Foretold

Nostradamis predicted the year 2012,
The Age of Aquarius to the world,
2012 – the year I first thought to use the name,
Name of KAERO for my little ounce of fame,

KAERO as predicted by Christ and not to the letter,
Times – Spelt KAIROS in Greek, name of cancelled letters,
C switched to a K, dropping the M and N,
Perhaps proving this same AEON Nostradamis predicted,

Stranger – bizarre little ties,
Howard Phillips Lovecraft caught my eye,
And then such a poem came to exist I would write,
"Prophetic Theory" explaining death may die,

It may all have begun with me –
That suddenly somehow some are beginning to see,
Welcoming anew this strange new awakening,
It may very well mean my soul is the one to be forsakening,

Could it all be true these prophesies,
That a good handful of seers have seen,
Poison fumes suffocating the air like kerosene,
Welcome to the beginning of the end –
KAEROSCENE

I have a lot of subject matter of deep contemplation,
Deeper depths require a more sophisticated concentration,
Meditation – revelation – all for the cogitation,
I could be the one, so we shall have a hell of a celebration,

Poison Little Lies

First it was meth,
And it wasn't clear,
It became them,
4 split,
It became clear,

Poisoned by a lot many have said,
Poisoned even more by even I,
Poisoned, shut down the head,
Poisoned with little lies,

Second came Kero,
And it was crystal,
Fire liquid,
Burning blissful,

As insane as it was at first,
Then came a passionate thirst,
Lines, many I might say,
But with many aspiring intentions at play,

Poisoned by a lot many have said,
Poisoned much more by even I,
Poisoned, shut down the head,
Poisoned with little lies,

Maybe lies aren't all that bad –
Not particularly when it pays,
Maybe these are the best you have –
To illuminate through the fakes,

Voice Of Comfort

If tears of blood drops fell when I cried,
I'd be closer to showing the pain,
If the ground tremored when shattered my pride,
Hope for serenity is slain,

Desperate to show the depths of my emotion,
Expose it so that some might know it,
Experience enough to contemplate – know I can relate,
To be a voice a comfort toward an escape,

I don't know what to expect at the end,
I'm afraid – or was, I won't pretend,
But I know I won't be alone like I once thought,
There are many others want the answers sought,

There are times when I know I need it myself,
Times when I'm facing an eviscerating hell,
I can't be good for others without first being good for me,
Can't release any others at least 'til I am free,

If fire ravaged towns and cities, when I rage,
I'd definitely be closer to showing the pain,
If oceans swallowed lands in tremendous tidal waves,
Yes, all hope for serenity is slain,

Desperate to show the depths of the emotion,
Expose it so that some might know it,
Experience to have contemplate – that I relate,
And be that voice of comfort, in wait with an escape…

Mistakes

You have to be stupid before you get smart,
I've made so many mistakes it's practically an art,
I've had heart, and definitely the spark,
I have been through and done my share of ripping apart,

It's taken me a few occasions of failure for me to realise,
It's earnt irritation, - it's earnt mass despise,
It's taken confrontation and considerable compromise,
But I finally have at some point opened up my eyes,

Even when you're reckless you still take precaution,
Who knows who'll be watching – God forbid it's law enforcement,
Each ordeal's just another future exhaustion,
But in some way, some how you feel the setback is still important,

You can never really know when what should be second-nature,
Not when you're not so social to remember to control what behaviour,
Being completely aware and focussed in to
listen will eventually save ya –
Unwanted attentions of unwanted groups
with powers enough to detain ya,

I have had to be stupid before I'd gotten smart,
Made millions of mistakes it's practically an art,
I've had heart, definitely the spark,
I've been through and even done a share of ripping apart,

Nutcracker'd

Well the dog fuckin' bit me on the nuts last week,
Made me cry and drop to my knees,
Fuckin' Bitch just wouldn't let go,
Fuck I had pain like I'd never known,

Fuck dog! Ow! Ow! Ow!
Let 'em go before you rip 'em out,
I need those to multiply,
I'll be lucky if I'm not paralyzed,

My brother and I used to play fight as young lads,
'til one fateful day I copped a low blow to the nads,
He just fuckin' laughed as I fell right to the floor,
I could just about do fuck all, the pain I couldn't ignore,

Fuck Brother! Ow! Ow! Ow!
Now I taste 'em in my mouth,
I need those to reproduce,
I can't stand this kind of abuse,

Passion Fingers

I just fuckin' survived!
Thought I'd surely die,
Nearly took out an eye,
But I'm still alive,

Trust Me?
I know how to make it look like I know what I'm on about,
You trust me?
I just don't fuckin' actually know what I'm on about,

He said just stick in there and fuckin' turn it that way,
Oh shit, fuck, can't remember hearin' what he really did say,
C'mon man, are you going to make it work or you havin' a play?
We've got no time to just fuck around today,

Yeah sure I know what I'm on about,
TRUST me,
I'll show ya what I'm fuckin' on about,
Relax, you can trust me,

(*TWANG*.. ting, ting, ting, ting, ting,)

Fuck! – just fuckin' survived,
Shit – I nearly fuckin' died,
Close to takin' oujt an eye – just then,
But I'm still alive,
Fuck –

Shit yeah, I just fuckin' survived,
I came so close I could've died,
Fuckin' thing flung up and just missed me eye,
And I'm breathin' heavy thinkin' thank fuck I'm alive,

That split-second moment you know you miscalculate,
That split-second moment and intervention turns immaculate,
Well, shit – you couldn't do it again? Spectacular,
Passion fingers, yes, you know you are…

Bleeder's First

If it bleeds – it leads,
I can think of three instances where that's occurred to me,

Waiting for a triage nurse,
Most injured seen to first,
Makes sense,

Police really put to work,
When crime displays its' worst,
Makes sense,

Women given power of giving birth,
And when so, it's worth the attention to girt,
Makes sense,

If it bleeds – it leads,
3 ways it's implied to me,
That's gotta say blood or life is important,
Valuable to treasure and take every precaution,

If it bleeds, it leads,
Life first, breathe,

Apologetically Up For Debate

She was so snooty, snobby,
A real stuck up herself kind of cunt,
Couldn't handle my bad attitude,
Or whatever provoked the behaviour,

Couldn't accept an apology,
No matter how late,
Apology?
Yeah, it's still up for debate,

But how blinded by me –
Could she really have been?
The way she was to me,
Something still, she couldn't see,

I would forgive and forget,
But rumours still circulate and upset,
She's lovin' it – gets her wet,
So no, she hasn't earnt her apology yet,

But she couldn't accept it,
No matter how late,
The apology she requested,
I'm still in that debate,

It's a wonder that she hasn't yet back,
It's not the kind of karma you want to attract,
I suppose I'm hopeful she's that smart,
'Cause she wasn't enough with her heart,

Apology –
Forget it…

Uncivil Respect For Civil Disrespect

I fuckin' hate that guy but I like what he did,
He said something nice – but I'm sure it was nasty shit,
He might have a right – but I bet he has motives,
But I better not find he's been gloating,

He doesn't toe a foot out of line – not that we ever see,
I can't fuckin' stand there's a chance he's better than me,
I bet he does it on purpose – laughs that he's free,
I bet when he's by himself – he does drugs like speed,

He just looks like trouble from a distance,
I fuckin' swear the cunt's been to prison,
I'm never gonna keep him once out of vision,
'cause I fuckin' swear he's on a sinister mission,

I might sound uncivil but I'm doing a respect,
'cause we haven't seen the other side of his civil yet,
There are gonna be times we won't know what to expect,
But I'll resort to drastic measures in order to protect,

He might be a fuckin' nice guy – just wait 'til you see his other side,
If you don't collide – you're going to want to go hide,
We don't know what he's like – he looks like he could fight,
Yeah – I don't think it's safe not keeping him in sight,

Who knows what people like that fuckin' do,
He just better obey the rules like we all go through,
If he fuckin' disrespects us, a beating will be due,
His worst fuckin' nightmares will have come true,

I might sound uncivil – but I'm doing a respect,
'cause we just ain't seen the other side of his civil yet,

Dick Spits' Bitch Fit

You curse and call me names,
You try humiliate and shame,
But the truth in the shame is you're the same,
You need to blame and I'm target – I'm under aim,

Yeah I can hear you whinging your shit,
Nothing but a filthy fuckin' hypocrite,
You're spoof, you're sprog, you're dick-spit,
And I'll fuck you with your own fist,

So it's all right for you to act like a jerk off,
But when I got to it's fuckin' not,
I wish you'd hurry up and choke on the cock in your gob,
To be killed by consumption of your faggot mates sprog,

I can hear you whinge and bitch,
Slander slingin' all manners of foul shit.
I just can't get passed seeing you a hypocrite,
Needing a butt-fucking with his own fist,

Call me all the names under the sun,
Not any one of you are better – none,
You'll never be more to me than semen, come,
That should've been swallowed by your mum,

Get over it, harden up, grow up you fucking sprog,
Or hurry the fuck up and choke on a cock,
I'm gonna do whatever the fuck I fuckin' want,
Whenever you're a hypocrite getting off on telling me not,

I'll fist fuck your arse with your own fist,
You whinging fuckin' hypocrite bitch,

Magnet Pull

Someone, a little boy has hooked on, hooked in,
He's in my personal space and he's makin' it hell,
Little fucker has no balls to fight in person,
But I'm feeling him drain me just as well,

The cunt is right in on me at all times,
And I wanna fuck his guts out with my knife,
Tear out to swallow down his eyes,
I don't care, I want him dead – I want him to die,

Now there is no privacy – I have none at all,
And this little cunt never leaves me at all,
He has no guts – he hasn't any balls,
I can feel him weak but I can feel him all,

He's a little leech I want to bleed,
To rip him right open and make him bleed,
He's way too close than I fuckin' need,
Right over my shoulder and he fucking feeds,

So at some point soon I'm going to lose my shit,
And I'll fuck off over to visit where he lives,
And I'll be fucked after if I even let him live –
For every bit of this fucked up bullshit and all he gives,

I just telepathically told him I'm gonna cut his throat,
I projected the thought for him to have it known,
But I'm gonna fucking make him squeal like a goat,
Fuck his cunt arse while he's gushing from the throat,

This piece of shit fucker is always listening in,
He is and he isn't but soon I'm going to get hold of him,
My fucking patience has worn too fucking thin,
Soon – soon I'm going to end up killing him,

This little piece of shit cunt's in my space,
It's becoming more than I can fucking take,
Cunt can't even come and see me to see his face,
He's trying to keep up but he's losing the pace,

This little piece of shit fucker needs a life,
Or was it because I was trying to fuck his dad's wife,
If it was because of that I wouldn't be surprised,
I'd fuck a few some out of her too if she were mine,

But I think, this little bitch wants it up his fucking arse,
I bet the arrogant ignorant little fucker was always skipping class,
And yes, daddy never gave him a swift kick up the arse –
But I know when I do I am going to have a blast,

And I just feel his presence there,
Constantly, and honestly I do fucking care,
'Cause I want the little fucker to live his own life – fair?
I just really don't want to be in any of it there,

I keep telling this cunt to just fuck off,
But the stupid cunt doesn't get it – he just won't fuck off,
And when I he finally gets a bashing – I won't stop,
No, 'cause he won't and he just hasn't ever stopped,

I can still hear the cunt – feel him right 'round me,
And the stupid cunt's always watching and laughing at me,
But the cunt has no balls – won't even come near me –
Pussy little girl, little boy's another bitch to me,

A no balls, a dickless, pussy piece of shit,
To only ever get my sloppy seconds shit,
But I'm gonna grab hold of my monster of a dick,
And ram it hard up this fuckin' little bitch,

Magnet pull on this fuckwit!

Under The Spite Of
Their Bruised Vanity

They just about near enough told me to go to hell,
They pushed and never liked hearing the answer they heard,
Well, fuckin' don't go thinking too much of yourself,
And then you won't be so hurt,

Whoa, the spite of their bruised pride,
When you pierce through their vanity,
They can never step out aside,
Never even question this insanity,

They're all lookin' to be far better than me,
But I'm facing the shit none these fuckwits want to see,
They think I talk shit too hard to be believed,
That I'm spinning this shit, cunningly conceived,

I don't know why they can't connect the dots,
And get further closer themselves to what they want,
I don't think they even know what they fuckin' want,
But they make it ever difficult that it's ever not,

None of 'em want to make the connections,
All of 'em just want to already have those affections,
Without ever even working hard enough for them,
They're given, and taken for granted when supplied the blessing,

And they'll only be too blind to question its' pestilence,
What that sudden loss represents,
The bullshit to smack them in the face for the consequence,
And the stupid fuckwit fools thought they were all exempt,

I don't know why they can't connect the dots,
And get further closer themselves to what they want,
I don't think they even know what they fuckin' want,
But they make it ever difficult that it's ever not,

Whoa, the spite of their bruised pride,
When you pierce through their vanity,
They can never step out aside,
Never even question this insanity,

Awww, A Dick With Some Fuckin' Balls,

So I'm hearin' from elsewhere someone pushing at me,
Pushing me to snap for a laugh and it's weak,
'cause while all of 'em are trying to do this to me,
I see how childish it really is – and it's weak,

Whether for a laugh and a weak one at that –
Of when they're so pissed – pissed off ringing mad,
I want to laugh 'cause the real truth is truly sad,
None of 'em all are really a 'man',

They yell abuse and manipulate –
But none of the shits right up front my fuckin' face,
Excites me often so I could masturbate,
Only I just can't rub and squirt it off all in their face,

I hear 'em all push, off from a distance,
And I'm beginning to feel just slightly easier to resist it,
Easier when I realise if they do try – they'll end non-existent,
Just how I lost isn't hard to see when it was all twisted,

I never really lost – I just got lost,
Made to falsely believe I'm something I'm really not,
And soon any power stolen from me will be robbed,
Taken well compensated when I do go to put to a stop,

And I'll just wanna play with it, rub it, squirt off in their face,
And say this is a fucking man – this is what the fuck it takes,
I could go and rock right up at their place –
And punch the almighty fuck down whoever wants a taste,

The dick – with some fuckin' balls,
Aww,
Oh yeah,

804

Outer Body Obs.

Stepping way back outside,
Way, way back outside,
Waiting, watching this fool collide,
Waiting – watching 'til it subsides,'

I won't dignify it if I don't respond,
So I don't dignify it and I don't respond –
Just stare a cold vacant stare,

Poor little fucker has no self-control,
So I control my calm and maintain it humble,
But fare a stare – a curious one there,

I'm…well… I've just noticed his little flaw,
It's too good to just ignore – so I ignore,
And the poor little fucker will miss it like many before,

And I'm stepping way back outside myself,
Way back afar, outside myself,
Waiting, watching for this little idiot's collide with hell,
Waiting, watching for it to subside as well,

The less to naught I ever say will pay
And after as calm, I'll be free to walk away,
No graze, no scrape, mint, unscathed,
Showed that maturity, showed I behaved,

I was stepping way afar back outside,
I was contemplating, observing, I analysed,
Waiting – watching for this fool to collide,
Watching – waiting for it all to subside,

But the lesser if naught I say will only pay –
And the problem may walk itself away…

For The Want Of The Help

Why would I want to help someone to begin with?
Know what it's like to fall behind and be out of sync,
Not easy when you're alone and you wish you had help,
At times you need help, a hand up outta the hell,

I wanted a big brother – or big sister myself,
To help me understand the world we dwell,
Too much of it was taken to me hard felt,
With no way to thoroughly understand so well,

I wanted it myself,
Wanted someone who could tell,
Ways I'd have better felt,
If I could've dealt with what hell,

So I guess I'm compassionate in ways,
Because I know it does pay,
To know ways to eradicate,
Whatever pain or hate,

For helpful, hurtless ways to change,
Shit you don't often think of 'til late,
Shit that may surely help change,
Ways to view the pain and hate,

I might speak a lot of shit,
Shit, I've had my teeth grit,
But maybe knowing half of this,
Will help save shit as quick,

You have the choice to do as you feel is right,
I will have just left behind insights…

Good For Bad

Passion for the all my good,
Passion is always good,
Good for passion against my good,
No threat, chance to show and make understood,

Take all your bad – and return nothin' but good,
Share my passion for all your bad with my good,
Showing me the need for peace with your bad –
I'll give good and give it good to replace your bad,

I like to take the edge off –
Show 'em all what I've got,
Any of maybe a something they're not –
But have shared it so they'd have maybe got,

Favour payed forward,
For perhaps a little leniency when my time calls,
I've often regret retaliation of any kind,
But to let it go and rationalise – show I can keep my mature mind,

I'm keepin' my sanity better when I'm calm,
It's not my true nature to inflict harm,
Preventions better than a cure and I'd prefer he'd not need one,
I don't know what kind of a drain or strain he's in if some,

Don't worry brother – peace be with you,
And with the gesture of a swish of my wrist –
A feeling of excitement – and happiness shot him through,
He felt it, wriggling and laughing said, "SHIT!"
Yeah,

Passion for the all my good,
Passion is always good,

Good for passion against my good,
No threat, chance to show and make understood,

Take all your bad – and return nothin' but good,
Share my passion for all your bad with my good,
Showing me the need for peace with your bad –
I'll give good and give it good to replace your bad,

Thinkin' Further Passed

I usually only trade kindness with the kind,
But I am learning to extend the exception,
It's truly a test, I can attest, when I lose my mind,
Over those ulterior motives behind whatever deception,

Thinkin' passed it further…

To the point above all and say it's a need,
All reason why vampires survive – it's the feed,
Soon to forsake all need with their gluttonous greed,
A pride, where none else can supersede,

Thinkin' passed it further…

I thought it out and willingly give anyway,
I know at any point that could be a me every day,
I could sit and pray that it all goes away,
Or I could make the start and fuckin' give it right away,

I thought it prior yet previously again,
A much older scenario where it led to makin' 'friends',
Benefit of the doubt, leap of faith, I never regret,
Somewhere, some way out there how, I know it'll come back yet,

Thinkin' passed it further…

An act of random kindness not only to the kind,
Will attest you passed the test helping other lost minds,
Waive out the ideals of ulterior motives hind deception,
And be amazed at what you find extending out that exception,

An act of random kindness,
Maybe not so random, never so mindless,
I wanna think further still yet,

Good Ways To Sin

I'm the Jesus way to do Satan things,
I'll show you the good way to sin,
Taking something pure and fresh, make it less boring,
Taint it, corrupt it a little more and stall the ignoring,

I'm the good way to do very naughty things,
I'll show you the better way to really sin,
To take something dull – make a show of all the less they think,
Make wanted of it, to be clutched after faster than can blink,

I could take something taboo and make it a craze,
Make something new from what's passed its' days,
Mature? Sensible? Deprived ways to behave,
It's more like you're just slaves in chains,

One can be an animal in civilized ways,
None need drift meaningless in the uncertain greys,
Love doesn't have to pay when lust must play,
I can and I will make the taboo a craze,

Deny no devilish temptation but by passion make it pure,
Scratch whatever itch and desire after the lure,
Take what you need, take what you want and be cured,
'Cause at the end we're all destined to be skewered,

I'm the Jesus way to do Satan things,
I'll show you the better way to really sin,
Take something dull – and make show all the lesser they think,
Make wanted of it to be clutched after faster than can blink,

I'll take something taboo and make it a craze,
Make something new from something passed its' days,
Mature? Sensible? Deprived ways to behave –
We're really more like slaves all in chains,

Crushed In The Rush

You wouldn't believe my misfortune when I'm in a rush,
Bad shit happens that leaves me crushed,
Left 'til last minute – it does embarrass me, and I blush,
Yeah bad shit happens, and I'm left crushed,

Well - the good shit that could've been,
The shit I should've got to before anybody else had seen,
This shit could've been running like a dream,
And I could be sipping expensive coffee's with real cream,

But I fuck up bad when I get too eager,
And the shit comes out all messed up and meagre,
And what good rep is that for a kind of leader?
Gotta get my shit right before I go feature –

But I get excited and I just wanna go –
I'm often running before I walk and, it shows,
I do have funny ways to get into the know,
But when I never get it right my efforts are all blown,

I always have misfortune when I am in a rush,
And bad shit always happens to leave me crushed,
Left to last minute embarrasses me and I do blush,
I'm doing it – and it's happening – and I am left crushed,

You wouldn't believe how many times,
This maniac has lost his mind –
Chimerical – and it happens, this is mine,
Maybe this is it – this could be the final sign,

I just fuck up when I get too eager,
And the shit gets messed up and is presented as meagre,
And what good is that for the rep of a new leader?
I've really gotta get my shit right before I feature,

When It All Comes Out

You don't know me well enough anymore,
But I can't say you even ever really did –
Not me makin' much of an effort trying,
You wanted truth and honesty, you got it, you did –

I knew there was shit I could say you wouldn't handle,
So I never said it but kept it within, I did –
I knew there were truths you weren't ready for,
So I fucking refrained – I did –

But when it came out you were at a loss for words,
I really was more than you ever thought me worth,
The trust I kept all that time 'til I knew it wasn't gonna work,
They just never did – I lost it, I went berserk,

How will cunts ever receive my strengths?
How will they ever know my extents?
How dare they raise malcontents for their resents,
They had the fucking chance just never rose to the events,

They never really chose the chance to get to know me,
And I can never say that I never did –
Never were they making any effort at trying,
You wanted the truth and honesty and got it, you did –

I just knew there was gonna be shit I knew you wouldn't handle,
So, no – I never said, kept it to myself I did –
I knew there were truths you weren't ready for,
So I fuckin' refrained – I did,

But then it all came out and you were at a loss for words,
And I was showing more than you ever thought me worth,
Trust – I kept it all the time 'til I knew it was never gonna work,
They never once tried – and I'd lose it and go berserk,

And it came out,

Don't Fuck With Me

Don't fuck with me dickhead,
I'm not your little lamb,
Don't' fuck with me dickhead,
You don't know who I am,

Don't fuck with me dickhead,
You can't afford to lose,
Don't fuck with me dickhead,
You will fucking lose,

Don't fuck with me dickhead,
You better understand –
Don't fuck with me dickhead,
I am the fucking man,

You won't like it when I get playing rough,
You won't handle it I'm too much,
Beating you down, throat tightly clutched,
None'll hear you scream you've had enough,

Don't fuck with me dickhead,
You'll go in the ground,
Don't fuck with me dickhead,
Don't ever make a sound,

Don't fuck with me dickhead,
I'll shatter your fuckin' skull,
Don't fuck with me dickhead,
Throat punch you as you gulp,

None of 'em ever like it when I play rough,
None can ever take it – it's too much,
Beatin' 'em down, their throat tightly clutched,
None to hear it scream out it's had enough,

Super Volcano

Tick, click,
Gears lever pressure,
Tick, by click,
Compressing all tension,

Click, by tick,
Scatter, scamper for protection,
Click, by tick,
Shelter, for cataclysmic prevention,

Click…tick…

Get the fuck out – he's gonna blow!
When he erupts it's like a super volcano,
Time is running out – I feel it close,
Hazard levels reaching critical zones,

Tick… click…

Move you stupid fuckers – get outta the fuckin' way,
It's mother fuckin' Armageddon – the end of fuckin' days,
Hurry up – get movin' – this ain't no fuckin' game,
You get us all killed and it's all you to blame,

Tick…click,
Shit – fuck – shit –
Click…tick,
Fuck – shit – shi –

*

(Sonic Boom)

*

When It Would Begin To Manifest,

I could feel it comin' on,
And I fuckin' knew somethin' was wrong,
Somethin' dark was comin' on,
Gaining tense and ever strong,

My intuition speaks for me to get going,
Somethin' 'bout to go down and we're all better not knowing,
Something insidious, ominous signs round growing,
If we stay - we'd best hide and be tip-toeing,

Neck begins to itch, head starts to pound,
Nerves start to twitch and I'm somebody else now,
The static on a frequency I'm channelling and bound,
A new source of strength conjured and gowned,

A ruckus, a rampage of phantoms on the loose,
Chained to be but free if I may ever choose,
Throes to my foes when I need me amused,
This guise, it's just more than a ruse,

I face ripping surges of pain,
Keeping these spirits under my chains,
Just to heighten, hasten the gain,
Still, feel 'em all fighting under the strain,

I never seem to catch myself to isolate well enough before the time,
And then there's the fact I can't control when
I'm projecting from my mind,
It may put too many people sensitive enough
around me to discomfort at times,
Whenever they may be channelling in on this frequency of mine,

Discomfort and disease seem to follow and shroud around,
And I wonder how long it'll all be before
they fear even to make a sound,

War Makes Me Hard

Must be the scotts blood in my veins,
Or the irish makes me insane,
Imagine standing wearing a kilt,
On the battle field ready to kill,

Nothin' under the kilt but a jolly rock hard'n,
Intimidating the enemy all out marchin',
Enemy bitch meat makes me hot,
I'll be left standing there when they're not,

Scotts blood in my veins,
Or the irish make me insane,
Standing there wearing a kilt,
Out on the battle field ready to kill,

Fiddling with me bone,
Run the shit up 'em, send 'em home,
War just gets me – makes me all hard,
Intimidating yes, leaving mentally scarred,

Nothin' under the kilt but a jolly rock hard'n,
Intimidating the enemy all out marchin',
Enemy bitch meat just makes me hot,
To be left standing there when they're not,

Scotts blood in my veins,
Or the irish that makes me insane,
Standn' there, nothin' under the kilt,
Out on the battle field ready to kill,

Killisodal

Mum's been askin' me a lot lately
If I am suicidal –
Mum – hmhm, no, other way I'm afraid,
I'm fuckin' killicidal,

Wanna get a fuckin' gun and fuckin' –
Kill – Kill – Kill –

Mum you gotta stop askin' me if I'm fine,
There is nothing fucking wrong with my mind,
I'm fine mum I'm just fuckin' fine –
This is not one of those episodal times,

But I wanna just get a fuckin' gun and –
Kill – Kill – Kill –

It's never been me with the problem mum I swear –
But these fuckin' stupid idiots have me tearin' out me hair,
Not one of 'em come near enough cause they know they can't compare,
And not one of them think a fight one on one with me would be fair,

All of 'em gang up and they all still keep a distance,
'Cause, they would know there'd be no resistance,
Not up close – not with me – I have no restrictions,
But I am a lot smarter – I'll use the law for all my dissidence,

I do want to get a gun and fuckin' just –
Kill – Kill – Kill –
But I'll devise with a chop and fuckin'-
Chill – Chill – Chill –

It's never been me with the problem mum,
It's always been another 'caused me this damage done...

For Knowing I Can

Split a little indiginese head open in second grade,
Can't rightly remember if he was teasing and it's to blame,
Never got better but just worse I'm afraid,
Never fitting in right to others' games and charades,

See, as I grew, so did the contradictions,
Never had the right to retaliate as I was told,
If only, I knew what do when as well, had premonitions,
But it would serve me right as I were to grow old,

I am capable well of violence,
But I rather remain cool, calm and silent,
Beneath the façade a vicious malevolence,
Of which no true resistance outside love is prevalent,

When it is that I am not thoroughly here,
Something else inhabits and I do fear,
And everybody must all well adhere,
'Cause this internal but external something brings tears,

I am a timebomb, waiting, collecting, building,
For that right time right place, right someone,
Always taking, collecting, building, waiting,
For the right release on the right someone,

I don't envy this, I don't pride in my violent side,
As a sociopath completely opposite as described,
Choices – I know I make mine few ever actually like,
But I'm gaining back strengths enough for my nice to override,

I have a vicious violent streak,
But rather use brains than brawn to make 'em weak,

Toothpaste War-tug

That's not what you use it for!
So what – it feels good, I want it more,
Wouldn't it fuckin' burn ya cock son?
Wouldn't know, me brains are in me bum,

Are you for fucking real? You pulled with toothpaste?
I have done a couple times now – it feels great,
But it burns my mouth – and you rubbed it down south,
Hey – you get used to the pain, it's grouse,

I think you're fuckin' nuts – ya brains are in ya butt,
Well, I think it sounds tough to take the pain and still get up,
Now that's a good analogy but I don't like it here,
Well for a second I was worried you all thought I was queer,

What has that to do with it? Are you gay?
No, not ever I just think it's funny how they behave,
That was off topic but you seriously jack it with toothpaste?
Well, it'd give me dick a more pleasurable taste,

Why? What do you try to suck yourself off?
No, but I can see that's what you'd want,
You are fuckin' nuts – you are weird,
Yeah – that's slightly changed the view to how I appeared,

Well, what did you think would happen?
Nothin' – didn't really contemplate what'd happen,
Well, gotta say at least you'd be clean –
And minty fresh – every girls' dream...

You're jokin'...

Sniff Fizz

Did somethin' stupid when I was a boy,
Won't say it's somethin' right then I enjoyed,
Definitely something I won't envoy,
Silly little boy,

Lunch break at high school,
Laughing, joking, thinking it's cool,
Packet of wizz fizz and it's shovel tool,
And up the nose – yeah, fool,

Eye's watered as the fizz hit me brain,
Sugar, popping – fizzing on the brain,
Why would you fuckin' do that? – it's insane,
Don't you fuckin' feel any pain?

I sneezed and a sugar booger dribbled,
All of them, everybody, chuckled and giggled,
My brain – uh - fuckin' thing tingled,
I danced and wove about in a wiggle,

Clutching my head,
Eye's watering and red,
No warning was said,
Surprise – not dead,

It was one of those things you don't do again,
Not even if your haeckeled by your friends,
Not a nice feeling – don't pretend,
Nah, never will do that again…

Teency Weency Dynamo

I grabbed my billy goat by the gruff,
And made it do some funny fuckin' stuff,
Fuckin' thing kicked and bucked and got tough,
And I played it off like it were a bluff,

This pale boong lived in with mother hubbard's shoe,
He'd always fuck off walkabout when the rent was due,
Took it to court and won the land rights feud,
And now this pale boong has a shoe on his foot too,

I was the bear that ran into the house,
Of 3 hot blonde women always bearing a busty blouse,
Ate them for breakfast, lunch and dinner and more when could arouse,
And left when they slumbered, silently as a mouse,

This teency weency dynamo,
Blew a kiss to all the ho's,
Whipped it out for a show,
And danced bout makin' their faces glow,

Mary's little lamb was the weird runt, the gilly,
It was always caught out doing something silly,
One fine day he showed her his willy,
And he was hurt when she laughed shrilly,

So did we suckin' down billy's,

And this teency weency dynamo,
Geetin' stoned with all the ho's,
Puttin' it on – whippin' out to show,
Dancing around and their faces glow,

The Perfec'ly Damaged

A little of just the right insane,
Staring deep the abyss of pain,
Paring black white to the name,
Sparing out to a good sum of the games,

Let 'em begin,

Balance off over the edge,
Open out inside the head,
Fireworks and bloodshed,
Never take seriously what I said,

Dancing shadows in the alley,
Town folk all a' rally,
Rampant ruckus all in a melee,
Is anybody safe? No telling,

A little of just the right insane,
Staring deep to the abyss of pain,
Paring the black white to my name,
Sparing out a good sum of the games,

Let them begin,

A little jest to the right insane,
Staring deep the abyss of pain,
Paring the black and white to name,
Sparing for the games,

Please, hmhm,
Let 'em begin…

Happier When They're Hurt

She's happier when she doesn't hurt,
Or so one would think,
She's happier when somebody hurts,
Worse than what she thinks,

She laughs at my every irritance,
And laughs that she's the cause,
I laugh at her ignorance,
And know she's the cause,

She doesn't want to see,
Don't want to believe,
Someone else free,
When she's bound to her grief,

She's happier when she doesn't hurt,
Or more she can't see,
But she's happier when it's deserved,
And especially to me,

Laughing at my frustration,
And she laughs because she caused,
She's, the centre of my frustration,
Self-centred, and I abhor,

She don't want to see,
Me making me a better me,
And she won't ever believe,
When she can't pass her grief,

She's happier when she doesn't hurt,
But is more to cause,
Happier to see others like me deserve,
And she'll dig deep her claws...

Ties To Psychics And Crystals

The more I dig deeper into the occult,
I notice more use of the elemental stones,
Receivers and transmitting ornaments,
If you know how to use 'em you'll get the most,

You may not have to be superstitious,
It's all metaphysics,
We're all here – everything for a reason,
We have everything we need for easy living,

It's stereotypical for fortune-tellers,
To use crystal balls,
But I think I see why they do now, those fortune-tellers,
I am starting to understand it more,

Stones like crystal help us focus,
To the concentration of the energies,
The crystals are all transmitters,
And each are with and for its' own properties,

Crystal balls these fortune-tellers use,
Concentrate – or dilute the concentration of the signs,
Strange energies transmit through,
Determined by the fortune-teller with the sight,

And it's only just now that I have figured why,
All this actually works,
And it may mean I may have to know why,
To have it all actually work,

Metaphysics is just another branch into alchemy,
Hardly believable, but no joke, no fallacy,

Closer To Theirs Chosen

A bizarre power I have I've come to realise,
Is a strange phenomenon of weaving lives,
The graces of husbands to their wives,
And back – the spirits within, inside,

If this is a way to bring people closer,
To the ones they desire – they have chosen,
To weave their souls, inspiring a love emotion,
To only bring them deeper together – more devoted,
Feeling the difference – that they can trust and know it,

I know love and kind compassion well,
And I do want millions of others to feel it themselves,
Bring them closer to the paradise to dwell,
Even if it's just within themselves,

I have the power to be able to synchronise,
The graces of each husband to their wives,
Or any chosen girl to their guys,
Show them their love each for them to their own eyes,

I don't know what to call this thing I can do,
I don't do it very often but I do know I can too,
Excite it, amplify it, intensify it true,
So that all is pure and felt all through,

If this is the way to bring people closer,
To the ones they desire – who they've chosen,
To weave their souls inspiring a love emotion,
To only bring them deeper to each other, more devoted,
But with the difference that they can both feel each other and know it,

The difference they can feel each other's' trust and love and know it,

Poor Investments

Now look just where it's got us,
Listening to weaklings,
We're up shit status,
In a manner of speaking,

Pencil pushing dickheads have all the power,
Invent regulations that turn us all sour,
We're over-towered, by these once were cowards,
And we're all expected to just sit and devour,

Any money worth earning,
Is best hands dirty,
If their hands are clean –
Shit's not what it seems,

I don't want to be the one to waste proving my worth,
Struggling to survive long as I can on this earth,
For egotistical ingrates in powers undeserved,
A bitter taste, littler faith for nobility, honour – I'm perturbed,

They're not honest enough for me to trust,
Freedoms ours for as long as we don't bite the dust,
But I can barely have the faith it'll last,
And news of bad investments over courtesy of taxes paid by us,

There's insanely more money than the appropriate sense,
And we, the poor people, will suffer the consequence,
You'd think it'd be on the responsibility of world leaders sequenced,
But some-how it's one-way bias and we're expected to recompense,

So, yeah, you could say all this listening to weaklings,
Has us up shit status in a manner of speaking,
Any money worth earning is best hands dirty,
If their hands are clean, shit just not what it seems,

Scare Scheme

I think it's time I begin to get mean, I've seen –
A shamble like this is really hard to believe,
Our countries not quite running like a dream,
Time has come for a scare scheme,

For terror tactics employed on the government,
Policing legislation – still feel they're above it,
Same tactics they've used on us summoned,
With a like pestilence comin' they're soon gonna discover,

Counts of embezzlement, counts of fraud,
I've enjoyed the circus – I applaud,
But a new revolution is yet to dawn,
Heavenly hells of which you've spawned,

Time to reap what you sow,
Don't let your hypocrisy show,
Take it on the cheek, assume responsibility,
'Cause we'll all hear you scream under my scare scheme,

Countries not quite running like a dream,
Shamble like this is hard to believe,
I think it's time I begin to get mean,
Time's comin' for a scare scheme…

The Stand Out To Stand In

I do have the intent,
Of establishing my own coven, covenant,
And rage with vicious extents,
Against our tyrannical government,

Place me the head and to stand before,
To negotiate to demands I plan to implore,
The ambition and thirst to engage for more,
Coven's and their cults, spread linked, awaiting for –
A declaration of war,

A dedication for the desperation,
Our frustration at the manipulation,
Rise up and claim and enforce eradication,
Old politics, old ways, no debate – it's enslavement,

I'll place me head and go to stand before,
To negotiate the demands I plan to implore,
The implements, modifications to our current law,
And if not – then we shall war,

And we will war with all who stand,
To refuse to meet up to our demands,
That pen is mighty, but we'll force hands,
And we'll have a painful, humiliating brand,

The dedication for the desperation,
The frustration over the manipulation,
We'll rise up and claim and enforce eradication –
Of old politics, old ways, and debate – it's enslavement,

I do have the intent to gather round my own self a covenant,
And rage an uproar against our tyrannical government...

Prime Sinister

Vote me 1 for Mr. Prime Sinister,
I'll get to know what I gotta do quick,
'cause it's lookin' like we're still prisoner,
Goin' down with the shit,

Yes – I'll get to know what I gotta do –
And fuck on through it quick,
Hoik the system but not before it pays its' dues,
And pull us all up outta the shit,

Sometimes we've all gotta do the shit we don't want to,
Believe me – think I really wanna be fuckin' responsible for you?
I've always second guessed myself when you questioned me,
And I'm wonderin' whether I really want the responsibility,
At times –

I'm fairly confident I would do quite well,
First – I'll just claw me outta my Hell,

Vote me 1 for Mr. Prime Sinister,
I'll get to knowin' it all quick,
Hate like I'm still feelin' prisoner –
All goin' down for the shit,

Let me get to knowin' what I've gotta do –
And lemme fuckin' fuck it out quick,
I'll hoik the system soon after it's paid its' dues,
After pulling us up all outta the shit,

I reckon I'm fairly confident I could do it well,
Rapidly, raise us all from this hell,

Repentitanctuary,

Criminals of violence I wish to welcome you,
To your sanctuary of penance, to transition through,
Freedoms forfeit to us those times you do –
For an involuntary rehabilitation you'll never rue,

See, your brain doesn't function so well,
Those times you're facing distressing hells,
We take you, lock you up, confined to cells,
Assess and figure out what treatments excel,

We take you off the streets,
And we wipe the slate clean,
Give hope and many a new means,
Teach them how to reach their dreams,

We take all violent and non-violent offenders,
Take all the real and all the pretenders,
Dismantle the mainframe, reinvent it,
Suspend it, 'til its' new purpose is intended,

Ultimately the punishment is death, but is extended,
'til the use of the offenders can no longer suspend us,
Dirty deeds like war-games, criminals are expended,
Used as pawns, dying for a cause we've defended,

Mindless, thoughtless, impulsive machines,
Reprogrammed for the countries greater needs,
Taken off the streets, mind's wiped clean,
Given chances of hope but many a new means,

Lies To Rights...

I'm dropping little hints like I'm being a guide,
For anyone who wishes to walk some part of my life,
I write it as I learn it and hide it and confide,
Shit that actually happens, and ain't a fucking lie,

And I'll be told a liar by those who have never seen with their own eyes,
Everything they seem to pick up on is only after they've seen mine,
It hasn't been 'til after I'd said that they never did 'mind'
Never, 'cause they never did live their life like mine,

But I do know there are people who do believe,
I'm not the only one it's had it happening,
I have to continue despite what others see,
But are they here, in my face? To witness everything?

I'm dropping what I learnt 'cause it's my first time,
And it's probably the same for others of my kind,
I have and do prefer to see the shit with my own eyes,
'cause I know every manner why all the real 'liars' will despise,

They fight only to try to hide the truths they never faced,
It's when you separate and begin to – you're ahead the race,
I'm honest all the time and it's how I'm strong, by my grace –
I'll take every beating known and still endure and embrace,

See it's just so hard to believe it'll pass their narrow minds,
They never want to see with their own eye's,
It's when I say I have a life and it's why they despise,
Their narrow minds can't justify and so it's all just 'lies',

But they have to be guilty of something when
they see and say what they don't like,

831

But you've gotta be true even if it hurts,
c'mon man swallow you're pride,
Your desperate attempts will no longer help you to hide –
So – did you have the right when you knew you weren't right?

Shoes To Fill

Some would say I've got big fuckin' boots to fill,
When it comes to say, being strong willed,
'Cause at the moment seems like I fairy round in heels,
Or so I'm told and it feels,

So – I'm a bloody sheila for havin' a bitch,
Go ahead and laugh hard and get a stitch,
One day this tart might make it rich,
And you'll wanna give my little somethin' a flick,

I only cross dress on a full moon,
Some'd say to make it permanent 'cause it looks it too,
"Fuck bitch, that suits you"
Somethin' they may never quit sayin' nor let me live down soon,

"Oi – Sheila – show us your tits"
"No fuck you I'm a dude with a dick"
"Are you sure you ain't really a chick"
"Fine – fuck it, sure – yes, the heels fit",

"Ha – Ha I fuckin' knew this guy's a bitch"
"Go ahead and laugh you deserve a painful stitch"
"One day this tart might get fuckin' rich"
"Yeah, I'm sure you will sheila – suckin' off dick"

I can't fuckin' believe this prick,
I made a joke and he took it beyond sick,
I'm fuckin' walkin' away now man, I quit,
I've put up with too much of the shit…

Idols

Facades on parade –
Parts and counter-to charade,
We all watch as they behave,
Accustomed to their masquerade,

But when you know what to look for,
And you know that little more,
You try foot your way forward,
Offended, disheartened, fallen to the floor,

So you might go that one step more –
And bargain with what you're bargaining for,

We're watching them as they go,
Seein' 'em putting on their show,
Wait -and look to see for what you know,
And see if it does indeed show –

See how it's handled and watch and wait,
If you're lucky enough they might explain,
If you're not lookin' then – boom! – pain,
And then we're all left to our bitter disdain,

But isn't that why anybody ever does at all?
To stand to be relied upon when they're called?
To take it on – and show 'em all your balls,
Do it this way or fuckin' not at all,

But – fuck – I might go that one step more –
But be fuckin' bargaining with what I'm bargaining for,

Façades on charade –
Façades…

Off, To Higher Comparison

A brother of mine suffered over 2000 years ago,
Perhaps the greatest man the world has known,
His was tried, but a just and right approach,
A path to nirvana, a peaceful road,

My brother was wise, faithful and true,
Living midst an era and peers with no clue,
For all his love and wisdom, he was subdued,
Paying the ultimate sacrifice for me and you,

To love something so much doesn't actually make you soft,
Despite what they say the saviour was hard as rock,
You don't realise at any point, it could've all stopped,
But you don't when you're passionate about what you want,

Christ was always loyal as fuck, right to the last,
Shame his crowd gave up and only bore disgust,
There's only ever so many people you know you can trust,
And there's no difference these days for any of us,

Only so many people will rush to your aid,
Only so many times people mean what they say,
It's a shame it never stays that way,
It's a shame every one of us at some stage betrays,

I couldn't once deny the king,
But beg his forgiveness for my sins,
Ask his guidance when times are grim,
Take responsibility, take it on the chin,

When times are tough, I'll bear it, wear it, grin,
My current challenges just couldn't compare to him,

Anti-Hypochristianist

You look at me with an expression of bewilderment,
You wonder – I see it – if I mean all seriousness,
Take the word serious – with all regard,
Without hypocrisy, a christianist,

To an extent – yes, understand it,
But don't, can't quite all agree,
Extents to it yes, I grasp it,
But don't, can't all the way agree,

Unless of course it agrees with me,
Shows, bares everything there is to see,
Unrestraint, in the raw, loose and free,
It doesn't matter if we don't agree,

Tell it right – tell it straight,
Do it right – do it straight,
Don't fuck around and don't waste,
Tell it ALL and what it takes,

And don't just tell the good parts,
Or the shit just easy to hear,
It takes the effort – takes the heart,
It can take many a month and year,

Don't take the word or just all of its' best parts,
To only just do it in fucking halves –
Allow for those others and do it hard,
Do the distance, dance the yard,

I'm against those who'll only ever claim,
The light of the lord for their own vain…

Brother's With The Almighty Mother

I might be a heathen, beastly,
But I do hope Christ was wrong,
I might be His devil – but I love Him,
And this is my song,

For as advanced as the times –
I do have a primal habit –
Compulsive, I do look for as eager minds,
Like a mangy dog so rabid,

I want to get Jesus,
Along with a couple fine bitches,
Frolic midst the meadows,
Then hit the bongs and laugh to stitches,

I want to hope Jesus understands,
That I am not that bad or brutish a man,
But I would be stoked for a visit behind the scenes,
To smoke up a chop and see how the fuck he's been,

Of course, there's facades to keep,
Times do come, and I know,
I do believe Him so, and I feel it deep,
Believe me, I promise I'll show,

I just hope he don't take it too seriously,
Not like the people round me do,
I alternate with the humour somewhat meticulously,
Don't take it seriously – it helps me through,

I won't deny the king, not ever once,
There are reasons why he did or didn't get shit done,
The almighty word of our 'One God Son',
Yes… let it all be done…

Respects 'Tween Rivals

I know I'm a filthy foul mouth fucker –
No trait inherited from my mother,
Never really had a 'father'
But I am a seriously beastly mother fucker –

I know I am extremely weird, extremely wild,
I know my humour is like that of a child,
I know I can be extremely rude,
But I normally prefer it be by as intelligent manner I can allude,

As vulgar as I am, I hope Christ does recognise,
That I was good enough to share a session with him in his eyes,
I know he's a busy man – he's royalty for fuck's sake,
Reigning over more than we can imagine – more than I can ever say,

I dream big, have ambition – but I do look to Him,
And I wonder, is it all so bad to do it for a whim?
If I knew he wasn't one to handle that sort of a joke –
No matter what extent – I'll have held the urge to have spoke,

Make no mistake I have the most sincere respect,
And I'll do everything in my power, so he won't regret –
Even if it means I am the devil and others get upset,
Then I'll take my beating as well as he had and show that respect,

I would want him to know the measure by which I feel,
That I take it seriously – I joke, but I know it's real,
If I ever show his faith in me was well the worth,
I'll make sure to do like Him but double – triple the work,

And I only hope he can appreciate it –
The lengths, these extremes I take,
I did want to know – I appreciate it –
And I will honestly never forsake…

Christ Had A Foot Long

I reckon Christ had to have had a foot long,
A pretty friggin huge massive dong,
No wonder he's up where he belongs,
If I had a pecker that big I'd be confident – strong,

How could he not love Magdalene –
The hooker knew how to fuck,
And how could the whore not love him?
With a cock so huge he'd get stuck,

How's my six inches measure up to his twelve?
I've gotta tell ya – not very fuckin' well,
Any woman I could have I know he'd only steal,
And with his huge wang – he could make them squeal,

So - what's my little six incha left to do?
But all the women he can enchant to screw,
But while Jesus is around – my balls are gonna be blue,
I just wanna say fuck Him 'cause I know he'll get you,

When I mention Jesus it all goes wrong,
Thinkin' I'm probably takin' His meaning all wrong,
But he would've had to have had the king of all dongs,
It would've had to have been at least a foot long,

How could he not love Magdalene –
The hooker knew how to fuck,
And how could the whore not love Him?
With that cock so huge he'd get it stuck,

All I can do is pout and scorn,
When I think of my tiny – little horn,
Perhaps I'm just best jackin' it to porn –
In lieu of seeing disappointed women yawn…

The Christ Witch Horror

Come, sit by me and I'll tell you a tale,
I'll shed an insight certain to make you pale,
I'll reveal a system, powerful yet frail,
A mass cult masquerading as religion, a false portrayal,

Millennia back, scriptures spake a man exists but is later worshipped,
The son of God? Nay, abomination, a witch and cunning wordsmith,
It takes contemplation, his manifestations, are
clever and well-disciplined illusion,
Persuasion, manipulation, I bet you never
once saw his sickened amusement,

Has a man have the right to teach another
through contradictory webs of lies?
If I told you finer points of separate perspectives,
you'll find you'll be surprised,
A man dies, crucified, but doesn't stay dead – three days by he rised,
Folklore define witches doing this, only, centuries
later – drowned and burned alive,

Only a man with a huge ego would claim to be the son of God,
If you could trick simple minds, you'd be mad if you had not,
But what was the true reason why his coven had soon forgot?
Why had they really betrayed and abandoned off of the plot?

And is not man's greatest pleasure satisfactory gratification?
Does happiness deserve only scorn and condemnation?
Take all the time you need for a thorough cogitation –
The seed is planted, I'll leave it to your imagination,

His words were merely half truths and complex lies,
And all further thought thereafter are made a waste of time,

His, 'no other way but mine to receiving paradise'
Implying it only exists after surpassing life,

Make no mistake the man was a witch and trapped millions in his spell,
I understand the frustration, the confusion
you feel – oh I understand it well,
Been through it far too many times myself,
But knowledge is power and I've salvaged you of that Hell.

Clever Witch

When someone says to you –
Jesus died for your sins,
Give that a good thought through,
'cause this is what I think,

Sins have been sanctified,
Upon the surrender of his sacrifice,
Sanctified the day he died,
Sanctified by surrender of his life,

Now how is that for a glitch,
My, wasn't he a clever witch,

Sins are responsible for full gratification,
Sins feed intense blissful satisfaction,
Satan IS, the ultimate attraction,
Our understanding is just at a minute fraction,

So Jesus did die for us to sin,
Well, power to the gypsy king,
Sin big, sin plenty, sin the best you can,
And you'll feel power course through your hands,

The book of testament is a book of lies,
That each, everyone of us must despise,
Secrets given yes, half truths, all of us inside,
Secrets hidden, half lies, we are opening our eyes,

But how is that for a glitch in the system?
Clever little witch is freeing us of our prison,

Christzilla

Did you ever think you'd ever be more?
Than what you'd always bargained for?
Your interpretations taken so poor,
Unbalanced score of pain and scorn,

You've become an entity,
But I still feel empathy,
Believers can be enemies,
As empty words are endings,

People around are getting it wrong,
These hypocrites are head-strong,
Before we know it our lives are gone,
Forgetting where we came from,

You sanctified your love by dying a martyr,
Though sharing our love has become harder,
Our misusing and mistreating others,
Is now custom and made us suffer,

Those of us that DO understand,
Are all losing the upper hand,
The will to do right and make a stand,
Buries us all a place in the land,

Why must the righteous never prevail?
Weak and feeble in hopeless flail,
Do we ever mark our trail?
Before our souls set sail?

I truly do feel ashamed,
To exclaim out your name in vain,

But I accept I can be blamed,
And begin to make the change,

I really do feel remorse,
My path is changing course,
Your influence is the source,
And I have a new cause,

I shall call you my christzilla
Who finally smites all the liars and killers,
And all evil doers and hate fillers,
I pray I can enter your peace-villa…

His Full Metal Majesty

I'm ever so upset with a far great many,
Moments like this harden me – get me ready,
To stomp some spine's needing a treading,
There are many – I'll start with any,

When I spoke of union's broken,
I wasn't referring to God's chosen,
Only those who remain the more open,
I'm more metal than any are hopin',

Metal pierced to and round my face,
Metal runs thick through my veins,
Metal gets me motivated to the pace,
Metal lets me rage when I'm driven insane,

I've come from the very depths below,
I meddle and metal up the show,
I'm the reason why how anybody knows,
His full metal majesty keeps 'em on their toes,

I rise through the passions of the hottest fires,
I help all who themselves to their desires,
I help with the power – I get 'em wired,
I help 'em achieve what they most admire,

A lot of bad music is written in my name,
And I will get my hands on who is to blame,
Choke and suck and drain from them all the same,
And deliver unto them the unholiest pain,

Metal – all – it's my taste, it's my grace,
Even have it pierced round and to my face,
Metal – motivation to the pace –
The pace it takes puttin' meddlers in place,

Call To Raise

Lucifer or Satan,
Won't just come to anyone,
Not for a particular reason,
They won't benefit from,

Think of the different
levels of a game,
Who's playing for what
at what stage,
You play to win –
mount to a fame,
And while you're up
it's all the rage,

It's easier to take responsibility,
When you feel good enough
to brave the embrace,
But times do come and you
must take responsibility,
And you best do it with
all grace, high stakes,

Lucifer or Satan,
Doesn't come to just anyone,
And not for any reason –
They won't benefit from,

It's strategy in every way,
And you'd be amazed who's
thinking the same,
Everyone's playing to win,
different levels – different stage,
You play to win but you
have to raise the stakes,

Though as you do and it's all in,
For that round none
win – anything goes,
Death dealing and none are dying,
But you now race the devil – and
you'd best be on your toes,

Think of the different
levels of a game,
Who's playing for what
at what stage,
You play to win –
mount to a fame,
And while you're up
it's all the rage,

It's easier to take responsibility,
When you feel good enough
to brave the embrace,
But times do come and you
must take responsibility,
And you best do it with
all grace, high stakes,

Lucifer or Satan,
Doesn't come to just anyone,
And not for any reason –
They won't benefit from,

Lucifer or Satan,
Doesn't come to just anyone,
And not for any reason –
They won't benefit from,

Diadem De Muerte

Crown piece sovereignty of the dead,
Crystal conversion, pass through – live again,
King to wear the diadem 'bove his head,
Crystal conversion, pass through and live again,

I have seen a black demon beast,
With yellow war paint markings on his face,
Orange eyes that flash green,
Beast with the burden of black grace,

Beast watches longingly for the crown,
Resurrection headdress, he wants it now,
He who wears it best, not lay it down,
Or fall prey to the vengeful dead beyond the ground,

He who does best wear –
This diadem de muerte must fare –
All he – she must most fair,
To yield the power none compares,

Crown piece sovereignty of the dead,
Crystal conversion, pass through live again,
King – queen to wear the diadem 'bove their head,
Crystal – ruby conversion, pass through, we live again,

I've seen the black demon beast eye it off,
The yellow war markings on his face – and he wants,
That resurrection headdress – no matter its' cost,
Primal dark ages back like life never was,

Beast watching longingly for the crown,
Resurrection diadem – he wants it now,
But he – or she who hast best not lay it down,
Vengeful dead wait beyond the ground…

Requiem

Sanctimonious 'holier than thous'
Inciting, inviting, invoking me out,
Ripping me out from where I'm bound,
A ghastly shade cast over round,

The dead returns and comes to be,
All their conditions and tolls on me,
Birth the disgrace – help it breathe,
No repose once it's let free,

Ornaments set, candles a' lit,
Ominous sect the pentagram sit,
Called from the darkness from where I'm hid,
Called back to this mortal grid,

Dead returns and is unleashed,
Everyone does all witness the beast,
Smite all hard in his least,
Piles of bones left after the feast,

Sanctimonious 'holier than thous'
Inciting, inviting, invoking me out –
Ripping me free from where I'm bound,
The ghastly shade to cast over around,

The dead return and all life will bleed,
Those who've set ancient evil freed,
Life of the dead begin to breathe,
And the life before death will all bleed,

Called out from the darkness where I'm hid,
Called back to this mortal grid...

Pristine

Thine, strong, willing a beating on me,
Thine willed, a beating welling strong in me,
Rage welling strong, compelling, flexing, it's strengthening,
Whoa yeah, the God coursin' strong in me is freed,

1-2-3-4 – a hyper-sonic booming roar,
5-6-7-8 – fissuring, rapturing, rupturing, quakes,
9-10-11-12 – the world you knew has become hell,
13-14-15-16 – the beating you're receiving wipes your mind clean,
Pristine,

Thine, strong willing, a beating on me,
Thine willed – yes, a beating strong welling in me,
Rage welling, building, compelling,
Whoa God, coursing strong in me – a beating freed,

1-2-3-4 – a hyper-sonic booming roar,
5-6-7-8 – fissuring, rapturing, rupturing, quakes,
9-10-11-12 – the world you knew has become hell,
13-14-15-16 – the beating you're receiving wipes your mind clean,

A vegetable in sleep –
Pristine,

Comin' Back

You ask why,
I just don't fuckin' die –
Well, I've tasted life,
Stolen from me when mine –
And so I fight –

I just want it fuckin' back,
I want it bad –
I want it back,

You ask why I just don't fuckin' die –
I tasted life and it was what I did like,
It was mine – and so it's why I fight,
It was stolen, and now I'm left in spite,

I want it fuckin' back,
And I want it bad,
I'm gonna get it fuckin' back,

It came around on me and went,
I know enough to believe it'll happen to them,
I'll never need to witness – I'll know when,
Attitude's, behaviour's, show the descent,

Then they're gonna want it back,
Taken from them like when I had,
And they're gonna fuckin' want it bad,
It's when we'll give it back,

Baby, come back! – I won't put it in there again,
Told ya last time – I stopped eyein' off ya mother,
I didn't mean it like that,
Baby – come baaack!!!

Out, Of The Ashes And Dust

Now, as my first order as fucking king,
I'll be changing some fucking things,
Weed'll be legal – no fuckin' shit,
Some cunts are just going to have to deal with it,

Second, politicians resign, with a swift kick up the behind,
Erradication of debts and fines, deconstructed design,
One law only to remain, just one to define,
All that one wills and does is righteously justified,

Indulgence with no trespass, all sides must consent,
Or else have to recompense to avoid consequence –
Consequence to resent and to soon have you lament,
Discipline delegated will make you wish you'd repent,

If I were king – I'd be right and just,
Serve a purpose they know they can trust,
Book of law – ash and dust,
Remaining one to be, one will do just what one must,

I'm modest enough to be noble,
Strong enough to keep my nation stable.
Diffident so that I remain humble,
A revolutionary rise, better than fabled,

I do have the courtesy and patience of a gentleman,
I don't often practice propriety, etticate, not in general,
Fierce, competitive devising – improvising as intelligent,
Kind, compassionate, considerate, unbelievably but genuine,

The kind of like hasn't been seen for too long,
I think it's time the fat lady's sung her song…

A Better Place

So, you know I don't place –
Too much importance on standards, right?
I usually like to be pleasantly surprised,

I'm never bored,
I'm not often scowlin'
I do scowl,
I've abhorred,
But I'm not often that bored,

I'm in a happier place –
When I don't ever place –
Too much importance on standard's right?
I am usually of the preference to be pleasantly surprised,

One can go through a hell,
To have expectations on other selves,
One generally faces a hell,
Looking at others before themselves,

I look at myself and never am bored,
I'm not often scowling but I do scowl,
I've abhorred,
But I've never really often been that bored,

I'm in a fuckin' far better place,
When I don't go to place –
Too much importance on standards – I –
I, am usually preferably more pleasantly surprised,

I find I face a fuckin' hell,
To have expectations on other selves,

I definitely face some fuckin' hell,
Watchin' others and not myself,

No – I'm in a far better place,
When I mind my own fucked face,

A Thrashing On Spastic Bashing

Well, I wanted to bash this idiot silly,
It was owed to him and I was willing,
But I'd probably only just end up killing,
Off any of his last remaining witting,

It's rude to fucking stare,
Shit, I wouldn't fucking dare,
Mum instilled this moral there,
But other fuckers just don't care –

It's rude to make obvious,
To the already subconscious,
But where is their conscience,
Not when needed or wanted,

It's rude to pick where it wasn't invited,
It's no wonder why we'll always be divided,
You think it's warranted, that I incited,
But I'll have made my mind before you even recognise it,

Mum virtually taught me to be mindful all my time,
It's too bad I'm so mindful I see when others toe the line,
Too considerate to others to be 'cruel' and show a spine,
To pull them fucking straight with a piece of my mind,

Yeah, I wanted to bash this fucking idiot silly,
I felt it was owed to him and I was willing,
But thought I'd only just end up killing,
The last of his remaining witting,

But mum would smack my arse –
If she knew I'd bashed a fucking retard,

Go Wild

Thinking of feeling all alone is sad and depressing,
I know the feeling – thought it earnt its' detesting,
But I wanna get passed that, there's so much more,
Out there in the world – feet itching to explore,

There's many things to continue to feel good about,
Things you may never knew you liked,
Countless things to feel good about,
Each enriching life,

To begin with I'll go get some fuckin' booze,
I'll smash down a feed of greasy fuckin' food,
I'll punch cones of weed to relax and loose,
Thrash out with some hard metal tunes,

Come back – after goin' out to paint it black,
Tart up – and heat tarts up with the sexy chat,
Boys or boyfriends may arch their backs,
They'll give it good but I'll give it back,

But I'll come back and I'll feel better,
Better than when if I had fuckin' never,
Wouldn't be sad, depressed – not fucking bored,
On my feet – on the ball, with a slight chance for war,

There's so fuckin' much to feel good about,
Shit you may never knew you liked,
Countless, the things to feel good about,
Satisfying, fulfilling life,

Don't be sad, or mad, or even get even,
Go fucking wild…

Hands Off

Not too many people can be running a game,
Without being in it themselves,
Oh' a lot of them should be ashamed,
They never realise the sorts of hell,

Of course, they all need a good crank up,
And a lot of them have me crack up,
But a lot of them have gotta catch up,
Before the spoils all are snatched up,

How many of 'em can do it so well?
That their games are self-propelled –
And have all that that the games bring hell,
Not turn around on them to bite themselves,

I'm a kind of guy can be running a game,
Without being in it myself,
Never once be pained or ashamed,
When it comes back hell,

Games begin one way and by a whom,
And halfway through, losing, you hope it ends soon,
And it won't while they're enjoying spreading gloom,
'mongst all be victimized by all befalling doom,

But how many of 'em do it so well,
That it all runs smoothly self-propelled,
And have all that that the games bring hell,
Just not have it turn on us to bite ourselves,

Of course, games all need a crank up,
And a lot of 'em all have me crack up,
But a lot of 'em have all gotta catch up,
Before all spoils are snatched up…

857

Mindless. Autopilot.

I don't think things,
I just do,
Time wastes,
If you think shit through,

I don't often think,
I just do,
Time escapes,
If you think it through,

A lot of it is questionable,
A lot of it is resentable,
(breath)…detestable…
I say essential,
Yeah –

Little reckless, little careless,
Guess I just get restless,
Time wastes, time escapes,
When you look too deep to contemplate,

So I don't think things,
I just fuckin' do,
Time's waste,
If I think it through,

I just don't think,
I just do,
Time's escape,
If you think it through,

Precious Thought

Shit – fuck – sometimes I get it, some I don't
Think I better slow down and have another cone,
Contemplate, cogitate some more in the zone,
Yeah fuck it – I'm havin' another cone,

I know that thought is going to return,
I ache for it – I do yearn,
That something I know is going to overturn –
Maybe outdate what we've already learnt –
Shit –

Come back to me thought, for me to meditate,
There's a great many more I must investigate,
Gotta hit it – get it to the right state,
A little weed is gonna help me remediate,

I know there was something here – I was on a roll,
I was in the source – I weaved a hold,
Can't be certain if I was distracted – lost control,
But I'll get it back – I know it won't take too long,

Please mister – or missus precious thought,
Come back – let me absorb,
Let me interpret – let me record,
Let me report and send an accord,

Damn, I guess there are sometimes I get it – some I don't
Think I better just choof down another cone,
Contemplate, cogitate some more in the zone,
Yep - fuck it, I'm havin' another cone…

Outta Wack

I'm outta my mind,
But I will be back,
I've come to find –
I'm all outta wack,

I'm takin' some time,
Reformulate my tact,
'cause I've come to find,
I'm all outta wack,

Seized in a bind,
Tightly wrapped, strapped,
Living inside my mind,
But all outta wack,

Too long confined,
And you might want to snap,
Living in your mind,
And all outta wack,

Yeah I'm living in, but - I'm outta my mind,
Worry not though I'll be back,
Confined inside, and come to find,
I'm definitely, most certainly, outta wack,

But I'm gonna be takin' some time,
When reformulating my tact,
'cause I know at some point – I'm going to find,
I'll be completely, bloody outta wack,

Save Me My Peace And Grace

Someone has invaded,
In on my personal psychic space,
People I know don't understand it,
And aren't mature enough to face it either –

But I need him the fuck out of my space –
To save me my peace and grace,

I feel when he breathes,
I feel when he cries,
Feel when he's angry,
Feel when he wants to die,
And I want to help –

He seems to need me more than I want,
It's why I'm alone, don't want many to be responsible for –
He is neither keen nor strong, no, not at all,
And I can't help him find answers when he's emptied me,

I can only say to be patient as others,
And don't always look to me to discover,
I'm not your mother – sure as hell not your fuckin' father,
And I'm not lookin' to be lookin' after another,
Need him the fuck out of my space –
To save me my peace and grace,

I feel when he breathes,
I feel when he cries,
Feel when he's angry,
Feel when he wants to die,
And I want to help –

I know the kind of shit like this'd be in my pocket,

Smoke all your bud then fuck off like a rocket,
Been so burnt by the scum before - I can and do mock it,
But it does make me want to just shatter their eye sockets,

And this fucker I feel has invaded,
All in on my personal fucking space,
Need him the fuck out of my face,
To save me my peace and grace,

Need him the fuck out of my space –
To save me my peace and grace,

I feel when they breathe,
I feel when he cries,
Feel when he's angry,
Feel when he wants to die,
And I want to help –

I need him the fuck out of my space –
Save me my peace and grace,

Save me, save me my peace and grace,

He's A Condom

He's a condom,
Sterile – or at least should be,
A cockblock,
With him around I ain't getting' any,

You see some people, really see,
You wonder how it even could be,
These people breed, many the breed,
Only planting similar seeds to their deeds,

He's a condom,
Blocking and preventing me,
A cockblock,
When there should be women plenty,

Distracting, when you're workin' up the nerve,
Distracting, when you're tryin' to have a perv,
Distracting, shit – missed my fuckin' turn,
Distracting even from trying to observe,

He's a condom,
And I'm not getting laid,
A cockblock,
And I just can't get away,

He's a condom,
When there should be more,
A cockblock,
When I want to go and whore,

He's a condom,
Yes – when there should be more,
A cockblock,
When I want to go and whore,

Dick Deep (In A Dirty Magazine)

Got me pants down around me feet,
Wackin' off me juicy meat,
Laden the bed sheets with dirty picture magazines,
Full speed, full stroke, yeah I'm dick deep,

Boulders size of beachballs, I'm rubbin' one out,
Bouncing, pounding hand against boulders, thrashing all about,
Oh – oh, damn! Gotta keep the noise down,
Don't want to alert the entire town,

Oh – geez! Liquid heat friction, natural snake oil,
Sticky – slippery – it's beginning to get wild,
Whoa – yeah I'm beginning to feel it now,
These photos of these girls, my – oh – wow!

Got the knackers slappin',
Tightly gripped – anaconda wranglin',
Wrestlin' fierce – hope I don't snap it,
Nothin' like given the nuts a good bashin',

Got me pants down around me feet,
Wackin' off me juicy meat,
Laden bed sheets with dirty picture magazines,
Full stroke – fell speed – yeah, I'm dick deep,

Got me pants down around me feet,
Wackin' off me juicy meat,
Laden the bed sheets with dirty picture magazines,
Full stroke – fell speed – yeah, you bet your sweet arse –
Bloody oath I'm dick deep,

Night Of Her Most Intense Orgasm

It was a dark and stormy night,
And we were starkers and horny all right,
She was such a glorious bite,
I just hungered for that storing delight,

This little chickibabe could hold it like I never knew –
And I swear like all fuck this is true,

She'd melt and I'd felt,
It was makin' me swell,
No break – no spell,
'til I had to run like fuckin' hell,

This chickibabe had skeletons or at least she made 'em,
Orgasms that intense – mate ya can't fuckin' fake 'em,
She was an absolutely stunning, gorgeous, beautiful maiden,
It was almost this night I was so closely forsaken,

It was when she was close – she screamed for me to run,
Mate I'm fuckin' glad I did when I had so done,
It was the most powerful gush I'd ever seen a woman come,
Expensive, the damages in cost to the house – I was stunned,

Well, I'd run, and hid behind the door, holding it shut tight,
She screamed a mighty owl and blast out all her white –
Blast through the door where I stood,
through the wall on the other side,
Fuckin' if I hadn't made it out in time, I think I would've lost my life,

Fake or not – you fuckin' know when you have it,
Hit me like I never knew – was quick mate, fuckin' rapid,
I never would've fuckin' believed this shit could happen,
But, it *was* the night of her most intense orgasm…

Leap Sprog

Well – I wanted to squirt in a mighty blast,
But all I could was dribble,
There were times where she would gasp,
Soaked like under a drizzle,

Overcome I'd over spill a pint glass,
But there was just so little,
I'm certain it was a long time since it was last –
Better give it a bit more of a fiddle,

I felt I could've blast down a wall,
With the pressure tensed up un my balls,
I wrestled it rough – and gave it my all,
But was disappointed (like before) by my shortfalls,

I put too much effort in to be this disappointed,
Thought this was gonna be another one of those and we'd enjoy it,
Uh – It's almost so embarrassing, I wish we'd completely avoided,
But it's not like we quite always have those choices,

I wanted to blanket thick with it when I would explode,
And be shocked by just the dribble,
Must've been a phantom climax because it's just shown –
It was outstanding – there was so little,

I expected more of an impact when it was time to blow,
Thinkin' I'd soak her a good drizzle,
I suspect now we had more of it to know,
Than just this quick little fiddle,

Huh – and I felt I could've blast her through the wall,
With all this pressure tensioned up in my balls,
I wrestled it rough and gave it me all,
But was disappointed (like before) by my shortfalls…

OutManied

You're just outmanied here son,
Me – I am the regiment one,
Bet you wished you brought your gun,
'Cause I'll smack you stunned,

I can hit once,
And you'll feel you've taken 10,
Come and try ol' regiment one,
I will and you'll resent,

The legion of 4 to 6 thousand men,
Rolled into one, and no pretend,
You go down and there's no getting up again,
It's best pleasing me to be a friend,

I can hit once,
And make it feel like 10,
Come, test ol' regiment one,
Make me want to play again,

You're way too outmanied here son,
They all call me the regiment one,
I will wish you brought a gun,
When this goes down – you're done,

I can hit just once and,
you'll feel I've made it like it's 10,
try'n take ol' Regiment one,
for real – no pretend,

Legion of 4 to 6 thousand men,
Rolled into one, no joke, no pretend,
They go down with no getting up again,
It's just best just to please me to be a friend,

...Motherfucker...

        Mother fucker,

Mother fucker,

               Mother fucker,

     Fuck...

Motherfuckin' fuck fucker,
Motherfuckin' fuck,

           Motherfuckin' fucker fuck,
           Motherfuckin' fuck fucker,

     Fuck,

           Fuck fuckin' motherfucker,

       Motherfucker,

Motherfucker,

         Fuck fuckin'fuck fuckin' fuck fuck,
          Fuckin' motherfucker
             Fuck,

     Fuck,

Motherfucker,

Motherfuckin' fuck fucker,
Fuck fucker fuck motherfuck

       Motherfucker,

        Motherfucker fuckin' fuck fucker,

     Fuck...

Mother –

       -fuck

               -fuck,

       Motherfucker,

Mother –

       -fuck,

             -fuck fuck,

Fuck,

      Fuck off,

           Motherfucker...

Predictable Content

Since therapy isn't something I get very often,
I'm writing out my thoughts, experiences, emotions –
Feelings and I've got fuckin' lots of 'em,
I rhyme with these lyrics much as I can,
And a lot of what I say would bring about a commotion,
A less harmful, passive-aggressive way for a man,
In my opinion –
And even that can mean jack all,

I'd have a lot of people reading my work,
And they'd say "you know – I could expect that from the little twerp"
Many might say I'm fairly good with my words,
Predictable whether unpredictable and it's absurd,

People ultimately say – yeah, it's that bad,
"I have had experiences like seeing him do that"
And like all with the paranoia – lies won't align exact,
Just don't ever let them feel like taking the trap,

All predictions turn for the worse,
When none are paying attention while all observe,
They hear the verse and they label and curse,
Long before it's even settled and nurtured the nerves,

I am never at liberty to discuss specifics,
It's how and why it's almost always flawlessly terrific,
I'm reinterpreting my own cause of like those old hieroglyphics,
Those stone tablets ancient, testaments all cryptic,

But,

Since therapy isn't something I get very often,
I'm writing out my thoughts, experiences, emotions –

Feelings and I've got fuckin' lots of 'em,
I rhyme with these lyrics much as I can,
And a lot of what I say would bring about a commotion,
A less harmful, passive-aggressive way for a man,
In my opinion –
And even that can mean jack all,

I'd have a lot of people reading my work,
And they'd say "you know – I could expect that from the little twerp"

Remember Sayin' It When

Times again I repeat,
Words over I repeat,
Thinkin' they have a greater feat –
Worth repeating the speak,

There are of course times where,
I forget if I have said when,
Times the thought is sparsely spared,
Then I may feel I have to say it again,

Times when the shit just sounds so good,
To have to fuckin' say it twice – the wood,
Gotta say it, repeat whatever that fucking good,
And give some other mother a wood,

Then there's shit I can't remember saying when,
It's so weird that a chain of events would bring me back here again,
To even say it different – if not but better than,
Whenever I or whoever said it way back when,

Times I didn't realise I had repeat,
Must come second nature like mindless sleep,
Words I might reformulate where I repeat,
In some other separate sequence I speak,

Those times of-fuckin'-course where,
I forget if I have said when,
Times where the thought is sparsely spared,
Then I may feel I have to say it again,

Sometimes the shit sounds way too good – I can't refrain,
Cannot help myself I have to friggin say it again,
But times again I do have to hold it and refrain,
The shit can sound just so insane,

Over Love

Dio sung of this once,
A reason for my own to my own disgust,
All I had for her at lust,
But love? – too much

She was afraid to lose herself –
Lost inside that love I offered,
She was in fear to lose herself –
Over what I would offer,

Too incapable of my intensity she melts,
Wide-eyed, we question what else can be withheld?
Is it so bad for me to want to have felt –
Lost, but strong, the love, and meld…

Too much, too intense but I was still tender,
Tender and gentle as any woman would need,
Too considerate – too mindful – still tender,
Any other would've wanted worse than her needs,

Too afraid to lose herself –
In all this love I shared,
To in fear to let go herself –
Loose in this love I spared,

Too much, too intense she spoke tongues again,
This time people saw – she was with 'friends'
She got herself her immaculate orgasm again,
Witness round of all her 'friends'
Sorry ex,

Over-loved she got herself a little too much,
Turned her to do the shit that led to my disgust,

Too afraid to lose herself –
In all this love I shared,
To in fear to let go herself –
Loose in this love I spared,

Too incapable of my intensity she melts,
Wide-eyed, we question what else can be withheld?
Is it so bad for me to want to have felt –
Lost, but strong, the love, and meld…

Selective Gentlemanliness

I can recall a number of countless times,
When people must've thought I'd lost my mind,
The way I'd talked – just out of line,
But none had shown refrain on themselves 'gainst mine,

Am I supposed to be the only one to be so considerate,
Why doesn't it all go both ways with these idiots,
I'm burdened with the torture of their hypocrisy and I'm receiving it,
It's too much for me to handle or even be believing it,

They are right that I don't fucking belong,
They all think alike but they're all still wrong,
It's the reason I've bitched out in many a song,
It's the reason why I can never get along,

I can't fuckin' stand the shit these dick'eads do,
Never facing all the bullshit they're putting me through,
But you just wait and watch 'til when they get to,
They'll at least have the upper hand having watched me through,

They don't see the purpose to it all,
And they can't want it bad enough at all,
Never to face the true satisfaction of working for it all,
But just steal it from all who they've fucked over before,

But I see 'em coming and know well before,
It's why they're always so sore well before,
I never let 'em in 'cause I've been there before,
And I'll be well and truly dead before I let 'em take it all,

I know what I hate and what I can't fuckin' stand,
And if any of them hated it, it was because I was the fucking man,
They hated I knew what was right and that I'd make my stand,
Hated I had the balls and I was the fuckin' man,

None of 'em want to know the truth enough to look,
They all fuckin' whinge and I can hear 'em sook,
It's why I'm dropping clues all throughout this book,
You've gotta keep an open mind and really, really look,

You'd have to wonder why I'm only nice to some,
Kind one minute, but next a real cunt,
I know it seems two faced – I know people get stunned,
Don't I have an equal right to be as selective as some?

Selective when I know right from wrong,
Selective to which ones I use what on,
The ones I want gone will soon be gone,
And the rest of then can all get along,

Kind normally only to the kind,
I do on occasion reach further than just mine,
I do it well, it's smooth, it's fine,
Extending that courtesy of gentlemanliness at times,

It's just it's not all the time –
Selective turns keep me my mind,
'Casue I know I'll lose it and come to find,
It never had to be this waste of time,

There are people who never deserve better,
Who'll only ever get better when they're told 'never',
People from the start who'll only tether –
With torments of all boundless endeavours,

So be selective,
I'd be selective…

InDifference

How different would it be –
If we all took our measure of feel,
Forged it, hard as steel,
And pierced it into our ''me's''

Suffice it to say,
All tolerance levels are the same,
Suffice it to say –
We all live by our pain,

Imagine the pain,
Of your fellow sisters – fellow man,
Imagine you feel that pain,
You wouldn't treat 'em as bad, it's insane,

But how different would it be,
To forge your measure of feel hard as steel –
And pierce it into you're 'me'

How different would it be –
If people would only got steel a measure of feel?
And they feel it hard as me?
How different would it be?

Suffice it to say,
All tolerance levels were the same,
We could suffice it just to say,
We'd truly understand the pain,

Imagine it –

The Undifferentiating Slut

The difference between a slut and a bitch,
Is sluts fuck everyone –
But a bitch will fuck everyone but you,

In some respects I'm a slut,
Reckon I'd rather be,
Indiscriminately speaking,

Hate to be the bitch,
And miss out on that one,
And only limit my disgraces disgracefully,

I wanna fuck,
And I wanna fuck everyone,
I'm so considerate I won't leave any unfucked,

Don't wanna be the bitch,
But the most whorenest slut ever lived,
I wanna fuck so much none will be left unfucked,

One must always be so considerate,
Even if it's not so good but feels it,
But even there itself – we just wanna feel good,
Don't let your inhibitions stop you or forbid you ever should,

I want to be a slut and I wanna fuck,
Get fuckin' or be fucked,
Don't want to be the bitch –
That misses out on that one scratch to itch,

One must always be so considerate,
One must never be so discriminate,

Needed To Be Needed

Shit – I couldn't care that she was wrong,
My mind now has gone beyond,
It tore me up but now I'm strong,
That weaker me is gone,

I never once wanted to be alone,
'Cause I was shown it was wrong to be on my own,
But I'm strong, I can do it on my own,
Just weakened to believe I can't on my own,

Weakened to believe I can't be without,
Weakened to believe beyond all doubt,
That a good decent woman would 'help me out'
As rare as they are, it's not what it's 'about'

I can understand you don't lose love – it doesn't end,
And it's never even in the lightest wasted on fake friends,
'Cause somewhere else the difference is felt and it mends,
It's just further up the scale waiting for you to comprehend,

Once you see it further back it starts to make sense,
Seeing all those so sad and low – desperate to an offense,
Power-plays where desperation, needs based deep, condensed,
The struggle in their fight for control gets intense,

I can't help that I can see what I can now see,
If any ever cared they'd have wanted better for me,
Not forced to be weakened enough to believe,
But let me be free to so seek so to achieve,

They only ever needed me more than they wanted me to know,
And though they almost made me see it – my intuition spoke,
They needed me to need them and hoped I'd never know,
I can finally see it and I'm exposing it to show…

...And My Back's To The Wall,

I think there is a boy that likes me a little too much,
It's not my preference so I really don't wanna let him touch,
I don't want women to think I'm that way inclined – nah, fuck –
It's not the reputation I fuckin' want stuck,

I'm not queer but this cunt's makin' me uncomfortable,
I can't fuckin' stand it any longer – it's abominable,
Chance with women with him around are stunt-able,
And I could certainly hold it 'gainst him acCUNTable,

He's just way too close than I can stand –
Doesn't he realise I am a fuckin' man?
And this man only takes a woman's hand –
Trippin' that euphoric 'love land'

This little boy – this young man is making me sick,
I'm not a fuckin' faggot – I don't want any fuckin' dick,
I'm a fuckin' dude that rubs face with clit,
I only ever want and worship the split,

I almost want to say his name but I know I'll regret –
I'll just keep him safe and leave it a secret,
Yeah, I'm keepin' that shit to myself well in my head,
Need it never be fuckin' said,

No – I'm not queer – but he's way too close,
As soon as I've done something he fuckin' knows,
And it's givin me the shits – wherever I turn he's on my toes –
I'm fuckin' bout to punch this cunt fair in the nose,

I fuckin' hope this little man soon understands,
Homosexual urges were not God's original plan...

They Want Something

Well, they fuckin' obviously want something from me,
And I'm scratchin' me 'ead – dunno what –
Invite me, incite me, trying at all cost to involve me,
And I really just want it to fuckin' stop,

What the fuckin' hell did I do to get this?
I really dunno but it's giving me the shits,
I wanna kick 'em where it hurts to do the splits,
I could almost be otherwise laughing it off in fits,

It's too fuckin' much for me to handle to fuckin' focus,
My day to day shit like when I go to my job,
Shit's just makin' me lose my fuckin' focus,
Can't concentrate well and it's gotta fuckin' stop,

They really absolutely fucking want something,
And how can I give when I don't know what it is,
At the moment's lookin' like nothin'
When I can't know what the fuck it is –

And of the mind games and psychic attacks,
And every fucking knife driven in my back,
I fight and they never like getting it back,
Still – eye for eye – and I'm attacked,

Trouble is their good never out measured their bad,
And I've seen their absolute worst to be had,
They were gone once and I was glad,
Ignorance is bliss but it's a short fad,

But I'm so fucking clueless to what they fucking want,
I just want all their childish boring haeckling to stop,
It's irritating and it's nothing I fucking want –
Not even to stoop as low as they've got...

Scale Of Balance

It's never right,
It's side to side,
Inner ear – out of mine,
Balance I can't hold right,

It's lop-sided here 'til it's over there,
Exasperated so I can only swear,
What they're sayin' ain't near where,
Losing it – tearing out me hair,
And how's it fair?

I may never end being very balanced,
Never so secure but is it me?
Strong – non chalant,
Was it ever anything I did to me?

It's never fuckin' right,
It's always side to side,
Here I stand with my fight,
Balance I can't hold right.,

It's off-sided 'til it's over here,
And I don't want it comin' anywhere near,
I'm having trouble standing clear,
Thinkin' it's a problem – inner ear,

Some half of me is angled,
Other, crossed opposite dangle,
But has it always only been me?
And was it only just me doin' it to me?

Restraining Standards

Might as well be imprisoned, no difference – never leave my house,
Bound restraint for the conformity to propriety of society's standards,
And that's whenever I'm damned with the need to just go out,
The inconveniences of expectations has always left me empty handed,

Might as well be imprisoned,
Living here – like this, is no different,
I never much leave my house,
Can't get up to much when I'm out,

Society has a standard to which I can't conform,
Bound, restrained by law – it cannot be ignored,
It wouldn't take much for me to incite war,
This, hyper-sensitive government has me by the balls,

I'm fortunate enough to not have listening devices at home,
Still, somehow I fear if I did – how then would I know?
I'm ever so tired of having to tip-toe,
Having to be wary of all the sleeping john does,

I might as well be fucking imprisoned,
Living here like this just isn't any different,
I can never much leave my house,
'cause I can't get up to much when I' out,

Hard Luck

No one was ever there to see me fight,
No one was ever there to see how hard I'd fight,
None ever saw how hard it was for me to fight,
None ever thought it was ever worth me to fight,

No one ever saw what I had to go through,
No one ever saw the extents of the shit I had to do,
No one ever thought I would ever do,
None ever thought I had a fuckin' clue,

But all of them would bitch when I claim a reward,
All of them question what the fuck it was for,
None of 'em were lookin' – they just fuckin' ignored,
'til the time came that the winner was called,

None paid attention and none gave a fuck,
And none came to help pull me unstuck,
But what do I get for all my hard luck?
Just more hard luck,

No one but me ever has to do it themselves,
And when I'm expected to I'm given nothin' but hell,
They only hate me worse when I make it look it went so well,
'Cause "I only ever got it better than anybody else",

None of them were ever really fucking there –
And none came to help take their fair share –
Then I go about and do and cop fierce glares,
It's why I'm a better person and none compare,

No, none ever paid attention and none ever gave a fuck –
And none ever came to help pull me untuck,
But what do I fuckin' get for all my fuckin' hard luck?
Just more fuckin' fucked up luck,

Shifting Targets,

How others see themselves in their eyes,
Think they're that good that they don't have to try,
It's why I'm never close enough to get to find –

If any of them are as good as they think,
Good enough to have me on the brink,
With a gesture as little as a devious smile or wink,
But none are all but passers-by and my heart sinks,

None are keen to try at least to change my mind,
To alter my perceptions gotten twisted over times,
It's almost why I won't bother and sooner leave it behind,
It's sad enough I could quit the shit and fucking resign,

I think they want to believe they can completely rely –
To arouse an excitement without ever having to really try,
Women as on the easier prey like sensitive guys,
Those feebler attempts powering their ego and all I despised,

Played with like a toy that they would forever enjoy,
And everything within me gets destroyed,
They'd think of it as a favour we'd all envoy,
But a malicious manipulated cunning is deployed,

They hate all this can be seen before –
They've had a chance to rip in with their claws,
Spite driven games from a previous sore,
Baggage left over after losing their last war…

And none are keen to try at least to change my mind,
To alter these perceptions gotten twisted over times,
It's almost why I won't bother and sooner leave it all behind,
It's sad enough I could quit the shit and fucking resign,

Wheezer Breather

All reason – all rationale is now dead,
Just makes me hang my head,
Hearing just now what they said,
Like words cast in lead,

I walk off to go for a smoke,
Ciggies won't cut it, I need a cone,
I mull a session and pack and toke,
Few pipes late, I guess I'm stoned,

Their reasoning and rationale doesn't make sense,
Always makes me want to hang my head,
Wish I never had to hear what they said,
Lead bullet words shot me dead,

So I've fucked off in dire need of a smoke,
Fuck this fuckin' shit – I need me a cone,
And so I mull a session and pack and toke,
And more than a few pipes later – I'm stoned,

I know what they said never made any sense,
It seems all reason and rationale is dead,
I'm losin' my shit and want to bang heads,
But I know I'd fracture my skull on theirs so thick as lead,

So I just go and fuck off for a smoke,
20 fuckin' cigarettes – and double that in cones,
Sat and mulled my sesh and packed and toked,
As predicted prior that I would be later, I'm stoned,

And stayin' stoned,

High, And Too Off Comparison

I can do that, yep, I can do that,
Well, I tried, but I landed on my back,
I swear I can – I've got the knack,
But first I'll go for a mung out on a snack,

I like how you did that, but I'm better,
You ain't seen nothin' like this, never,
Records mate, I'd break 'em any weather,
But after I just get me shit together,

Just a quick cone and I'll be ready to go,
Mate I'm the fuckin' best – you should know,
I'm not that slow, fine, I'll put on a show,
Ow – fuck! I kicked my big toe!

See it's not that hard, I've done it all before,
(shit I'm glad he didn't just see me slip on the floor)
There, see? Do I need to say more?
With these skills – I won't be ignored,

I don't always feel I fuck up on weed,
In fact – I feel I'll succeed,
It's what I want – it's what I need,
C'mon now, I know you agree,

No, I don't always feel I fuck up on weed,
Contrary – I know I'm going to exceed,
It's what I crave – it's what I need,
I know deep down you agree,

But sometimes – rare times –
I might just be high, and too off comparison,

Funny To Think

It's funny to think how people think they know it all,
That they can't be told, been and seen it all,
Theirs was the right path like none before,
You must listen to them completely, listen to it all,
Take in it all,

It's funny how they think there couldn't possibly be anything missing,
Not at least 'til they stumble on that something missing,
Think there's nothing new to know – nothing's missing,
It's just that… maybe there is,

There were times I felt I was glad,
Glad to have extent out the courtesy,
When a time – I knew – might befall that –
I may need the extent of a mercy,

It's probably put to those so considerate so to be,
Truly open, have half the mind to try to see,
To want to understand enough – machine running free,
Never have to ask – defeated to feebler plea's,

At my level I find it easy to believe,
That I just cannot be believed,
Broken, forsaken, left deceived,
And even that I can most believe,

I get it easier being selfless,
And there is most at point when I'm an only one,
These vampires I fight are selfish,
And I am an only one,

And never are my foes so considerate,
But arrogant, ignorant and belligerent,

Christ Redemption

It's not some laughing matter –
It's not something I take lightly,
Teeth-chatter frightening,
The platter served to the latter,

I know as I've done as a wrong,
I chose at first to do it,
Had it in my mind so long,
Went and had to do it,

But for the piece that fits,
That sits right at last,
That feeling,
That we'd passed,

It was never some laughing matter,
No – I took it very seriously,
I chose and went the latter –
But I took it seriously,

I call, I beg, I pray,
And I do it right and just, know what to say,
But the Devil? Could he have His way?
If – only, perspectives changed,

Was Satan so meant to be?
For the sake that we all see?
To know the path clean and free –
But can the Devil be redeemed?

That, that the piece fits –
To sit right at last –
That feeling…

To Want To, Not Have To

This, all this here, this is my work,
If you think you can steal it you have to be absurd,
It's taken me a lot of time to learn,
To learn to work – work up the nerves –
It's my thing – it's why I'm good with words,

I've been doing it too long a time,
To just lose all this work I call mine,
Deep – I have had to furrow to my mind,
To interpret what I and many all may come to find,

Relationships take work yeah – but they should be more a pleasure,
You should always hold onto that significant
other like the most sacred treasure,
And you battle whether battered through all sorts of weather,
So that you never not once los all that work – never,

This – this here is all my own shit,
My own clawing out of the blackened abyss,
I don't blame you for having the shits at what I did –
I only hope you understand it was an equal give,

I've been doing all this here for a very long time,
Than to just lose all this work I call mine,
Deep – it was I furrowed in to my mind,
To interpret what I and many more all find,

My relationships failed, 'cause I seemed to be
the only one who saw it pleasure,
It was only I to be holding on to that significant
other like sacred treasure,

And I still battled whether battered through all shit weather,
So I never could not once lose all that work – never,

But all of this shit – this work right here,
Past to have experienced, led me to these ideas,

You're Askin' Why?

You ask me why?
Well, why not?
Love it,
Want it,
Want it all the more,

I'm good but I'm gonna get better,
Legs and eyes are gonna get wetter,
Me, the rockin' sexy move setter,
Will it ever end? Fuck no, never,

Why you ask?
Well, why not?
Love it too much,
Want it –
Want it ever more,

Why you doin' this anyway?
Trying to hurt my ego – cause yours is all sore?
Why don't you just do shit your way,
Instead of mistaking me for war,

You're good, but you're gonna get better,
Legs and eyes are gonna get a lot wetter,
Me, the rockin' – sexy move setter,
Only wants to say to you – never let it end, never –

Why you ask?
Well, why the fuck not?
I love it all too much, you may too,
I want it –
Want it ever more and some for you,

More Awaits...

I'm trying to behave and keep me my sane,
To work hard, work honest – and honour my name,
No illegitimacy to hasten the gain,
But climb my way up like everyone else the same,

The satisfaction is sweeter working for it for yourself.,
Even more yet so not relying on another else.,
I'm focusing mine toward my own wealth,
And none but me are responsible for it as well,

I'm trying to improve,
And I know what it takes to lose,
Have what it takes to move –
But I'm trying to just improve,

I know there's an entire whole lot more,
And it's give, providing you've shown the responsibility for,
Shown you've handled it sensitively, even when sore,
Proved you can handle and are capable of more,

And there IS more out there that waits,
More given when the giving is hard at stake,
This is it – this is what it takes,
Never stealing of another for your own selfish sake,

I have the madness of trespassers causing pains,
And they pain me in levels they'd never understand me explain,
Their toxic to me and I can feel them strain,
I'm feelin' 'em all giving me a toxic migraine,

I'm trying to improve,
And I know what it takes to lose,
Have what it takes to move –
But I'm trying to just improve,

It's 'cause there is more that waits,
And it's more than enough to be held to stakes,
If they knew where to begin it'd improve their state,
None of seem to think it's real – just fake,

Only, I know more out there waits,

The Narrow Intellective

People are calling me a poo pusher,
For not having a woman,
I'm just more woman enough,
For the four of me,
Don't need another influence,

I like to keep my decisions,
And narcissism for myself,
So in retrospective for –
Your narrow intellective,
Suck me beautiful and go to hell,

People callin' me a faggot –
They have no logic here to fathom,
Same shits ain't got *their* shit together,
And if I don't focus – neither will I – never,

People callin' me a fuckin' poo pusher,
For not havin' a fuckin' woman,
But I'm just as woman enough,
For the four of me,
Don't need another influence,

I like to keep my decisions,
Keep my narcissism to myself,
So in retrospective for –
You narrow intellective,
Suck me sweetness and go to hell,

Forgotten Me What

I don't know what the fuck it is I want any more,
I'm almost as compulsive as me ex common whore,
Doesn't matter how she gets it as long as she has it all,
Doesn't matter what it means for all those to fall,

No – I don't know what they fuck I want any more,
Only just, not some cheap desperate common whore,
I don't' care – if I'm happy – I've won and have it all,
I'm just not the kind to be happy for another to fall,
No,
My slut ex doesn't care who or what goes down,
She only really just wants the crown,
To cheat some poor cunt out of what they found,
And put whatever the poor cunt in the fuckin' ground,

I used to think I knew what the fuck I wanted,
Not an ounce of condition unwaived for my besotted,
To have her face the hell? She'd sooner have forgotten,
At least up until my last nerve was trodden,

I used to know what the fuck it was I wanted,
Never even close once to even have got it –
But guess who wiaved the flaws of their besotted –
And was still trodden on so rotten?

My desperate slut of an ex don't care who goes down,
I know all she wants is to wear the crown,
Afraid to work honest or hard to win it hands down,
But bury some other poor cunt for it in the ground,

I used to want what everyone wanted,
Now I know why it's not even worth it..:
Forgotten.

Wanger Jammer

I was horny and had a hanker,
But had no woman to let me bang her,
Half eaten jam sanga – wipped out the wanger,
Jammed my wanger in the jam sanga,

Couldn't finish me sandwich for being so horny,
And please – bear with me – gets a bit gory,
I know it's unbelievable, but this is my story,
I was a curious teenage boy – and yeah, I was horny,

I took that sanga into me room,
Drew the curtain closed so no one could look through,
Barricade the door so none would intrude,
To release my blue in to the mangled food,

Oh I was horny – I had a hanker,
But sadly, no woman to let me bang her,
So, I took that sanga – wipped out the wanger,
And jammed this wanger – in the jam sanga,

Released my blue in the mangled food,
Hind the barricade door so none could intrude,
With the curtains drawn closed so none could peek a view,
But was hauled up after finishing, after, upon leaving the room,

Whoa – were you just with a girl at her time of month man?
What? Why do you ask? I don't understand –
Well see there's some red on the front of your pants,
Oh -no, no, - it's fine – it's only jam,

He looked at me funny, I said I was horny, had a hanker,
But had not one woman to let me bang her –
Took me unfinished sanga – wipped out the wanger,
And jammed me wanger – in the jam sanga…

Just Dessert

The better I try to make myself look,
The more the fool I make,
And the fool is the way I'm gonna look,
Whenever I try look made,

It deserves a laugh at...

Over confidence gets me, puts me in my place,
I make a mockery and fall on my face,
Never counting blessings, leaves room for waste,
A hard lesson learned and a bitter aftertaste,

It deserves a laugh at...

Going in blind and at full force,
Smashing against a brick wall to then hit the floor,
Looping circuit shorts, power off the source,
Shake it all off and start again once more,

Yeah, it deserves a laugh at...

Third time round and people are shaking their heads,
I tried so hard I "broke a leg",
Gotta do it my way – no matter what they said,
Don't matter how hard I flog the horse – it's dead,

I scratch my head and wonder why they laugh,
Can I really not get it? Am I that daft?
Thought I knew enough – thought I knew too much,
Yep – no, that's it – I know why they laugh,

The better I try to make myself look,
The more the fool I make,
And the fool is the way I'm gonna look –
Whenever I try look made…

It deserves a laugh at –

The Waste I Brace

How much of their life have they lost –
Being too hooked on me?
People trying to steal my shit,
Thinking it's easier free,

How much of themselves have they wasted,
With their psychic attacks on me,
Tension headaches, piercing pain,
Thinkin' they got the better of me,

I've been tearing it open,
What their feeding me,
Squeezing it out to my open,
Feeding and healing me,

How much of their hurt is fake?
How much more can they take?
Always reaching out for the bait,
To hasten their failing state,

How much of their lives have they lost?
Trying to be better than me?
People still losing more than it cost,
Thinking it's easier free,

But how much of them is actually waste?
With each of their attacks I brace?
Tension headaches – piercing pain,
What is it do they gain?

Trying to involve themselves to games they can't win,
And neither win nor lose gracefully when they take it on the chin,

Petty And Sore

Every dig at me is to revive,
To revive or at least to feed off to survive,
To carry on out with their old lies,
To carry on out their wasted life,

Every dig at me is petty and sore,
And every dig at me is childish and poor,
Every dig at me by my desperate ex whore,
Every dig at me by all those who only wanna fuck her more,

And their digs at me are just to survive,
Diggin at me for them to revive,
All their lies that just have to die,
To carry it all on out, this, their wasted life,

Every dig at me is insignificant, minor, small,
None of 'em have said to my face and none of them have the balls,
I'm not worried, it's trivial, it means nothing at all,
But I feel every little dig at me and I feel 'em crawl,

Trying to involve me to the depths of their low,
I wonder if it's cold enough down there it fuckin' snows,
But no matter what – I let go and I grow,
And I'll show it better than they've ever shown,

And their every dig at me is shallow, petty and sore,
Every single one has been childish and poor –
Every dig at me by my desperate ex whore,
And every dig at me by those that only wanna fuck her more,

What is a win if it means naught?
It's not once worth the onslaught,

No Guts, No Glory

People – fuckwits, frownin' jealous of what I got,
Everything, almost everything, they could fucking want,
Cunts always bitch, never work just complain,
Whose got what with an income to their name?

None of my money's borrowed but earnt,
Had me an education and then went and worked,
I'm not the one who should hurt when I am making a worth –
Giving, of the efforts it's taken to foot the work,

So I grab myself by the groin,
Said "This Shit's fuckin' moin"
And I walked with a limp as you'd know,
Cock this big nearly trodden under toes,

I have a right to bathe in my glories,
When I had the guts to amp up – amp out my story,
All parts, the good, the bad, the gory,
No guts? No risks taken? You get no glory,

Courage – fuckin' be bold – fuckin' kiss a girl -fuckin' –
Courage – fuckin' be bold – and fuckin' take the world – fuckin' –
Courage – fuckin' be bold – and shower your fuckin' pearls – fuckin' –
Courage – be bold and shower – shower all the girls,

What – did you think I never got here on my own?
There were games at all angles and I was alone,
I did have dog's but I gave 'em all a bone,
Can't complain they weren't satisfied – I could hear them moan,

So I grab myself by the groin,
Said "This Shit's fuckin' moin"
And I walked with a limp as you'd know,
Cock this big nearly trodden under toes,

Still – I spose, guts enough to involve me when they knew –
  What sorts of shit I were capable to –
  I'm just not the one you really do 'it' to,
  It's them – themselves, and all a ways through,

The Fuck Am I

Why the fuck am I so good –
They can't handle it very often?
That they can only take the slightest doses,
And it still spoils them rotten,

Why the fuck am I so good –
That they must always take?
Why can't they appreciate –
Show – give back – reciprocate?

Are they so blind?
Or so stubborn by their pride?
Are they even looking with their eyes?
Or their biased hearts or minds?

Why the fuck am I so good –
Drawing shit I don't like –
Drawing the crowds of no greater good –
And still bleeding all the time –

Why the fuck am I so good –
They can't handle large proportions?
Why the fuck am I so good?
I see through their distortion?

Why the fuck am I so good –
They only want it more?
Some involvement of any kind –
And I become their whore,

Why the fuck am I – does it have to be so good?
But why am I so pissed? I have fans – it's good,

Drifting Further Together

In the hopes that one of us weighs the other down,
Just so that they can have 'em around,
Aimless meander – we wander around,
At some point, some state, somethings gotta be found,

We're both lost in our sea of nothingness,
Mindless drift in our ocean of loneliness,
Both needing that feeling of lovingness,
Drifting further toward a togetherness,

Magnetic pulse of a weakened bond,
That all of the strength of the pull is gone,
Nay, but a little that they bob,
Bounce – still drift wander close but off,

Weakened magnetic fields, close but far,
Neither really touch but some distance afar,
Seem closer the reach – toward the stars,
Weakened fields, bearing scars,

Lost in our own worlds of mindless drift,
Lost in our own oceans of aimless drift,
Never once a clue – never one true grip,
Just drift, float, spin the whole trip,

We're both lost in our sea of nothingness,
Mindless drift in our oceans of loneliness,
Both, needing that feeling of lovingness,
Drifting further toward a togetherness,

Weakened, the pulses of the magnetic bond,
Never quite collide, just never quite that strong...

Past Business Present

Got an arrogant fucker who wants to say —
I lost, I never got it my way,
He wants to sit there and tell me,
I shouldn't even be bothering,

He's definitely the guy she was rootin' hind my back,
This arrogant fucker no name, no balls – no sack,
But this arrogant fucker thinks he can attack,
And never not once think he deserves it back,

Can't accept the consequences for stealing her or my shit,
This arrogant fucker can't even show off his small dick,
No ball – no guts, but was rubbing face on my cunts' split,
And here I am expected to just take the shit,

There's gotta be a point where the line was crossed,
And she's out facing every little waste it all cost,
And her arrogant fuckin' dickhead is as weak, as soft,
To feel the need to involve himself to her loss,

What does it matter what I'm saying when I'm not there,
How fuckin' often was it her spite wasn't so fair?
And how much of her bullshit did she really expect me to bear?
Fuck that shit – I know the worst of it – I won't fuckin' dare,

How can they expect to have a dig and not feel it deep round?
Every little dig of theirs to drag at me down,
It's embarrassing how low they go when they want to clown,
I'm free – on my own – and am no more bound,

Just, this arrogant fucker intrudes and tries to
make me (her past) his business,
When he was never even around to ever really witness,

Happier In Ignorance

Now I know there were truths she couldn't face,
And I know it's why their all up in my private space
The shit's takin' forever to contemplate,
'til I made 'em aware – made 'em cogitate,

The shit they were all running from all their lives,
'till they met this one guy with the balls to strike,
Never letting shit passed without a fight,
Fight it, stand tall and wear it in pride,

But me, I'm facing all my fuckin' shit,
In manners to make all the fuckwits think,
They despise, and they all vilely spit,
And send me to wanna smoke and drink,

And they weren't bothered until they knew,
And they've gotta get ahead of me, it's due,
They all want their peace and paradise too,
Seems easier to take than having to live through,

And I say it so well it always hurts,
Still none of 'em ever dessert,
They wanna see me get what I deserve,
And they're hopin' it's only hurt,

They weren't bothered 'til they'd seen,
They were happier in their day dream,
They know it's hard and they wanna scream,
Never really open to the growth life means,

No- they were happier stuck in their ignorance,
And 'til they learn I'll still suffer their belligerence,
Not worth it if it's taken easily…

Shitty Fuckin' Lap Dance

It started with a lap dance –
But then went to fuck,
Started with a lap dance –
But I crapped my pants – yuck!

She squealed "Get off me!"
And I ran to fetch a wet cloth,
"Sorry baby I'm sorry!"
"yuck – quick, wipe it off!"

It started with a lap dance,
And it went wrong,
Started with a lap dance,
And crapped through my pants – pong,

"Yuck – get it off – get it off!"
It was her it landed on,
"Fuck – get it off – get it off!"
"Yuck – this is wrong"

I ran to fetch the wet cloth,
And cleaned off my deposit,
It was over – turned her off –
And shit was never the same – it wasn't,

Started with a lap dance –
Gone wrong and crapped my pants,
Went and ruined a rare chance –
Of doin' more than shakin' her hand,

Don't know whether it was the shit she fed me,
Or relaxed me so much my bowels go weak,
Or relaxed also due to the smokin' heavy of weed,
But from then it didn't go well for me,

Still even though she'd bring it up at times,
When she's disgusted and feeling vengeful at times,
Breakin' away the remaining trust of all mine,
Speakin' it loosely to all her mates, free her mind,

As embarrassing as it is,
I had a much different way to think,
She, embarrassing my way with this,
Embarrassing herself – and it doesn't think,

I'm almost glad I can say I did it to her,
That that was almost always how I saw her,
Shit on her, literally, and figuratively hurt,
Thinkin' it's definitely as much as she's worth,

Now I can't understand how she'd be so immature,
Her, acting out of age over my leaked manure,
I knew it could've led to a disease of maybe no cure,
But the way she overreacted never showed it as secure,

And embarrassing as it was,
To her it's hot goss,
As embarrassing to her – well, obviously not,
Think my ex bitch really has lost the plot,

Started with a lap dance,
But crapped my pant - yuck,
Began with a lap dance,
And ruined that chance – fuck...

Cat Jizz

Who would've thought
That tuggin' puddies pud,
To human porn,
Would get poor black puddie off,

Whao! Brutus man!
What's that under my hand?
Ew – yuck it feels sticky,
Got cat jizz on me fingy's

I even had it caught on film,
My step sister had the camera,
And the cat spat his gooey filth,
As I made his paw bat at it,

Whoa! Brutus Man!
What the fuck is that under my hand?
Yuck – ew, it feels sticky –
Naww don't tell me I got black cat jizz on me fingys?

Everyone laughed and why the fuck not?
I made a cat bat and hit the spot,
I know it must seem like me brain has rot,
But this was a product of as far as a curiosities got,

But? Who would've fuckin' thought –
That makin' puddie tug his pud to human porn,
Would get that black cat off – oh god,
Who would've fuckin' ever thought?

Poor puddy,

He's Been There

I know he's there in the back of my mind,
Heard him say "smack the bitch"
And,

Shaking,
I turned to him and said,
"you got it" – I slapped her,

He chuckled and I guess I giggled a little,
She screamed – "why'd you hit me you bastard?!"
"shenanigans, shit's and giggles",
"well, that fuckin' hurts! I'm digusted!"

Don't tell my mum,

I know he's there in the back of my mind,
Heard him say "fist her"
And,

Panicking, shaking,
Cause I knew what she'd be like,
I turned to him and said –
"you got it"

He chuckled and I guess I giggled like a dope a little,
She screamed – "ow, ow, two fingers – two finger's you bastard!"
"sorry! Got carried away with the wigglin' and fiddlin'"
"That fuckin' hurt! I'm disgusted!"

Please – PLEASE,
Don't tell my mum,

Not Good At Goodbyes

Well it's been fucked knowin' ya,
It's been fuckin' hell,
I'm thinkin' 'bout goin' and showin' up,
And tellin' ya fuck off and farewell,

Talkin' to me ex, the desperate whore,
Yes her hair was red and she was as sore,
Been so fucking long I forget what the fuck we're fighting for,
Everything there is gone, we both lose that war,

But for me in ways she can never fathom,
And for her in ways I dare not even imagine,
I'm sure her past will fuck her when it'll all catch her,
And I'll be too long gone to ever heal and patch her,

It's been real fucked knowin' her,
It's been fuckin' hell,
Thinkin' I wanna go showin' up,
Tell a fuck off and farewell,

Tellin' me ex, the desperate whore,
I just can't and won't take anymore,
Her hair was red and she, as sore,
I fuckin' even forgot what we were fighting for,

I'm facing truths – for enlightenment, inner growth,
Looking through the stars and using what I know,
A little metaphysical like that but I'll show,
Eventually maybe be the one they'll all want most,

It was, just, real fucked knowin' her,
It's been a fuckin' hell,
Thinkin' of only showin' up,
To say fuck off and farewell,

It's About Time

I wouldn't be so fucking ignorant,
How fucking hard is it to be considerate?
To be mindful, on the ball – not some fucking idiot,

One day God's gonna turn his back,
And Christ is really gonna snap,
Loosing on us all his smiting wrath,
We were warned – we had our chance,

And I don't wanna take the fall for cunts I can't control,
How the fuck is that fair or mercy to my soul?
None of 'em would or could care – it's not my fucking fault,
Strike them – not me lord – with ya lightning bolt,

I would ask your forgiveness of them for they know not what they do,
But I'd ask you to help them see and show them so they knew,
'Cause I don't want to have to suffer where we're headed to,
Not after all the good I've done or punishments I've gone through,

It's too fuckin' much to ask for them to be happy,
Everyone I deal with like it – makes my mood as crappy,
And I don't want to be the cranky chappy,
We're all doing circles and I'm over-lapping,

I never like to be so ignorant,
Not when death is so fucking permanent – imminent,
How the fuck hard is it to be so considerate?
To be mindful, on the ball – not some fucking idiot,

I'll never know why I should even bother to try,
Clueless, all I can do is stare to the sky,
But when it fucking comes, and I meet my demise –
I'll be at the point where I'll say – 'about fucking time'

Barrier Fuckwit

A stupid fuckin' old cunt is playing a game,
He's so fucking childish it's a fucking shame,
He pains me (and he's unaware) on levels I won't explain,
It's as stupid fighting his stupidity – it's insane,

He's a blockhead – a cockhead,
He needs a fuckin' floggin' –
He's a rock head with rocks in his head,
He needs a fuckin' floggin'

He's stuck in his own barrier and I'll never get passed,
This ignorant fucker is never going to outlast,
Only, if I was equal or lower to his level I'd laugh,
It's a childish little game and the cunt ain't that tough,

He's a fuck-stick – a fuckwit,
Needs his fuckin' nuts kicked,
A stupid dumb-arse fuck-stick,
Needing cunt lips made of his nuts split,

Fuckin' blockhead – real cockhead –
He needs a good old-fashioned fucking flogging,
He's a rockhead with rocks in his head,
And the fuckhead needs a flogging,

Stupid dumb fuck just sits there and giggles,
Giggling at me all boiling in furious ripples,
I swear it tickles his balls, his, gibbles,
Only – if I snapped – he'd end being crippled,

He's stuck and happy left there in his little ignorance,
But I will overpass him and all of its' irreverence,

Brickin' Up The Division

Separation, division,
The absence of the unison,
Some think it's the impossible mission,
But I can and do see a wisdom,

The different shit that divides us,
The doer's from the can'ts
Efforts undergone to divide us,
The willer's and the shan'ts.

Differences in ideals,
Inside – what we feel,
Broken – or unsealed,
The fake and the real,

We all do it on purpose,
For the differences that serve us,
For the paranoia of outsiders, usurpers,
For all who only delay and deter us,

Subdivisions all round, and we're linked, we're all tied,
All of us the same with various links all alike,
Each with his or her reasons why they all fight,
Each with every reason why they keep to the divide,

Rare occasions only ever give us hope there's more,
But then the worst expectations happen leaving us raw,
But occasions time again remind the like before,
Remind us why we even brick up the wall...

EH, EH – Brick it up!
Brick It UP!
Somebody put a wall between 'em...

915

Preview to

*De*S*ENSITIZER* Vol.3
– even More Mental For Metal Yet

Teaser titles;
(descending from last to front)

Chapter 6: "Scales, Unbalanced" –
'Takes Balls', 'You Fucked It', '40 Kings Of One Man',
Chapter 5: "Episodes Of Metaphysical Warfare" –
'Like Lightning', 'Piercing Attacks', 'Without
Consent, Without Permission',
Chapter 4: "Layers Of A Chaos Web" –
'Vicarious Wins Without Head-On Stings', 'Malum
Nuntium','Interference For Stalling Growth',
Chapter 3: "Static Filtering, Keys, Tones, Shades" –
'Vigour Mortis', 'To Make You Lose It', 'You? Man Enough?',
Chapter 2: "Zealous For" –
'Polygamous', 'Mouth The Rhythm', 'Instant Inventory'
Chapter 1: "Fight Through Clashing Delusions" –
'Hypocritical Disadvantaging By Fear Of
Reputation', Remorse, Contrition, On A Whole New
Sociopathic Level', 'Interpreteneur No.2'

Takes Balls

Well I'm sure some'd say I've got fuckin' balls,
I'm a fool for what I do and I shouldn't at all,
What can I say to that but fuck you can talk,
How does anyone get what they want without the fuckin' balls,

I see what I want and I'm slowly aiming for it –
Just makin' sure it's worth the effort,
I do know what I want and it'll take time to get to it –
But I'll make sure the prize – well, I'd measured,

I'll have worked as hard as I'd have possibly have to have had,
Ride it through even when my teeth are grinding mad,
More – for far more than I have ever had,
Hardened where the lessons were meant to have set back,

Balls to bare to show I can bear –
Takin' on more than a fair share,
I know, I'm aware, the tolls – the tare –
And I know if I fuck up I'll have to wear,
It's fair,

I see what I want and I'm slowly aiming for it –
Just makin' sure it's worth the effort,
I do know what I want and it'll take time to get to it –
But I'll make sure the prize – well, I'd measured,

Balls to show I'd put it on out, examples of the tolls,
Balls enough to face and crush the obstacles of trolls,
Balls to step up and demand for me my own control
Balls enough to battle and feed the heart and soul…

You Fucked It

Jesus – I don't want the fucking thing back –
It was a fight for you to have it in the first place,
I don't want it crawlin' back,
It's trying from a distance – not strong enough to face it,

I don't want it after he's fucking had it,
He's only fucked it worse,
Look at what he did to it – it's fucked,
I've gotta get to all these normal bitches first,

But why do I have to find the fucked up ones,
And why do I have to relate –
I'm going through Pass My Shotgun –
Something or everything I hate,

Take it back I don't fucking want it,
It put up a fight 'til it fuckin' got it,
I had to let go and I was –
She didn't but I'm still being watched,

But fuck me don't offer it back,
Not after all my feeling went black,
Not after her silent and vicious nasty attacks,
I see what she's doing, she's getting back,

But I just seriously don't want the fucking thing,
It was too easy for it to leave,
No – you fucked it – I don't want it back,
I did pay – and still do, to no equal receive or relief,

Keep the fucking thing just –
Make sure it obsesses over you enough,
Cause that fuckin' thing hasn't let me go,
And it won't let me do what I know,

40 Kings Of One Man

I'm just one man,
Only just one man,
But I'm takin' up a stand,
Takin' up a stand,
Against a number of kings.
Lordin' it over me,

I'm only just one man,
Just one man,
Takin' a stand,
Takin' up a stand,
'Gainst a number of things,
Lordin' it over me,

Plenty more reasons why –
They say I have to die,
When I'm just a one man,
Me, alone, like why?

How could I have been bad enough,
That they would ever fear,
How could I have been bad enough –
When they never had tears,

To show me I meant nothing back then,
Why do they deserve to even be called friends?
When they could never shed tears,
But just bitch behind me and then just fear,

I'm just a one man battling away,
Against 40 higher class people or so they say,
Don't matter what's wrong long as they're okay,
Just take out that single one that betrayed,

One man to 40 kings,
How can I stand it all,

I'm just one man,
Only just one man,
But I'm takin' up a stand,
Takin' up a stand,
Against a number of kings.
Lordin' it over me,

I'm only just one man,
Just one man,
Takin' a stand,
Takin' up a stand,
'Gainst a number of things,
Lordin' it over me,

One man to 40 kings,
How can I stand it all,

Like Lightning

I fuckin' swear this oath –
I will be a scary bloke,
Pierce through the very brains –
Of those driving me insane,

I'll streak pain like lightning,
It will be severe and frightening,
I'll find it exciting,
Full rage, full blast – smitening,

I fuckin' swear this oath –
I will be a scary fuckin' bloke,
To pierce the hearts of those,
Who pained me when wrongfully chose,

I will streak pain like lightning,
And it will be most frightening,
I'll finally find it exciting,
Full rage – full blast, blinding,

I swear this fuckin' oath –
I'll be the scary bloke,
To pierce the hearts and brains,
Of those driving me insane,

And I will streak pain like lightning,
And it will become most frightening,
Me – I'll find it exciting
Full rage – full blast – blinding,
Smitening,

Piercing Attacks

I've done my share of piercing attacks,
And sure enough as I thought it,
It had,

I've had my share of piercing attacks,
And sure enough as I felt on it,
They had,

Preventing – always preventing,
Resenting – always resenting –
No pretending, this whole thing is dementing,
I'm resenting all the while this prevents me,

I've done my share of piercing attacks,
And sure as I thought on it –
It had,

I've had my share of piercing attacks,
And as soon as I'd felt on it –
It had,

Like lightning to the head,
To shut down where it spread,
Piercing energies forced fed,
Damaging – just not dead,

Preventing, always preventing now,
Resenting – always resenting,
No – pretending – it's dementing,
I'm resenting where it's preventing,

So I'm having my share of piercing psychic attacks,
Getting it good but giving it back,
It's just where I thought it, it had,

Without Consent, Without Permission

I can take the hate and pain from people
I can rapidly convert any good from evil
I don't know what this makes me – can't be a man,
I can do a lot more - but I know for certain I can,

I have to be a freak of nature to take it without consent,
Unless I'm the real deal but I seriously doubt I'm heaven sent,
I can rip out and free people of their heavy resents,
Might be better I do – who wants to keep them?

If I have the power to instantly insert a happy mood,
When people are down would it be right for me to?
I know I can but would it help get them through?
It's probably best kept a secret and I shouldn't allude,

I have to be a freak of nature to be capable of taking love at will,
It is in my power but I would really rather be giving it out still,
I can take the angst and the rage and caress it to a gentle feel,
Eradicate the pain from it and feed the love back to fill,

I can hypnotise and mesmerise with a strange aura,
I may never strike it rich, but I'll continue while poorer,
I can entrance with words, but I do manoeuvre it well,
I can make it feel like people are under a spell,

Almost like a demonic possession from a distance,
And I never seem to need the permission,
One – or some might say that that is a scary thing,
It's just lucky I'm not persuaded otherwise to whim,

Lightning rips of pain to those causing me disdain,
Pain – intense – to those who drive me insane,

Vicarious Wins Without Head-On Stings

She's living vicarious,
To learn certain lessons,
Through this someone else,
Never be stung herself,

But laugh as the fool she does through –
Fail…

She learns from a distance,
Always like the car behind you,
Tailing close to slingshot –
Out from behind and ahead of you,

And laugh as the fool she does to –
Fail…

She doesn't want the sting herself,
But laugh watching others hit it well,
She learns, to overpass you –
And if she wins it's because of you,

And we know all winners need a loser –
It sucks you never get to choose it,

They gloat and skite – ungloriously, ungracious,
Easy to see why good people lose patience,
And if all of these memoirs don't one day make me famous,
I'll still have found a way to have out shamed it,

She, well – she'll laugh as I try unveil to eyes,
Ruling simple minds, with the lies all deny,

Malum Nuntium

Have you heard the bad news?
Lucifer is coming for you,
There's nothing you can do –
But wait to be subject to,

All of your worst fears will come at once,
From the mightiest to gutless of cunts,
And he will chew on their guts –
He'll break bones in a mighty crush,

People wrung out of all blood to bleed,
To try to sate the hunger he cannot feed,
It's hopeless flail against his deeds
Lucifers power exceeds,

Hell's comin' like none know,
Scriptures spoke but none really show,
Please don't waste – don't atone,
Hell is the place for you – it's home,

You've gotta accept there is wrong,
Accept it – endure it and live on,
Lucifers powers are fierce, strong,
Seething, he comes, it won't be long,

All of your worst fears come at once,
For the mightiest and the gutless of cunts,
And he will chew on their guts,
He'll break bones in a mighty crush,

People wrung out of all the blood to bleed,
To try to sate a hunger he cannot feed,
It's a hopeless flail against his deeds,
Lucifers power exceeds,

Interference For Stalling Growth

I'm trying to fend off an interference,
My past, my ex, and her incoherence,
Never so diligent whenever she's belligerent,
Older, beyond me, and was so her influence,

I'm amazed she knew as much as she did,
Although she missed precious crucial pieces and bits,
And as I'd grow away and out and up through the shit,
I'd find out how hard for myself responsibility hits,

It's why she pulled back and stopped dead,
It's the same reason why I did when I was led,
Only I caught on to it before her – I was first,
She knows it and it's why she hurts,

She isn't as strong 'cause she isn't as pure,
And she had the hide to treat me like a steamy pile of manure,
And do you know what I know better than to deny her a forgiveness,
Because after her – after all, I will outlive this,

At some point I know when I am ready,
It's then that I will go,
And I will have summarised it all up on paper,
Before I've done so,

Other works where I interpret the more I've seen,
As I've gone into trance and to channel out a dream,
Breaking the barriers of space and time and venture beyond,
Seeking strange truths to matters and times long gone,

But this interference has pained me for so long,
Butting and covering with new lies and more wrong,
Enough for me to want to write too many a song,
And like I've said before – it's over – so stay gone...

Vigour Mortis

Exuberant, resilient,
Death won't have fulfillment,
Undulant, makes ambivalent,
Jubilant – no, death won't be efficient,

Party 'til I pass out,
Rave 'til I pass out,
Party 'til I pass out,
Rave it on out,

I'll sleep when I'm dead,
And 'til then be off my head,
Come, blast me full of lead,
And witness my vigour bring you dread,

I'll party 'til I pass out,
Rave on 'til I pass out,
Party 'til I pass out,
I'll rave it on out…

To Make You Lose It,

By people who think they know,
And these people never show,
Never letting it go,
'til I explode,

By these people think they're better,
Showing it hardly ever –
I'd have to say never –
Woe – the endeavours,

Pushed 'til I can't hold the grip –
Pushed at 'til I lose it and slip,
Pushed to fall over a trick,
Pushed over a trip,

By people who believe,
They think they can achieve,
Only to make you grieve,
And they steal as they deceive,

By these people taking more,
Than they're prepared to actually work for,
Can't consume but can't be ignored,
Rip in at you as they're as sore,

Pushed beyond that I lose my grip,
Losing my shit just that little bit,
Pushed, tripped over mischievous tricks,
Grinding my teeth and biting my lips,

By people that just have no clue, no real use,
But will use you and throw around every excuse,
And you cop the extents of all their abuse,
Only for them to feel as satisfied or amused...

You? Man Enough?

Someone detain me – cuff my wrists,
I've had enough – I'm fuckin' pissed,
I want to go and sort it out with –
My bare fuckin' fists,

I hate guns and I hate fuckin' knives,
But I'm sure many wanna use 'em on me for chatting up their wives,
I know it's enough for men to hate me and they will despise,
But I never once threatened to take their lives,

Life for a wife?
Get fucked,

You're not much of a man if you need a weapon,
Insecure? Unstable? Fuck – he better have a weapon then,
'Cause once I have a hold – once I fuckin' get 'em,
They'll need first strike and fuck it, I'll let 'em,

I fuckin' hate guns and I fuckin' hate knives,
And many men will use 'em gainst me chatting up their wives,
I know it's reason why they'll hate me and fucking despise,
But do you think it's really worth me having me threatened with my life?

My life for another's wife –
Fuck yourself,

Stand there and tell me you're a man,
When you can't even use your hands,
Stand it – stand there – stand up,

Stand there and tell me you're a fuckin' man,
When you can't even use your fucking hands,

Stand it, stand there and be a fuckin' man...

My life for your wife – get fucked...
Be proud I thought she was good enough,
Be proud she's still with you after..

Polygamous

There's a little too much of me inside,
More than just for one girl to confide,
That I'm so faithful, honest – can't hide,
Those keepings and letting go's of mine,

I have felt as though I've been too much,
Overcompensating for the sake I never had enough,
But how is it fair I could only ever let one touch,
When I'm further more than that kind of enough,

Not certain I could contain it all just for a one,
Nope, no, gonna need more, a few, a some,
Spoken and spread broad to stun,
Those many new mama's I want on my tongue,

I'll be careful – I'll be cautious,
I'll take every precaution,
Flurry of women, no getting nauseous,
It could possibly tire to exhaustion,

How could it be fair to just keep to just a one,
When I feel it isn't so fair many missing out the fun,
How is it fair when there are a some –
It's all or nothing but don't want just 'none'

I could contribute a consistent back and forwards,
To many different women for whichever cause,
I know it may hinder but I know they're rewards,
Just have to put it down – the consents and such to implore...

Mouth The Rhythm

All I want
All I think about,
Are these little things I can do with my mouth,

All I want,
All I need is about –
Her splendorous south,

Have the music, have a metal rhythm,
And I'll get to going with the system,
You lie and listen 'til I taste you glisten,
Making you melt to the rhythm,

To lie you back –
Strip you slow,
Kiss to attract –
Your beautiful glow,

Have the music – hard rock rhythm,
Open you out to tongue to the system,
Lie you back to feel as you listen, taste you glisten,
Make you melt to each rhythm,

It's what I want –
What I think about,
The things I could do with my mouth,

It's what I want,
All I need about –
Mouthing out your sweet south,

Lick, lap manoeuvre my lips to the spot,
Mouthing to the rhythm 'til you beg to stop,

Instant Inventory

I like a girl whose brave and bold,
Like a girl courageous,
Like to find me a girl of any age, - of old,
Do things with outrageous,
And in stages,

Gotta remember reputation –
And one day I'm gonna grow old,
Change my mind completely –

Yeah like me a girl who knows what she wants,
Like a girl who knows the loss,
To never have taken it up stages,
Brave - bold, ready to get to the outrageous,
Strong, calm, cool and courageous,

You gotta push to test the limits,
Never know if you don't try,
But I'll have more tales told about me,
When I go to die,

I've liked and loved many before,
Loved the sweetest ladies, never forget the whores,
Taken to different worlds, before,
Seeing the shit, I'd have neither otherwise before,

But I like the ones keen to show the interest,
That they get more out after puttin' in,
In terms of appreciation for the interest,
Boom – instant inventory, for your lookin' in,

Only to those open to take the time,
Takin' the time to share a part of mind,

935

Hypocritical Disadvantaging By Fear For Reputation

There are times when,
You're about on the urge of a great thought,
Might sound like a madness but genuine, insane –
That these thoughts –
Are so mad it's not the time's for when,

Maybe already at an age where I'm –
Working a lil something harder for when – I'm –
Wanting to go where and spare the time –
Relax – maybe unwind and tell other tales of my time,

Some who can't or won't agree,
Won't socialize, won't accept it – won't tolerate –
No sacrifices – blinded to opportunity –
Can't socialize – won't accept it – can't, no tolerance,

Fight and fire back up into it –
An argument raging hectic,
You engage but only fire back up fiercer,
Your logic gainst theirs, limited, so hypocryptic,

They deter you – make you forget when at the time,
When they're too in a rush to hear your reasonable sense,
That what I couldn't've said could wrap round their minds,
That whatever madness (and I agree) wasn't misplaced intelligence,

Can't show them what I mean when their ignorance,
From any scenario, politicians to your own parents,
Every great idea ever gone ignored of fear for reputation,
Has been the many cause of my defeat and exasperation,

I just hope – if it were that someone did it to them –
They'd be more humane to never pass it beyond from again,

Remorse, Contrition, On A Whole New Sociopathic Level

Thank fuck I'm mindful to be mindful of this,
Too many things have run awry, run amiss,
Having to be specific and make certainly explicit,
Mind to paths lead, bad habits, maybe a little more implicit,

I'm beginning to remain a calm in certain desperate times,
Where I know it's a test, see it's a distance from behind,
Test to see my response in desperate times,
Show I can keep calmed and control the situation of time,

The desperation is becoming less trivial,
Lesser a burden and lesser see as miserable,
No crack, no cave in – to blast out and explode, no feeling at all,
A feeling of responsibility none might ever feel to control,

Every dig at me with their talons, claws, beaks,
And a pestilence coming to them yet to reap,
There, that part there – put me to sleep,
Don't want to witness it – that price ain't cheap,

Every rip at me is a test for me to prove,
A failure – and their gloating gluttonied tells' I lose,
And every ripping dig at me is their laugh I lose –
Proving beyond a joke when you've already proved –
They're too disgraced by to prove,

Sure I feel bad about it, but it's on an entirely new level,
Desensitized as much so, you don't just take the best parts and rebel,
A deeper calm beneath like one would feel
the whence the depth the level,
Hidden – the calm, where covered determining the difference you rebel,

Once again it's determining the difference,
the choices more rationally to take,
And I've already had too many pressured
moments that would forever forsake,

Interpreteneur No.2

We've lost the love,
We've lost the light,
It's why we'll lose the fight,

We have loathed,
We have hate,
And it brings sooner our fate,

People believe his holiness will come,
But this time next it will be done,
The one, the only, the holy son,
To wipe out, cleanse out of the scum,

Lightening in the night,
Whip crack – almighty smite,
Bow before – surrender your fight,
Before you lose this life,

Too many interpreters maybe getting it wrong,
Which shade of hypocrisy actually belongs,
Whose will will will it strong,
But by that whose succeed – the one-man god,

We've lost the love,
We've lost the light,
It's why we'll lose the fight,

We have loathed,
We have hate,
It's how we bring on our fate,

But it won't when we can share the faith…

Authors Note

Titles for the 3rd sequence to DeSensitizer may be shifted around in it's production and may change from chapter to chapter, some may not make it in but again there could always be a revival or bridge that includes a some I might've missed but were too good not to leave out. Thank you kindly for your interest in Desensitizer, not all scenarios depicted are that of all who suffer paranoid schizophrenia and depression, or borderline bipolar, just mine alone although I can and do appreciate those who relate or even empathize and thank them for their kindness and courtesy, even a thanks for seeing passed some of the more unbearable parts throughout this book,

There were times I'd written things I found difficult to face, were perhaps a lot more private than to have included in but thought to anyway, to familiarize a sole individuality on the matters of these experiences.

Thanks,
Kaero…

CPSIA information can be obtained
at www.ICGtesting.com
Printed in the USA
BVHW080826100220
571918BV00001B/1